W9-AHH-374

Set the Stars Alight

SET THE STARS ALIGHT

AMANDA DYKES

THORNDIKE PRESS
A part of Gale, a Cengage Company

Unless otherwise indicated, Scripture quotations are from the King James Version of the Bible.
Scripture quotations labeled NIV are from THE HOLY BIBLE, NEW INTERNATIONAL VERSION®, NIV® Copyright © 1973, 1978, 1984, 2011 by Biblica, Inc.® Used by permission. All rights reserved worldwide.
Thorndike Press, a part of Gale, a Cengage Company.

Thorndike Press® Large Print Christian Fiction.
The text of this Large Print edition is unabridged.
Other aspects of the book may vary from the original edition.
Set in 16 pt. Plantin.

**LIBRARY OF CONGRESS CIP DATA ON FILE.
CATALOGUING IN PUBLICATION FOR THIS BOOK
IS AVAILABLE FROM THE LIBRARY OF CONGRESS.**

ISBN-13: 978-1-4328-8315-7 (hardcover alk. paper)

Published in 2020 by arrangement with Bethany House Publishers, a division of Baker Publishing Group

Printed in Mexico
Print Number: 01 Print Year: 2020

For our kids.
Wonder-filled adventurers,
what a gift you are!
The Maker of the stars is
the Maker of your hearts,
and oh! how He loves you.
May this truth set the stars alight,
all your days and every night.

And for you, dear reader.
Wonder is a mighty thing,
a weighty thing,
a truth-filled thing,
a lifting thing.
Given to buoy our hearts
and hopes and spirits.
Hang on to it, brave ones.
And more — hang on to the Giver of it.
Though darkness may fall
and times grow hard,
hold fast to this given light.

Every good and perfect gift is from above, coming down from the Father of the heavenly lights, who does not change like shifting shadows.

James 1:17 NIV

The fair breeze blew, the white foam flew,
The furrow followed free;
We were the first that ever burst
Into that silent sea.

— Samuel Taylor Coleridge,
from *The Rime of the Ancient Mariner*

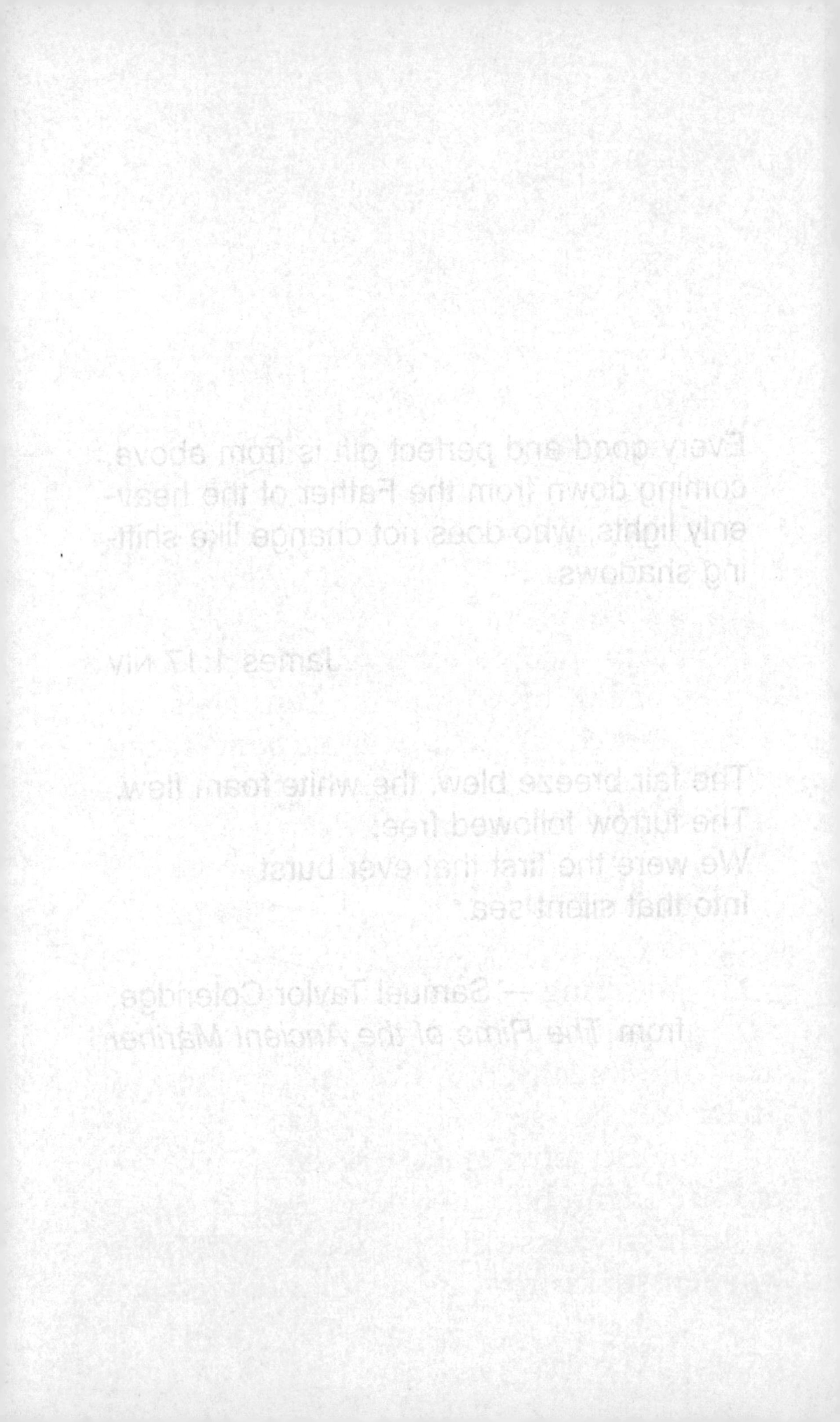

Prologue

London, England
May 1987

The smell of cinders permanently etched the abandoned Bessette Match Factory into the minds of all who passed. If asked about the factory, people rarely remembered the details of the brick towers, iron gates, and black-painted sign with carved letters, their gilded edges now gone . . . but they inevitably recalled the general specter of smoke and soot — a vestige of industrial revolutions and factory strikes and all manner of Victorian lore.

The towering roofline dwarfed the homes and shops that, over time, had popped up near the vacant building in old London Town. Yet not so long ago, for over a century, the Bessette Match Factory, Purveyors of Pure Light, had produced the metal hum of industry, issuing a steady stream of wooden sticks from its depths. Those sticks were then sent to the glass house. Not a house of glass, but a brick outbuilding whose walls housed the glass-grinding quarters. There the sticks were treated, their tips dipped in powdered glass, glass born of fire — and to fire they were destined to return.

Once they were cloaked in chemicals, the strike-anywhere matches were bundled and sent off to Market Street and Covent Garden and on to the Lake District and the dales and the seaports circling the green island nation, until parlor fires and hearth fires and cooking fires and fires of camps all owed their warmth to that match factory.

But time swept through, as time does. Two world wars embedded themselves into the souls of the land, and with war came new innovations promised to cast out darkness. Great Britain learned to twist light bulbs into sockets and fill hand torches with batteries, until that steady stream of matches from the factory slowed to a trickle and then . . . to a stop. The Bessette Match Factory, Purveyors of Pure Light, gaped empty for a year . . . then two . . . then three decades.

Until one drizzly May morning in 1987, when Gerald W. Bessette, reluctant inheritor of "The Fossil," as the family had come to call the factory, visited the place with a land agent to see what could be done about selling.

Blinking into the darkness as they entered, he kicked something that caused him to stumble. He retrieved the culprit: a hand torch, the very thing that had led to the factory's demise. He flicked it on and by its tired beam saw blankets and boxes spread everywhere — evidence that people had moved into the old factory, set up camp on the lower levels.

Torch in hand, he had what he would later call his "light-bulb moment." If people were already living here, why not capitalize on that? Gerald W. Bessette left the factory that day with a vision of pounds paving his every step and set to transforming the place with the help of his family's coffers. A few dozen well-placed walls inside the expansive complex, bricks scrubbed clean of soot until they shone red against the grey sky, and clever wording to make the lofty ceilings sound like echoes of palace living instead of a thoroughfare of chilly drafts, and the Bessette Match Factory became Candlewick Commons: Fine Flats at Fulham.

Toward the end of the project he hired a local watchmaker, one Simon Claremont, to repair the broken tower clock that looked out over the concrete courtyard from above the arched entrance. And finally, on an unremarkable Tuesday afternoon almost a year after Gerald started the reconstruction, the two men stood on the roof, waiting for the clock to strike three and prove itself repaired.

"This marks the end of an era," Gerald W. Bessette said, clapping the watchmaker on the back as if they were old school chums. "Workers once tuned their ears to this very tower to keep watch over the beginning and end of their toiling each day. And now" — the man spread his arms wide, as if unrolling the horizon of the whole city — "it marks the beginning of a new epoch. A time of . . ." He furrowed his brow, apparently having used up all his words to capture his grandiose swell of feeling. "A time of something really, really good."

With a nod, Simon walked to the clock, tightened a gear in his pensive way, and stood back, waiting. Seconds ticked on . . . and the clock struck three o'clock right on cue, limping its slightly off-kilter song into the world in between Big Ben's own declarations pealing down alleys and avenues across the Thames.

"Ha!" Gerald W. Bessette pumped his hands into the air in victory. "New life, my friend." He surveyed the brick building beneath them, its wings that cloistered three sides of a courtyard, and the small cottage standing squat and humble at the far corner of the land, beneath the property's lone tree.

"That'll be the caretaker's quarters," he said, pointing. "Glass grinder's cottage, it was. But now it'll be hearth and home to some lucky soul who'll keep this place hale and hearty."

Simon narrowed his eyes, his gaze landing upon the sleepy cottage with its dripping glass windows, squat brick walls, and arched black door. "A thing of beauty, that is."

And Gerald, whether swept up in the grandeur of his kingdom or recognizing a visionary and able man all wrapped up in one package, shrewdly offered the position of caretaker to his new friend, insisting that he could still keep his shop on Cecil Court, only a few minutes' walk away.

And so it happened that Simon Claremont, watchmaker, story keeper, last of a dying breed, came home to Candlewick Commons with his wife, Penny. And a little over a year later, as they each neared forty, they added the surprise and joy of their lives: a wee bundle of a daughter.

"Lucy," he said, as they stood over her bassinet by the light of the fire on their first night home from hospital. "Her name is Lucy." He placed her in her cradle in the glass house, naming her *light* itself. For her life, they were sure, would mean something.

One

Candlewick Commons
London, England
2000

To step inside the watchmaker's cottage was to step outside of time. Lucy grew there, a waif of a thing and a solitary soul. Her mind was full of wonderings and wanderings. She spent her days at school, and her afternoons circling Candlewick's round courtyard fountain as she studied maps or read books.

Her evenings, however, were magic. Each day, as the sun began to set over Candlewick's towers and the stars began to appear, and flats across the courtyard were coming to life with the blue glow of tellies, she returned to the glass house and felt the rush of the city drop away. The cottage was a place where tales spun inside every dusty shaft of golden-hour sunlight. Where each evening, stories and riddles were told around flickering flames — crackling hearth fire in winter months, pirouetting candlelight in the summer.

They had no telly. She sometimes burned with embarrassment when she couldn't join in the conversations at school, but in the moment, in the warm glow of their cottage home, she did not mind. The mellowed wooden floors creaked with the rush of her feet, racing to turn off the lamps and leap into the embrace of the old stuffed armchair in the corner. Her young fingers wrapped around chipped mugs of chamomile or, on Sundays, sipping chocolate. "Monday is upon us," her mum would say with a conspiratorial wink. "We must prepare. Chocolate all 'round."

The watchmaker would invariably dust off his hands after laying the fire, plant a kiss on his wife's rosy cheek, and look his daughter in the eye. "Make a friend today, Lucy?"

He asked every day. Sometimes it bothered her. She did not mind being alone. "Just wait," he always said. "The best of friends come in the unlikeliest ways." He always winked at Mum when he said it, and she'd swat him playfully with whatever she had in her hand — usually a dirt-smudged towel. She always seemed to be loosening the roots of her lilac plants.

They had met when she'd been up a tree — literally — at Kew Gardens, obtaining a sample of lichen for a study. She'd dropped the bit of green moss, and it had landed on Father's hat below, where he'd been studying a sundial. And the rest, as they said, was history.

But Lucy did not climb trees or study sundials. She did not have a "thing," as most people seemed to. She kept waiting to find it, looking out over the Thames, or over the sea when they were on rare holiday, wondering who she would be. Sometimes she searched in books, pulling them one at a time from the shelves of Candlewick's reading room.

One day, after returning from school, Lucy ran into the reading room, pulled out a book, and walked through the tunnel that led to Candlewick Commons' front doors. She always shivered as she passed through. Not so much from cold, as from the distinct impression that the tunnel was a portal to a dragon's lair, and its many windows reached story upon story into the sky.

Passing through the massive front doors, she entered the garden courtyard, where she liked to read while circling the fountain. " 'All the world is a stage,' " Lucy read aloud, trying to keep from chucking the book into the fountain. Chopped up in strange lengths of lines, it made no sense to her. Whoever had given a pen to this man Shakespeare had made a massive mistake.

"All the world is *not* a stage," she argued right back at the book. And with her nose buried in the offending pages, she collided with something and only had time to think one thing on her way down — that something was *tall.*

Not having far to fall, she hit the ground before her counterpart, and when a boy landed next to her, all limbs and glasses, they looked at each other wide-eyed for a moment. When her haze lifted, Lucy made to speak, but the boy — dark-haired, brown-eyed, a year or two older than her ten years — beat her to it.

"Sorry," he said.

American. His *R*s dug deep into the word, mouth as wide as his eyes when he spoke it. She attributed it to his accent but would later come to learn it was just him. Wide-eyed, wide-worded, wide-hearted.

"Sorry," she echoed.

He stood, reaching first for her book, which had fallen near the fountain and was catching stray water droplets on its aged pages. He pushed his black-rimmed glasses up as he read the title. "*As You Like It.*

What's that mean?"

Lucy shrugged. "I *don't* like it."

He seemed to remember her presence then, nearly tripping over his lanky legs all over again as he reached a hand to pull her up — the first instance of many times in their lives.

"Why are you reading it if you don't like it?"

Lucy blinked, embarrassed to admit she had just liked the way the gold words shone against its old blue spine on the shelf. And more than that, it had been on the upper shelf, meaning she had an excuse to climb the rolling ladder. All her schoolmates had swing sets in their gardens or nearby parks. She . . . she had a fountain in place of a merry-go-round and a rolling ladder instead of monkey bars.

But she was full of rebellion against Shakespeare's words and refused to play a part by giving some more logical excuse as to why she was reading this old play. So out of sheer defiance against the bard, she said to the boy, "I'll show you."

He followed her through the "dragon's lair," up the corridor to the north wing, and into the tower that had been made into a quiet gathering place for the community, complete with two wingback chairs and an oversized fireplace. She showed him the ladder and the high row of Shakespeare volumes lined up like royal sailors in their navy blue and gold. She climbed dark rungs to replace the book, then came down and gestured for him to take a turn.

Pulling out the fourth volume, he tossed it down to her and pulled out another for himself. Planting themselves in the old wingback chairs facing the cold fireplace, they took turns reading random lines and allowing the other to spout off a retort.

" 'You speak an infinite deal of nothing,' " the boy read.

"Yes, you do, Mr. Shakespeare," Lucy said. The boy grinned.

Lucy read, " 'What's past is prologue.' "

"I think you mean anti-log," the boy said, and they dissolved into snickers over their own cleverness, neither knowing what a prologue was. This continued — one of them vaulting a line into the air, the other taking a crack at it like a cricket player — until the tall windows let in less and less light, the night calling them each home.

"Hey," the boy said, as he stopped at what she assumed was the long hallway to his flat. "What's your name?"

"Lucy."

"I'm Dashel," he said. "Dash." He walked

away in exactly the opposite speed of his name, slow and thoughtful, looking over his shoulder and offering a clumsy wave.

The next night, when Lucy and her parents sat on the porch of their little brick home, eating cinnamon toast and reading from *Peter Pan* as the crickets began to sing, she saw that same thoughtful walk in silhouette, going round about the fountain.

"Sometimes stories are more real than you think," Father said, gesturing at the book in Mother's lap. "Take the lost boys, for instance." He tipped his head toward the fountain. "And take that boy. I thought he might just come 'round."

"You know him?" Lucy narrowed her eyes, looking between the boy and her father's laughing eyes.

"Who do you think told him he should go to the fountain yesterday?"

"But . . . you were at the watch shop then."

"Yes, but you weren't." He had a glimmer in his eyes, one that turned to compassion as he looked again at the boy who was casting furtive glances their way. "He spends every night alone in that flat. Lives there with an aunt . . ." He looked ready to say more, but a cloud crossed his face and he simply said, "She's not there much. So I may have told him in passing when to happen upon the fountain."

Lucy's heart beat quicker. "What exactly did you say he'd find, Dad?"

Her father shrugged mischievously. "A shooting star."

"Dad!" Her eyes grew wide in embarrassment.

"What? It's what you are, Lucy — light on the move. What else would you call that?"

Lucy groaned, dropping her face to her hands. Her father . . . Would he never tire of writing a fairy tale with his every word?

Mum tipped her head toward the fountain. "Why not go and invite him over, Lucy?" She had the prettiest hair — golden and wavy, where Lucy's was black and straight around her freckled face. Cruel irony for a girl named after light. The only thing they shared were wide eyes, "bluer than blue," Dad liked to say.

And so she invited the lost boy into their circle. That night, and the next, and the next — until it was just expected that Dash would be there for dinner each night. The brother she'd never had. The friend she hadn't known she'd needed.

Two

London
2002

"Hey, Matchstick Girl," Dash said one night. He had learned that her bedroom was once the place where sticks became matches, and the name had stuck. "Did you hear about the supernova?" He was always asking about some astronomical wonder or another.

She gave him a sideways glance and a half smile, which she knew he would take to mean "no" as well as "please tell me everything you know about the supernova," and he proceeded to fill her head with scientific jargon she hardly understood until he finished rambling, out of breath and red in the face with excitement.

Pausing in the dragon's lair she tilted her head quizzically. "And now . . . for us mere mortals, if you please?" Dash was brilliant. And she suspected he had no idea at all.

"Lucy." He shook his head back and forth in mock disappointment, but she knew he relished this part most of all. "A supernova is a gigantic burst of light like you've never *seen* before."

"You haven't seen one, either."

"No, but I will, one day."

Once inside the cottage, Lucy's mother placed a mug of chocolate in Dash's one hand, and her father a screwdriver in the other, and they set to work building the telescope Lucy's father was coaching them through. As they worked, Simon the watchmaker told his riddles, and Penny the gardener propagated lilacs and schemed great schemes for fountains, follies, and all manner of courtyard beauty. For many years ago, Gerald W. Bessette had seen her green thumb, dubbed her the resident gardener, and increased their stipend.

At precisely seven o'clock, the watchmaker packed away his tools and opened a palm toward Lucy as if to give her the floor. She stifled a smile, put on her serious face, and pulled the watch on its long chain from her pocket. With a quick snap, she held it out for all to see and uttered her favorite words in all the world: "Let the story . . . begin."

And with that, the walls fell away from their narrow cottage and imagination swept them to far-off lands, the world around them transformed in Father's rugged cadence. The growl of the Underground beneath them tumbled straight into their tale as the sound of the waking dragon. Or the roll of a storm-tossed ship. Or once, even, the dwellers of an underground city.

"Pay attention now." When Dad said things like "Pay attention," he made it sound like an invitation.

Mum chimed in. "Pay attention. From the Latin *ad tendere.*" She loved her Latin. She pronounced the scientific names of her plants as if they were magnificent treasures, not just clumps of soil and plucky seedlings clinging to her knuckles.

"What's that mean?" Lucy asked.

"It means *to stretch toward.*" Mum slid a plate of lavender short-bread beneath their noses. "Pay attention to those cookies, too, will you?" She winked.

Dad cleared his throat. "As I was saying . . ."

"Oh, hush. Time enough for biscuits, too." Mum placed one in his hand.

He ate it in one giant bite and returned to his story. "Now, picture it, children." He ran his hand around a yellowing globe. "Here we are, this tiny island nation. Green and lush, surrounded by ocean. And here"

— he slid his finger across the ocean, down, down, until he tapped the desert stretches of Australia — "nearly the bottom of the world, is another island nation. Forget the trees and grass of England. Imagine sand and rock the colour of rust. The only trees in sight are those made from metal, by man, for shade. The outback stretching as far as the eye can see."

Lucy felt parched, envisioning it.

"Here," Dad said, "light is born."

A myth, then. A legend of the sun's birth, or fire's origin, or . . .

"Coober Pedy," he said, leaning forward. "The underground city."

"Like Poseidon's palace?" Lucy remembered his story of jeweled iron and coral, twisting together into a fortress under the sea. She inched forward. "Or the Shadowlands, or the Deep Realm, or Bism!" Mum had finished reading them *The Silver Chair* only last week.

"Or the Dwarf Cities," Dash said, reaching for *The Fellowship of the Ring* and leafing through it. "The realm of the Longbeards. What was it called? Doom . . . Kaddoom . . .

"*Khazad-dûm.* Beneath the Misty Mountains. Yes, like all of those . . . but real."

Lucy felt reality push back against his

claims. "But you said light was born there. We know that can't be real."

"Have a listen. There at the bottom of the world, you might go travelling across the desert. You might see signs of life. A lemonade stand sitting empty upon the stretching desert plains. Trucks abandoned, no driver in sight. A cross aboveground — but no church to be seen. Heat scorching the earth, dust storms tearing across the land with a mighty *roar*!"

Dash jerked his head up as Dad hollered the last word.

"Where are all the people?" Dad asked, palms up.

"Beneath ground," Dash said. "But why?"

"You are a scholar of the highest pedigree, Dashel Greene. They live there — they have their doors in the hillside and have dug homes for themselves right out of the earth. Hollowed bookshelves out of the limestone walls, vaulted intricate carved ceilings in their church to rival the artistry of the Sistine Chapel. Rooms and reaches and swimming pools and everything you can imagine, all there underground. But why, you ask?"

He waited. His watch tick-tocked, spinning a spell.

"Water runs down into the earth there. Seeks out all the cracks and chasms, the broken places, and sinks deep, bringing with it mineral deposits. It lands in voids — empty places caused by faults, the shaking of the earth. Or places fossils once lay. The water does its good work, depositing something called silica, then just" — he raised his hands and wiggled his fingers, as if performing a magic trick — "vanishes."

"You mean evaporates," Lucy said. "The water evaporates."

"Isn't that what I said?" Father winked, his dark bushy brows scrunching. "And what do you suppose it leaves behind?"

"Mineral deposits," the girl said. "You told us."

"Yes, Lucy. But don't you miss the wonder, all covered up in the big words. Peel them back and see what lies beneath."

"Beneath the mineral deposits?" Dash furrowed his brow. "You said it yourself. Darkness and emptiness."

"Indeed there would be, if not for the miracle. The darkness is filled . . ."

Dad reached out his arm, beckoning his wife's hand. She laced her fingers into his, smiling and keeping his secret. She had heard this before.

He held her hand out toward them as Lucy held her breath, heart beating.

"With light," he whispered. He turned

Mum's hand this way and that, letting the pale light from the room's solitary window skim over the gem on her finger. It lit into an explosion of colour beneath its cloudy surface.

"They are mining opals, there in Coober Pedy," he said. "Just think. In the dark, beneath the scorching heat and sandstorms above, they live cooled by the earth, and pull colour and light from its belly."

Mum laughed. "You make it sound so fantastical."

"Ah, but it is. You remember that, children. You mine for the colour and light in the dark, in the harshest terrain. Because these truths . . . as dazzling to the mind as they are . . . are only echoes."

"Echoes of what?" Lucy was always anxious to cut right to the heart of the matter.

"The truest story of all."

And so it went, night after night, story after story stitching Dash into the fabric of their family.

It seemed things would stay that way forever. That they would always be together like this. But something changed for Dash as time ticked by.

"Why do you study the stars, Dash?" Lucy had asked one day in the reading room when she was thirteen and he fifteen. They were sitting sideways on their chairs, legs draped over the wingbacks' arms, feet almost touching. And yet even so close, she felt the distance growing between them, attributed it to the galaxies holding so much more than she could.

He shrugged.

And she waited.

He turned a page.

She cleared her throat.

At last he swung his legs over the edge of the chair to sit properly. "I don't know," he said, looking at her, then out the window. "I guess . . . my relatives, they bounced me around so much when I was a kid after Mom and Dad . . ."

Here, Lucy sat up properly, crossing her legs in the chair, giving him her full attention. He never mentioned his parents.

"Wherever I moved after that, everything was different. Time zones. Weather. Buildings. Food. Music. All the things that tell a person what home is. It changed every time." He dropped his gaze then, staring at his black Converse shoes. "Except the stars."

Lucy ached for him. Wished he would have a home with them forever, that he wouldn't always have to wait to enroll for school each year until the last second, unsure of whether his aunt would continue to be based out of London or move on, as she often spoke of doing, to New Jersey.

"The stars are your home," Lucy said quietly, wanting him to know she recognized this truth he had shared and would hold it carefully. Maybe she was younger than him, but she could still understand. And her heart was for him.

He shrugged again. "Yeah," he said. "I guess."

He returned to his study of black holes, and she lifted her book to read again, too, but watched wide-eyed as the years continued on and Dash drifted farther from her still.

His teachers saw special things at work in his mind. Words like *genius, prodigy,* and *untapped potential* floated around. Lucy's mum had gone to parent-teacher meetings in his aunt's stead, for she traveled away from home more and more for business. Lucy attributed his intelligence to all that time alone spent in books, with entire universes as his constant companions.

They moved him up, made provision for him to begin university classes at sixteen — one of them being a class on Shakespeare.

One night, Lucy vaulted a Shakespeare quote at him — something about the stars — but instead of taking a crack at it in their usual fashion, he had just looked up at the stars and quoted one back.

" 'I am constant as the northern star, of whose true-fixed and resting quality there is no fellow in the firmament.' "

His eyes were sad, then, as he turned to her. Her chest ached, and her hand wanted to reach out and take his — to squeeze away the loneliness of his pain-filled life. To banish the heartbreak of a father who had left him, as she'd eventually learned, of a mother who'd given herself to a substance that had taken her from him, and of the aunt who did not care to even know the nephew who had dwelled beneath her roof for a quarter of his life.

Something changed in that moment. Many things changed, actually, knocking into one another like the swirling lines of dominoes they had once filled the courtyard with. The breath went from Lucy's lungs as she saw before her not the lost boy, but the young man, whose gaze no longer lingered on his oversized feet through thick glasses but lifted to the horizon, to the sky above, searching.

And as he lifted his gaze to these new horizons, he was looking right over her. Past her.

She felt for the first time the irony of a

love that had been there, subterranean, for longer than she'd known. Love that was already beyond her grasp.

She was too late in realizing, too young to do anything about it. And too dim to compete with the stars that had captured his mind. As his professors put it, his bright future was limitless. Meanwhile, her teachers said things of her like "her time will come" and "still waters run deep" and "she will find her place."

The sadness in him gathered something fierce up inside of her. "Dash," she said.

"Hmm?" He didn't look at her. Only out the reading room window, past the city lights.

She didn't know what she should say. What could she offer him? "That Shakespeare quote . . . Do you mean you are constant? Because you are. There's nothing you can't do if you set your mind to it. I believe that, Dash. You can do anything."

It broke her young heart to say it, for she knew that in all likelihood, his limitless potential would take him far from her. Probably for good.

"No," he said. "It's just . . . alone. The star, I mean. In that quote."

"That's not true." She stood, her book thudding to the ground. "It's surrounded by lots of stars. You're surrounded. I mean . . . by us. I mean, you . . . and us." This was not going well. *Stop flopping over your words like a fish out of water.* She took a breath. "You're not alone, Dash. You're ours."

He did not look at her for a long while. And when he did, it was from a far-off place. "You have a good life, Lucy."

"*We* do, Dash. It's yours, too."

He shuffled his foot, his height no longer lanky but sure.

"You . . . live in a fairy tale."

The words slammed into her. "No I don't," she said, defensive for her, and for him. Fairy tales did not feel like this.

"It's not a bad thing," Dash said. "It's just, not many people live in a family like yours, Lucy. Stories by the fire and dinner under stars and all that. It's good. I mean, it's amazing. Hang on to it."

His eyes pleaded with her, and her ribs ached in silent reply.

"I-I will," she said, her voice small, with a sense that she'd been uninvited to some very deep place inside of Dash.

She wanted to knock him on the head, get him to understand that her family was his, that this life was his, too. But he had shadows in his past, and there was a part of him he did not want to let her into, judging by his abrupt jump to his feet and quiet stride away.

Their meetings changed after this. He studied the stars, then their galaxies. She fought the dreadful anchored feeling of being left behind, throwing her heart and mind the other direction — into the deep, deep depths of the sea. She pulled books of maritime history, shipwrecked mystery, ocean currents from the shelves and always, always the mystery of the lost ship HMS *Jubilee,* which had made an appearance in several of her father's stories, and whose disappearance gripped her imagination.

She hated the new distance between them, and hoped that somehow, someday he might let her back in.

THREE

"Hang on to it." Dash's words about her family followed Lucy to the seaside in his place that spring. But how was she supposed to do so, when Dash — an integral part of her family — was slipping farther away? Though he was meant to come with them, at the last moment his attendance was specially requested at a maths tournament.

In spite of his absence, Lucy enjoyed a glorious week, with days spent reading her atlas, the ocean itself climbing sand to greet her toes, chasing wild flora with her mother, and marveling at the skies with her father. She packed for the return home with mixed feelings, but she was eager to see Dash and her cottage filled with the love and laughter of family.

They loaded the suitcases into their borrowed car through a downpour of rain, Mum blessing the skies for not unleashing until today. As they approached London,

Mum turned to smile at Lucy in the back seat. "How about we repot the French hybrid lilac when we get h—"

And all went screeching and black after that. Bits of sirens and raindrops breaking through. Glimpses of Father at Lucy's side as she lay in a strange white room. Bright lights and the smell of rubber gloves and medicine.

And finally, the waking up to what was most certainly no fairy tale. A home half-empty. The French hybrid shriveled crisp and brown in its too-small pot.

Father stroked her hand gently as they sat side by side in silence each night as she slowly came to understand . . . Mum was gone.

No longer a child at fourteen, but feeling more lost and childlike than ever, she began to understand that it wasn't just Mum she had lost. She pruned and deadheaded the lilac, watering it, repotting it, moving it from sunny spot to sunny spot as the light shifted. But it would not come back.

And neither would Dad.

He was there . . . but he was gone. He smiled at her, but the smile was so unnatural, so untrue, that it broke her heart over and over again. Gone were the riddles and stories.

Gone was Dash, except for the books he left on her doorstep. He did not know how to enter their broken lives any more than they knew how to bring him back in. Not with Mum gone.

Light itself. That was what Dad called Lucy. So one day, when he did not even get out of bed, she put on her best dress, brushed her stick-straight black hair, and pulled down his cup from the kitchen shelf. It had a coating of dust inside, so she rinsed it, dried it, taking care around the chip, and brewed him his favorite chamomile, just as Mum used to.

When she cracked open the door of her parents' room — *his* room, she reminded herself — she found him sitting in the dark, holding Mother's watch. His chin trembled and he moved the back of his fist over his eyes, stifling a moan that sounded, to Lucy, like all the pain she felt caught up inside of herself. He took the face off Mum's watch, stopped the ticking hands, and clicked the tiny, fragile face back in place with a click so soft and final it made Lucy's hands shake.

The cup echoed her trembling upon its saucer, and Father saw her for the first time. His eyes grew wide and pooled deeper with tears.

"Oh, my girl," he said in a ragged, shuddering breath. And that was all. She sat on the edge of his bed and leaned against him, feeling the tremble of his chin upon her head, the silent tears baptizing her hair as his large palm ran itself over, and over, and over her head, pressing her close to his broken heart.

"I'm sorry," he whispered.

She whispered the same. But it had not been enough . . . for then, he was gone.

"A week and no more," he explained, "and I'll come back ready to be the father you deserve, Lucy."

She had not understood. Even after the kindly Mrs. Richards, who lived on the third floor in Candlewick, came down to stay with her in Father's absence, explained. "He just needs time, dearie." She was kind but a stranger, when all Lucy wanted was her family.

And so she took herself to Dash's door once again. Not to summon the lost boy home . . . but clutching hopes that the lost boy could help her find her way.

Four

Dash answered her knock, beheld her with solemn face, stepped into the hallway, and closed the door behind him, as if he refused to let his own flat's emptiness seep into her newly acquired emptiness. There was something new in him. Where before they had shared camaraderie, now his presence held protectiveness, too.

"Dash, I . . ." Lucy's voice burned. She had not spoken of her grief yet and did not know how to put this great billowing pain into words. "I don't know what to do." It was all she could manage, but he took up where her words failed.

"It's okay, Matchstick Girl," he said. "Come on."

Just two words: *Come on.* No treatise on healing or hope, no magic cure . . . but somehow they infused her with hope all the same. As if this boy, who knew how to be alone and still live, was promising to show her how to be okay.

They stopped to tell Mrs. Richards where they were going, and Dash grabbed Lucy's atlas. After proper instructions for when to be back, Mrs. Richards waved and watched them from the gates of Candlewick all the way until they disappeared down the street.

Lucy looked at the calendar at the ticket window and thought how strange it was to see a date there when time was all a blur, when she did not even know what day of the week it was. *August 28, 2004.* The numbers baffled her.

What baffled her more was how Dash, at sixteen, felt suddenly so grown up. Though she had traveled the Tube many times over the years, she saw a different side of him as he navigated their journey as one accustomed to fending for himself. His slim height looked solitary but assured here in the crowd, rather than gangly as it did at home. Perhaps he had been right — her life had been a fairy tale, compared with his.

And now he could show her how to live the other sort of life.

She followed him down into the station's maze of stairs and passageways, past a busker fiddling a folk tune that sounded like it belonged more at a country ball than in a sweaty dark tunnel.

As she stood at a fork in the station, wondering which way to take, Dash leaned down and whispered, "Greenwich." A thrill went through her. For while Greenwich was not far, it had felt in all their armchair conspiring like a distant promised land.

The Tube swayed and clicked along, beginning to feel like an embrace around her broken self. Dash opened the atlas of oceans in Lucy's lap.

"Are you shore you want to bring this big book?"

Lucy gave a confused look. "What? You're the one who said to —"

His deadpan face flashed mischief. "Shore," he said. "Get it? Oceans . . . shore . . ."

"Oar not," she said dryly.

"Whoa, way to *barge* into my joke, Matchstick Girl. *Sea* what I did there?"

It was the silliest thing. Puns cheesier than the Harrod's cheese counter. But for the first time in weeks — she felt her spirit lighten. Even a smile began.

And then, right in the middle of a pun spree sprouting the beginnings of hope . . . the Tube stopped. The lights cut out, speed slowed . . . and then nothing. Just darkness, too many stories beneath the sunlight and fresh air above.

Slowly emergency lights clicked on, giving a yellow glow to the worried murmurs coursing through the train. Someone mentioned the Twin Towers attack from almost three years before. Was this . . . *that*? An attack?

Lucy slammed her atlas shut, every muscle going tight in her body.

"Hey," Dash said, leaning close. "Fear knot."

Lucy swallowed.

"Get it? Knot?" He tapped her atlas.

Lucy tried to keep from shaking, but her hands trembled. The last time everything went dark . . .

She pressed her eyes closed, willing away the visions of sirens and the smell of rain. It was more than a memory. It was as if the Tube had slammed her right back into that car crash. She felt too small, not enough for this. Her breaths came quick and shallow.

Dash laid his hands on hers. "It's gonna be okay, Matchstick Girl. Probably just a power outage. And what does a power outage have on a girl who is . . . How does your dad say it?"

"Light?" She eked the word out.

"Light *itself*. Listen, we're gonna be okay. Here." He reached for her atlas, and she hated how childish she felt. Opening the book between them, he looked around. "Look at that." He held up a hand at a sign touting Jubilee Line. "It's meant to be. Show me where you think the *Jubilee* is." He tapped the atlas. It was open to the page showing the South Pacific.

"Not there," Lucy said, feeling her hands begin to steady as she flipped the pages, showing him her most recent theory about its location — the Strait of Gibraltar.

They passed two hours turning pages and swapping theories, until the stalled Jubilee Line felt more like a safe hideaway than a threat to her life. He leaned in close and told her of a poem he'd learned in school.

"A poem?"

"Relax. No Shakespeare, I promise. It's called 'The Old Astronomer.' About a brilliant astronomer on his deathbed. Near the end it says, " 'Though my soul may set in darkness, it will rise in perfect light; I have loved the stars too fondly to be fearful of the night.'

"See?" He gestured at their dim surroundings, the darkness. "Nothing to fear here." Offering theories about deeper meanings, they talked on about the poem. It felt magical and heavy. She didn't quite know what to do with it but wanted to love it, for Dash's sake, for the way he'd seen her through the grip of fear and not made her feel ridiculous. She felt her being return from that faraway cold scene of the crash and back into the present.

When the Tube finally started moving and they emerged in Greenwich, blinking in the sun, a joy overtook her like none she'd ever felt, to be in the wide world again. This place, high on a hill and looking down on London Town, held hope. Home to the National Maritime Museum *and* the Royal Observatory, with the prime meridian splitting time right between them, it seemed to declare that Lucy and Dash, though on diverging paths, need not be so separate from each other after all.

But two things had changed forever down in the Underground. Though they had weathered the ordeal and she had risen to the surface triumphant in the journey, from that point, small dark spaces clawed at her, made her feel trapped and breathless, a second away from returning to the moment that had taken Mum. And that day she stopped seeing Dashel Greene as the lost boy. For he had found her in the dark, and given her a home.

FIVE

The watchmaker changed, too. Though he phoned every night, counting down the days until he'd come home and assuring her he loved her, he never told Lucy where he'd gone. When he returned he was different, somehow. Present. Scarred and sad, but . . . he was hers again, claimed back from the dark place she had found him in.

Dash came again to the evening fires, and while it took some time for the stories to resume, her father began to instruct them on the art of riddle-making, as if it were the most natural thing in the world with which to break the silence.

"The secret to a good riddle," he told them one night, his voice trying and not quite succeeding to reach the peaks and valleys of his old magical tone, "is to begin at the end. Know what your answer is, and slowly drop clues. Your listeners won't know they are clues, of course — not until they lean in."

He swallowed, managing to find a smile. He played with some gears on his small worktable, piecing cogs together until they fit just so, taking them apart, doing it again. "That's what your mother used to say." He put his hand on his head in thought, subconsciously rubbing it as if Penny had just plopped a clump of lichen on his hat from a tree, this time from way up in heaven. "What was it she called it? To stretch toward."

"Ad tendere," Lucy said, her heart quickening at being able to offer her father this gift — a lost phrase of her mother's. How horrid to lose those details in the fog of grief. Loss upon loss. She vowed to breathe life back into her father whenever she could.

"That's it." He smiled in earnest this time. "Pay attention. Make a practice of digging for clues."

Lucy glanced at Dash, who shared her concerned look. Neither of them, apparently, quite understood what Dad was getting at.

Lucy fixed her eyes on her father, eyes wide and waiting.

"So," he said, "riddlers we shall become. Something to set our hands to. I shall give you two clues, and you shall find a story.

And along the way, we will dig for light. Continue to tell the stories of this world's wonders. I think we could all use a bit of that, don't you? Some reminding of what the Maker of such a world can do?"

He looked so fragilely hopeful then, all Lucy could do was nod, though she still did not understand.

"Good," he said, ruffling her hair. "I think it's our duty to keep the stories, to pass them on. It is our duty — and our honor. In a world as dark as ours, we — that is, *people* — forget how to see the light. So we remind them by telling the truth, fighting the dark, paying attention . . . setting the stars alight. There are things shining brightly all along, if we will notice."

"You make it sound as if we're in a battle, Dad."

He folded his fingers around her small hand. "So we are, my girl. So we are. But it is a battle that can be won by holding fast to hope . . . and light. We'll keep telling the stories, finding the clues. Gather them up, Lucy and Dash. Taking note of the good, the true, the just, the miracles hidden at every turn is like . . . a deliberate act of defiance against the darkness. Build a . . ." He paused, searching for a word and not finding it. "Your mother was always the one with the words. Gather the stories into a . . ."

"Compendium?" Dash offered, pushing his glasses up as if unsure whether he should speak into this moment.

"Yes!" Dad pointed at Dash. "A compendium." He blew his cheeks out. "You kids have had more than your fair share thrown at you. Stick together. Gather the clues. Don't give up. And remember — every good riddle has a safeguard built into it, a way for the seeker to solve the riddle, when all else fails." He grew serious again. "If ever anything should happen to me — if my stories should stop — watch for the safeguard. It'll come."

Six

And so began the gift. Dad giving, and giving, and giving them stories. True ones, made-up ones, and some a mysterious mingling in between. *"To remember the God who is coming, and coming, and coming to find your heart,"* he'd said. *"Wherever you are, whatever's happened. With every miracle around every ordinary corner."* It did not feel like he was riddling them, only continuing his nightly stories.

As she grew, it felt as if he was withholding some great story behind them all, but she began to understand that the stories were perhaps his own way of fighting the darkness. But even more, they were his way of giving her a way out of hers. They reached into her grief, spinning one step at a time into place, forming an invisible staircase out of the pit she had found herself in. And Dash was always there too, always faithful.

Until one day the thread between them

was snipped. Cut quick, when Dash did not come. When she went to fetch him from his flat, the door stood propped open, revealing dark emptiness, with moonlight falling across the cold floor. Lucy felt for the first time what Dashel had felt all his life: forgotten.

She had turned to go when a scrap of paper on the table caught her eye. She knew it was for her before she even read her name, printed there in his stick-straight writing. Dash always wrote with fine-tip permanent marker. *"No sense writing something down if you don't mean it,"* he'd once told her.

Unfolding it now, her heart sank at the sight of only a few lines. She didn't know what she'd hoped for. A novel? A letter? A map to find him, perhaps?

But instead, it read:

> To the Matchstick Girl. I had to go . . . my aunt had a job offer she couldn't say no to, over in the States. She said it was time I returned to my roots. I know my roots are here, if they're anywhere — right out by our fountain — but I've got to go. I'll write as soon as I can. I won't say good-bye to you, because I know it'll never be good-bye for us. Not ever.

And that was it. She turned a circle, slowly, in that empty flat, hating the paper in her hands. Anger boiled up in her at Dash. For leaving, for not saying good-bye, for so many things.

When she and her dad looked through the telescope that night, she missing Dash and his glasses and his supernova quips, he tried to encourage her as she had him in the midst of his darkest hour. "When things seem dark, Lucy, that's when you fight for the light."

The next night she'd found a book on her pillow, tied with a length of twine and a lilac tucked underneath. Dad's work again, with a nod to Mum in that lilac.

Into the Void: The Search for the HMS Jubilee, bound in scarlet.

"Dad," she said, warmth in her voice at his thoughtfulness in hunting down a book on one of her favorite subjects. She dove in, devouring the accounts of seafloor searches, underwater trench excavations, all in search of the famed lost ship that had vanished with a traitor aboard during the Napoleonic wars.

True to his promise, Dash sent a letter from New Jersey. A few lines meant to be a friendly hello, but only enlarging the hollow place inside of her. She tried to hide it but felt Dad's compassion as he watched her, the determined set of his jaw.

A year later a postcard from Harvard in Massachusetts announced he'd been admitted to the astronomy and astrophysics programme. *Next stop the moon! But not before stopping back at Candlewick to pick you up, Lucy. If you're not diving the ocean depths and finding the lost ship* Jubilee *by then, that is.*

His words made her smile, that time. Less of the longing, more of a joy for her friend. For his dreams, his home in the stars. Time, as she had learned, did soothe the rough edges away from wounds, even if the wounds still ran deep and a distant ache remained. And the pain was once again stifled by the appearance of another book on her pillow, a biography of the traitor Frederick Hanford, the man who absconded with the *Jubilee* and disappeared without a trace.

She heard from Dash a few more times over the years, and soon she was neck-deep in her own studies at university. She wondered, sometimes, looking up at the domed ceiling in her beloved Oxford library, how Dash was doing.

And she wondered where he was when she desperately needed him more than a decade later. For as Dash found his place in the world, the watchmaker had fallen ill. Lucy declared she would put her master's degree on hold, but Dad didn't allow it. "I'm not going anywhere," he said stubbornly. "Chase that mystery, Lucy. Find your answers."

She was researching the *Jubilee,* and it gave her father, in particular, a spark of joy to see the elements of his fireside tales igniting a flame in her.

But Lucy was as stubborn as he, and so they found a middle ground. She moved home, working on her thesis from afar with special arrangement from her mentor and professor, Dr. Dorothy Greenleaf, and she tended to the watch shop at Cecil Court to be nearby on Dad's bad days.

She got lost in the pages of the British Museum's reading room for hours at a time, emerging to lay the fire at night when the watchmaker no longer could, his health failing faster. She sat beside him when a stroke stilled the work of his hands, but not his heart, and she filled the silence with her own stories procured from the annals of history.

It was Lucy who "put his affairs in order" — the doctor's words, uttered with compassion, shattering her world with one gentle blow. And it was Lucy who, walking the rooms of the too-empty cottage at thirty years old, felt her pocket watch's warm, engraved metal slip from her hands and fall to the ground. It sliced through those old dusty sunbeams and winked back at her from the creaking floorboard. In that same spot where Dash used to sit, glasses sliding down his nose as he worked the screwdriver to adjust the telescope they were building . . . before he disappeared.

But when she knelt to retrieve the watch it would not come. The chain snagged, caught like her heart, stitching itself to this place. With fingers long accustomed to coaxing delicate parts to cooperate, she eased the chain from its splintered captivity . . . and stilled.

It was no splinter at all. It was a carefully notched pull, spun on its wooden axis as if to point at the darkness beneath. Holding her breath, Lucy lifted it and pulled out a brittle envelope.

Every riddle has a safeguard. Dad's writing scrawled upon it from a time when his hand was much steadier.

Opening the envelope, she found a faded watercolor picture of a stone-clad structure — part of a castle, perhaps. It looked as if it might have been painted from a rooftop, for dark sky pinpricked with starlight served as a canopy to the seascape below. The scene sent a shiver up Lucy's spine. Five white sea stacks rose from the churning black waves like so many bony fingers, such that any ship would be dashed to pieces if it sailed into them.

At the bottom of the painting, studied handwriting — perhaps a bit shaky — spelled out three words. At first she thought it to be the name of the building pictured or the harbor in view. But instead the three words read to her narrowed eyes, *The Way Home.* The right half of the painting was torn clean off, and part of the building with it. And in the bottom corner where an artist might have made his mark, a single initial: *J.*

The rumble of the Underground shook right through the floor and straight into Lucy's veins, thundering with her pulse. She slipped the painting into the envelope, this vestige of life and mystery. It meant something, and she must know what it was. As the shaking walls stilled, in breathless anticipation, Lucy opened her watch and spoke into the room full of memories:

"Let the story begin."

Seven

Edgecliffe Estate
East Sussex, England
August 1802

The wind rose again in the night, and with it, Father's temper. The two were inter-twined. A gale bellowed down the cliffs to the sea below, snatching up its fury in swirls and delivering it back into The Admiral's soul. Cannon fire in the English Channel beyond rolled in like thunder, echoes of Napoleon's ongoing war.

Orange fire glowing from the hearth behind him, The Admiral stood at the window in his study as a man far from home, commanding a battle he could not see. Lamenting his absence from it, and the way the endless searing pain in his leg caused a pain deeper than the physical. It took him from that war, shut him out of it.

The cannons, and the wind, and the fury

of it all would pour out on whomever was around.

On this night, Frederick Hanford was determined it would not be him this time. He would not wait for his father to summon him for an inquisition.

He always made demands like, *"Boy. Name the sails."* And Frederick, nameless in the angry great man's presence, would recite them like cogs in a machine. *Mizzen. Mizzen topgallant. Main topsail. Fore topsail.*

Sails that infused Frederick with the majesty and adventure of what awaited him out there in the great blue, someday. He knew them all, knew them perfectly.

But perfection did not satisfy. Father would not even look at him. Never acknowledge his good studying. Onward to the next thing. Name the decks. The guns. Captain of the *Victory.* The *Orient.* The *Ville de Paris.*

On, and on, and on it went. Glass catching firelight, firelight catching that word. *Boy.* As if he were just a tool in The Admiral's arsenal, his one remaining campaign in Great Britain's war.

In the past, the hollering had most often been met with another sound — the ivory-keyed piano. Father, in the west wing, poured amber liquid to fuel his tirade. Mother, in the east wing, sat at her instrument and countered the yelling the only way she knew how: Handel's *Messiah.*

She, playing her part alone, had sent her notes down the corridor. An invitation to the man whose heart and hand she had won playing that very piece at a benefit concert for the London Foundling Hospital.

And not long afterward they'd had a son. But war, injury, and the loss of his place commanding his ship all but killed her husband. The void had run so deep in their home — with these three souls spread to the far corners of Edgecliffe Manor — it felt hopeless. But she'd done what she could — played her notes, always from the refrain: *Let us break their bonds asunder.*

She'd played them with passion, conviction, desperation. And perhaps more than anything else, with the effect of a long, flowing garment tossed up in the air like a sheet in the sun, falling over the yelling to dampen it. To breathe beauty back into the night.

Maria Hanford had not been the sort of mother who would sing Frederick a lullaby or draw him into an embrace, but these late-night concertos, he knew, were sent to do battle on his behalf. Fierce in their beauty, just like her.

Though Frederick had not known the reason at the time, as her end approached, the notes tumbled down the corridor with more desperation, colliding with Father's yelling as a force sent to shatter the pummeling words, to wall them away from her son. The two forces had done battle there, right outside his bedroom door, tangling in the night.

It was thus that he would fall into a fitful sleep and forget, for a spell, the darkness that shook the age-old walls, sometimes turning in his hand the old sixpence his mother had slipped him once to buy a peppermint stick in the village. A peppermint stick would be gone in an instant, he'd known, but a coin, he could keep. Hold. Slip beneath his pillow to run his thumb over and pretend instead it was his mother who ran a thumb over his cheek, as mothers in the fairy stories always did.

He'd wrapped his thoughts in her notes, let them bury the cannon fire in the distance, and the shadowy someday of his future among those cannons.

Now that his mother's notes had fallen silent — consumed forever by the fever — The Admiral's amber liquid flowed more abundantly, and the wrathful words bellowed freely without any music to fight back.

So this night, when darkness shook those walls again, Frederick slipped inside them . . . and escaped. The house had been built with priest holes, hidden passageways, and secrets in its very stones. For the first time, he thanked the heavens for his dark suit of mourning, the way it blended him into the night.

He knew not where he was going as he stumbled past St. Thomas's chapel and its graveyard with weathered tombstones sticking up into the night like crooked teeth. With wide young eyes and shaking hands and legs, he wandered on in the dark through cliff-side pasture paths and stick-built gates, growing more and more fearful as the harsh night descended.

But kindness, as it happened, did not reside only in Handel's *Messiah.* It also dwelled in the blistered hands of a shepherd who gathered up Frederick's shivering body from beneath the lone yew tree as if he were a lost lamb. He brought him home to a single-room cottage, laid him on a mattress of straw before the crackling fire.

In his nine years Frederick had never known such warmth. Not from the fireplaces of all the twenty-seven chimneys that turned his own home's roofline into that of a fortress. Nor had he ever experienced the odd sort of light that seeped into his soul when woken by the sound of laughter.

"He looks lost, Father," a voice sweet and gold as honey said.

"And well he might be," the man responded, casting a shadowed look through a small window.

Frederick rubbed his eyes, sitting up to take in the scene: mottled walls with stonework breaking through plaster. The room was simple and bare, its only adornment two small windows, with light spilling in as if from heaven itself.

A door creaked open, bringing with it air so fresh it seemed to clean his soul. The sea mists had not yet burned off the pastures. How early was it, here in this other world?

"Eggs," a new voice said. A woman. The mother? The ache inside him yawned as Handel's *Messiah* tiptoed through his memory. He watched as she cracked an egg into a steaming pot hanging over the crackling fire.

"We've got a double yolk today, we do. Must be the hens knew we had a young guest with us."

Frederick's still form filled with shame as he watched the family's flurry of activity. He stood, his unpracticed hands fumbling to pull the blanket over the makeshift straw mattress. Was this how one . . . made a bed? His face burned. Here he was nearly ten years old — a man, according to Father — and a heap of straw made him glow like a hearth fire.

"Never you mind, dear," the woman said, placing her hands gently about his shoulders and guiding him to a table of weathered wood. "Time enough for me to do that later."

The shepherd stood from the stool at Frederick's side and strode to the door. "Sheep are callin'. The day's a-wastin'."

In the silence that followed the shepherd's departure, Frederick swallowed, trying to find words in this new place.

That honey-filled laugh sounded again. "Cat got your tongue?"

"Hush, Juliette." The mother swatted the girl playfully with a rag. "You'd do well to learn a lesson or two from him on how to hold your own tongue." Her words were strict but her tone was gold, offered with a wink. "Heaven help us, the girl comes into this world with the sea flood, and she takes the force of the sea with her wherever she goes."

Frederick tilted his head. "Sea flood?"

"Aye. Surely you know of the great sea flood?"

When his silence answered to the contrary, she leaned in as if to impart a great secret.

"Every eighteen years, the moon draws closer than any other time. Like a great silver dish in the sky, it draws the sea up higher . . . and higher . . . and higher. All the fisherfolk around clamber to see it. Legend has it that to be touched by the spray of a sea flood wave is to be granted good fortune all the days of your life."

"And . . . Juliette was sprayed?"

She laughed. "Oh my, no. Juliette was born the night of the last sea flood. Folks like to say the moon and the waves delivered her right into our arms."

She shook her head. "I know 'twern't the moon, but I do believe the sea got caught up in that girl's soul. 'Tis in her, the force and the call of it. She vows she'll be there to meet that tide, next time it do come 'round."

Frederick gulped. A great silver moon . . . What might that look like from his rooftop telescope? "Will it be soon?"

"Aye, the wink of an eye, and the stretch of an eternity. Another ten years. But mark my word, our Juliette will make good on that vow."

"Aye," Juliette chimed in from where she placed carrots upon a plate. "That I shall."

"Now," her mother said, tugging the girl's plaited copper hair. "Give the boy a bowl and be on your way. The pigs need feeding and they'll have it from none but you, you sprite-o'-the-mist."

The girl slid a plain brown bowl his way, running her finger around the rim and skipping over its three chips. "Do take care with our fine china," she said with a wink and skipped out the door, her mother shooing her and whisking the bowl away from Frederick. She moved it to the head of the small table, replacing Frederick's with one that bore only a single chip on its rim.

Steam curled from a poached egg within. Double yolk, indeed. It looked for all the world like a king's feast, his stomach coming alive with a vengeance after last night's wanderings. He thought of the breakfast that Cook laid out every morning, silver-domed dishes piping with sausages and potatoes and all manner of offerings. Never did he remember wishing to inhale them as he took breakfast alone each morning. But the simple fare before him now summoned a growl from his belly, the likes of which could've shaken the earth.

Frederick watched as the woman pulled a single cob of corn from another pot over the fire and harvested its kernels into a bowl. She heaped at least half into his bowl, dividing the remainder among another three bowls.

"Please . . ." His voice broke, muddied from the long night as it scraped past a soreness. He cleared his throat. "Please, don't trouble yourself for me."

The woman paused with a dish she was drying in her apron and looked him full in the face. "Master Frederick."

He hung his head. "You know . . . who I am." He heard the heavy defeat in his own voice. If she knew he was the son of Sir Barnard Hanford, she would know him as the servants did — for he heard them, when they did not know he was near, call him the "sea brat."

"Too much salt air's addled him," he'd heard a footman say once. *"Wanderin' the cliffs like a banshee, never knowin' the work it takes to keep the land beneath his feet alive."* The man had spit in disgust, and Frederick had begun letting his wanders take him farther inland, to watch as the tenant farmers toiled over the land. Was it true? Did those who worked on his father's land break their backs, only to live on a handful of corn kernels for breakfast?

"Ah, now don't let the gloom settle over your bones so," the woman said.

Gloom in the bones . . . He had never

heard the phrase before, and though it was a sad one, it comforted him to think that somebody understood him.

"To be known is no shame. You eat up, Master Frederick."

But the gloom did settle in his bones — the heaviness piling upon him until he felt physically weary. He nudged the bowl away from himself, looking toward the door where the others had disappeared. "Might I . . ." His formal speech sounded sharp here. "Would you mind if I . . ."

She laughed, an easy sound like the rolling tide, and lowered herself into the chair beside him as it creaked beneath her slight form. "Out with it, then. What's it you want, child?"

"To help," he blurted, the words sounding foolish. What did he have to offer? And yet . . . how could he not?

Understanding eased the lovely lines around her smile. "Ah," she said. "Juliette'll be slopping the pigs, and Tom — that's my husband — and Elias will be feedin' the sheep. The porridge'll keep, but eat that egg before you go. They'll show you what to do."

Frederick made quick work of the egg with a tarnished tin fork and set outdoors, where the mud was gloriously thick and the sun shone bright.

He watched as Tom filled a trough with straw for the lambs who were nudging their way toward breakfast. Perhaps he imagined it, but the man seemed to slow his work, never saying a word but casting a glance at the spare shovel, then sending a grin Frederick's way. An invitation.

Before long he was transferring armloads of pokey straw, doubtless bungling the job at every turn, but something about plunging his strength into the dark earth was a balm to his soul.

Juliette seemed less than pleased that her shovel had landed in the hands of a spoiled sea brat. "You're always tellin' me not to hold the shovel that way," she said, crossing her arms.

"Juliette, my girl," Tom said, a glimmer in his eye. "Come here and I'll show you how to hold it."

"You *have* before, Father." She looked offended, but there was a spark in her spirit mirroring her father's, as if she knew he was up to something. She drew near to him, stepping with caution toward his open hand. Another step, another — and he reached out and smudged her cheek with mud.

"There, now," Tom said. "Fit to be mistress o' the land."

She shrieked feigned anger, the smile across her face entirely consuming.

"Not the likes of me," she said, and it was with pride, this proclamation that she was unfit to be mistress of the land.

Somewhere in Frederick's young mind, her words stung.

"The day I become mistress of the land is the day I can fly!" She launched a clump of mud at her father, pleased when it landed on his shoulder and splattered his face.

Frederick could see by the look on the shepherd's face that he relished their banter. He rested his chin on the shovel, his head feeling heavy and foggy after the work, and laughed quietly as he watched father and daughter splatter each other with mud. They heard, and the two of them turned on him, exchanging a conspiratorial glance.

"No," he said, but felt something come alive in him.

"Aye," Juliette said, and drawing back her arm, sent a glop of mud flying right at his shoulder, hitting its mark expertly.

This was foreign to him. Had he ever known larks such as this? With another child, no less? Some instinct overtook him, and he stooped to gather soggy ammunition of his own. But could he truly take aim at a girl? Smear her, most literally, with mud?

He glanced at her father, as if to ask permission. The shepherd tipped his head as if to say, *Only if you dare.* All the permission he needed.

What followed was joy. Pure, wild, unabashed. Mucking about with two people he'd never met, who by rights should despise him, the way Father's tenants were wont to do with his family.

And yet here he was, sun splotched, dirt streaked, and happier than he'd ever been.

A sudden clanging sounded, tin bucket against fence, and Frederick turned to see a boy about his age. He was tossing grain on the ground for the chickens and looking none too pleased at the scene before him — despite the smile pasted on his ruddy face.

"Who's this?" He dipped his head toward Frederick, never taking his eyes from him.

"I'm . . . I'm nobody," he said, his tongue feeling thick as his thoughts. The boy's manner made Frederick feel three inches tall, an imposter here in the barnyard.

And wasn't he?

The shepherd, Tom, drew up next to Frederick and put an arm around his shoulder. The effect was that of a protective cloak. The boy's stare flicked to Tom, whose face showed only welcome to them both.

"This is our friend," Tom said simply. "As

are you, Elias. Thanks for that." He pointed toward the bucket, and Elias's manner was suddenly humbled. Frederick wondered what tale he'd stumbled into here. What was the story behind Elias's immediately humbled manner? As if he owed his life to the shepherd.

"Look at the lot of you!" Juliette's mother stood in the door of the cottage, shielding her eyes and shaking her head. "If you think you're coming back into my house tracking the whole soggy pasture in with you, you'd best think again. Wash up and come get some breakfast."

Juliette and Elias — apparently a hired hand, though something about the way he kept his eyes fixed suspiciously on Frederick made him seem more a guardian — rounded to the trough where a pump waited. They each splashed water on their faces and hands, ruddy from its cold. Frederick followed suit, and when he opened his eyes, droplets clung to his lashes and framed the view before him. A daughter. A father. A friend. A corner of the world where all was right, and that picture bolstered him so that he felt perhaps he could go on after all.

He could face the bellowing at night, even without Mother's music. This memory would now be his song. He inhaled, trying to affix every bit of it to his mind. And as each detail found its place there in the forever-place inside him, he felt something foreign. A fullness in his lungs, a tingling in his fingers. A buoyant heart. Courage.

Courage is a hefty thing, he thought, for though foreign strength flowed through him, so did a heaviness. Heavier with every step toward the stone cottage. So heavy he became dizzy with it. So dizzy he became hot with it. So hot he burned, until there on the threshold of the shepherd's cottage, it pulled him into a sea of black.

Muddled sounds and patchwork pieces of faces clouded his consciousness. The shepherd, lifting him once again. Juliette, running away from her home and toward his. Light and darkness, and light again, and darkness once more. These were days and nights passing — he felt it more than knew it, somewhere in the middle of it all. Fires crackling and low voices murmuring saying things about "fever" and "like his mother, poor soul." Vaguely he became aware that the fireplace he lay by was no longer the shepherd's, but one of gilded ivory. *Edgecliffe.*

He felt homesick.

And yet he was home.

In his ebbing haze, all he could think of

was the darkness of that soil and the white of the sheep. How good God must be, if God be real, to let him know the shepherd's family, to have spent a night by their fire. To have experienced something true and good before leaving this earth. Somewhere in the distance, a church bell rang haunting and slow. A death knell. Was it his?

But visions of the soil rolled on, so rich he could almost smell the spice of it. And though it felt like heaven to him, he knew this did not align with what the Scriptures said of heaven.

The days and nights stewed thick together until slowly, slowly he was drawn out, and morning dawned with a strange clarity. Pale light reached past heavy scarlet curtains. The window was cracked open, letting in the call of the sea beyond, beckoning him back into life.

Days followed as his body tried to catch up to his spirit, which wanted out of this place. Back to the pastures, the cottage, to the people who had known who he was and gave him the gift of home despite it.

When at last his legs were strong enough to carry him across the land, he slipped back into the passageways behind the manor walls, escaped back onto the pastures, urged his weakened limbs to carry him swiftly to the yew tree and beyond. Determined to once more set his eyes on a good and true thing — on that family.

But he slowed as he approached St. Thomas's chapel and the old graveyard, seeing a tiny clutch of mourners in the distance, gathered around a grave. A cloud of black in human form. A sight he would have retreated from only a month before. But now?

Cloaked still in his own suit of mourning, and having come so close to death himself, he felt kinship to these people. He watched on as a small form — a girl — dropped to her knees before the grave.

As the curate retreated from the gathering and people began to disperse, a woman laid a hand on the girl's shoulder, stooping to say something to her. Slipping a bouquet of white daisies into the girl's hands, and waiting.

When the girl did not budge, the woman slowly, sadly stepped toward the fresh grave and laid her own single flower upon it. Turning to go, she stopped to lay a hand upon the girl's head, to stoop, leaning in until their foreheads touched and the girl's cheeks were cradled in the woman's hands. She spoke in a manner gentle and broken and strong all at once, and rose again.

A hollow pit began to open inside of Frederick, a suspicion that he knew this clutch of people. He did not want that to be true. For that would mean the shepherd . . .

He gulped. Could not finish the thought.

A boy lingered near the church. His stare bored into the green grass at his feet as he slowly closed the gap between himself and the girl. His hand reached for hers. She pulled back and he waited, unspeaking. Moments passed until he reached again, and this time the fortress that was the girl eased, ever so slowly, as she laid her head upon the boy's shoulder.

Her form did not shake with sobs, as Frederick had seen some do. It held fierceness as an armor, but a fleeting softness, a crack in her armor, reached out, up through the rich green grass of summer on the hill, up its rise, and straight into Frederick. Like calling unto like, a grief he knew too well knocked at his heart as if to say, *You are not alone. I am here, too.*

And for the first time since his mother's music went silent, Frederick was not alone in the world.

When the girl and the boy climbed the hill arm in arm, she with hollowness in her green eyes, she met his gaze . . . and grief lit into ire.

Pounding inside him urged him to reach out and speak the words — *You are not alone. I am here, too.* They pounded the more when he saw, without a doubt, that it was Juliette and Elias.

He summoned the words. They sat on his tongue like arrows ready to sail into her world, but he stopped. For what if they pierced when they landed, rather than bringing comfort?

He took a step forward. Swallowed. Opened his mouth to speak.

"I-I'm sorry," he said, voice breaking. Heart raw, hanging in those words offered to her into the brittle air between them. He inhaled, summoning courage to offer everything he could. "You are not alone," he said.

Elias shot him a look as if to say, *What fell on your head, you brute? Of course she's not alone. I'm here.*

He swallowed. Against all sense, he continued, if only to give her what little he had — understanding. "I —"

She held up a hand. Silenced him and spoke so low her words could have been cannons dropping slow and solid into the depths of the sea. "It should have been you."

Frederick flinched.

Juliette leaned in, fierceness wrapping her like a serpent around a pole, squeezing vehement words in a shuddering whisper and leaving no room for doubt. "There in the ground. It should never have been Father. And it wouldn't have been Father if you hadn't come, bringing the fever with you."

The words pummeled him, his foot stepping backward. This was a horror he hadn't even considered. That good shepherd was in the ground . . . because of him?

Elias was tugging gently, making to lead Juliette away. A flicker of apology crossed his face, a hint that he, perhaps, did not arrive at the same conclusion as she had. Even so, he would not bring his eyes to meet Frederick's.

Juliette turned to go, one end of her russet shawl slipping from a shoulder and dropping to the ground. Unthinking, Frederick lunged, face hot, snatching it up from where it dragged in the dark earth, tucking it back around her.

She recoiled at his touch and spun to face him. "Be sure of this," she said. "You and I shall never" — she gritted her teeth — "*ever*, speak again." She spat on the ground beside him and left, never once looking back.

The wind that was always tormenting Father flew up the cliffs and into Frederick. It drove him as he ran numbly, blindly, unheeding that he was headed to the very place that would make that girl despise him all the more.

And there, kneeling beside the grave of the kind shepherd dark against green earth, with the cannons of the war rolling gunpowder thunder across the sky, Frederick buried his own tears.

"Anything." His voice choked. "I will do anything you ask of me, God. Undo it. Take me into the earth instead. Bring that girl life once more. Somehow . . . help me make it right." His chest squeezed around the words as they came out flat, insufficient for the burn inside. "Help me. Make it right." This, he repeated, willing the words to be enough. Realizing they never would be.

The prayer was broken and messy and held none of the rhymes or verses that his governess had taught him to pray before bed and meals. And yet, jagged as it was, it was the truest prayer he'd ever known. It mingled with exhaustion as he repeated fragments of it, clutching earth until sleep overtook him right there beside the shepherd's resting place.

EIGHT

Edgecliffe Estate
East Sussex, England
August 1805

Everything changed for Frederick the night of the disappearing light.

Three years had passed since the day at St. Thomas's graveyard. And the silence of the corridors of Edgecliffe was nearly as bad as Father's yelling had been. It drove Frederick, twelve years old, night after night to the stone stairs of the east wing. He climbed and climbed until he burst out into the night upon the roof. Here, tucked behind one of the twenty-seven chimneys, was his secret world.

It was simple, yet it was everything. A chair with a wobbly leg, rescued from the cobwebbed attic. A stockpot salvaged from Cook's castoffs, large enough to hold his own small fire, its smoke curling up against that chimney, so none looking on from afar would imagine it belonged to the vagrant fire of a runaway in his own home. And the book. Always the book, with quill and ink kept beneath the chair to inscribe in it.

Twelfth of August, 1805. The quill scratched its song against the waves that came gently tonight.

Skies: He squinted at the sky as Reskell, his tutor, had taught him. *Constellation Draco in the sky. Constellation Gemini dimly visible.*

Giving his eyes time to adjust, he strained to see the twins within that constellation. Brothers Castor and Pollux, from the stories of yore. Inseparable. He knew they were stars, not people, but the theme of brotherhood drew him deeply. What would it be to have a friend? Much less a brother? The sort to stand fast with you in battle. He knew only solitude in his home. And though he did not mind the quiet . . . the isolation sometimes pierced.

A look over to the parapet where a lopsided weathervane creaked a slow turn, then stopped. *Wind: North.*

He thought back on the day's lessons regarding angles and equations. What was it Reskell had said? He lifted his quill to record it. Words from Galileo Galilei, whom the tutor was forever quoting.

"Mathematics is the language with which God has written the universe."

He didn't know whether he believed that. Pythagoras's theorem certainly didn't smack of the divine. Even so, Frederick knew the working of numbers would serve him well once he boarded Admiral Forsythe's ship, once his father pronounced him ready.

Still, if Galileo had been correct, he was surely only partially correct. Frederick thought back to what he'd seen in the library today and recorded it:

Millie the parlormaid makes landscapes with the ashes before she sweeps them from the hearth.

He only knew this because she'd been called away before she'd swept it up, and he'd happened into the library and found a scene of beach and waves, finger-traced into a canvas of ashes. When she'd returned and seen him studying her work, her face had burned redder than coals. She'd swept it all away quick as a wink before disappearing with only a *"Beg pardon, sir,"* and a hurried curtsy.

He could not account for the reason, but that scene in ashes had risen up to challenge him. *See,* it seemed to say. *Open your eyes. There is goodness here, right here, right in the ashes.*

He opened his eyes there on the roof. Above, the night sky spread like a star-flung canvas. Beyond, the sea rolled its waves. And there, across the meadows and headed for the seaside cliff, a light. Bouncing like a lantern-in-hand.

Which was entirely wrong. None in this village of fishers and farmers would be out this late. Certainly not at the cliffs, which were notoriously perilous to any who did not know their terrain intimately.

He lifted his spyglass and trained it toward the light.

But he saw nothing. No light. Had he imagined it?

He lowered his spyglass and narrowed his eyes, scanning. There — silhouetted black against the dark blue waves and reflected sky, he saw the figure of a boy.

From such a distance Frederick could not make out much, but he saw the lad stoop near the ground. He was close to the cliff edge. Too close. Frederick nearly hollered out for him to stop but knew his voice would not reach across the expanse, nor be heard above the waves crashing upon cliffs.

The boy looked over one shoulder, then over the other. And then he clambered over the edge as if it were his homeland. Frederick knew that spot, had been warned away a thousand times. The cliff had long been receding, rocks falling into the ocean below, carrying any soul foolish enough to tread there right along, too.

Down went Frederick's stomach, straight into a hard pit, and down went his body, through flights of stairs and dark corridors and out into the night below, racing across land soggy from the day's rains. He arrived with shoulders heaving at the cliff's edge.

He pulled up, slowing at a safe distance.

"H-hello," he said, his voice faltering pitifully on the wind. He cleared his throat. "Hello," he said, this time forcing boldness. "Are you there?" No answer. "Are you hurt?" Still, nothing. "I say, are you hurt!"

He splayed himself down upon the ground, feeling cold water seep through his nightshirt. He dreaded what he would see. For it could only be a body, broken on the rocks below. Or, if by some miracle, the boy had caught a branch or stronghold on his fall, what then? What would Frederick do?

When he finally gathered the courage and peered over the cliff, he was met with only a yawning black night. The moon was bright enough to show that no body lay broken, and for that he was awash with gratitude. No boy hung precariously in the balance, awaiting his help, and for that, chagrined though he was to acknowledge it, he was disappointed. He'd thought, perhaps, he might help someone. It would be a nice feeling, he imagined. Something to . . . to matter.

Eventually, he wandered his way home, but sleep did not come that night. Frederick stood watch on his rooftop, chased by doubts over his own sanity. Had he really seen someone out there?

The next afternoon, Reskell was in a delighted froth over Pythagoras. It was getting late, and Frederick was losing all hope of leaving Edgecliffe while the daylight lingered.

He lifted his eyes to the old clock and then transferred his gaze to the looming portraits of Britain's Triumphant Three, the men who had been touted as the great leaders who would put Bonaparte in his place. First, Admiral Horatio Nelson, his portrait gallant in full navy dress, painted so after the Battle of Nile. Second, Father, illustrious hero of Cadiz. Serious. Pockmarked. Proud of his show of courage and cunning in that battle's victory — which was also, as it turned out, his last battle. As the nightly tirades at Edgecliffe had attested for so long.

And last, Admiral Cuthbert Forsythe, who had earned a place in the proud land's hearts and history with his triumph at Malta. This man had agreed to take Frederick onto his ship, the HMS *Avalon.*

"Anyone would be lucky to sail with Forsythe," Father had said. *"Mind, he's not to be crossed. He once threw a fresh-arrived sailor in with the pigs his first night. Said if he was intent on acting like the prodigal son, he'd sleep with the pigs."*

Frederick gulped at the thought. And yet it also conjured the heartwarming memory of a certain mud battle he'd been a part of, once upon a time.

"Do pay attention, Master Frederick," Reskell beckoned. "I know squares of numbers aren't as riveting as watching the sails in action, but if you want to keep your wits about you on deck, absorb these equations as though they are your very lifeblood."

Frederick heard his tutor's voice but the words skipped over his consciousness like gulls upon wind. Pevensey Bay was whitecapped and churning, and the frigate beyond the sea stack rocks was being tossed like a plaything. He narrowed his eyes, tracing its structure. He tried to count. Was it a thirty-two gun? The *Lively,* perhaps? Or no. He squinted. Counted again. Thirty-six guns. The *Dryad,* he'd wager. It'd been seen in Portsmouth recently, and that wasn't terribly far. He reached for the telescope lying on the windowsill.

Reskell put his thin body between Frederick and the telescope. "You'll not board that ship, nor any of His Majesty's vessels, if you can't calculate knots and plot routes. It matters not who your father is, nor how many captains he knows. None of them want a man who doesn't know his way around the rigging when other boys have been at it since nine and ten years old. If you have any hope of excelling in His Majesty's Royal Navy, I suggest you make a quick study. As I was saying —"

"Upend the sand timer at the same moment the chip log is submerged in the water. After the thirty seconds' sand is up, count the knots that have unraveled in the rope attached to the log. This is the speed at which the ship is traversing the ocean." Frederick rattled off the answer he'd memorized from Reskell's manuals late into the night — and thought again of the disappearing light. His foot bounced, awaiting Reskell's response. Awaiting his freedom.

The sound of the surf filled the silence, and Frederick felt the man's astonishment before he looked up and confirmed it in his bespectacled, slack-jawed expression. Father had had the man shipped in from Portsmouth, pilfered from the teachers at the Royal Naval Academy, and he'd arrived at Edgecliffe with low expectations for his lone student.

Reskell blinked, clearly unable to reconcile how those words had transmitted themselves into his feckless young pupil's equally feckless brain.

"But . . . we've only just begun with measurements. How did you know —"

"Grant's *Shipman's Guide,*" Frederick said. He leaned over and tapped the leather-bound volume. "Lifeblood. You said it yourself."

His foot twitched, awaiting the words that would set him free. He'd used his time on the roof last night to affix facts to his memory, in hopes that he might break free of the schoolroom today. It was August thirteenth. The single solitary day of the year he had somewhere he must be.

But his liberation was not so quickly won. "Very well," Reskell said. "On to history. The HMS *Jubilee,* as we read yesterday, was a gift to the kingdom from Denmark. A proud tribute to our continued successful —"

"Sisterhood at sea."

Reskell narrowed his eyes suspiciously. "Yes. But what you haven't learned yet is that on her maiden voyage from Portsmouth, she listed and nearly dashed against East Sussex's very own white cliffs — the Seven Sisters. It was so ornate and gaudy that she served little function but as a spectacle. The historian Peabody said the Seven Sisters looked like veiled mourners that day, stretching into the blue sky above a ship sure to sink."

Frederick's foot tapped faster. Time was wasting. "But she was saved from sinking," he said, hoping to usher in the end of Reskell's tale of the *Jubilee.* He had read the chapter detailing her unfortunate history for just such a moment as this. "Right? She limped back to Portsmouth and was permanently anchored in port, becoming perfect in her gaudy idleness to play prison to traitors awaiting their trials, attracting all the more attention to the treasonous souls she held, framing their disgrace." He spilled the words in a rush, letting the *Jubilee* vanish in the waves of his mind. A fact memorized, recited, and now dutifully disposed of. He would have no need of this knowledge again.

Reskell assessed him and something very nearly conspiratorial appeared in his narrowed eyes. "I see you have been studious of late, Master Frederick."

Frederick waited, breath bated.

"Very well. Go."

He went like the wind itself, tearing over meadows and moors. With their low rises and stretches of great empty space, they felt more like home to him than anywhere upon this green earth. He did not belong in Edgecliffe. No more than he belonged in the village, Weldensea, or Bexhill beyond it.

Years ago he'd asked his governess what made a moor a moor. She'd laughed and told him he asked the strangest questions, that he may as well ask what makes the sea the sea, or England, England. Those had sounded like good questions to him, but he did not say so. When her laughter evened into a sigh, she answered, "A moor be a lifeless place, Master Frederick. There's naught that grows there but prickly things."

And to him, the moors came alive that day. He, even so young, knew what lifeless felt like, and he determined that as long as he was able, he would not let the moors feel that gaping, empty chasm.

So his feet flew through the moors whenever they could, fast and furious and full of life. Just as they did now. Just as they would for as long as —

A snatch of swift motion from the direction of the sea cliff stopped him. A form, strong but wiry, coming from the same place the boy had disappeared the night before. Here he was, in broad daylight — and coming at Frederick full force, head down.

Frederick turned to stop, letting his feet slide across the boggy expanse and willing his body to miss the lad.

But it was too late. He collided pell-mell with him, toppling the boy straight into the muck. They both tumbled to the ground, a tangle of limbs.

"So ye be at it again," the boy said. He sounded young for one so strong. Frederick was splayed across the mud, face down.

"At what?" he said, attempting to get to his knees. A foot upon his back stopped him.

"Snatching my sheep like a common thief." The foot went hard into his back, but Frederick resisted, pushing back and raising himself up as the boy's spit landed beside him.

The heat of injustice began a slow boil inside Frederick. "I would never do that." He turned to face the boy and found a fist in his face, positioned to blow. The face behind it was contorted into hatred, covered in the tar-black of the moor's mud.

"Then explain why you were runnin' like God's wind to my pasture. Explain why your footprints mark this land betwixt, too many times to count."

"I owe you no explanation," Frederick said, the boil inside simmering until he clenched his own fists. He took a step back. "But I am no thief."

He turned to go, but the arm upon his elbow whirled him back around. In that motion, the boy's cap tumbled off, unleashing long hair copper as a farthing and plaited unevenly, eyes green as an angry sea. This was no boy at all. It was the girl, Juliette Heath. The same girl whom he had watched from the corridor windows these past three years, whenever she happened to the pasture beyond with her flock. Her father's flock, as was. There were times they'd nearly crossed paths over the years, but he'd been careful to stay well out of her way. She'd made it very clear she wanted nothing to do with him — and staying away was the only way she'd left him to honor her. That, and the bells she knew naught of.

"It's you," he said.

"Yes," she said, eyebrows raised. "I do appear to be myself. What of it?"

"I . . . just . . ." His tongue was thick, the anger inside replaced by the old shame he knew too well. He'd killed the girl's father, when it came down to it. There was no returning from that.

Her fist clenched tighter, and her wrist — the single spot on her not covered in mud or boy's clothes — was marked with the crimson of a fresh cut from her fall.

"I meant you no harm," he said. And the moment the words were out — the second he saw the ire in her emerald green eyes deepen to a flash of grief — he wished them back. She'd taken them to mean a pain much deeper than the surface wound. She grieved over the wound he could never undo. He hung his head.

"Well, now you've done it," she said. Her jaw jutted out as she crossed her arms.

He was afraid to ask. "Done what?"

"Made me break my vow. I swore we would never speak again. Remember?"

How could he forget? He nodded, scuffed his boot. Three years ago to the day. She, more than anyone, knew what today marked.

"I wasn't stealing your sheep," he said. "Has someone been stealing your sheep?"

She averted her eyes and shrugged one shoulder. "Two are gone."

But that was not an answer, not really. He waited.

She sighed, exasperated. "They may have . . . wandered while I was away."

"Where were you?" He offered the question slowly, keenly aware that he was treading on thin ice and that any misstep would send this exchange crashing into the frigid depths. But perhaps, if he could keep her talking . . . it might help. Somehow.

"Out in the blue," she said, as if it should have been obvious that she'd been at sea. She sighed again and began walking toward her flock.

He jogged to catch up. She didn't bite his head off, merely gave him a furtive glance. As good as an invitation, coming from her. "You were at sea?"

"Only in the bay. Mr. Swain lets me go out to the frigates with him. He's a pilot, you know."

He did know. From the schoolroom window, three flights up in the west wing, he'd often watched Swain's pilot cutter dart out to the bigger ships. He boarded the frigates to help guide them through the currents and hidden rocks of the coastal waters. 'Twas a common practice for captains to entrust their vessels to local watermen to pilot these waters. In truth, Frederick envied Swain. The way he, a common fisherman, could spend his days pulling fish from the sea and, just like that, be onboard some of His Majesty's finest ships, beside captains and admirals whose names the whole world knew. It was honest work, adventurous work, and watching Mr. Swain made Frederick itch to get out to sea all the faster. To feel the thrill of churning waves in a groaning city with wooden walls. To chase down enemies, bring justice. All the things he could not do here on shore.

Juliette spoke on. "I keep watch aboard his cutter while he pilots the frigates."

Shock sputtered from Frederick.

"You find it funny," she said. "Yes, I suppose navigating treacherous waters in Pevensey Bay, where tides grow larger than the sea cliffs themselves, is something to laugh at."

"You misunderstand me," Frederick said, gathering his wits.

"Oh?" She stopped, turned to face him. Her brow raised, a challenge. "Please, do enlighten me."

She made a sight, stray hairs tangling above her head in a haphazard halo where her hat had been. She was a force to be reckoned with.

He paddled about in the muck of his mind for some appeasing explanation, but knew she would see through anything less than the truth.

"You . . . you're a girl."

She stared. "I don't think the boat much cares whose hands guide it, so long as it reaches home," she said. "Anyway. It brings in an extra shilling, and for that Mother and I are grateful."

Frederick's throat burned with responsibility for their situation. But something else in him battled to meet this fiery soul's challenge. He narrowed his eyes, looking at the hat clutched in one of her hands.

"The boat might not be bothered, nor I, but I'd venture a guess its owner doesn't know he's taking a girl to sea."

She narrowed her eyes. And he saw it, hiding behind the hard exterior. A flash of something — fear?

"You'd best take care in that getup," he said. "Keep watch for the press gangs. They've been spotted hereabouts in the last fortnight."

This, she laughed at. "If they want to kidnap me and put me to work on one of His Majesty's ships, I welcome them. I would be a powder monkey to put all other powder monkeys to shame." She spoke so lightly of the position he himself was headed for . . . and it smote him. He yearned to be at sea, yes, but could not pretend that the task of funneling gunpowder into cannons in the midst of battle did not shake something deep inside him.

Footsteps pounded behind him. Frederick knew, by the way Juliette's cheeks flushed and the corners of her mouth turned up into a smile, that it could only be one person. He'd seen Juliette and Elias walk these moors arm in arm, day after day, year after year — climb down cliffs, duck into the sea cave in the cove below, scale trees above, splash in streams while running through fields. He'd seen the way the fierceness of her seemed to soften in his presence. The way she could sock him on the shoulder in jest, and an hour later, lay her head on that shoulder as if it were the truest home she knew. Frederick was glad of it — she deserved something good.

Frederick took a step back and turned. Indeed, it was Elias Flint. The boy drew up between them, casting a wary glance at Frederick. A quick look at Juliette, and the two seemed to speak in some secret language. He raising his eyebrows, she lifting a shoulder, then shaking her head sternly.

"Your mum has a hot kettle ready," he said to her, offering his hand.

He thought of how his own father rang the bell for tea as if it were a weapon of precision. When he summoned the creaky tea cart in the drafty climes of Edgecliffe so that he could drill his son in the science of strategy over a game of chess, it held none of the warmth promised by Juliette's mother's humble kettle.

It had been only a couple of days ago, in front of the chess board, that Frederick glimpsed what he thought might be an inkling of pride on his father's face. He had positioned a pawn so that it placed his father's king in check.

"Ah, the humble pawn," The Admiral said. "Now you're thinking like a Hanford. Use the thing they least expect, the humble to do the work of the mighty. That's my son. Leave off there. Next time we play, your pawn will overtake my king. And that's what you'll do someday, Frederick. You'll step into my place. The way of the Hanfords."

Of all the pomp and plans in that speech, only three words had landed deep inside of Frederick: *"That's my son."* He thought perhaps someday, if he distinguished himself at sea, he might see those words spread across his father's countenance. What would it be to make him truly proud of Frederick?

He watched Juliette and Elias go. He had heard Elias now lived in the sheepherder's shed only a stone's throw from the Heath home. It was a common expectation that someday, when their ages caught up to their hearts, the two would wed, keep sheep, and lead a good life. He thanked heaven that God had seen fit to give the girl a safe place in this cold world.

Encouraged by such a promise, Frederick climbed the rise to the church. The stone structure perched on a hill awaited him, just as it had the day the shepherd was buried.

Three years ago, Frederick had awoken from his graveside slumber, heaviness draping him in silence. The sun was sinking over the horizon and into the sea.

Something was wrong.

In truth, too many things were wrong to be counted. But the stillness — only waves in the distance marking time — unsettled his soul. It was the silence. He recalled the way, after his mother's burial, the funeral bells had rolled their slow, mournful toll over the hills of Pevensey Bay. It had stirred something in his young heart, this invisible thing that gave voice to loss. But none had rung for the shepherd. He was certain the sound would have awakened him if they had.

He took himself to the chapel, silhouetted against the grey sky, and found it empty. The vicarage, likewise, lay silent to his knock.

Now looking back on that moment, he

wondered at the blind fervor that had overtaken him. He'd been desperate for those bells to be rung, to fill the day before it ended, to send the shepherd out with a song as he crossed into eternity. It had felt as if he were drowning and those bells were air. And if he felt this way, mustn't the shepherd's family, also? And mustn't he be the one to give them that air? He who had stolen air and life from the man?

It was this strain of clumsy thought that sent him running toward a figure down the lane. It was Elias, hands in his pockets, sadness his cloak.

Frederick caught up to him and spoke past his burning lungs. "Why . . ." He stopped, momentarily halted by Elias's narrowed eyes, the way he stepped back as if Frederick carried the plague. "Why did the bells not ring for him?"

A single derisive laugh. Elias shook his head slowly. "It costs money to ring the bells."

Frederick cast a glance back at the church.

"Money they don't have," Elias said. "No thanks to you."

The talk of bells costing money had been as foreign to Frederick as any talk of money. With Edgecliffe's silhouette looming large in the distance, he suddenly felt small.

Ashamed. How had he never considered such?

Elias turned to go.

"Wait." Frederick reached out to touch the boy's shoulder. He dug in his pocket and found the sixpence piece his mother had given him. The one he had clutched as if it were a lullaby all his boyhood. Holding fast for just a moment, he reached out his hand to offer it.

Elias recoiled. "Best to keep your distance," he said. "No money can undo what's been done."

As Elias walked away, Frederick realized he was right. The truth of it made him wish to vanish entirely. Instead, he did the only thing he could think of. It would not take away Juliette's loss, but it was the only offering he had.

He'd made his way back to the chapel, took hold of the worn rope, rough against his young hands, and pulled. It was, he feared, the most unnatural performance the bell tower had ever known in all its time keeping watch over weddings and wars, fire and funerals. There in the hands of a boy who had nothing, they rang out in clumsy cadence for the shepherd.

He dropped his coin in a wooden bowl near the door and left.

Having saved a few coins, he'd repeated the act the next year, and the next, though first arranging for the ringing and its payment with the vicar — swearing him to secrecy. Perhaps it was not done, the ringing to mark an anniversary of one's passing, but it was all he could think to do.

Last summer he'd realized that, with his impending journey to sea, this might be the last time he would be there to arrange for the ringing. He would have to find another way.

So for six months, whenever he could spend the day away without it being noticed, he'd donned the oversized garments of a field worker and gone to work with the tenant farmers.

He'd asked them to call him Fred. They had, none the wiser that they were breaking ground next to the young master of that very land. When he offered no surname and fell into the River Welden while trying to pull a rock from the soil, they pulled him out with hearty laughs, gave him a soggy slap on the back, and christened him Young Freddy Rivers, who came to work the land a few days a month.

He received his meager pay along with them. And with each crack in that ground, each mass of earth moved by his own growing arms, the words of the footman — *"never knowin' the work it takes to keep the land beneath his feet alive"* — faded. He was proud to know, at least a little.

So now he entered the vicarage carrying a satchel filled with coins from his own hard work. He rang the bell, shook the vicar's hand, and left the satchel with the man's assurance that every thirteenth day of August for the next ten years, the bells would ring whether he was there to do so or not.

"Ye be careful, lad," the vicar said in parting. "There be press gangs about. Took two fishermen over in Bexhill just yesterday morning."

"They'll not take the likes of me," he said. "They want sea knowledge in a man's bones, not just in his head." Frederick tapped his skull ruefully. "They'll be sticking to the fishing harbors and merchant vessels."

He thanked the vicar and left the churchyard. Senses heightened after the vicar's warning, he froze when he heard a twig snap from behind the yew tree. He swallowed. But stealth was not the way of a press gang, not from the tales he'd heard. Theirs was the way of brute force.

He began again, shoulders forward and

ears trained behind him. If there was anything to be wary of, he would hear it move again.

Or speak.

"Stay away," a voice said. That of a boy, trained low into that of a man.

Frederick turned. Elias Flint stood beneath the falling dark, his very presence shadowed.

"You stand on Hanford land," Frederick said. " 'Tis not for me to stay away."

"From her." Elias stepped closer. "Stay away from *her.*"

He did not need to say who *her* was. Frederick had no intention of going anywhere near the girl in question. Even so, the insolence of the situation drew out what little Hanford pride he possessed.

"*I* did not go anywhere near her," he said. He gestured a hand broadly over the moors, over Edgecliffe. "Hanford land, as I said."

"Oh, aye. Hanford land, which you know so much of."

He did. He knew every inch of it. He'd seen to it. Hiking across meadow and moor, watching the workers in the fields, witnessing the sheep shorn and the mill grind and the way the work-worn savored water as if it were the sweetest thing in all creation.

But that was not what Elias meant.

"You've no business here," Frederick said, and turned to go. Elias blocked his way.

"Swear it," he said. Something in the protective timbre of his voice gave Frederick pause. This was not the act of a jealous boy. There was nothing of envy or possession in him. Instead it was protection — tempered by something unspoken. Elias closed the gap between them, gripped Frederick's forearm with strength of a boy the land and sea were turning into a man.

Frederick yanked himself away, jutted his jaw out. He'd sworn to stay away long ago, but this demand rankled.

"What do you mean by *it*?" Frederick had little patience for talking around something. Especially when it was important.

For the first time, Elias's guard flickered. His eyes darted out beyond the cliff.

"You . . . When she sees you it reminds her." He swallowed. "It hurts her."

Frederick stared at his boots, his fists uncurling. "I know," he said, pride dissipating. "I did not mean to come upon her today," he said. "And I will do all I can to not see her again." Truly, he had no desire to. He wished them both happy — and wished himself away. Far away. "I will join the navy soon," he said, "and be gone."

Elias relaxed. "Good," he said. "Her

mother ails. She does not need this." His eyes raised and lowered, scrutinizing Frederick's lanky form.

And with that, he was gone.

But that night, from his chimney watch, Frederick saw the light again.

NINE

The figure — Juliette Heath, he now knew — disappeared again over the edge of the cliff. Frederick was ready this time. Lantern, rope, and club in hand, for he did not know what would await him.

Minutes later he was once more at the cliff's edge, flat upon his belly, squinting to see in the moonlight. This coast was riddled with sea caves, each of them storied with pirates and smugglers and even soldiers convalescing after battle. But none of those stories centered on the cave below. Though it was striking, the mouth stretching to great heights, it was so shallow that it held none of the reaches and caverns that drew smugglers, even if it were reachable by ship. The sea towers out in the breakers beyond kept it useless for all underhanded purposes.

But there was the wiry figure, clambering up with a swiftness that showed this was a place frequented. Who would it be but

Juliette? As she reached the cliff top, gripping what appeared to be a scroll, he hid himself and then followed her back the village way. Halfway to the village she crouched, pulled a rock from the seawall, and slipped the scroll inside. With a furtive look around, she stole farther down the road and into the village, where the tavern windows glowed bright. She ducked inside.

"Stay away." The warning pierced his thoughts. He strode into the tavern. Yellow light and stale air scented with the musk of fishermen and sheepherders at day's end mingled with a fiddler's tune. Metal cups clinked and sloshed, and a woman carrying a tray with a teapot piping steam from its spout wove around the bustle without spilling a drop. Frederick scanned the booths, the stretch of the counter, the corners . . . but to no avail. He did not see Juliette.

While moving along the perimeter, he grew keenly aware of the way conversations halted and eyes grew wary at every table he passed, and he willed himself invisible. He felt heat creep up his spine but forced himself onward. If this was no place for the likes of him, it was tenfold no place for the likes of Juliette Heath.

There. In a shadowed room beyond. She, in her boy's getup and with the brown hood cloaking her further, gave over a paper and held out a palm. A man who looked too polished for his shadowed corner said something, his countenance grim. He leaned forward. Juliette spoke, thrusting her open palm farther toward him. Tension swarmed between them until finally, the man slowly reached into his navy coat pocket and withdrew a dull coin. Holding it as if to show who held the power in this arrangement, he finally deposited it in her palm and waved her away with a flick of his hand.

Sickness turned in Frederick. These wars were not just fought out on the open sea. Yes, England had filled the English Channel and beyond with her "wooden walls," her mighty fleet of ships. They gave chase, battled, captured enemy ships, brought in prize money, took ground one waterborne vessel at a time. But this war was waged on land, too, through secret missives, codes spun into letters, signals given through lights and flags and he knew not what else. *Espionage,* Reskell called it. Bold of him, to use a French term in times like these.

Fishing harbors were primed for such activity. And a girl desperate to bring food to her ailing mother's table, a girl with a countenance fierce as the north wind . . . was she, too, primed for such? Frederick swallowed. The burn of responsibility raced down his spine.

Juliette placed her fists on the table. She had made good study of the ways of a boy. A man, even. If he didn't know it was she beneath that charade, he never would have guessed it.

She turned suddenly. Frederick swallowed, sure he had been discovered. But no — her hood was draped low, her pace swift, and she was gone into the night.

He followed. Outside, the air slapped his cheeks with coolness and cleared his head. He looked to the left and saw her turn around the corner of the cobbler's stone shop. He started out at a slow run to catch up but was careful to stay far enough back that she would not notice.

She would not appreciate being tracked — most especially by her sworn enemy. But if she was in any danger, caught up in something dishonest . . . the thought pounded that this, too, was his fault. If she still had a father to provide. If her mother had had an easier time and was not ailing. If the coin to run a home and feed two mouths did not rest on Juliette's shoulders — a child still and unable to earn wages as a man could . . . All this, and more, urged him on.

But as he rounded the corner, he heard a scuffle. Black-booted men emerged from the shadows. "Oy, stop!" one said. "By command of His Majesty's Navy."

The vicar's earlier warning whispered down the dark alley: *"There be press gangs about."* Bile rose in his throat, thinking of Juliette landing on a ship. She would be thrilled, no doubt. But she did not know what he did, what the son of an admiral knew — of maggots in bread and floggings and maneuverings among crew and bullying and worse. The fate of an unprotected girl aboard a ship of men. Things unfit to be spoken. Scars that ran far deeper than skin.

Not her. The thought fisted his stomach. As she turned to run, his feet flew into motion. *Not her.* Not this.

"Stop, I say!" a man hollered after Juliette. She ran around the back of the cobbler's shop, where a hill rose behind. Good — she would disappear there. Hide among the gorse shrub or outwit their maneuvers.

But a sickening *thud* sounded as she collided, instead, into a man coming from the opposite way. They'd cornered her. They had a quota to fill, hands needed in order to set sail once more. And if that meant capturing boys from the tavern in the night, that's what they would do. It was legal. Somehow, this *kidnapping* by infamously brute force was sanctioned by the king. And what then? Would this news break her mother?

He was nearly there. All he could do was run faster. Heart pounding, he hurtled himself into their midst. "Stop." His shoulders heaved as he uttered the word with more force than he believed was inside him. A force that reminded him too much of his father. *Pretend you're him.* That was the sort of force it would take to stop these men who were, after all, performing their duty.

One of the larger men raised a club. Gritting his teeth, Frederick reached for the yelling that once filled the halls of Edgecliffe. But just as his voice gripped those corridors of his childhood, it wasn't his father's wrath that he took hold of. It was the notes of Handel's *Messiah* marching their steady strength, billowing into something perhaps stronger.

"Take me," he said. Blinking as the words registered. Then standing straighter, stretching to the height of the sacrifice.

And for an instant everyone froze.

"Take me instead," he repeated.

The men stared. One of them started a low, rolling laugh. Something dark. Frederick turned his head to whisper fiercely, "Run."

She hesitated. What was she waiting for?

"Go," he said, desperate. What was this — some show of misappropriated courage?

"Aye, we'll take ye, boy," the tall man said. His figure was reaching and shiny — not the sort to instill fear or acquiescence in his targets. Less like a brute and more like a — well, an oar. If a man could resemble an oar. But his presence was commanding, and the thick men about him awaited his direction.

"Come," he said. "Both of you. Count yourselves lucky. You're bound for the HMS *Avalon*." He gripped Frederick around the wrist.

Cold fear buried itself in his belly. Not for his own fate — for he had been bound for the *Avalon* anyway, once Father thought him ready. He thought of his father's assessing gaze, the way he raised a brow whenever he sat in on Frederick's tutoring session and proclaimed his disappointment in his son without uttering a single word. Yes. It was better this way. He would go now. Find sea legs. Earn respect outside the schoolroom, ropes and gunpowder in hand. And most importantly, he would let no further harm come to the girl whose childhood he'd ended.

He had no weapon. No cunning words. The only thing he had was the logbook in his pocket, and what was he to do with that? Toss it at someone's head and hope the paper cut the man deeply?

He thrust his free arm out, palm up. Blocking their way to Juliette while offering all of himself. One final try. He turned to look her full in the face — if her face he could have seen, beyond the shadow of her hood. He saw only resolution in the posture, defiant as he hissed through his teeth one last time. "Go to her."

Surely this would move her. To plead on behalf of her mother. "Who will she have left, if not you?" He hated himself for the harshness of those words, but the sickness inside abated when she turned her head toward the hills. Toward home. Good.

But her way was blocked now. The man from behind was encroaching, raising his own club.

"Don't ye think of runnin', now," he said. "Come along quiet and ye'll know no harm from us."

"Speak for yourself," another said, and made for Juliette's head. Frederick lunged to block them, face colliding with the man's fist. Pain exploded in his lip. He flinched but opened his eyes to see the man yanking back Juliette's hood.

Only . . . it was not Juliette.

The taste of blood filled Frederick's mouth as he locked eyes with Elias Flint.

What followed was a blur of ropes burning wrists, the two boys bound for the HMS *Avalon.*

Ten

Greenwich, England
2020

Lucy paced the gallery, her ballet flats tapping lightly on the museum floor. There was something magical about any museum after hours, but this one in particular . . . She paused at the *Implacable*'s stern, which protruded straight out from the wall of the National Maritime Museum as if the ship had sailed out of the Napoleonic wars and right into the building, where it decided to make its resting place.

The stern's reaching windows, which had once looked out over expanses of sea and battle, now looked out over the museum's ornate display of gilded riverboats and storied uniforms, history breathing around every corner. She ran her hand over the *Implacable*'s surface. What waves had crashed against this ship? What lives had it once housed? What history had it altered, forever? It was just wood, built into a boat, painted and sealed. But the thought of a single ship's significance to time sent a thrill through her. That was why she was here.

She checked her watch. Any moment now, the committee would summon her into the lecture hall to present her proposal. If all went well — *Please, God* — she would be on her way to finding the lost ship *Jubilee.* And who knew? Perhaps one day it, too, would be housed in this hall of history.

She rested against the wall beside the *Implacable* and took a deep breath. Silence stretched from floor to glass ceiling. She was alone again, but she could do this.

"The disappearance of the HMS *Jubilee* has long perplexed historians," she practiced. Closing her eyes, she saw the speech scrawled out in her script on the white-and-blue graph paper left in scads from Father's stores of it. "When a traitor during the Napoleonic wars was caught in the act of transmitting information proprietary to His Majesty's Navy, he was held aboard the *Jubilee* in port until his trial. The ship vanished when —"

A door creaked across the gallery, and a balding man with round glasses and the dark uniform-suit of a docent nodded congenially at her. She waited until his footsteps receded and continued her practice in a whisper.

"If the committee finds it fitting, I would submit this proposal for research into Hurd's Deep in the English Channel. Though explored before in search of traces of the *Jubilee,* recent developments in technology mean that a second trip, if funded, could reveal the whereabouts of —"

"Miss Claremont?"

Dr. Pomeroy, the chair of the Committee for Maritime Archaeology, leaned out from the lecture hall. "The committee will hear your proposal now."

Lucy smiled and nodded, inwardly quelling the barrage of doubts that swarmed. *They'll never award the research funds. It's a wild-goose chase. Who are you to put yourself forth as a scholar?* They came in a steady stream, punctuated by the clicking of her shoes, that door drawing ever nearer, ever larger, until she was inside.

The tiered rows of green chairs sat empty, and at the front of the lecture hall, Doctors Finchley and Muller sat shuffling papers, murmuring to each other. Stage lights poured over their solemn faces seated behind a long console carved with renderings of Norse, Greek, Roman myths. Seas tossing ships. Leviathans rising from the deep. She could almost hear the crash of waves and sense the scores of years gathered in this place, of the ships and swords and uniforms that lay on display just outside that door.

Horatio Nelson, for goodness' sake. His belongings, his uniform — the greatest fighting sailor in Britain's history — and here she stood. Plain old Lucy who, being a Londoner, had been to the sea only twice in her life. She felt dizzy.

"Pardon?" Dr. Pomeroy raised his bushy eyebrows. He'd sat next to the others as she'd pondered.

"Oh . . . nothing."

"Something about Horatio Nelson?" His smile was broad in a kind way.

She gulped. She hadn't meant to say that out loud. "I was just thinking about the amount of history gathered in this museum."

"Ah, yes. A humbling thing. But this is the place many of their ideas were born, too, so don't let their legacies intimidate you. We've all been in your shoes, Miss Claremont."

She eased at his words.

The other two committee members, however, seemed less amiable. They watched with skeptical gazes. The clock's ticking in the corner grew louder. So loud it threw her right back to when she was fourteen years old, the Harrison clocks at the Royal Observatory just up the path ticking right into her soul with their volume. Dash beside her, seeing something in her come alive.

"Miss Claremont. The floor is yours," Dr. Finchley, a woman with white-blond hair pulled back severely into a bun, said.

"Thank you," Lucy said, her mouth dry. "The disappearance of the perplexing history of the . . ."

No. That was all wrong. She paused and cleared her throat. Thrust her hand into her pocket, feeling the old pocket watch, seeing her young self unfold a story with delight and mystery. *Let the story begin.* She took a deep breath, and started again.

"Members of the committee, thank you for hearing my proposal this evening. The HMS *Jubilee* has perplexed historians for over two centuries . . ." She felt the story of that ornate old ship come alive inside of her. Felt it roll from her tongue, the magical pull of the mystery of a traitor that all children learned by fifth form in school. Even the open and close of the door from up and behind her didn't pull her from the narrative. It barely registered. The passion of the project swept her away, and she saw in the glimmer of a smile on Dr. Pomeroy's face that it was — at least she hoped — contagious.

She finished, breathless. Waiting.

And now for the real battle.

"I would be honored to take your questions," she said. This, she knew, was where her proposal would sink or swim. And her future along with it.

The committee asked about the research of Vincent Ashford, the renowned expert on the *Jubilee* from decades past, how hers would differ. They inquired as to the vessel she wished to commission for the purposes of research in the Channel.

And then, with a shuffle of papers, they asked the question she feared would be the proposal's death sentence.

"What is the pecuniary implication of this proposal, Miss Claremont?"

It came down to the money. She gulped and named a figure larger than she had a right to even speak.

But they did not react. Nobody lost their hat or gave her the immediate boot.

Dr. Pomeroy leaned forward, hands clasped upon the mahogany table. "If I may be candid, Miss Claremont."

"Of course," Lucy said.

"This is a gross amount of money for

research that may or may not have sufficient evidence. Your theory is compelling. If it proves true, it would be seen as a risk most worth taking. But as you must know, the committee's funding is limited, and there are a number of scholars vying for the stipend."

"I understand."

A soft rustling sounded behind her, and she remembered the opening and closing door. Who might it be? Who even knew of her proposal, other than Gerald Bessette? She prayed he had not come. Though he treated her with a fatherly kindness, she cringed at the thought of her failure being so visible to such a successful man.

She knew this was where she should remove herself with dignity, let the idea die. But in the same way the stars were home to Dash, the sea and the *Jubilee* were home to Lucy. A wave of homesickness lent her boldness.

"If I can provide more evidence, more research. If I cross-reference in detail Vincent Ashford, show how this proposed expedition —"

Dr. Finchley loudly cleared her throat, cutting off Lucy's desperate plea. "Sadly, Miss Claremont, without empirical evidence at the front end — something more substantial than process of elimination — we cannot in good conscience distribute the funds to this project. As intriguing as the idea is, we have a reputation to uphold and a duty to respect the foundation's donors, who encourage us to allocate money to low-risk, high-impact endeavors."

Silence. The clock's slow ticking. Her mind scrambling, coming up empty. All of it pointing to one thing: defeat. Heat swept her face, her being.

"What if there was a co-researcher?"

The low voice came from the shadows behind her. She turned, straining to see a man stand, his stature tall.

Whirling, she took in the faces of the panel. They looked as befuddled as she felt.

Dr. Pomeroy leaned forward. The tall man emerged from the shadows. He wore a baseball cap — navy blue with an orange star and a big *H.* Khakis and a black fleece pullover made him look very . . . unacademic. Something about the man felt . . . familiar. And yet so unfamiliar.

He walked down the stairs and stood next to Lucy. "If I may . . ."

She stared straight ahead, focused on the committee, debating whether to feel faint hope or absolute indignation. A stranger presuming upon the proposal she'd slaved over for months — years! — during evenings in the cottage and the slow hours at the watch shop, which, sadly, had been plentiful as of late.

She drew herself up. Waiting. Well aware that the proposal was likely dying on the spot.

"And who are you?" asked the third committee member, Dr. Muller, his German accent thick. He chaired Oxford's archaeological arm. "Forgive us, but we are unaccustomed to proposal proceedings being open to public contribution. Most unusual. *Most* unusual."

The man beside her withdrew his hands from his pockets, looked long at Lucy.

Unable to resist, she finally turned to him. There — beneath the bill of his baseball cap — she saw the brown eyes she knew better than her own reflection. Matured by years passed, but with that same earnest depth and spark of mirth.

He seemed to be giving her this chance to see him before he spoke his name. Her heart, in response, tumbled about, madly trying to find a place for itself.

"Dashel Greene," he said, keeping her gaze, letting apology fill his entire demeanor before turning to face the committee.

After a silent conversation with his colleagues in which they'd shrugged, raised eyebrows, and nodded respectively, Dr. Pomeroy said, "Well, Dashel Greene. Speak on."

Dash strode forward, reaching them in three lanky steps, and pumped their hands in his familiar friendly way. Asking their names, offering his. "Dashel Greene," he said, reaching the third and final member of the committee.

"So you have said," Dr. Muller said. "Several times."

Dash bobbed his head. "I did. Forgive me. I've come as one who has great interest in Miss Claremont's impressive proposal," he said, stepping back to join her.

Lucy was speechless. She felt her eyes widen, told herself to stop this, to take back her presentation from this boy — man — who had vanished for so long with little more than an email in over a decade.

That wasn't *entirely* true. He had done more than that. And she felt a tug of shame, for hadn't she been just as remiss in dropping their communication?

But he was here now. Despite it all.

Dr. Pomeroy looked to the other committee members, and asked, "And you are . . . ?"

"Doctor of Forensic Astronomy," he said.

"Ah," said Dr. Pomeroy.

"*Forensic* astronomy," said Dr. Finchley, as if he'd just said he ate beetles for breakfast. "Are the stars committing crimes, now, that we need celestial detectives?"

Dash let out a hearty laugh and pointed at Dr. Finchley. "Good one. I like it."

Dr. Finchley was not amused. She waited, and Dash cleared his throat and pulled into a professional mode Lucy had never seen from him.

"Forensic astronomy is sleuthing using the sky. We use what we know from science, history, observation of the night skies, to help bring answers to unanswered questions. Sometimes it's art." He gestured. "When was Van Gogh's *Evening Landscape with a Rising Moon* painted? Sometimes it's crime. What time was a crime committed? Abraham Lincoln, when he was a lawyer, even used the position of the moon on the night of a crime to prove his case. And sometimes it's history. How is it possible that in the midst of the Civil War, Stonewall Jackson was shot by his own troops? I'll tell you. Or rather, forensic astronomy will. A full moon caused him to be unrecognizable in silhouette.

"Forensic astronomy uses calculations, logbooks, sky charts . . . and so much more." He was looking, in his impassioned explanation, more like his boyhood self. She half expected him to turn and ask her if she'd seen any supernovas lately.

But what did all this have to do with her? She was relieved when Dr. Finchley asked the question that plagued her.

Dash smiled at Lucy before beginning. "I have a shared interest with Miss Claremont in the *Jubilee.*" Shared interest. That was putting it mildly. A vision flashed of the two of them crouched on the reading room floor following one of Father's tales of the *Jubilee,* the oversized atlas open to the English Channel, and each of them using shells from the bowl of peanuts they were munching on to mimic the *Jubilee,* to play out theories. *"We'll figure it out one of these days, Matchstick Girl."*

"You remembered the *Jubilee*?" she whispered.

He beheld her with solemnity. "I'd never forget."

"Forgive us," Dr. Pomeroy said. "But in the interest of time, could you tell us of the merits of your research? Your credentials? What your background and experience might lend to this research endeavor?"

Dash appeared at a loss. And suddenly Lucy felt a wash of compassion for him.

Perhaps he had not achieved his dreams, after all this time. So much promise — and so much pressure he had put upon himself to live up to those labels given him. *Genius. Brilliant. Prodigy.*

"H-Harvard," she spat out, eager to take the pressure off of him.

"Pardon?" Dr. Pomeroy, friendly as he was, seemed to be growing impatient.

"He went to Harvard," she said. "Isn't that right, Dash — Mr. Greene?"

"Yes." His answer came slowly, as if he were weighing what to add. "Well, here." He thrust a hand into his pocket and removed a folded rectangle of paper.

Unfolding it into its full size, he slid it across the desk to Dr. Pomeroy. "My résumé."

Lucy couldn't see much, but she saw enough to know it had been handwritten in his trademark permanent marker, stick-straight, just like Dash had always written. What had he done, written it on the train ride here? Wherever he'd come from?

The man placed his wire-rimmed spectacles on his nose and looked dubiously at the makeshift résumé. But his eyebrows raised halfway through reading it, and he opened his mouth to speak.

Dash beat him to it. "In addition to what

you see there." He seemed flustered. "I'm currently the astronomer-in-residence at Stone's Throw Farm near Weldensea, East Sussex."

Dr. Pomeroy narrowed his eyes, looking confused. "A farm. Indeed," he said. With a twinkle in his kindly eyes, he added, "Does that account for the handwritten résumé?"

"Most unusual," Dr. Muller added. "*Most* unusual."

"Ah, I apologize for that," Dash said. "I don't travel with a printed résumé but thought it might help. I can email a typed one, along with my *curriculum vitae,* if it helps."

They all sat a little straighter at the familiar and academic Latin phrase, and Dr. Pomeroy slid the résumé down the line.

Each professor took in its contents, and each had that same eyebrow-raising moment.

"And you plan to lend your expertise to this project . . . how, precisely?" Dr. Finchley asked, ever the skeptic.

Lucy couldn't blame her. She wanted to ask Dash a few questions of her own. And yet with his unexpected arrival, a tiny flicker of hope had entered the room.

"I can provide empirical evidence in the form of historical and contemporary star charts, the tracking of tides as dictated by the lunar pull and cycles."

The woman nodded. Lucy bit her tongue, waiting.

"I propose a brief recess," Dr. Pomeroy said. "Shall we say . . . ten minutes? We'll have an answer for you both then."

An answer. Lucy had not expected this. She had thought — hoped, really — they'd take more time to consider, to be pulled in by the magic of the legend. But what she spoke was, "Perfect."

Numbly leading the way from the room and back out into the gallery, she stared at the wall of large white bricks across the way, heard the door latch heavily behind her. And felt the weight of Dash's presence beside her.

ELEVEN

She could not look at him. Did not know whether to slug him or give in to the tears pulling hot at her eyes. Dared she ask him *Where were you?* Or should she just do what she wanted most — hug him? She wanted to pull her old friend in tight and never let him out of her sight again.

But she did not know him anymore. She was certainly not the same person she'd been at fifteen, the last time she'd seen him, and she couldn't expect him to be, either.

In the end, simplicity won out. She turned to face him, to offer the most basic courtesy she would offer a stranger — which was what he was.

"Thank you," she said.

He searched her, then stuffed his hands in his back khaki pockets and bowed his head until his baseball cap bill hid his face.

"It was a great presentation," he said, "and I didn't intend to interrupt. It's just" — he looked at her again — "you deserve this, Lucy."

His voice speaking her name felt so foreign. She did not know this voice, deepened and full. And even if she had, he had rarely called her Lucy. It had been Matchstick Girl or, occasionally, Lu. But more often than those he'd greeted her with the illustrious "Hey" — which he had somehow infused with all the warmth in the world.

A thousand questions rolled through her like an unseen avalanche. They tangled and fought and twisted into something so complex, the only one she could retrieve was meager. "How are you here?"

He looked over his shoulder, as if expecting the big oak door might hold the answer. "I . . . follow your work," he said.

"You do?"

"Of course I do."

That smote her. She could not say the same of him. The thought had arisen, many times over the years, that she should find him. To see what he was up to. A couple of times she'd given in and done Internet searches. Found him at one observatory, and then another, doing research stints. But without fail, those times left her feeling heavy and alone. Forgotten. So she had stopped torturing herself.

"I saw online that you were presenting a research grant proposal tonight. So I came."

She shook her head. Like it was as simple as hopping on a train. Which, come to think of it, perhaps it had been.

"You said you were at a farm?"

"Yeah. You'd love it, Lucy. It's a sheep farm over near the Channel. But with the farm side of things slowing down, they've diversified. Now they run it as a tourist-type thing. People come and help with the sheep and pay the farm to get to do it. Ha! Ironic, right? But it's the novelty. People would give anything nowadays to get away from the craziness of their everyday lives. Even pay to go be farmhands for a week. Agritourism. They do campfires at night. Tea in the afternoon in this gazebo in the middle of a meadow. They lead walks along the Seven Sisters — those famous white cliffs down there — and they poke around the ruins of an old estate. They even arrange for the visitors to work on a fishing boat for an afternoon." He grinned. "You'd love it. Your parents would have loved it."

Her smile vanished.

Would have loved . . .

He knew her father was gone. Of course he had known. . . . There had been that email afterwards. And the document he'd sent. His version of a sympathy card, she'd guessed. It had meant more than all the sympathy cards in the world. But hearing him say he'd known and hadn't come scooped out a hollowness in her.

She changed the subject. "So . . . they have a resident astronomer at this sheep farm bed-and-breakfast?"

"That part's my fault. I needed a dark-sky place near the Channel to do some research, so we struck a deal. They let me plant myself there and do my thing, and in return, I do a star party for their guests once a week. And . . ." He leaned forward, as if about to impart some great treasure. "There's scones."

She laughed and had to keep herself from punching him on the shoulder, a gesture so familiar it had become a part of their shared language. A laugh with a sock. "Scones, you say."

He grinned, his old dimples appearing. She had never thought of Dash as handsome, never had occasion to weigh whether he was or not. He was always and ever just Dash. Her Dash. So close and so much a part of her that to consider whether he was handsome or not would be as laughable as considering whether one's own arm had any particular amount of worldly beauty.

But looking at him now, as a stranger appearing from the literal shadows, she felt an odd sort of pang in realizing the boy next door really did hold that boy-next-door charisma. Familiar and handsome, friendly and kind.

And bold. Taking over her proposal like that. It smarted, when she thought of it that way.

"Listen." He lowered his voice, nearing her. "If they say yes to all of this, there's a place for you there, Lucy. You can stay there, and we'll do our research and we'll find the *Jubilee.* I have some theories, and I'd love to get your take on them."

"I can't, Dash. I have Dad's shop. I have to find a place to move, and I just . . . I can't just pick up and leave." Hadn't that been her life? Anchored, always. Steadfast. Minding the shop. Staying close to the nucleus of her world, where she belonged. The outer edges of that world called her, but such things weren't for her.

"You don't have to leave forever. The watch shop . . . Is there any way you can close it for a week? Maybe two? We can hang a sign on the door. You'll have to close it up if you get your funding. Your dad used to close it up once in a while, right?"

He had. There had been a time when he'd

closed the shop for a week or more to take a holiday, but that had ended when . . .

It still hurt to think of their last trip to the beach. But for a time before he'd died, he'd hung a sign on the watch shop that read "Time waits for no man, but neither does tea." Then he'd stuck on his old tweed cap and walked down the street all the way to the Charing Cross Café. She'd gotten used to his weekly declaration. *"Off to a café for a date with an apple and a friend."* It had done her heart good — and challenged her to seek ways to chase hope and community, too. She hadn't succeeded, but it had inspired her nonetheless.

"He would understand," Dash said. "What was it that plaque on his wall said? *Tempus Truth* — time is truth — something like that?"

"Tempus custodit veritatem," Lucy said. The motto of the Worshipful Company of Clocksmiths, a society so old it nearly predated London itself. Dad had been proud to be a member of something so full of tradition. She'd grown up watching Mother knot the black-and-silver diagonal-striped membership tie. Loved the picture of him with the other members, arms looped about one another in their fine suits. Loved hearing him tell of the three ways to become

a part of the company — patrimony, servitude, or redemption. That is, to be born into it, earn your way into it, or — most remarkable of all — sponsorship by a member who is also a member of the royal court. "*Remarkable, Lucy. It's an echo of the true redemption — who they are covering over who you are, making a way in.* Tempus custodit veritatem."

"Time is truth's keeper," she said.

"Right! Exactly. He would want you to hunt down the truth. Time was made for truth."

She remembered this. His exuberance. The way an idea would fill him, spill over, and pull everyone around him in, too.

"You won't have to pay for board. I'll get you in under my deal with the farm siblings. Two sisters and a brother. Did I mention there's scones?"

"It's England. Scones are everywhere."

"Not like these. Come on! You can sleep and eat and study and find the *Jubilee* and get back to the shop and do whatever you need to do. Badda-bing, badda-boom."

She laughed through her nose. She couldn't help it. He was his old incorrigible self, his enthusiasm contagious.

"I —" Her breath hitched. It was crazy. She couldn't do this.

The door creaked open, and Dr. Finchley presented her pinched face in cold invitation. "The committee is ready for you."

Lucy looked at Dash. Dash looked at Lucy. The two of them looked at Dr. Finchley, her expression unreadable.

Back inside, the air was warm from the lights shining down on the committee. Lucy and Dash stood side by side, facing the members as if they were a jury.

Dr. Muller spoke a few words about how highly unusual this request was, and Lucy lifted her chin to keep it from following her sinking spirits.

Beside her, the back of Dash's hand brushed hers. For a split second, her fingers ached to lace themselves to his, like they had in the Underground when everything had gone black. As if her fingers sensed home nearby.

But she straightened those fingers, schooling them into submission.

"However," Dr. Pomeroy interjected. "In light of your impressive claims, Mr. Greene —"

"Highly impressive. Highly impressive." Dr. Muller wrinkled his forehead, looking again at Dash's résumé.

Dr. Pomeroy continued. "We are prepared to offer a one-month extension. If within that time you are able to document convincing evidence that links your two schools of study —"

"Maritime archaeology and forensic astronomy," Dr. Finchley clarified.

"Yes. Then we believe this will be something truly . . ." He let his voice trail upward as he deliberated on the right word. "Remarkable."

"And if there is enough evidence to suggest concretely the whereabouts of the *Jubilee,* we will fund your request in full."

Lucy's heart raced. She bit her lip around her spreading smile.

"Aw, that's great," Dash said, taking his cap from his head. His hair stuck up in the back, every bit the mad scientist. He never had been polished or professional. And apparently degrees from Harvard and roving astronomer positions hadn't changed that.

"Yes, thank you. Truly," Lucy said.

"You won't regret it," Dash said, about to become effusive, if the glimmer in his eye meant what it used to. So before he could bring the whole building down around them in thanks, she nudged him and led the way out, tilting her head for him to follow.

"We shall see," Dr. Finchley's crow-like words followed them out.

Outside, the evening burst upon them in a

baptism of fresh air and hope. It was summer, and that meant evenings stretched long and clear. Greenwich Park was vibrant green, a clash with the state of her mind, which was muddled over what had just happened.

"There's your place," Lucy said, pointing in the direction of the Royal Observatory. After he first introduced her to Greenwich all those years ago, they'd hopped the Tube and come here several times before he'd disappeared — she getting lost for hours in the displays at the Maritime Museum, he scribbling down notes and calculations at the observatory.

And always, they'd end the day at the prime meridian. She'd stand on one side of the line, he on the other, and they'd high-five one another — Dash's idea. *"Can't keep us apart,"* he'd once said. *"Even in different hemispheres. Time starts here, you know. Greenwich mean time and all that. So we're high-fiving"* — he held his hand up with a cheesy smile — *"right where time begins."*

That had been a lifetime ago. And they'd proven the contrary.

No one said anything more as they now walked to the Underground in the softening light. Standing on the platform, he broke the thick silence. "Come with me, Lucy.

Please. A month is so short, and we've got a lot of work to do if you want that grant. I've got some business at the Royal Observatory tomorrow, and then I'll show you the way. If you can. If you want to."

It was just a train ride. A simple *yes* would begin the journey. But it felt as impossible to speak as it would to proclaim herself royalty. It wasn't what she did.

"Even if I shut down the shop, I have to be out of the cottage in a month's time. Mr. Bessette has been kind to let me stay there as long as he has, but he's hired a new groundskeeper, and they'll be needing to move house soon."

In truth, the household furnishings would stay with the cottage, and she'd already packed most of her personal items. Mr. Bessette had offered her a small Candlewick Commons flat at a good rate, but she hadn't been sure she wanted to stay in the area. She'd made no other plans — but she wasn't going to admit that to Dash.

She expected him to protest, to pipe up with his enthusiasm and list all the reasons she could — should — travel to the farm, all the ways it could work.

But instead she saw understanding in his eyes. "I'm sorry," he said. And she knew he truly was. It was the house, and the life in it she was leaving behind, and all the loss — especially of the past two years.

"I'll bring the packing tape," he said. "I'm good at moving. Put me to work."

Her throat grew tight. She nodded, eyes stinging, his kindness touching a place in her she did not often visit. "Thank you, Dash."

"I'm serious. How can I help?"

She thought of the document he'd sent her. The one he'd created and reached out with, emailing her out of the blue. He couldn't have known it would reach her just as she was about to toss her phone into the Thames in sorrow and frustration. Had no way of knowing it was what had brought her here, to the committee, dreams in her hands.

"You already have helped, Dash. More than I can say. Thank you for coming all this way, for doing what you did. I'm sure we can collaborate via email, perhaps phone or video, if we need to. And if you'd like to come back next month, I'll pay for your train ticket."

He narrowed his eyes. This, he did not understand. He looked crestfallen.

"Okay," he said, stuffing his hands back in his pockets and turning toward his platform.

"I guess . . . if you need anything, you know where to find me."

TWELVE

That night, Lucy could not sleep. Her dreams, when snatches of sleep came, were those of heavy blackouts beneath ground in the Tube. Dash's hand reaching for hers, comfort in the dark. One of those moments so deeply etched in her soul, it would be a part of her always, though years upon years had passed.

But wasn't that what he'd done again? Showed up, emerging from the shadows . . . and brought hope? And wasn't that what he'd done two years ago, when she'd been blindly wandering the banks of the Thames?

The Thames had drawn her when she realized she was now an orphan.

She closed her eyes around the memory. . . .

Orphan?

Was that a word people used anymore? Was it not reserved for the pages of fairy tales and Dickens? Certainly not used to describe a grown woman. Lucy knew it was ridiculous, but the question plagued. So she sat, garbed in a simple black dress upon a bench near the river, and pulled out her phone.

A man looked up briefly from his book stand beneath the bridge — first at the children playing jacks on the sidewalk, then over at Lucy. Her cheeks burned as if he could see what she'd typed: *orphan definition.*

He went back to reading and so did she.

Orphan: a person whose parents are deceased.

Doubtless, the term was normally reserved for children, but an orphan, indeed, she was. Lucy Claremont, student of maritime history, proprietor of the family watch shop, and . . . orphan.

The river flowed on by, whispering assurance that if this was true, she was certainly in the right place for it. Oliver Twist, David Copperfield, Little Nell, and a plethora of other Dickensian waifs trod this soil before her, and people loved them still. Never mind that things usually ended tragically for them. Dickens wasn't around. He wasn't here to write the end of her story.

But who was?

She picked herself up and shuffled along

the Thames, watched the evening lights come on, strung between lampposts and flower baskets. Listened past the noise of the buses and traffic, until she could hear the whisper of the water.

What had Father called this river in his stories? Her mind was a muddle of grief and graduate studies and she couldn't pin down the right word. Magic . . . magic kingdom. "No, that's Disney, you fool."

A wide-eyed girl looked up from her place at her mother's side, and her mother held the girl's hand tighter.

"Sorry," she said with a small wave. "Never mind me." She hadn't meant to speak aloud. She was losing her mind.

The Hidden World?

No, that wasn't right, either. She stopped on the riverbank and watched the currents weave to and fro. "What are you?" she asked, careful to whisper this time. "What's your name?"

She could not find it. She remembered the stories Father had told of this river — of how people had played cricket on the bottom when it had dried up, and held ice festivals on its surface when it had frozen over. How they'd defeated hopelessness by doing something within their impossible circumstances.

She remembered how the stories made her feel. Full of longing, like she'd missed the times of yore and wonder and was born instead into a time of plastic and speed. Father's magic was tucked, always, in the past. Her chest burned and she sniffled. It was ridiculous that she hadn't cried at the funeral but was sniffling like a baby an hour later over lost fairy tales.

Grief did that, apparently. Snuck out of hidden exits.

Fear gripped her deeply. What if she never remembered? And worse, what if this wasn't the only one of his stories she had lost in the muddle?

She closed her eyes, a sickening darkness gripping her stomach at the realization: She could not remember the stories. A few of them, perhaps, but . . . there had been so many. They melded together, covered over in an iron blanket of grief that would not let her in.

It was too much. To lose those, too.

So she stood there. She and the river and a thousand stories and losses in between — and she wept. She wept for Father. For Mum. For the stories, the world they so longed to give her, and the way it was lost to reality. And for the boy who once sat beside her in that fragile place of hope . . .

and who was long gone, too.

Her phone dinged. She raised her arm in blind instinct, pulled it back as if to throw it out into the dark waters, let it sink to the bottom of the place where people apparently celebrated with picnics and cricket. Happy things for a happy time.

It dinged again. Incessant. She pulled her hand back farther, but hesitated. And just as she was about to vault that portal to constant connection into a watery grave alongside the impossible picnics and cricket matches — she looked up and back and saw three words on the screen:

THE HIDDEN KINGDOM

Her heart thudded. That was it. The name Father had called the dried-up Thames, the words her mind had failed to excavate. And now . . . here they were, shining bright in black letters upon a white ribbon of email notification on her phone?

Surely not. This was a break with reality, some grief-induced delusion. She clutched the phone against her chest, pressed her eyes closed to give them a fresh start. Opening them, she turned slowly, taking in the signs all about as a litmus test.

Waterloo Bridge.

Southbank Book Market.

These, she knew to be true. So perhaps,

just possibly, her imagination wasn't just conjuring things out of desperation. With some trepidation, she peeked again at her phone, and there were the words, as clear as day in an email notification:

THE HIDDEN KINGDOM

"But that's impossible," she whispered. Unless Dad had somehow scheduled an email to be sent, before he . . .

No, he had been a pen-and-graph-paper user for everything from gear schematics to market lists to letters to his friends. He would as soon have known how to schedule an email as to turn back time.

So it hadn't been him. And it wasn't her imagination. That left just one possibility, the only other person in all the universe who knew Dad's name for the dry bed of the Thames.

Her heart tripped about in her chest, like a stone skipped upon the rippling river. Swiping her thumb across the screen to unlock it, she opened the full email.

DEAR LUCY,

The air went out of her, years falling away. Dash had always typed in all capitals — and she had forever given him a hard time about it. He was such an easygoing soul, it made her laugh that his writing looked like yelling. But some things did change, it seemed, in half a lifetime. She felt as much a stranger to him, apparently, as he did to her. He had never called her Lucy.

Her eyes devoured the lines as fast as she could skim them, then returned to savor them slowly.

DEAR LUCY,
I DON'T KNOW WHAT TO SAY. I WISH I COULD SAY SOMETHING TO MAKE IT BETTER . . . BUT I KNOW THERE AREN'T WORDS. I WISH I COULD BE THERE. THERE'S NOWHERE IN THE UNIVERSE I WOULD RATHER BE THAN AT YOUR SIDE. BUT . . . I KNOW I'M A STRANGER TO YOU NOW, AND THIS ISN'T THE TIME FOR STRANGERS.

STILL, THERE WAS A TIME WHEN YOU WERE THE ONLY FAMILY I KNEW. WHEN YOUR PARENTS OPENED THEIR DOOR TO A LOST KID WHO DIDN'T KNOW UP FROM DOWN, AND INSTEAD OF TELLING HIM TO PULL HIS HEAD OUT OF THE STARS, THEY GAVE

HIM THE FOOTING BENEATH HIS FEET TO SEE THEM CLEARLY, AND THEIR MAKER.

YOUR DAD TOLD US OF THAT HIDDEN KINGDOM AT THE BOTTOM OF THE RIVER, AND IT ALWAYS SEEMED TO ME TO SPEAK OF A KINGDOM OF HOPE. EVERY TIME I LOOKED AT THOSE MURKY RIVER WATERS IN THE YEARS THAT FOLLOWED, I GRINNED LIKE A FOOL, THINKING I KNEW SOME BIG SECRET THE REST OF LONDON HAD NO IDEA OF.

YOUR PARENTS GAVE ME A HOME, WHICH I HAD NEVER KNOWN. THEY GAVE ME A HEART, WHICH I HADN'T KNOWN POSSIBLE. AND WHEN I THINK OF THOSE STORIES YOUR DAD TOLD US, I WONDER IF WHAT HE WAS REALLY DOING WAS GIVING US HOPE. OR WONDER. . . . WHICH MAYBE, AFTER ALL, ARE SORT OF THE SAME THING.

I WON'T PRESUME TO KNOW WHAT YOU ARE FACING, LUCY. I

CAN ONLY IMAGINE. BUT BECAUSE OF WHAT HE GAVE ME, WHAT YOU GAVE ME, TOO . . . MY HOPE IS THAT BY RETURNING HIS STORY TO YOU NOW, IT MIGHT OFFER SOME SMALL LIGHT INTO YOUR WORLD.

YOU WERE LIGHT IN MINE.

SINCERELY,
ALWAYS,
DASHEL GREENE

She read it again, tracing her finger over his name. How they would have guffawed as kids if they'd imagined him writing her a letter one day and signing it *Dashel Greene.* How many Dashels did he think she knew? But she sensed it was less about clarity of identity, and more about somber respect, that he signed it so.

So many questions fought their way from the screen and into her mind. It seemed he had at least visited London after first leaving. Why had he never come to them? Quick anger morphed into sadness. And he wrote of hearing of Dad's passing. How had he heard? Dad hadn't wanted to be in the newspapers, so she had never submitted an obituary.

Beyond her, the river sang, and the children playing jacks had moved on to a game of hopscotch while their mothers chatted away on a bench. Big Ben struck four o'clock across the river.

On its last strike, with a strange swimming sensation filling her chest, she let her thumb tap the link he'd included. A blue circle spun on the screen while a web page loaded. It was a shared document.

She laughed — it was fitting, somehow, that the kid with his head in the stars was now meeting her, quite literally, in the cloud.

She scrolled down, taking in his words, amazed that he'd turned off the caps.

COMPENDIUM OF WONDER

A collection of the
stunningly impossible to inspire

TABLE OF CONTENTS:

1) The Hidden Kingdom
2) (to come) The City beneath the Earth
3) (to come) The Stair in the Sky
4) (to come) The Ever-Rising Tide
5)

Number five was untitled. And for a moment, she felt bereft again, for the blank number. It could be so many different stories that Dad had told them. The salt mines that had housed thousands of books. The chimney swifts in America. *"Birds that'll take your breath away, flyin' into chimneys in swirling swarms like smoke in reverse."* Dad was the one who told her of Hurd's Deep — the trench that hid remnants of wars away in safety. She recognized the story titles but grieved again that she remembered so few details. When had this happened?

Just as she began to scroll down, to see if there was more information about number five, a blinking blue cursor popped up — and letters began to appear out of thin air.

He was here? Well, not *here* — but here in this shared document? Right now. This very instant. Remembering her dad on the day of his burial.

And suddenly she did not feel so alone.

Looking back to that day, Lucy understood he'd been fighting for light on her behalf, right there in a humble document. She hadn't responded to his email, didn't feel ready, but she'd watched that blue cursor write out his memory of her father's tale, The Hidden Kingdom, and after twenty minutes, the cursor disappeared.

The rest of the stories had never been filled in, but she had always harbored hope that perhaps, someday, Dash might write the rest.

The memories, along with Dad's twenty-four-hour clock marking time on the wall, lulled her to sleep, and she slept peacefully through the few remaining hours of the dark morning.

When she awoke, and before she could talk herself out of it, she packed a bag, locked her door, and pointed herself toward the Royal Observatory.

Thirteen

Weldensea
East Sussex, England

The village of Weldensea in East Sussex lay nestled at the base of Welden Hill. It was a corridor of brick buildings lining a cobbled street with bunting stretched back and forth above. Hanging from the cheery triangles of colour, a banner announced the annual Smugglers' Ball. A small breeze tumbled down the way, lifting the banner's corner in a welcoming wave.

"Where to next?" Lucy asked. "I assume Stone's Throw Farm is on the outskirts of the town." She guessed this from the farm's name.

"You might say that." Was Dash evading her question?

"Longer, then?"

"You could say that, too."

Fearing the reason for his evasion, Lucy scanned the quiet village for a taxi. A bus. A carthorse. Anything. And found only an older man putting out a sign in front of a building that appeared to be half inn, half pub with arched doors, red geraniums in black window boxes, a pirate flag waving over a blue coat of arms, and a gilded sign that read The Jolly Roger.

"Oy, Greene!" The man's hunched figure straightened when he spotted Dash. "See ye at the star party, then! Bringin' a bucket o' scallops."

Dash waved his appreciation.

"Scallops? You astound me, Dashel Greene," Lucy said. "Once upon a time, you'd not have touched a bit of seafood if we'd paid you a hundred pounds."

He shrugged, giving a good-natured grin. "They're fried. And they're fresh. Turns out those two things make a world of difference, and Sussex knows what it's about when it comes to seafood."

They left the village on foot, passing a hand-painted sign that read:

Stone's Throw Farm

Hot Breakfast

Wireless

And then, scrunched in at the bottom, added more recently, judging by the unchipped paint:

Weekly Star Talks given by Dr. Dashel Greene

A small metal sign hung below, waving in the breeze. It announced —

"Two miles?" Lucy filled her lungs to appear plucky and energized in a way she did not feel, and asked, "We'll walk?"

Dash shrugged. "If it's all right with you. People around here walk. It's the pace of things."

So they walked. He led the way, filling the silence by whistling a jolly tune with the occasional minor note thrown in. She followed, sometimes walking beside him, sometimes behind, and so very thankful he had insisted on carrying her bag.

His tune was fitting, in a way. All the sweetness of their youth, tripping now and again over a minor chord. Just like them. For who were they to each other now? A shadow. An outline. A question mark.

"Dash," she began, hoping to break the silence, erase a bit of that question mark with some sort of conversation. "What's the Smugglers' Ball?"

"According to the locals, it's the event of the season. They prepare for it for months beforehand. This whole coast used to be riddled with smugglers' haunts. One of them lies near the local chapel — St. Thomas's. It's an old tunnel that's since been blocked off and caved in, but the room is so large, they host a ball down there once a year. People dress up, they bring in an orchestra, the whole thing."

"In a cave?"

"Tunnel. Former tunnel. More like a sunken amphitheatre, mostly open to the sky. But before the cave-in, in Victorian times, they used to hold it beneath ground. Some royalty even came."

"How do you know all this?"

He laughed. "Spend five minutes at the farm, and they make it their personal mission to complete your thorough education on all things Weldensea."

His lanky stride paired with the downward slope were taking him faster, and she hurried to catch up. She saw they were approaching a building, but the sun broke through the clouds, obscuring a clear view. As they drew closer her nerves ramped up. Who was she to presume upon these strangers?

Dash stopped in front of a stone wall flanked by two pillars, a white picket gate creaking open to his touch.

Lucy's breath caught as she stepped through to hydrangeas in full bloom leading to a Dutch door whose top was flung wide open. Its white paint was chipped and all the more lovely for it. The farmhouse rose up from the ground as if it had grown there, stone by stone, over the course of a thousand lifetimes. Wisps of smoke slipped from the chimney as a cool breeze blew off the distant Channel, and every step ushered her into an unseen veil of cinnamon and allspice.

She ached so deeply, her feet slowed and finally stopped altogether.

Dash turned. "You okay?"

She blinked back the heat in her eyes, willing herself not to cry. "Silly," she said, shaking her head.

Dash tipped his head ever so slightly. She'd forgotten that about him, the way he would wait, the way he let silence invite talk.

She shook her head as if to shoo away the ache growing inside. "It's just . . . it's a home," she said, lifting one shoulder. Of course it was a home. She might as well declare the dirt brown and the buttercups yellow. Such a sparkling conversationalist. But she had not set foot inside a house that felt like a home in . . . well, not since her parents had gone.

But Dash did not laugh. He did not smile, or continue on. He took a step closer to her and held out his hand. "Yeah," he said.

"And they're waiting for *you.*" He said it as if she were a guest of honor, and not the orphaned spinster-waif that she was — in keeping with her Dickensian identity.

He held out his hand, and finger by finger she unwrapped her clenched fist and slipped it into his. And again, the disconnect hit her. This hand, offered to lend her strength, belonged to a man who knew her both intimately and barely at all. She swallowed and gave his hand a thankful squeeze before releasing it.

He rapped on the doorframe twice. When no one answered, he called through the open part of the door, "Hello? Anybody home?"

Hissed whispering sounded from somewhere inside. "Shhh! He'll hear you! And then what'll I do?"

"It's not *him,*" a second whisperer sounded, words forceful and final. "It's Dashel Greene."

"Dashel?"

"Dash. El." Now the stern one was speaking openly, and the voice was enough to strike fear into a fortress. "Dashel."

Clipped footsteps came, and a tall woman swung the lower door open. "Come in," she said. *She was silver,* Lucy thought. Cold silver. From the crisp silvery blue of her eyes to the long white waves of her hair pulled into a braid draped over her shoulder, she was aloof and crisp and cold like silver.

"Dashel Greene!" The first whisperer, Lucy presumed, came into view, all rosy cheeks and softness. Right down to her stature, which bespoke afternoons in a warm kitchen spent cooking up delicious things and tasting them along the way. If the first woman was silver, this lady was copper. Bright and cheery and warm.

"Clara, Sophie." Dash tipped his baseball cap at the copper woman, then the silvery one.

Copper Clara. Silver Sophie. Lucy tucked this trick into her mind, determined not to mix them up.

"You've come back to us at last!" Clara said. Her cheeks glowed, and she spun a plate in her apron as if to dry it, though it had to have been dried at least five rotations back. "Sorry for the whispering. We thought you were Roger, you see."

"*You* thought he was Roger," Sophie corrected. "And you know he was only gone three days."

"Was he, indeed," Clara marveled. "It felt longer. You mustn't leave us anymore, Dashel Greene. Far too much change here of late. But *this* looks like a wonderful change." She craned to look around Dash, her big hazel eyes blinking expectantly when they landed upon Lucy. "Who's this? Who've you brought to us?"

Dash cleared his throat. "This is the girl I told you about. Lucy Claremont. Lucy, this is Sophie and Clara Smythe."

Clara's face lit up. "Ah," she breathed, as if beholding the queen herself. "Lucy." She pressed a smile closed around her dimples and clasped Lucy's hand. "So you've joined us at last. Come, come, we'll have a tea."

Ushered past the wary gaze of Sophie, Lucy followed Clara inside. The woman's pleasant chatter faded into a hush as Lucy took in her surroundings. What was it about this place that quickened her soul so? She felt, as she slipped into the cool haven, that she was cocooned inside a place that changed people, harbored hearts, grew stories.

She drew close to the hearth and took in the way the plaster was cracking away from the stone walls. No attempt had been made to repair it, for to do so would strip the room of its airy charm.

But she was being silly. Places did not grow stories. Plaster did not make or break a home. She shivered away the notions that belonged more in a fairy tale than a farmhouse. They'd passed dozens of stone farmhouses on the journey down from London, but none of them had put a lump in her throat and made her close her eyes briefly to wonder why she felt like she had been there before, like Stone's Throw Farm had been waiting for her for a long time.

"Here we are." Clara pulled out an old wooden chair, its legs scraping the floor musically.

A basset hound in the corner tilted melancholy, vaguely curious eyes toward her.

"Don't mind her," Sophie said from the doorway, looking from the dog to Lucy. "She won't trouble us for long."

"Oh, I don't mind dogs," Lucy said.

"I wasn't talking about her. I was talking *to* her. Dear Beatrix." She knelt to jostle the dog's droopy black ears lightly and looked pointedly at Lucy, who gulped, taking her meaning.

"Hush, Sophie. She'll think you're serious," Clara said, bustling about the small kitchen.

Sophie raised an eyebrow that spoke very clearly. *And?*

Lucy's face flushed, and she folded her hands on the table to keep from fidgeting. It was an interesting table, covered in thick black paint, with gilded carvings etched into its legs. Appearing to have been hand built some time ago, it seemed oddly ornate in the otherwise homey farmhouse.

Clara slid a chipped red-and-white china plate in front of Lucy. A sailing ship emerged from beneath a crumpet piping steam.

Clara slid a jar on the table. "Midsummer jam. All our berries, in one jam. You'll not find that in London, or even Oxford, I'd wager." She winked. "Lemon curd." She gave a bright yellow jar a jingling stir with a spoon whose end was slightly bent from culinary misadventure. "And . . . clotted cream," she said, pulling a crock from a narrow refrigerator with rounded corners and a silver handle. Vintage design, they would call that in London. But Lucy had a hunch that here, it was simply the refrigerator hauled in sometime in the 1960s, awkwardly trying to find its place in a home built before electricity.

Dash poked his head through the arched stone kitchen doorway. "I'll just put Lucy's things upstairs?"

"Of course." Clara glowed.

"No." Sophie glowered.

Clara's wide eyes grew wider, and Sophie's narrowed. Lucy's neck grew hot, the currents of their unspoken battle raging right over her head.

"All the guest quarters are full, sister," Clara said with contrived cheer. She turned to Lucy. "Business is booming lately. Word of mouth and all that.

"Barnabas wanted to hook us up to the Intermet, but I put my foot down there. I don't have many rules, but I draw the line when it comes to invisible meeting places where you never actually see the person you're speaking to. Hocus pocus, if you ask me."

"Inter*net,* sister," Sophie corrected.

"Just so. The place people meet online. I said, 'No Intermet for us, thank you very much! People want to get away from all that! We'll be completely wireless!' And was I right?"

"Wireless, you say?" Lucy tilted her head.

"Right you are. No wires, no computers, none of it. *Completely* wireless. I even advertised that in the village, and folks seem excited."

"I do not think that means what you think it means," Sophie muttered. And suddenly the rough-edged woman seemed a little less formidable, quoting lines from *The Princess Bride* under her breath. Lucy determined to like the woman, whatever she thought of her. And she liked Clara all the more for her perception — or misperception — of what advertising wireless on their sign actually meant.

The clock ticked. Sophie cleared her throat. "The guest rooms are full," she repeated. "There's no room."

"Well, there — there *is* one room," Clara said, eyes wide with gentle pleading.

"Please." Lucy stood too quickly, knocking her chair over. She bent to right it. "So sorry," she said. "Don't trouble yourselves. I saw an inn back in the village. I can stay there and catch a train home tomorrow."

"No trains tomorrow," Sophie said.

"You'll *not* stay in that inn," Clara said. "That's Roger's inn."

What had she stepped into the middle of?

"Right," Lucy said, thinking back to the pirate flag and window boxes. She struggled to keep up, longing to restore the peace. "Who is Roger?" It seemed the most benign question to ask. Better than *Why not the empty room upstairs?*

"Roger Falke is the most maddening human being under the good sun," Clara said, picking up a broom from the corner and sweeping the neat floor in a bustle.

"He's also Clara's beau," Sophie said.

"Sister!"

"Yes, sister?" Sophie lifted a crumpet and

bit, unflinchingly deadpan.

Clara twisted her apron, flustered. "We needn't bore Miss Claremont with such talk."

"Please, it's just Lucy," Lucy said.

Clara nodded, her ruddy cheeks glowing redder after the mention of Roger Falke as her beau. She laid a hand on her sister's shoulder, her expression morphing, not into one of defense, as Lucy's would have, but one of tender compassion. "If not the room upstairs, then the spring cellar. Surely she can stay there."

Lucy gulped. Visions of a dark hole in the earth set the walls to closing in on her, her head to spinning. She shook free of the vision. *You don't know what the spring cellar is,* she told herself. Perhaps it meant spring, as in verdant life, birdsong, and baby ducklings. And . . . small spaces were essentially the same as big spaces. Same air, same molecules, same opportunity to be human and alive. She reminded herself of this, just as she did every time she got on the Tube, or went down to the basement, or found herself in any space that had her feeling fourteen years old again, the world closing in on her.

Cellar, though, she could not find a happy

potential meaning for. Only cold and darkness.

Yet even as Lucy battled to reconcile this new plot twist, Sophie's rigid stature eased, almost imperceptibly. With a curt nod, she moved toward a cupboard in the corner. The woman had a way of almost gliding — not in the graceful, practiced way of the ladies of gothic novels, but rather more like an apparition gliding over ice. She glided, procured a bundle of flannel sheets, and stole out a back door, casting a stained-glass confetti of light all about the floor in her wake.

FOURTEEN

"Please pardon my sister," Clara said, cheeks glowing even rosier than before. "She . . . she means well. The room upstairs . . . It's hard for her that it's empty. Hard for all of us, really. But harder still to think of someone new occupying it."

Lucy nodded, understanding the sentiment if not the story behind the room, wishing for words that might sweep away the awkwardness she'd caused.

When Clara turned again to the potbelly stove, Dash gave a half-shrug meant for Lucy's eyes only and followed Sophie with Lucy's carpetbag. It was endearing to see this astrophysicist, sleuth of the stars, whose mind operated literally in another galaxy, tromping through ancient farm muck to carry her disintegrating carpetbag to, apparently, the larder.

Clara opened a box of Yorkshire Gold, deposited tea bags in two cups, and poured steaming water from a copper kettle. The woman looked to be in her late forties and gave the impression that she'd been born and raised in a confectioner's shop and trailed a dusting of sweetness wherever she went. "Tell me, Lucy. What brings you to the farm?"

Such a simple question . . . without a simple answer. She took a sip of tea to stall, its scorching heat causing her hand to fly to her mouth.

"Oh, dear. You've burnt your tongue, I shouldn't wonder. I'm so sorry. Here." She nudged a plate toward Lucy. "Have a scone. It'll cure anything that ails."

"Stone's Throw Farm scones," Lucy said. "The stuff of legends."

This made Clara hoot with laughter.

The sweetness of the glaze brought with it a subtle airy sage taste. "Oh, my," Lucy said. "What is that?"

"Lavender, dear. Our secret." She winked. "You were saying?"

Right. Her reason for being here. "I've come to work with Dash on some research," she said. It was a truth, though perhaps less sensational than explaining about the atlas, the peanut shells, the *Jubilee,* and the compendium.

"That boy and his telescope," Clara said.

"He spends far too much time all alone out there with his head in the stars. It's good that he has a friend. Or perhaps" — she stirred her tea nonchalantly — "something more than a friend?"

Lucy nearly choked on her scone. "No," she said. "Nothing like that." She hoped her skittering pulse did not give her away, loud as it pounded in her ears.

"If you say so, dear."

A hush settled over the kitchen as Clara finished her tea and settled into sweeping the stone floor, shaking out a braided rug, moving in and out of sunbeams as she hummed a tune. The place had a magic about it, inviting imaginings about lives in other times, other cups of tea sipped in the kitchen, other bodies weaving through its sunbeams, warming by the hearth.

A cuckoo clock on the wall ticked the moments away, until Lucy became aware that she was being watched. It was an odd sensation. Not that sudden awareness that someone nearby has glanced over at you, but something distant and constant and deep. She looked around. The dog, Beatrix, snoozed. Clara swept. Lucy looked through a window.

There. On the green hill beyond, surrounded by a swirl of black-faced, white-coated sheep about her, stood a girl . . . or a woman. Her long black hair blew in the wind, her slight form still as she watched.

Lucy lifted a hand to wave, but the girl just stood there.

"Who is that?" she asked.

Clara followed Lucy's gaze. "Why, that's our Violette. She's my niece."

"Sophie has a daughter?" Lucy was ashamed at the surprise in her voice. Had she so quickly boxed the woman into a stereotype of a childless spinster?

"No, not Sophie's," Clara said.

Oh. Perhaps she hadn't been too far off after all.

"Sophie never had a daughter. Just a son."

Or perhaps she'd been very far off.

"I see," said Lucy. "So Violette is your brother's child, then?" Dash had spoken of their brother, Barnabas, who was away at a sheep show.

"Aye, she was Jonas's only child, and a comfort to us all after he passed on so young. My dear eldest brother. She came to us . . . oh, about twenty years ago. Just a wee fifteen years old. So young to be alone like that."

She shook her head. "But she's home with us now, and she'll have a home here as long as she likes. She's a quiet one, she is, but don't let that put you off. When you find a friend in Violette, you find a friend for life."

Clara's sweeping slowed, and she grew pensive but then seemed to shake off the mood as if it were a cloak and brightened. "Dash and Sophie will be finished preparing your accommodations by now," she said. "Such as they are." This, more quietly. "But it's snug, and the bed is comfortable, and you'll have birdsong to wake you in the morning. Not a bad lot in life, all things considered."

Lucy repeated Clara's assurances to herself with every step as they passed one stone building, then another, then one without a roof — thankfully they did not stop at that one — and then stopped at a stone pen containing a single pig.

"This is Salt," Clara said. "Odd name, I know, but it's a family tradition. None of us know why that is, but we carry it on, even so, and the pigs seem to like it. This here is Salt the Twenty-Ninth. Occasionally known as Morton."

Lucy patted the pig on the head tentatively, rather warming to his pitifully dirty snout. Then they continued on the path until a green knoll rose and a stream sang.

"Here we are." Clara hesitated almost imperceptibly before turning her gaze on

Lucy, gauging, it seemed, her reaction.

But to what? The stream, the tall grasses? She turned a circle, searching. Had she missed a structure? Her rotation complete, she looked quizzically to Clara, who nodded her forward. She took a step. And there, just beyond the tall grasses and a gentle bulge in the knoll, was a door.

A door in a wall, to be more precise. A door in a wall in a hill, to be exact. A grassy roof sloped over the stone wall, and the door was weathered and slightly warped beneath its white paint. A small square window looked as if it had recently been added, and for that she breathed a little easier. Perhaps it wouldn't feel entirely like a dungeon cell.

The door in the mountain was to be her temporary home, then. She half expected to see a hobbit pop out from this hill-embedded home.

"I know it doesn't look like much," Clara said. "But the spring cellar is one of the most unique spots we have here. Sometimes people request it specially. They like the coolness of it, and . . ."

Her cheery chatter faded as Lucy's old fear slithered out of its long-buried place. She shoveled as much feigned courage onto that fear as she could. *Dark is just dark. Small is just small. Don't make of it more than it is.*

She smiled and nodded, forcing herself back to paying attention to Clara.

"Truly, it's a delightful spot. I've spent many a happy afternoon jollying it up from the storage place it once was."

Storage. Dark. Doubts filled Lucy's heart, telling her this was perhaps her rightful place. Dark obscurity, her career about to be put in cold storage.

Dash opened the door and ducked out. "Oh good, you're here. It's ready for you," he said. "Sophie went to get some extra blankets."

Clara nodded. "It does get a little cold in there. And I know it's dark — but we tuck light in wherever light can be tucked. 'Don't let the gloom settle over your bones so,' my grandmother used to say, and so we chase it off however we can."

Funny words, that phrase — lilting and hopeful and shadowed, all at once. Lucy let them wrap her as she stepped inside and blinked in the darkness.

She did not see much, but was that . . . running water that she heard?

"That's the stream," Dash said, ducking back in.

The space was more comfortable than she'd expected, a step down into the earth making the ceiling feel almost lofty to her

— and just tall enough for Dash's lanky form.

"This was where they used to stick stuff to keep it cold," he said.

"Such a technical explanation from the astrophysicist." Lucy laughed lightly.

Dash smiled and shrugged. "No need to overcomplicate something so simple and effective that it's sheer genius. If you ask me, we don't even need a refrigerator. They could keep all the milk and eggs in here and be just fine. Stick the stuff you want extra cold right into the stream. Put the rest on the shelves and call it good. Right?"

Lucy inhaled spiced, earthy air. The stream babbled along, and as her eyes adjusted, she took in little outcroppings of stone jutting out from the mortared walls here and there. Perhaps they had once housed food, but now they were stacked with books, each of them with jars containing tiny fairy lights in place of bookends.

The space was tight — just big enough for a cot. Or rather . . . What was that? She squinted. "Is that a hammock?" she asked of the platform hanging from four thick ropes that looked as if they'd been taken straight off a ship. Sheer fabric hung alongside it, lending airy elegance to the rustic feel. Throw pillows piled at the back of the bed against the wall, and an old trunk stood on its end as a bed table of black painted wood and gilded carvings that looked quite aged. A partner, perhaps, to the kitchen table in the farmhouse? Lucy reached out and switched on a hurricane lamp, warming at its soft light.

"Not quite a hammock," Clara said from the door. "It's a cross between a hammock and a wooden swing. A hanging platform bed, Barnabas calls it. I drew my vision for the place, he made it real."

Lucy shook her head in wonder. "I can see why people request to stay here," she said. Despite it being dark and a little claustrophobic at first, it felt . . . safe, with a sprinkling of magic and an invitation to linger and rest. That window to the outside would be her sanity, she knew. A portal through which the weight of darkness was lifted, and that made all the difference.

When was the last time she'd rested? It seemed a foreign concept, and she suddenly felt an aching tiredness.

"You rest awhile, dear," Clara said, as she entered and fluffed up a few pillows on the bed. "You look like you could use a wink or two."

"Oh, but there's so much to do, I couldn't possibly —"

"Take it from me," Clara said, laying a hand on Lucy's shoulder. "When you're so busy you can't possibly rest, that's when it's most important to throw caution to the wind and take a nap. Here." She patted the mattress on the platform and waited until Lucy sat, feeling the lull of the gentle sway of the bed.

"We'll catch you later, Matchstick Girl." Dash winked and vanished through the door. Clara followed, but just as she was about to close the door, Lucy stopped her.

"Please," she said, "would you mind leaving that cracked open?" She flushed, embarrassed and feeling approximately six years old. "I love the fresh air." That much was true. And the last thing Clara needed was the full explanation, saga that it was.

Clara smiled and left the door ajar, and soon Lucy — who twelve hours before had stepped away from the only home she had ever known, was nearly jobless, and pretty much one hundred percent alone in the world — was laying her head against a feather pillow impossibly soft, sung to sleep by a stream running through her own bedchamber, with the best friend she'd ever known whistling a tune somewhere in the green meadow beyond.

Fifteen

HMS Avalon
The English Channel
August 1805

The only person Frederick might have called friend was half-enemy. But Elias was the only soul he knew here and felt for all the world like a best chum. A best chum who was nowhere to be seen.

Sails snapped. Masts groaned and swayed, reaching up into the impossible beyond. The HMS *Avalon* was a floating monarch worthy of its legendary namesake, a vessel where one could well imagine the sword Excalibur being forged, as it was said to have been on King Arthur's mist-shrouded Isle of Avalon.

Through his schoolroom telescope, Frederick had often admired the gold-on-black paint, the wall of windows that reached the heavens, and the sails that layered one another in perfect symmetry, looking like angels' wings. He'd watched the crew —

like little ants from so far away — traverse rigging so swiftly and seamlessly, it seemed an art.

When he pressed his eyes closed now, ignored the burning rope rubbing into his wrists tied behind his back, he could still see it that way — majestic. But here on the grand ship's deck, the stench forced his eyes open, his whole body lurched in a gag. Though the *Avalon* looked a stately queen from afar, up close she was a rank cesspool of hundreds of men living close, farm animals kept in the hold for future meals, and the aftermath and byproducts of both those things mingling to create a putrid odor.

And yet, here he was, lying on the deck of the ship he'd dreamed of boarding for so long. Did it matter, then, that he'd landed here by force? He felt . . . robbed, somehow. With a little more time he could have stepped onto this vessel in honor, his place secured, his father's good name preceding him, making a way for him at Admiral Forsythe's table. For the man was known to be kind to the young members of his crew, unlike many of the tyrants at sea.

"Oy," a man with skin as tanned and weathered as a saddle said, "you lot stay put 'til Reynolds can look over ye." He strode off into bright sun.

Another gag seized Frederick's body, clenching his stomach and releasing it only at the sound of jeering.

He closed his eyes, saw the diagrams Reskell had made him label twenty times over. He was on the forecastle deck. Ahead, past the bow, the Union flag rippled its blue-and-white into a grey sky. Shouts sounded all about — above and below, beside and beyond — this place where he and Elias had been deposited along with three others. Two of them were boys who appeared two or three years older than him — fifteen, perhaps? They looked none too pleased to be here but appeared to be quite at home at sea. They took twin stances, legs spread wide and standing as sure as if they stood on solid ground. Frederick forced himself to his feet and moved to imitate their stance, surveying the swift movements of the seamen, the low conversation of officers on the quarterdeck. The ship tilted and splayed him flat on his stomach.

"Green as green water," someone said, and Frederick watched their boots carry them past his face.

But where was Elias? Remorse filled Frederick when he thought of having placed himself between the press gang and the likes of him. He scraped sheer will together, dredging it past a dark force gathering inside him, bent on making him retch.

A hand thrust itself into view. Weathered but scrappy, dirt outlining fingernails where skin was stained with black ink.

"Come on, then," a voice said, gravelly and buoyant all at once. A hand made for Frederick's rope with a knife so swift he didn't have time to register panic. The rope snapped loose and relief flooded in.

The hand appeared again. "Give me yer 'and."

Frederick looked up into the face of a man who was all points. A dark beard, peppered with white, combed into a triangle, whose tip reached his chest. Moustache groomed into thin points stretching past the edge of his face, one end bent, apparently from the misadventures of the evening before. He was a caricature in human form, with a once-ivory cravat that looked to have come from a tailor but now bore layers of dust and grime that bespoke a long time between washings.

"Wh-who are you?" Frederick sputtered, taking the man's hand and glad for the strength it offered as it lifted him to his feet. If he could but imitate that strength, he might make it two minutes without flopping like a fish out of water. His words were floundering, too. Father would be raising his eyebrows at that. "That is, to whom do I owe my thanks?"

"Killian Blackaby, at your service," the man said.

"Killian . . . Blackaby?" Frederick didn't know why he repeated the name, other than it seemed a name that should be spoken, a name one would spot more readily on Father's bookshelves rather than onboard a man-o'-war.

The man seemed pleased, and took the repetition to mean he'd been recognized. "The very same! Glad to see my reputation precedes me."

"But I didn't . . . That is, I don't . . ." Frederick's head throbbed.

Killian Blackaby beamed, and he bit his tongue. Best not take the man's pleasure, when it cost him so little.

"Did you see another boy, Mr. Blackaby?"

"What, those two louses?" He thumbed toward the seaworthy fellows. "Louses," he muttered. "Blouses. What a rhyme. If I but had my quill to write it down . . ." He patted his trousers and jacket as if their pockets might hold such a thing. "Or paper, at the very least."

Frederick thought to the logbook he'd

stuck in his jacket pocket yesterday. A lifetime ago. He bit his tongue. For all he knew, the man would abscond with the whole lot.

"No matter," the man said. "I'll keep it in the locker." He winked, turning toward the side of the ship. Frederick hastened to stop him, horror reaching his toes. Did the man mean to toss himself overboard?

"No, don't!" Frederick planted himself in front of the man, who lifted a quizzical brow, as pointy as his beard. "It's not as bad as all that. Please don't jump."

"Jump!" Mr. Blackaby hooted. "Indeed not. Not with a rhyme like that pounding to be writ down."

"But you said . . . the locker. Did you mean Davy Jones's locker?"

The man stooped, and Frederick despised the way it made him feel a child. He did not need to appear any smaller or less capable than he already did. "The locker is what I call this." He tapped his forehead. "The place ideas go to . . ." He waited.

Was Frederick to fill in the blank, then? "To die?"

Killian Blackaby took a step back, hand to his chest as if Frederick had dealt him a blow. "Certainly not! To be kept safe from that fate. A balladmonger needs a healthy arsenal of rhymes."

Frederick had never heard poetry described as weaponry before. But it seemed fitting for this pointy man. "I see." Frederick shook his head, clearing the fog again. "But no, I wasn't referring to those boys. Another boy. Closer to my age. Looks as if he ate anger for breakfast."

Killian Blackaby hooted again, and this time it drew stares from the seamen about deck. "Now, that's another one for the locker. Mind if I use that?"

Frederick shook his head, and it throbbed the harder.

"Eh? Was that a yes?"

"Yes," Frederick muttered, pressing his eyes shut as the odd man turned away.

"So, what's your plan to get us out of this mess?" *Elias Flint.* Frederick searched for the source of the voice and saw the boy sitting with knees wide, wrists resting upon them, and leaning against a spool of rope as if he were merely soaking in the sun in a pasture somewhere.

"*My* plan?" Bitterness swarmed. Frederick crossed the deck to stand, arms crossed, in front of Elias. *Don't fall. Don't fall. Do. Not. Fall.* "*Your* plan, more like. I'm not the one who got us into this mess."

"No?" He opened one eye, squinting, then

shut it again as if Frederick did not warrant open eyes. "You think I didn't see you there, following me in the dark?"

"Why did you not say anything?"

"Why would I? Besides, you're the one who tipped them off, led that crew right to me."

That wasn't true. Frederick's jaw clenched, injustice mounting into a boil.

"Thought you'd be a brave defender, did you? Win Juliette's heart by freeing me from the big bad press gang?"

Frederick's brow pinched. "What are you talking about?"

"I heard you. *'Go to her.'* Telling me over and over to go to Juliette. As if she's not the very reason I stayed."

The pieces began to fall into place. Frederick had *thought* he was telling Juliette to "go to her." To her mother.

But it had been Elias, whose countenance now twisted in disdain. "As if she'd even think twice about a useless nobody like you who wouldn't know a shovel if it hit him in the head."

Something hot billowed up in Frederick's chest. He didn't care what anyone thought of him, and he certainly had no eyes for Juliette Heath. But he had made a promise to a grave, and it was solemn and so far from what the scoundrel implied.

"Stand up." The words barely slipped past the prison of Frederick's clenched teeth.

"Why." Elias's reply was so dry, it tossed oil on the fire.

Frederick strode over and gripped the boy's elbow, pulling him to his feet. "Because I'll not attack a sitting duck."

Elias sputtered laughter.

"Defend yourself," Frederick demanded, fists rising, circling in some instinct he knew nothing of. If he'd had a sword, if this were a fencing match, he could parry, plan, strategize, and advance with precision that would leave Elias no hope. But he had only ire and knuckles and a smirking target. And the old familiar swelling up inside, urging him to fight for justice, no matter the cost.

Elias's smug expression flickered almost imperceptibly into concern, his muscles stiffening. But the dubious look he gave Frederick told him he did not believe he had anything to fear.

"What?" he said. "A boy like you going to do me in?"

Frederick's fist shot back and let loose. Even as it flew through the air he knew it was wrong, knew he should halt, knew a thousand other truths that fell away in the wake of that fist. Only one word blazed, fueling the fire: *Boy.* He was eight again, his father running him through masts and decks and captains and calling him boy. Never looking. Never seeing.

Boy.

And finally, he was not a boy. He was here now, on the *Avalon.* Owing to none but his own foolhardy antics for thrusting him into the clutches of the press gang. Frederick's body took over as if to pound that word straight out of the world.

Pain split across his knuckles. The sight of blood at the corner of Elias's mouth sent remorse pummeling through him.

Elias touched his mouth, withdrew his hand, and stared at the red. An eerie stillness overtook him. Frederick had seen it too many times to count, looking out from his window over Pevensey Bay. The calm before the storm, and all one could do was brace for impact.

Frederick clenched every muscle, jutted his jaw, and stood — he hoped — like a man. But the rage of a child flared when Elias threw himself into him. Frederick did not register the pain, other than the way each blow contained rage. They were down. Blind limbs launching, bodies colliding with the deck, a fog of shouts and jeers mounting.

A pair of grimy hands circled around Elias, pulling him off Frederick. A sturdy force pulled Frederick back likewise until the boys stood facing each other, each shackled by a man, shoulders heaving. Killian Blackaby grinned from his place binding Elias.

"Some entrance." Blackaby laughed, and the man behind Frederick tensed. Something about the man's silence, along with his iron grip, sank sickness into Frederick as he realized what he'd just done. All these boys — and men — had just been witness to his very first act upon the great *Avalon.*

"Yes," the man behind Frederick said, easing his grip around Frederick's elbows as his breathing slowed. He hung his head.

His sole hope now was that Admiral Forsythe had not also seen this disgrace.

"I do not permit such . . . spectacles . . . on my ship," the man behind him said. Frederick let his head fall lower and, as he did, saw Elias from the corner of his eye. He stood taller. Face ruddy, eyes wide. He gulped. And for the first time, Frederick felt . . . *like* Elias. It was a brotherhood he did not wish to acknowledge. He, too, gulped. Turned. And lifted his gaze to meet that of the man whose portrait hung on his schoolroom wall. Admiral Cuthbert Forsythe.

Sixteen

"Y-yes, sir." He stammered, loathing himself for it. "My apologies."

A few stifled snickers slipped through the crowd, which had otherwise become thick with silence.

That silence grew until Killian fairly burst forth from himself, apparently one of the rare breed who could not abide the absence of words. "Killian Blackaby," he said, his greeting almost as explosive as his stride, pumping the admiral's hand with no regard for the decorum that should preside over such a meeting. "Purveyor of Ballads. At your humble service. Humbly at your service. At your service in any humble way you choose, Admiral." God bless the man. He was succeeding not only in making a spectacle of his own self but, Frederick sheepishly hoped, also in erasing the spectacle of his own making.

Forsythe, bedecked in gold buttons, medals, and fringes upon his navy suit, was what Reskell would have described as "Gravitas, embodied." The very soul of dignity. He surveyed Killian from head to toe, then Frederick, Elias, and finally, the leader of the press gang, who was much more reticent than he'd been the night before.

Forsythe's expression seemed to question the haphazard lot of sea urchins the press gang had brought him. He looked Frederick over. "How old are you, young man?"

"Twelve, sir."

"Far too young."

Frederick knew twelve was not the youngest the waves knew, and he was nearly thirteen. And yet . . . was there a note of compassion in the admiral's voice? Frederick could but hope.

Admiral Forsythe turned to the press gang leader. "This is what you bring when I request seaworthy men?"

The leader, whom the others had called Smith, wavered for the first time. "The county stock was limited, Admiral. Other press gangs gone before us an' such." He ventured a half laugh that flopped like a cold squid upon humorless decks.

Admiral Forsythe spoke not a word more. Only turned to climb the steps to the quarterdeck. In his silence, he communicated more than all the volumes in the Royal Naval Academy in Portsmouth could have. "The sailors aboard the *Avalon* will not resort to violence amongst themselves," he said. "Show them the sty." And with hands clasped behind his back, he disappeared behind a mast.

"You heard the man!" the press gang leader barked. "No room for your rows here. To the meat grinder, and then down to the hull with ye. You're in for it tonight. Slap you in the stocks or worse after a scene like that, like as not."

Or worse. The admiral had called it the sty. Frederick had read of ship discipline. Of running the gauntlet, of leg irons, floggings, being left to blister in the sun where all could see a man's shame. Which of these, he wondered, did the admiral mean? His stomach betrayed him, but it was empty, and for that he was thankful.

The "meat grinder," Frederick learned, was the maze belowdecks where new seamen were catalogued and assessed like livestock. Eye colour, hair colour, temperament — Frederick catalogued as *about as lively as a clam,* and Elias as *suspected unruly* — and whether or not they were seaworthy.

They apparently were, for they were

ushered farther into the belly of the whale, where the sound of fiddles and rowdy voices faded and they heard the lower grunts of swine.

"Here ye be," Smith said. "Accommodations for the night."

Frederick nearly tripped in the dimness over something warm and large and full of deep-snouted grunting. "That's . . . that's a *pig.*"

"Aye, so it is."

"Right brilliant of you to say so, too," Elias piped up, crossing his arms in his maddening fashion.

"I just thought . . . Well, I thought the admiral meant something else when he said *sty.*"

"You'll find Cuthbert Forsythe to be a man who says what he means."

As Smith turned to go, Elias strode over to the beast, who lay in contented reverie in his own filth. "Escaped the sheepfold to land in a pigsty. Just my luck." He gave a mirthless laugh. "What's his name?"

"Name," the man said, as if it were the most preposterous notion he'd ever heard. "*Salt.* And it's a 'she.' "

"As in, 'a sailor worth his salt'?" Frederick bent to scratch the animal on his head. He looked at him with a fond affection in his pitiful animal eyes.

"As in, 'salted pork.' " The sailor filled the cavernous sty with laughter and departed, shouting after them to clean up the place but good, lest they end up with lashings for their row, rather than this kinder punishment.

What a world it is, Frederick thought later, when they finally lay down after six bells of the dogwatch. If he were at Edgecliffe, he'd have been waiting on the rising of the midnight star, but here he was three decks below the night sky, hundreds of men sleeping or working in the columns of space above him while he cleaned and fed his own future dinner rather than tracking stars.

Bone-tired when all was said and done, Frederick struggled to climb into his hammock — his own future coffin, should he meet his end at sea — swaying barely above the fresh straw and the muck hidden beneath it. It was in this fashion, morose as it was, that he recorded that night in his log.

In the days and weeks that followed, he stayed awake as long as he could in the minutes just before sleep to record a line or a page — whatever he could muster to keep himself sane.

September the eighth, 1805

Dined with Salt.

Fiddles above, fighting off strong head-winds.

Smith keeps us in the hold, going on three weeks now. He says Elias and I are of the same country stock, from East Sussex, and therefore we are as good as family and may as well stay here.

Does family make one wish to poke one's own eyes out?

September the twenty-first, 1805

Mal de Mer. Seasick. Wouldn't wish this upon Salt. Or even Elias. (Debatable.)

October the first, 1805

If I had the seasickness badly, Elias has it ten times over, and the sea is making the most of it, tossing us with a vengeance. Water seeps into the hold and the stink from Salt is worse than ever, but she looks apologetic, poor old girl. She does not know her fate. What sort of life is it, to spend every waking and sleeping moment in a dark hole, awaiting the day you die?

Then again . . . perhaps we are not so different from Salt.

Gave my crust to Elias. Even wretches need strength.

Every night without fail, he goes up to deck and points himself homeward and just . . . watches. I know what he's thinking of.

Or rather . . . who he's thinking of.

I think of her, too. I think of how to get him home to her. It seems the right thing to do. For I have taken, again, something good from her.

October the fifteenth, 1805

The admiral had us into his quarters to dine. It seems he's had a letter from his old shipmate, Barnard Hanford, letting him know his son had been among those pressed into service.

Barnard Hanford — Father — did not likewise send a letter to that son.

Since they came up together from the days of powder monkeys and beyond, the admiral felt he owed it to me — and my bunkmate, apparently — to give us a proper reception. "I have strict admonitions from your father to treat you as any other powder monkey," he said when he issued the invitation. "But he did not strictly forbid me giving you a decent meal. I know what you eat down in the hold."

And so we scrubbed the stink of the manger from our clothes as best we could and dined on mutton and butter and biscuits, with chandelier overhead and views to the ocean beyond. He keeps a grey mourning dove in a cage, and I asked after it. Most captains and admirals keep some exotic pet from their adventures — a monkey, a parrot — but this creature was so quiet and unassuming, it did not seem the sort to play mascot to a grand ship like the Avalon.

He said he observed it, on shore in Canada. It was wounded, or so he'd thought. It seemed to have a broken wing, limping away as if to escape him. He later watched from some distance, and the dove tucked her wing in just fine, returning to her nest of young ones. She had been attempting to distract him, a threat to those in her care.

The next day, he had returned to find her wounded in earnest, her nest empty. Some creature had gotten to her, and the mourning dove, bereft of her fledglings, was earning her namesake.

I asked why he kept her. He said, "Any creature willing to sacrifice herself for one weaker is a creature with truer heart than many a man I've met. I kept her to let her heal. I keep her to protect her. And I keep her to remind us."

I thought of his fighting tactics. The way he infamously puts the Avalon in harm's way when smaller ships in the fleet are in danger. And I counted myself lucky to have been pressed into service on a ship with such a man.

Nights in the hold with a smelly pig and a smelly would-be comrade did not a pleasant slumber make. Frederick had realized early on that the answer to maintaining sanity was the same as his methods at home. So tonight, like so many nights before, he wound through the labyrinth of the ship, up and up, until the night sky burst upon him with fresh air that blew the cobwebs and stench-laden clouds right out of him. The dogwatch was on — those latest hours when the sky was darkest, the ship seemed small, and the sky seemed big. He did not know the crew taking the watch this night. Even after months aboard in tight quarters, there were new faces at every turn. Five hundred, he'd heard, all in different shifts and roles, making the ship run like clockwork.

Though he knew his fellow sailors hardly at all, if he looked higher — above the rigging, above the billowed, taut sails, above the crow's nest — he spotted his only true friends, scattered across the dark sky like diamonds.

Orion. Ursa Major. And faintly — way up north — Draco. Warriors of the heavens, whose reaching expanse made this never-ending war seem small. Made him smaller still, and glad for it.

Like flames drawing a winged creature, they summoned him. He was thankful, suddenly, for the swabbing of the decks and mucking of the stalls, and how they'd toughened his skin enough — left it with screaming red marks and thick blisters — so that he might now ascend the heavens, as it were.

He'd fallen at first. Picked himself up. Slipped. Caught himself. A wrestle with the ropes, which for a long while he'd lost. But he'd thought of a girl with freckles splashed across her face, how she'd take on the world, and that had fueled him. If a girl could man a cutter on her own, he could climb rigging. He'd kept at it, again and again. He'd gathered stares from the sailors on watch, but no one stopped him. And when nightly he stole above deck to practice, until the ropes no longer tangled and ensnared, their stares of amusement had turned to nods of respect.

Tonight, the higher he went, the more the ship's rocking amplified, flinging him about like a plaything. His hands and feet flew over the rigging like a spider over his web, until at last he reached the crow's nest, naught but a man-sized barrel with its top cut off, lashed to the mast pole.

Betimes it was occupied by a sailor on watch or a sailor relegated to a place of assured seasickness to school his unruly behavior. But tonight it was empty, and it became his sanctuary. He imagined himself standing on Edgecliffe's rooftop again, far above strife and war, guarded by chimneys. Only here, he was hidden among masts.

Here he could look up and out and see an entire universe of black that would turn to blue come daylight — sky above, sea below, blue all 'round. In the light of the starry night he could only vaguely see the other ships of the fleet trailing behind, waves circling. How could he feel confined, with such a view? In the smallest segment of the ship, he found boundless freedom.

He narrowed his eyes until they focused on the warriors of the sky — Hercules, Poseidon; and the brothers, Castor and Pollux, for whom he still harbored envy. But his mind was then drawn higher, to the One who created these stars that men assigned stories and names to. Here, he prayed.

In the midst of those prayers he finally fell

asleep . . . and awoke to dawn's light and a sound so sickening it could not be real.

The splintering force of cannonball on wood, embedded with frantic voices.

Just above him, something round sung through the air in a streak, its dark mass punching through a white sail and leaving a perfectly round, perfectly horrifying window to the blue sky above.

What ensued was chaos.

"She's gaining on us!" a voice called from the quarterdeck below. Frederick turned his head. A sail flapped aside to reveal the blue, red, and white of French colours on an approaching frigate.

He scrambled to the rigging, all limbs tripping to obey. But when he looked below, he saw the admiral commanding on deck. Men were climbing over one another to obey, to save their own lives.

Frederick did not know what to do. If he descended into the mayhem, what could he do but make it worse? But if he stayed hidden amongst the sails, he was naught but a coward. A deserter, on his own ship.

"Beat to quarters! Beat to quarters!" And there was the command. The decision made for him. Cannons would be fired. And cannons must be loaded.

Something inside took over, urging his feet

to action before his thoughts had time to match. The rigging flying by as he descended, he landed in a sea of missional confusion — every man on fire with purpose, and every purpose urgent.

Frederick spotted Elias, making a mad dash for the gun deck below. Sprinting to join him, Frederick leapt over sacks, dodged ropes, ducked around bodies intent on reaching their posts. Just as he reached Elias, he saw the officer of the watch opening wide his mouth, fire in his eyes, shouting for them to take cover. All of this in surreal motion, drawn out as if the urgency of the moment had muted the chaos, stretched time, and all he could hear was his pulse.

He threw himself over Elias. Knocking the boy to the ground as he'd wished to dozens of times before. Only now it was to save him.

Frederick collided with Elias — and Frederick's head collided with a crate, exploding into pain, but registering nothing but the destruction of the cannonball just feet away.

Elias squirmed to his feet. And as Frederick made to do the same, his head protested, the world spinning fast, red pooling where he'd collided.

One look at him and Elias braced his shoulders, guided him downstairs, tossed an empty sack at him, and pointed at Frederick's head, hollering something.

Frederick's thoughts were ringed in clouded black. What was wrong with him? He looked at his hand holding the sack, then back at Elias. Gripping the bag, not understanding, Frederick tried to shake clear of the fog. He stooped to grab at a bucket, slipped — and only then did he understand. 'Twas his own blood there, slicking the floor.

Quick motion yanked the empty sack, and Frederick lifted his head to see Elias had grabbed the sack and was tearing it seam from seam. He wrapped the rough fabric tightly about Frederick's head and thrust a bucket at him.

What followed was men becoming machine. Rolling cannons. Loading. Firing, to an upward eruption of black smoke. Yellow lanterns swung eerily above as the *Avalon* rocked and shook with shots fired, shots landed, men falling, cannons rolling. And firing. And rolling. And firing. Sick, odd silences, broken again by flashes of fire in the fray beyond. Shouts to "Hold steady, men!" made him stand tall, ignore the pounding in his head. Splintering blows until at last . . .

Silence.

The *Avalon* groaned an ancient, wounded groan. Guttural and waterlogged, like her men.

But though they be cut, and though they be worn . . . they were victorious.

It was not until later, far into the night, as Salt sang them to sleep with her lullaby of porcine snores, that Frederick looked over at Elias, and something changed. They were no longer boys. Nor nemeses. Nor even begrudging friends by default of being kept in a literal pigsty.

They were comrades.

"What." Elias's face was grim, staring at the dark ceiling. "What are you staring at?"

"Nothing," Frederick said.

"You're staring at me."

"Precisely."

Elias held silence a moment, then snorted at Frederick's dig.

Frederick looked at the ceiling, and spoke what he needed to. "Thank you," he said simply.

"For what?" Elias said.

Frederick shook his head, frustration climbing into his voice. "You helped."

"I saved you, more like."

Now Frederick sat up. "I saved you first."

Elias leaned up on an elbow. "You must've really knocked your skull hard if you think that. You'd have bled out if I hadn't tied you up like a mummy. With my hand crushed from someone tossing me to the ground, by the way." He held up his swollen hand, pressing his fist to his heart and pounding it for effect.

"And how do you think I got this head wound? Throwing you out of harm's way — that's how."

"Shut up!" The bellow came from above, the deep and groggy voice of a man dragged from his sleep. "Bickering like a pair o' green-bellied brothers! Git to sleep!"

Elias was silent. The silence grew thick. And then somewhere between the boy with the black eye as big as a saucer and the boy with the gunpowder sack for a crown, they must have seen themselves as they were.

Truth, as it is wont to do, speared the tensions, and laughter broke through its crack. They collapsed into their hammocks as if they were the beds of kings, for they brought solace to tired bones and souls.

After that night, Elias and Frederick were not exactly fast friends. One did not owe undying allegiance to the other in effusive thanks for saving his life. But two clumsy boys forced into manhood became something more.

Brothers.

Seventeen

A week later, Frederick felt Elias watching on as he scratched the day's entry into his logbook.

"You write," Elias said after a while.

Frederick paused, shifting his weight, unwilling to answer his obvious statement. He bent his head low, eyes straining to see in the dim light.

Elias lay in his hammock, uncharacteristically quiet. Not humming or being his usual bothersome self.

"You write, Freddy," he said after a few moments. "What do you write?"

Frederick gripped his book. "Things. And don't call me Freddy."

Elias screwed up his face at the evasive reply. "What *things,* Freddy?"

Frederick blew out his cheeks. He would tell him, if only to be rid of him.

"Just . . . ship's log type things. Headwinds, following seas, that sort of thing."

He left out the part about the stories written across the skies, the way he carved hope into these pages in the dark. "Letters to Father, sometimes." Letters that always went unanswered. No doubt The Admiral was of the mind that to speak into his son's life would be to interfere with the Royal Navy's further schooling.

"Ha!" Elias swung his legs over the edge off his hammock. "Letters. I thought as much. I have a proposition for you," he said, putting on an unnaturally proper tone.

Frederick slid a wary gaze his direction. "Do tell," he said drolly. The quicker it was out, the quicker he could refuse and be done with it.

"Write letters for me."

"To whom?" The question was out before he thought better of it. The boy had no family other than the band of smugglers who'd all but raised him, at least before Tom Heath had taken him under his wing.

"You're not the only one in the world with someone to write to," Elias said. "Don't forget" — he held out his hand nonchalantly, turning it this way and that as he examined the ragged bandage about his palm — "I can't grip a pen. Can't think why that is. This pesky war injury, I s'pose. Got it when a good-for-nothing —"

"Fine."

"What was that?" Elias stilled his hand, a glimmer in his eye. He was enjoying this far too much.

"I'll write your letters for you. Until your martyr there" — Frederick nodded toward his hand — "is healed."

Elias's face grew red. "Well, that's the thing, mate. Might need your help a smidge longer than that."

Frederick studied Elias, whose grim expression was suddenly full of shame. Understanding tugged at Frederick. "You don't write," he said, the realization dawning, and with it, remorse. He should've thought of that.

Elias's defenses were up. "What of it," he spat. "Not all of us are shut up with a four-eyed tutor all day. Some of us have lives to live, you know."

Touché. Frederick turned a page. "Very well. What should I write?"

"What? Now?"

Frederick nodded. "Unless you want to wait for your other hand to be smashed to smithereens, too."

The barb worked its magic. Elias took it for the invitation it was and lay back in his hammock. "Write . . . Dear Juliette."

Frederick's quill froze as a vision of a girl

with cheeks pink from sun and sea air, hair flying behind her wild and free, flashed across his mind. The laughter had gone from her because of him. And she'd once declared they would have nothing to do with each other, ever again.

He gulped. Would this be a violation of her intent?

"Well, go on." Elias circled his good hand in the air impatiently. "Write Dear Juliette!"

Frederick's quill touched paper. Long, slow strokes scratched black onto white until her name appeared before him, there in the dark hold. "What's next?"

"It's me, Elias." He said this with far too much pride, but his dirt-smudged face grinned on. "I'm here on board the *Avalon.* You always said I'd be a great man of the sea, and here I am."

Frederick snorted. "Great . . . man . . . of . . . the sea," he repeated as he wrote, eyebrows raised. "Very grand indeed. Shall I tell her of your bunkmate the pig?"

Elias rolled his eyes and gestured for him to continue writing. "I'll win our fortune yet — you'll see. We'll live far away in the Windward Isles, that picture we saw of the green islands in the West Indies. You'll see. Give your mother my fondest wishes, and . . ."

Frederick's hand flew to catch up, halting where Elias had stopped.

"And?"

He mumbled something.

"What was that?"

"I said, *wait for me.*"

The quill grew clammy in Frederick's hand, and he suddenly felt like an intruder. And worse, a liar. He'd given her one promise — the only thing he'd been permitted to give after her father's death. And he was not just breaking that promise, but inserting himself into the most private place of her heart. He had to apologize, somehow — to acknowledge he knew he was intruding yet would continue if it meant she might receive word from the one good thing she had left, besides her mother.

He looked over at Elias, who was tracing images into the air with a stockinged foot, his big toe poking through a hole. He . . . was her one good thing. The one reason she smiled. He and his big, fat, clumsy toe.

Well, he would break his promise if it meant giving her that. He thought a moment, scribbling Elias's closing words onto the page, then adding some of his own.

p.s. The scribe adds his well wishes for your sheep to never fall into thieving hands.

There. She would understand. Having been quick to accuse him of stealing her sheep, she would surely be just as quick to understand his words for the peace offering he hoped they were.

And so it began. The writing of letters that bridged the chasm between Elias and Juliette. Lost between ports for months, sometimes, he prayed they'd always find their way. Elias writing to Juliette — Juliette writing to Elias. News from home. New lambs, and farmers welcoming children, village goings-on, and her mother's health.

Frederick read Juliette's missives aloud in the dark hold, wondering betimes — with a hollow inside of him growing wider by turns — what it would have been like to have words written for him by such a hand. But he never let the thought linger, for her words were not for him. Instead he contented himself that the shapes of the letters — the jots and lines and crooked way she quirked her *S*'s — were for him. For she knew he would read them and Elias would not.

But the meaning beneath the letters, the

words with a heartbeat and a soul, was for Elias. Frederick drew strict boundaries around the stubborn thing that beat in his chest when it came to that.

So it went, him on the outside looking on — just as it always had been. Only instead of watching from the windows of Edgecliffe as Juliette and Elias traversed the fields, his panes were her letters as they traversed life.

He recorded whatever Elias dictated, from recounting heroic battle wounds, to the story of how they'd smuggled Salt to safety when Cook had come for her and they'd given their first prize money to purchase her. She'd written back, offering asylum for the hapless pig. She'd met them in Portsmouth when next they were in port and walked away with a rope tied about the squealing creature's neck, as if walking a pig like a dog down the dock were the most natural thing in all the world.

Frederick watched with amusement and respect at the girl's endless pluck as she nodded at curious onlookers. Gone was her boy's cap of yesteryear. Her auburn hair and rust-coloured dress tangled about her in the wind. When she tripped and fell, Elias was quick to leap over boxes and barrels to help her back up. She scolded him, but the look she gave him told Frederick she didn't mind that arm about hers, not one bit.

Good. This is good. Looking at the pair of them, Frederick felt certain their future was bright, and hoped, perhaps he might have had some small part in that. *Please, God.*

The hold had been too silent after Salt left, and the young men eventually migrated to the regular sleeping quarters, the days of being powder monkeys long behind them. As the years passed, the happy news from Juliette was mixed with sad news — her mother had succumbed to her long illness. Juliette's sorrow nearly broke her, but as she shared her heart, it was clear her bravery and faith sustained her.

Frederick watched as Elias took the news, gratefully accepted the heavy cloak of responsibility. But it changed him in a way Frederick couldn't quite put a finger on.

At eighteen, they were truly men now. Frederick had moved from powder monkey to seaman to petty officer and now midshipman. He was poised to become master one day. Elias, likewise, had risen up through the ranks, distinguishing himself on different fronts. Moving from seaman to petty officer, he'd been sorely disappointed to not yet have been promoted to midshipman. But he was determined, after midshipman, to someday reach the golden land of lieutenant. "You wait and see," he said. "My ship'll come in. I'll get that prize money and purchase a commission. Imagine that, Freddy. You, master, and me, lieutenant. There'll be none to stop us then, least of all old Bonaparte."

Frederick had written his father of the promotion to midshipman and — wonder of wonders — had received a letter in return, instructing him to stop when next he was in Portsmouth to see a Mr. Hogarth, with whom he had commissioned a portrait.

A portrait. This, from the man who'd been silent for years, but for his secondhand communications through Admiral Forsythe. From the man who could scarce look at a chess board after Frederick had failed to secure a brilliant strategy. His father desired a portrait . . . of Frederick?

Perhaps it was the shock of it all, but Frederick had obliged, wondering during the entire excruciating sitting if ever he would darken the doors of Edgecliffe again. Would he ever see the man who became more enigmatic with every passing year? He dared to entertain the hope that this portrait was, perhaps, a gesture. An invitation. An approval . . . at last.

But while Frederick allowed himself meager hope of reconciliation with his father,

Elias's sense of responsibility for Juliette — and their separation — weighed heavy on him. One evening, as they headed homeward from the Mediterranean, Elias asked to hold the quill himself and copied, painstakingly, the words Frederick had written for him to use as a pattern:

Dearest Juliette, it said, his letters formed with care, but a quaver here and there. *Will you marry me?*

He'd saved almost every penny of his prize money, was always, always counting the coin in his rucksack, and always looking grim afterward. But he'd finally done it — saved whatever amount he'd determined was needful to support a wife. And when they'd docked in Dartmouth, Elias had fairly dragged Frederick across the back-country roads of Devon, until they'd arrived at a church of stone on a hill and he'd taken Juliette to be his, forever.

Good. This was good. *Thank you, God.* Juliette's heart was secure with Elias, a man to love her as her father had.

A grey twist of melancholy settled into Frederick's breathing as he watched the simple wedding. He had thought once that he might marry, start a family. When he was sick with the fever as a boy, had even had a fleeting notion that the girl with freckles on her nose might fill that place in his life. But he had awoken to her hatred, and to the realization that she'd already given her heart to another.

When he'd made a promise at a shepherd's grave, he had promised himself one other thing: He would give that girl his estate one day. Whomever she was wed to. It was all he had to give, or rather would one day. And it would be hers.

So he had closed his heart away back then to the hope of marriage. For who would want a solitary soul like him who stumbled over his words and, even more so, over his feet on a dance floor? Who would want a man who felt more at home on a rooftop, hidden among chimneys watching the heavens, than at a dinner table among ladies and gentlemen, telling tales of daring? With no estate to recommend him, the answer was simple — nobody.

So he'd settled that truth in his soul, tied it up tight, and moved on. He had purpose. Justice to fight for. And that was enough.

A week after the wedding, he and Elias were back in their hammocks, and Frederick felt, at last, some sense of having done right. Somehow, with those letters flying over the years, he'd managed to help something good along in Juliette Heath's life.

Juliette Flint now, he reminded himself. And, he thought — looking at his boyhood nemesis stretched out with the length of a man, still tracing shapes and images in the air with his big old toe — in a way, he'd gained a brother. Which meant, by marriage, he'd gained a sister, too.

They were his family. In that realization he felt a swelling in the void he had long since resigned himself to.

And in that realization, fierce protection rose up. *I will guard him with my life,* he vowed. With no one else to hear, he promised solemnly to God above. If it ever came to it — which it very well could, in these times — it would be Frederick's life for Elias's. In a heartbeat.

Eighteen

Stone's Throw Farm
East Sussex, England
August 2020

In the four days since arriving at Stone's Throw Farm, Lucy had cross-referenced local records, visited a museum in Eastbourne that housed old ship's logs — nothing revealing anything she hadn't already known — and consulted with a diver based out of Brighton, who attested to having seen remnants of a shipwreck in Hurd's Deep consistent with a ship of the *Jubilee*'s era.

How to best retrieve the wreck became the most troublesome bit, however. Hurd's Deep, the deepest portion of the English Channel, was also the keeper of war waste from the two world wars, whose radioactivity was monitored annually. Obtaining artifacts from this burial ground for weaponry was a matter of national security. In spite of only finding remnants of hope through her research, Lucy was more convinced than ever that the *Jubilee* lay at the bottom of Hurd's Deep.

Dash was not as convinced.

"What if it's not in Hurd's Deep?" he asked as they walked a footpath to the west pasture. They trailed Sophie — who was going to set the leg of a lamb found hurt earlier that day — and two of the families staying at the farm, who were eager to watch the setting.

Dash was to assist if needed, and he'd pulled Lucy along to discuss the *Jubilee* as they went.

"Ah, but what if it *is*?" Lucy asked. "They've searched and charted the rest of the Channel, cataloguing wrecks and currents and every other possibility. There is no trace of it. Nothing in over two hundred years. So that leaves only two possibilities — the second having two variations."

Lucy's mind raced as she laid out her argument. "A, Frederick Hanford escaped aboard the *Jubilee,* and somehow, between all the fleets in all the navy, a one-man crew on a sizable ship with little to no rations or weapons made it out of the Channel and set sail to somewhere else in the world."

Dash shrugged. "Is that so crazy?"

"Nearly impossible. Aside from the improbability of him being able to crew the albeit small *Jubilee* on his own for any sort of distance, there's no record of him anywhere ever again. He would've at least shown up in folktales as the captain of a ghost ship or something."

"Okay, so what's the next possibility?"

"Possibility B is that with only himself to man it, the *Jubilee* wrecked soon after leaving Portsmouth. It was a distinctive ship, little more than a showpiece gift from Denmark. It was completely unseaworthy. So the authorities docked it in Portsmouth to be used as a prison ship, a holding spot for those facing the gallows. Water all around, leg irons and shackles and every security. A guard on deck every moment keeping vigil. They believed it was inescapable. Un-sailable if someone should attempt that."

"All right, so if he tried, it would have almost certainly wrecked, is that what you're saying?"

"Yes, either somewhere in the shallower, excessively explored and charted areas of the English Channel — or, specifically, in Hurd's Deep. But again, no wreckage has ever been found. Which is why Hurd's Deep is the only place it could be."

Lucy felt the excitement of the chase

catching up to her. "Do you know how rare it is, in this age of endless information, to have an honest-to-goodness mystery on our hands? And of this proportion! A national traitor." The excitement bubbled up inside of her, driving her on. "We could be a part of unearthing that story."

They walked on, through a wooden gate, slowing as they neared the spot where Sophie had stopped.

"Let me ask you this," Dash said. "What if the stars could help?"

Lucy turned her face up toward him, considering. "If they could . . . that would be amazing. But I don't see how. What could they tell us about a ship whose whereabouts we know nothing of?"

"You'd be surprised," he said. "Bear with me. And come to the star party. We'll take a look in the telescope and see what stories they have to tell."

They fell quiet as they joined the group forming around Sophie. At the same time, Sophie's brother, Barnabas, strode up. Barnabas had surprised Lucy — delighted her, really — upon his return from his sheep show the night before. She'd imagined him falling somewhere between Copper Clara and Silver Sophie on the personality spectrum. A steady presence to bring balance to two such extremes. Bronze Barnabas, she had dubbed him, before even meeting him.

But he'd blown onto the farm like a rogue wind, voice rough and deep with gravel, full of story and lore. Lucy imagined everyone he met was an old friend, whether he knew them or not, and it took some keen tracking to keep up with his runaway tangents. But she had quickly determined that, if people could keep up, they were in for an adventure, traveling alongside Barnabas. And he and Dash, heaven help them all, were thick as thieves.

Barnabas started regaling the family with tales of the landowners of yore, of secret pits where gargantuan dog-like creatures lived and lay in wait. "East Sussex be a place of mystery," he said. "Every stone and tree and shrub would attest to that if they could."

"And now," Sophie said, giving her brother a stern look, "after a few housekeeping items we'll proceed with the demonstration." Tall and willowy, beautiful and fierce, the woman was an enigma. Though Lucy guessed her to be in her late fifties, there was something ageless about her in the haunted way she carried herself. Older and youthful, all at the same time. As if searching this land, whose stalwartness grew right up into her. Rugged elegance appeared daily in her varying combinations of pearl earrings and plaid flannel shirts.

Lucy leaned in and whispered to Dash. "I can't get a handle on her."

He shrugged. "I don't know that anyone could get a handle on Sophie," he said, voice low. "Least of all her. But don't believe the cold exterior she plays up. There's more to her than that."

Sophie gave a few cautionary warnings to those who would be exploring the grounds later: to be wary of the cliffs and keep a safe distance, to take note of the blowhole, a hole in one of the cliff overhangs where high-tide waves could sometimes splash up through and onto the land around.

Lucy rather liked trading in the city warnings to *Mind the Gap* for *Beware the Blowhole* at the seashore. There was air and adventure in the warning.

Finished with her admonitions, Sophie knelt and gathered a lamb up into her reedy arms, and something changed. Gentleness entered the woman, like a thing long lost, finding home at last.

"Left on his own, this lamb's small bone may heal, but never quite right. She'd always be marked. Carrying a limp, perhaps walking akilter. But if we will take the simplest measures" — she picked up a thick, straight twig and pulled a bit of muslin from where it had been slung about her neck like a scarf — "she will mend. Dashel?"

Dash joined Sophie and slipped his arms about the lamb, whose little bleating was snatched into the breeze and carried straight into Lucy's heart. It did something to her, seeing the boy who had so longed for someone's arms to encircle him in belonging all his childhood, now encircle his own arms about this helpless creature.

"We wrap it snugly," Sophie said, winding the white muslin tightly around the lamb, tying it, and tearing off the excess cloth. "And then . . ." She searched the small gathering, skimming over a mother holding a babe and a father barely restraining an exuberant boy, perhaps six years old.

Barnabas knelt and spoke to the boy, whose eyes grew wide at the bearded man's deep voice. The second family present was a mother and her two teenage daughters, one of them feigning indifference as the other tried to restrain her own excitement about the "adorable sheep" who she wanted to "stuff in her pocket."

Apparently deciding there was wisdom in leaving each of them in their current roles, Sophie slid her gaze to Lucy. "A moment?"

she asked.

Lucy looked over her shoulder. "Me?"

Sophie waited, and Lucy joined her.

"Just hold this leg steady," she said, making to hand off the lamb's injured leg.

Lucy took a step back. "What if I hurt her?"

Sophie's eyes shifted back to Lucy, considering her. Lucy might have been mistaken, but there seemed to be a flash of understanding — or recognition — in the woman's face.

Barnabas sidled up. "We none of us know quite what to do when something is broken. Might be we'll make it worse. But if we do nothing, it'll surely stay broken. Ain't it worth takin' a chance on that?"

Lucy shifted her feet. Sophie pursed her mouth grimly. Dash cleared his throat. It appeared the three of them made for three broken souls, caught red-handed.

"Yes!" Barnabas barked past his dark bushy beard. "Answer's yes. So get the tape, and get to work, and this little thing'll be right as rain." He scratched large fingers clumsily over the lamb's fleece. It bleated in response, and Sophie glided into action. Pulling a roll of silver tape from her supply basket, she tore a length of it with her teeth and passed one end to Lucy.

Together, they worked to pass the tape over, under, and around the lamb's leg.

"There ye be." Barnabas clapped and spread his arms wide. "Take a broken thing, gather around, and wrap it. That's where it begins. And if you want to know what that looks like for us splintery humans who need some repairin' ourselves, join us two nights hence at dark o'clock for the campfire and star party. Yours truly builds the fire, and that one over there" — he pointed to Dash — "does the star things."

And with that, he was off. The young boy resumed his general exuberance, the mother knelt to show a flower to the baby, and Dash passed the lamb back into Sophie's arms.

She looked between the two of them, longer at Dash, and nodded. "Go on, then." No *thank you,* no *not to worry, the lamb will be on the mend in no time.* She'd dismissed them and was already off on her way to place the lamb with its mother.

Dash looked after her, concern carving his face.

"Is she always like that?" Lucy said.

Dash shook his head, then turned to guide them back toward the farm. "It's hard to know," he said. "I've only been here a little more than six months."

She knew it shouldn't, but hearing that

socked her in the middle. *Six months.* He'd been a train ride away for six months, and she'd never known.

"But she's quieter, lately. And maybe a little less prickly than usual."

Lucy couldn't help laughing. "Did you say *less* prickly?"

Dash grinned. "Well, anyhow. What's on the docket next, Matchstick Girl? Another museum? We've got" — he checked his watch — "five hours until dinner."

Lucy scanned the horizon. The Channel was frothy today, the sun causing it to dance a thousand watts per wave. "What's that?" she asked, her gaze pausing on a looming structure that'd been hidden from view by a grove of trees on the way up the path. From this perspective, though, it peeked out from far beyond that grove, as if the green leaves were stitches in its secret hiding cloak.

"Edgecliffe," he said. "Those are the ruins of the old estate. Barnabas leads a tour on Thursdays. He's got a whole reel of tales about it that he likes to string out, and the visitors soak it up. You should go."

She could well imagine that. She stepped to the right, hoping for a better view. Something about the place struck a chord inside her. The way it perched upon a white cliff, its stones keeping watch on the comings and goings of ships. What would it be like, she wondered, to live beside the ocean?

She had studied it in books — knew the difference between neap tide, spring tide, and everything beyond and in between — but on the East Sussex coast, with the village homes tucked into hillsides that seemed to roll straight down into the surf, and the shouts of fishermen below, decades erased and time slowed to a more rightful pace. The lives and the spray of the sea intertwined so intricately it took her breath away.

This was marine archaeology brought to life. The study of life in and around the sea. And Edgecliffe — the way it leaned in its ruined state to get a better view of the village below, as if an outsider looking in, seemed so . . . familiar.

"Can we go there now?"

Dash tipped his head at Edgecliffe. "Go there?"

She nodded, her heart beating quicker, her feet carrying her that way.

"Yeah," he said, laughing. "Looks like you already are."

Nineteen

He was right. She'd already turned down the path to Edgecliffe. Only a step or two, but it was as if some part of her had been wandering far from home, and this place . . . it was home. She couldn't explain it.

They arrived surprisingly quickly, passing few landmarks on the way. An old church. The grove of trees, which, it turned out, was actually one large, ancient yew tree, with varying generations sprouting up around it.

And then there they were, standing on the threshold, or on what had once been the threshold, of a veritable castle.

To the right hung a white plaque, carved with letters painted black.

" 'Edgecliffe Manor,' " Lucy read. " 'First built in the year 1400, the estate in ruins before you was built for Earl Radcliffe, around a preexisting priory that became the manor's ballroom at the heart of the home.

Centuries later it was owned by the respected admiral Sir Barnard Hanford. The estate fell to ruin after the disgrace of his son and heir, who many had expected would be the next Hanford to bring further victory to England during her wars with France. A fire broke out months after that son proved himself traitor to the king. . . ."

Lucy knew this tale. As did every British school child, as much as they knew of Horatio Nelson and the HMS *Victory.*

She surveyed the scene, tried to envision Frederick Hanford, whom everyone knew from the oil painting his father had had commissioned after his promotion. He seemed a solemn fellow, with his dark hair and blue eyes which always seemed, to Lucy, so sad. She'd wondered more than once what the reason for the sadness had been. And whether, perhaps, that sadness had been part of what had driven him to betray his ship. His country.

But he had, and so her compassion was short-lived. She'd seen a depiction of his home, but never in detail. And it had always been shown in its whole state. Never in ruins.

Dash stepped over the threshold and into what would have been the foyer, according to the map on the plaque. It showed where the grand hall had once stood, and each of its twenty-seven chimneys. She looked up to where a blue sky played ceiling where none existed.

She closed her eyes and tried to picture it as it once was. To hear what Frederick Hanford would have fallen asleep to as a boy. The waves beyond his window? Strains of music coming from a quartet in the grand hall? What were the sounds of childhood for an infamous traitor?

She opened her eyes and imagined what the manor had once been. Windows framed in stone. Earth and glass. *"Glass is a remarkable thing,"* her father had often said.

She shivered. Was that what was making this place feel so . . . so *known*? Snippets of memory she was pulling from her subconscious?

They poked about, rooks circling on high and gulls joining in chorus. Farther down, an explanation of the fire that took this place was detailed. Starting the night after the master of the house had passed away in his sleep at the age of sixty-eight. It had taken much of the old home, leaving nothing for any heirs.

Which mattered little, as there were none.

"Look at this," Dash said. "This was home

to an admiral from the Napoleonic wars, right?"

"Right," Lucy said.

"As in . . . wars against France."

"Right again."

"But this says when it was built, they used stone and flint imported from France."

Lucy laughed at the irony. "It was built at a different time," she said.

"You're a girl outside time, Lucy Claremont." And there it was again. Memories from the past — this time her mother's voice. What she used to tell her when she'd tuck her "old soul" daughter in at night.

"Matchstick Girl, Matchstick Girl, come and see the stars. . . ." That was Dash — well, young Dash — tossing pebbles at her window as if in a fairy tale, waving awkwardly at her from the garden behind the glass house in his gangly stance and thick-rimmed glasses.

This place was peppering her with parts of herself. She felt as if she'd stepped into a swirl of memories, all out of order, all pulling her in. But why here, why now?

"There's something strange about this place, Dash," she said.

"You can say that again. A lot of people think so. No one really owns it, for one thing. And that ball is held near here."

"The Smugglers' Ball?" She looked around at the rubble. "Here?" Tripping hazards everywhere, even for people less prone to stumbling than she. She thought to Dash's description of the ball on their two-mile walk from Weldensea. "You said people dress up for it. Did you mean fancy dress?"

He scratched his head, looking very much out of his element. He shrugged. "I guess it's fancy, from what the sisters say."

"I mean . . ." What was the American term for it? "Costumes? Period dress?"

"If you want to name it after punctuation, I'd pick a semicolon. Because it's semi-crazy."

This made her laugh. He confirmed that, yes, many people dressed in "olden days" clothes.

She picked her way across the place, imagining its glory days, watching the wind blow the cobwebs free from window openings. She leaned on one, breathing deep, and opened her eyes.

Below her lay a complex and curving bay. The deep harbor beyond the village, quite far beyond hollering distance down the coast. And closer, a sight that froze every bone in her body.

Five white sea stacks. Like so many bony

fingers reaching from the deep.

The breath went from her. Visions of the torn painting she'd found hidden beneath the floorboard of the glass house scrubbed over the scene.

It was the same. It had to be.

"Lucy?" Dash said, concern in his gaze. "What is that?"

"They call those The Towers."

She shook her head. "This is impossible." Too much a coincidence. To find this very scene in a painting that had slumbered, perhaps for her whole life, beneath her very feet, now rising to life before her? And to have been brought here by Dash, of all people.

"Dash." She turned toward him. "Please tell me. How did you come to be here?"

"I told you," he said, stuffing his hands in his jeans pockets and leaning against the bit of wall behind him. "I asked if I could come, and they said yes."

"But why Stone's Throw Farm?" She narrowed her eyes. Not accusing. Just . . . wanting to understand. To put her finger on this missing piece, the thing that tied all of these strings together. Her tides, the *Jubilee,* his stars, the painting.

He looked for a long while out at the sea, then finally looked at her.

"You know your father was the closest thing to a dad I ever had," he said.

She nodded. She'd loved their relationship. "He loved you like a son. So did Mum."

His nod was slow, as if it took work to draw it up the entire length of his tall form. "So . . . what would you do, if you received a message from a long-lost father, years after you had last talked with him?"

"I'd send him a message right back," she said. That was easy.

Dash shrugged one shoulder. "That's what happened."

"Dad wrote you a letter?" He was always writing letters. Scratching them out with fountain pen upon white graph paper, chuckling at his own jokes, sealing them up and whistling as he strode to Cecil Court's red-and-black mailbox. She didn't know how he'd tracked down Dash's address, but she could well picture him reaching out to his "lost boy."

"He found me in Houston where I was . . ." — he tripped over the right word — "studying."

"I thought you went to Harvard," she said, puzzled. Last she'd checked, Harvard was not in Texas.

Dash laughed. "I did. But you never stop

learning. And I was working there, too. When I moved again, he wrote me in Canada. Then Russia, the year after that. I kept expecting him to give up on me, but his letters followed wherever I went, no matter how often I could or could not reply. And then, when my next location had no mailing address . . . Now prepare yourself, Lucy." His grin dimpled with a mischievous secret. "He wrote me an email."

Lucy stumbled — caught her balance and laughed. "Dad?"

Dash nodded.

"My dad, who's never so much as touched a computer in his life?"

Dash tilted his head and pulled his mouth to the side until his cheek dimpled. "Maybe not *never,* so much as Wednesdays at three o'clock London time."

Wednesdays. *Time waits for no man, but neither does tea.* A date with an apple and a friend.

"Clever, Dad." She laughed softly. "A date with a computer and Dash."

"He paid a kid five pounds to set up an email account for him, and from then on, he wrote every Wednesday like —"

"Clockwork."

"Exactly."

"What did he write about?" The watchmaker was full of surprises.

"What he'd always talked about," Dash said. "Everything. And everything as if it was the most incredible miracle in the world. He asked about me, my studies. . . . He spoke of you, Lucy."

Her eyes pricked. She shouldn't ask, but it had been such a long time since anyone had thought of her, at least in the way of a parent for their child. How she missed them both. "What did he say?"

Dash's eyes smiled. Mum had always said, *"When that boy smiles, it's his eyes that smile most."*

"He spoke of your studies, your work. He was so proud of you. He spoke of you being as stubborn as ever and refusing any tea but Earl Grey."

The laughter felt good. "Long live the Earl," she said.

Then Dash's face grew more serious. "And he said he never could figure out how we'd drifted apart. He said my head was in the stars, always had been, and always should be. And that you, old soul that you are, are moonlight. Pure light in the darkness. But he insisted that the moon and stars aren't so different, our worlds weren't as far apart as we imagined them to be, and that someone needed to knock some sense into us both.

"I intended to come see you both, when I got back from that outpost. But I was too late. I read of his passing while I was away and sent you that email. But after that, when I finally returned to civilization, I didn't want to just plop myself into your world out of nowhere. I thought you deserved better, Lucy. I had trust to earn. I was a stranger to you. I know I still am. So eventually I moved here to be closer, to look for ways to build that bridge."

His words shamed her. He had deserved better, too. In this moment, that bespectacled kid waiting in her garden with his hands stuffed in his pockets didn't seem so far away. Her Dash.

Her head swam, trying to absorb it all. "But why to Stone's Throw Farm?" She looked out at the sea stacks again. "Why Edgecliffe?"

"Your father told me about the farm."

She swallowed, unsure what to say. "You said — you read of his passing? Where? He didn't want an obituary. . . ."

"When he went silent for so long, I went looking and saw it announced on the Worshipful Company of Clocksmiths's website," he said.

Of course. *Tempus custodit veritatem.*

Time was truth's keeper, in more ways than one, it seemed.

"I'm sorry, Dash," she said. "I could have reached out, too. I just thought . . . I didn't want to be a bother, and —"

"A bother?" He vaulted himself from his leaning position to stand at his full height. With a flicker of hesitation, he lifted his hand and let his fingers touch her jawline. Steady, kind, familiar — and yet . . . entirely new, this jolt it sent straight into her heart. It was the first time he had touched her in fifteen years, and something, in that small gesture, fell away. Broke into a chasm within that scared her, for it was the place she kept the treasures — and she had so few of them now.

"I was so stupid then," he said.

"Then?" She quirked a half smile, attempting to lighten the mood. "Only kidding, I was so shortsighted, Dash. It takes two, doesn't it?"

But he remained serious. "I've made a lot of mistakes in my life," he said, "and letting go of you was the biggest. I got busy with my studies, my head filled with hopes and dreams and reaching for the stars, and I lost sight of the moon in the process. The purest light I know. Your dad saw that. And he loved me enough to whack me over the head with the truth."

Lucy laughed past the cinching in her chest, and it eased the strain. "He was good at that," she said. "He gave me a few truth-whacks myself."

"He told me Stone's Throw Farm's view of the night skies couldn't be rivaled in England — and that you would be interested to know I'd found my way here. So . . . I came. And I studied the stars, began to measure their movements against those in local legends and lore. Which, let me tell you, is bountiful around here."

"Just ask Barnabas, right?"

"Oh, Barnabas'll give you an earful tonight after dinner, if you stick around. And I highly recommend you do. But there was one tale in particular that caught my attention. That of a local girl, born on a sheep farm at the time of the sea flood — a mega-tide that comes every eighteen years. She vowed she would be there to greet it the next time it rose, but that day, she just . . . disappeared."

"No one knows what happened to her?" Lucy's mind raced over the tales she'd studied of life by the sea — everything from riptides to sinkholes to collapsing roofs of sea caves made this a treacherous place. Treachery amplified, no doubt, by a higher-than-normal tide.

"Not a soul," Dash said. "I started studying records, studying tales, and though it's still more hunch than theory, I'm coming to wonder if her story could have something to do with your *Jubilee.*"

Now, that was a leap, and one that had Lucy standing at attention. "Why would a nationally known ship be tied to a nameless girl in a fishing village?"

Dash leaned in, mischief on his face. "Perhaps the better question," he said, "is . . . why not?"

Dad's favorite question.

"I don't know, Lucy. I could be completely wrong. But when I saw you were presenting at the committee, I hopped on that train. They should've listened to you. Your proposal was strong. *You* were strong. But foundations like those are notoriously conservative when it comes to risk-taking in their funding. And I thought — I mean, I hoped — we might be able to work together."

Lucy inhaled. "So here we are."

"Here we are."

"Dash . . ."

"Lucy . . ." he parroted, his playful side coming back. She was beginning to get used to him using her real name.

"Thank you for taking a risk on me. Really. I know where that meeting with the committee was headed, and it's taken me a while to catch up to all of this, but thanks. I mean it."

"You're welcome," he said, beaming.

"If we're going to be a team . . . I mean if we're really going to chase down theories and chart the tides and stars, there's something you should know. I'd never heard of Stone's Throw Farm until you told me about it. But this place . . . I mean this very spot looking out over the Channel, and the Towers . . ." She shook her head and plunged ahead. "I found a painting of this hidden back home." She told him of the floorboards, of the painting that she'd tucked snugly back in its hiding place.

"It was this precise view." She framed the empty window and the sapphire blue beyond it with her hands. "Only perhaps . . . up? Could it have been painted from the rooftop? There was a night sky, no ceiling."

"Did it say anything on it?" Dash asked. "An artist's name? Maybe we could look up the artist, find more information."

Lucy could picture the carefully scripted initial in the corner. "Just the letter J," she said. "And a title. *The Way Home.*"

They looked out at the choppy sea, gulls

tossing about above it and waves smashing over and over into the sea towers.

If that was the way home . . . then heaven help the sojourner.

Twenty

That night, after a dinner of shepherd's pie, they retreated to the cozy stone hearth for dessert. With a chipped china plate of sticky toffee pudding and a cup of garden-picked chamomile tea in hand, Lucy let the paying guests take the few chairs and chose instead to sit upon the humble hearth. There beside the warmth, it seemed a place where happiness was born. She sipped the tea — it wasn't the Earl, but she had never had chamomile so fresh and fragrant and found herself enjoying the sun-drenched blend.

Dash was out, charting what he called the summer triangle in his observatory. A family with young children lingered after finishing dessert, and the other families dispersed, all appearing both weary and happy from the day's adventures. Sophie bustled about with preparations for upcoming meals, and Clara fluffed pillows and settled into an armchair beside Barnabas's old wooden stool.

"Best make room," he said in his gruff voice, leaning over toward Clara. "Company's coming."

Clara's rosy countenance melted into a pool of horror. "Barnabas Smythe, you didn't!"

"Ah, but I did."

A knock sounded at the door.

Clara stood, looking around as if searching for a place to hide. Barnabas took her hand and guided her back to the armchair.

"Give the poor bloke a chance, will ye, Clara? You're as stubborn and flighty as a gull. It's just Roger."

A man entered, guided by Sophie, who for all her taciturn nature and stone-faced ways held a glimmer in her eye and spared a wink for her sister — followed immediately by a quick eyebrow raise that told her to *stay put.*

"Good evening, everybody," the newcomer said. "Barnabas. Sophie." He took his hat off and held it to his rounding stomach. "Clara."

She nodded and fell silent. Clara Smythe with pursed lips and silence was about as natural as snow in July.

"This is Roger Falke, owner of the inn in

town," Sophie said, and then introduced the visiting family. Roger's gaze landed on the only remaining guest in the room — Lucy.

"Oh, and Lucy," Sophie said, "in from the city."

Not "Dash's friend," or "here on research." Just plain Lucy, in from the city. Story of her life, wrapped in distant anonymity and disconnectedness since her father's death.

Sophie surely meant no harm, but her manner was markedly colder toward her than the other guests, and it stung.

But she would not sink into that now. "Pleased to meet you, Mr. Falke," she said, springing to her feet to shake his hand, then returning to her place.

"Please. Folk around here call me Jolly Roger," he said. "Named for my father, and his father before him, back and back as long as anyone on God's green earth can say."

Lucy tried to picture family gatherings in a cottage full of truly jolly Rogers. How the laughter must have tumbled from the windows.

"I, eh, I got somethin' for ye, Clara," he said, as he pulled a crumpled paper sack from behind his back.

Clara slowly held out her hands to accept the proffered gift. Opening the crinkling bag, her jaw dropped as if the crown jewels were inside.

She reached inside and pulled out a muddy lump. Turned it as if it were sparkling beneath museum lights for all to see, unheeding of the bits of soil that dropped onto her gleaming floor.

"Is this a snowdrop?" she asked, eyes wide.

"Aye," Roger said. "Or it will be, when you stick it in the earth wherever you like, Clara. Always seemed the right sort of plant for you, popping up to cheer up the world after winter's dropped down. And that there is the Weldensea snowdrop."

Her hazel eyes flashed sheer disbelief. "But that's impossible! The only place those are found anymore is atop the hill. That's much too far for you to climb with your lung trouble, Roger Falke. Why, the last time we were there we were mere schoolchildren."

"Some things are worth a long journey," the man said. "You know that, Clara."

He ducked his head, and Lucy's heart warmed at the way the man's face flushed deep red. He shuffled backward out of the circle of chairs, pulled a seat up to the table, and accepted a steaming cup of chamomile from Sophie. "Thank you, Sophie."

"A pleasure, Roger. You're always welcome

here. Always." This, with a drilling look at her sister, who turned the prized bulb in her hands. Lucy might have been mistaken, but there looked to be a sheen of tears over the woman's eyes.

"I'll be back in two minutes," Sophie said, slipping out the Dutch door with a tin bucket. "Going to water the dog. Go ahead with your stories, Barnabas."

Barnabas nodded, asking the guests what sort of tale they'd like to close the day out with. They bandied back and forth about giants and bogeymen, dragons of the land and sea, and legends. As they debated, Lucy pulled a book from beside her.

Life at Stone's Throw Farm, it read. She felt Clara's kind study of her and lifted her gaze, silently asking permission. The woman nodded, and Lucy flipped through an album that went from black-and-white photographs yellowed with age, all the way to Polaroids, glossy printed snapshots, and images more recently printed from a home printer. The mixing and mingling of the generations of Smythes warmed her. She wondered if she might spy a sneak appearance of some version of her father. How had he known of this place, to tell Dash of it?

She flipped through the images, each carefully labeled. Clara and Sophie as girls in their ruffled Easter dresses, out climbing Welden Hill. Barnabas and the older brother, Jonas, waving and grinning from a rowboat. A photo of Jonas on his wedding day with a beaming red-headed bride. That same couple, dated a year later, with a dark-haired baby in their arms — Violette. Lucy felt kinship to the girl, and her heart broke thinking of losing both parents at once, as Violette had, according to Clara's whispered explanations these past days.

And then another wedding picture. Sophie looking adoringly at a tall, thin man, kind in the face and with a lilt to his smile that seemed to harbor a sense of humor. Other pictures followed of the same man as his health rapidly declined in the few years that followed.

Clara had mentioned this, too — that Sophie's one true love had passed away young, the result of a genetic condition. She hadn't elaborated, but the pictures told the story of a courageous, kind man.

And then a picture dated three years later — Sophie holding a young boy with his father's grin. A toddler, and the paper next to the photo labeled *Jesse. 3 years old. Pride of his mother. Legacy and namesake of his father.*

A small paper fluttered out. Newsprint,

an obituary. The son Jesse, who had lived until only a few years ago.

Sophie, prickly Sophie, had loved deeply — and lost deeply. Husband and son, both. Lucy better understood, now, the abrasiveness that cloaked the willowy woman who held the strength of the land in her.

The photos continued for several years after that. Portraits of the Smythe children being assembled bit by bit in Lucy's mind.

Clara: bringer of biscuits and smiles and delight. Wholehearted cheerer at siblings' weddings, though never pictured with a special love of her own, living a full and beautiful life spilling light onto everyone around her. So many of her pictures, from childhood on, featured a ruddy youth who was unmistakably a younger version of Jolly Roger. They'd been inseparable friends, it seemed.

Lucy traced their childhood smiles and thought of Dash. A longing grew within her for Roger and Clara to mend this broken fence between them, and she thrilled when she saw Clara send a small smile over her shoulder to the kind man.

Flipping through the photos, she imagined Jonas, the oldest of the siblings, who never met a stranger. A man who lived bravely and fully and hard and good and fast, and wielded a paintbrush as well as an axe. He loved his wife and daughter, that small soul he carried more often than not upon his broad shoulders, but she disappeared from pictures when he and his wife met their tragic end.

Barnabas: serious-faced and bearded, his presence larger than life as he picked up hurt lambs and carried them far, regaling friends with tall tales, and lending his gruff presence to a masquerading softer side, where compassion ran deep.

And Sophie, with quiet strength and rugged beauty, had dared to love a man with numbered days. And when those days came to an end, she'd given every ounce of herself to the son he left, a son who later shared his father's fate.

All this she gleaned as these souls soaked into her heart's crevices. She sensed a family that knew great joy and deep loss, and that could perhaps understand someone like her. They seemed to make it their purpose to usher in people like her and make them theirs.

"And that's when the great sea dragon leapt over the stacks and disappeared into the cave, never to be seen again, the night of the sea flood. There's none who'll venture there now, for fear of knocking into one of the old sea towers and waking the dragon inside." Barnabas had the guests grinning at his telling of the local legend. "And if ye're lucky," he said, "or perhaps unlucky, you may just catch a glimpse of his tail swishing about when the sea flood comes again."

The door creaked open, and Dash entered along with Violette. Lucy had seen her several times in the past few days, always on the outskirts of the farm or disappearing into some hollow or hedge. "Building hedgehog homes," Clara had informed her. "Poor creatures are endangered, you know. Violette builds little hovels for them. Knows what it is to be without a home, I expect."

Violette looked upon them all seriously now and pulled up a chair against the wall, where the firelight cast shadows.

"Ah, Vi, my girl," Barnabas said, slapping his knee. "What'll I tell them next?"

Violette gave him a timid look that said she didn't appreciate being called upon. Lucy had yet to hear her say anything and wondered if she ever spoke at all. But the woman seemed content in her quiet life, overseeing the whole place, always at a distance.

Violette shrugged, stood, and left the room, and Dash picked his way carefully around the smattering of people and settled on the floor next to Lucy's hearthside perch.

"Our Violette don't talk much," Barnabas said, his voice low, in a rare tone of compassion, with none of his usual captivating bluster. "Sometimes you've lived so much life, the words just run out. But she's a good one, mark that. Still waters and all that." He leaned forward and whispered to Lucy, "She's scarcely left this farm since the day she arrived."

The girl — for Lucy thought of her so, though she had figured out that Violette was actually a few years older than she — reentered the room and settled on the floor. Something about her seemed as ancient and knowing as the walls that enclosed them. A direct contrast to her wide-eyed youthful gaze.

She pulled a handful of marbles from her pocket, opening her palm to the young boy in invitation. He clambered from his mother's lap and onto the floor, where he looked up at Barnabas. He'd taken a liking to the bearded man, who picked up a marble and showed him how to furl his finger to flick it.

"Right," he said, nodding approval as the boy mimicked the antic and set to shooting marbles with Violette, sending glass orbs skittering across the stone floor. "Now, last tale of the night. I think we need to hear one of those stories Dash is always talkin' about."

Lucy smiled, sitting straighter and filling with anticipation that she'd get to hear something important to Dash.

Her gaze landed on him, but the look on his face froze her smile. He caught her gaze with apology written so deep she could feel it stretching across the room. He dropped his gaze . . . and she realized no one else was looking at him.

They were looking at her.

She gulped. "Oh . . . me?"

"That's right." Barnabas slapped his knee. "Dash told us of your father's stories. And right sorry we are for your loss, I might add." Barnabas mingled his apology with his gruff speech, and she hardly had time to acknowledge it. "So, tell us a story, eh? We could use some fresh tales 'round here."

Silence blossomed. The fire snapped beside her, and she tugged at her turtleneck, which suddenly seemed to be tightening its grip on her throat.

She looked at Dash, pleading silently for him to take up the cause. Willing him to somehow understand what she had yet to tell him — she had lost the stories.

Her face must have been redder than beets. Throat thick, she silently shook her head. “I’m sorry,” she said. “I can’t.” To say more would be to unleash grief she had never given voice to, right here in a sea of strangers.

“Ah, never you mind.” Barnabas waved it off, his voice softer than usual. “You haven’t heard of Mad Kit Bill yet, I’d wager. I’d best be telling you all that tale, or he may be after ye on your way back to your rooms tonight.”

Lucy had no idea who Mad Kit Bill was, but she was thankful for the distraction he provided. She felt Dash’s gaze on her, concerned. Summoning courage to meet his eyes, she whispered, “I’m sorry.”

“I’m the one who’s sorry, Lu.” He hadn’t called her that in so long, and it held such tenderness. “I probably shouldn’t have told your dad’s stories without asking.”

She shook her head. “It’s not that,” she whispered, making sure to keep her voice far below Barnabas’s exuberant storytelling. “I-I lost them. The stories.”

He looked perplexed.

She drew in a breath. “I . . . can’t remember them . . . not in detail. After I lost him, everything sort of melded together into one big memory, and I-I can’t sort them out, Dash.” It felt both awful and freeing to confess it out loud, even in hushed tones.

He studied her, his concern deepening. And then, rather than trying to explain it away or offer a platitude of some kind, he just reached over, right into her aching confession, and took hold of her hand, with no apparent thought of ever letting go.

She looked at this foreign yet familiar sight and breathed in wonder. How was it that this man had stepped back into her life after so long but knew her so very, very well?

She focused, determining to enjoy what she was sure was a jest with the rest of the room. Instead, thick silence met her after Barnabas's prologue to the Mad Kit Bill story. And of all that did not seem right — the way Roger stopped puffing his pipe, the way the skittering marbles glinted as they rolled, seeming suddenly sinister — it was Violette's response that made something shiver deep inside Lucy.

Violette's usual silence was cloaked, suddenly, in fear. Something about this Mad Kit Bill had undone the girl who was all keen intuition and compassion for woodland creatures. She sat stiff as a board now, refusing eye contact with anyone.

So Lucy took the bait. "Oh?" She tried to sound nonchalant. "And who is this" — she forced herself to say his whole name — "Mad Cap Bill?"

"Kit, darling. Mad *Kit.*" The word *darling* sounded as incongruous coming from Sophie's bristly personage as sugar from a pepper shaker.

Lucy felt a quickening inside, one that picked up pace with the howl of the wind outside and the crackle of the fire within. She was at Dad's hearth again, soaking in his tall tales, searching for ways they might be real, at their very core. *"All stories — the very best ones, anyhow — may be full of fairy tales and nonsense and lore, but if they are to be lasting . . . they must have truth at their very core."*

Violette's unflinching stare at her glinting marbles told Lucy this was to be such a tale.

"Mad Kit Bill was a strange soul, indeed. Neither pirate nor wrecker nor smuggler nor brigadier . . . he blew in from nobody-knows-where and took to the village and the pastures and beyond like a bandit. He turned Weldensea on its head in one single night, and no one saw him after that."

"What is it he's supposed to have done?"

"What he did" — Sophie hammered that last word — "is he stole Salt."

Lucy felt her blinking stare ask the question for her, but when Sophie didn't elaborate, she asked, "He stole . . . salt?" She took a sip from her tea, hoping it would keep the incredulity from her tone.

"Yes," Sophie said. "Salt, the beloved pig and former companion of the late Margaret Heath, a shepherd's widow who may as well have been the entire village's godmother, the way she doted upon everyone with what little she had in the world. Salt had been her daughter's pet, you see."

Lucy nearly spat that tea right back out.

She thought of the peasants she'd read of from the Regency era. People like Harriet Smith, or . . . or Charlotte and Maria Lucas, all ribboned up in their bonnets and corsets and laces. Never would they have been seen with a muddy pig for a companion.

Lizzie Bennet might have, though, and that softened the idea. Just a touch.

"So Mad Kit Bill absconded with a pet pig named Salt." So far this tale wasn't sounding very ghostly. Certainly nothing to strike tremors into Violette.

"Aye, but that's not all."

"What else?"

"He stole up the rise, you see, right into Edgecliffe Manor, no one the wiser. Likely none would have known, had it not been for the famously meticulous steward who noticed the missing goods just as soon as the sun rose the next morning."

"He robbed the place, then."

"If you can call it that. Walked right past the butler's pantry. Left the silver untouched. Didn't bat an eye at the family jewels in the late mistress's chamber, it would seem. But took two dresses — the plainest she had. Robbed the servant's quarters of trousers and shirts that had gone unused for years, since most of the staff had been dismissed long before. Took a sack of flour from the kitchen, a hen from the hen house, and a potato plant from the garden, along with a satchel of seeds."

Lucy shook her head. "And that's why he's called 'mad,' then — for what he stole?"

"Aye, and for what he did with it."

"Which was . . . ?"

"No one knows! Disappeared without a trace, the only account of him an old woman who'd seen a man on the run across the meadows in the middle of the night, his back strapped with a satchel like a sailor's kit of belongings. *Mad Kit,* you see. And *Bill* . . . well, because someone named him that along the way. Mad is the only explanation if you ask me. If that was all the man intended on stealing, why not sack the village and leave the manor alone? Would've been a deal easier. Except perhaps the spirits . . . That might explain it a touch more."

"The spirits?"

"The Admiral's spirits. The master of the manor did love the bottle. The more so after his son turned up a traitor and disappeared in shame. When he woke the next morning, every bottle in the house had been emptied."

Dash let out a low whistle. "That's a lot of drink for one man."

Sophie laughed bitterly. "Tell that to the admiral. Tell that to Mad Kit Bill."

Clara twisted her apron in her hands. "Oof," she said, cheeks glowing. " 'Tisn't right to speak so of the dead. So long gone, and us with no way of knowin' what's true and what's fabled over time."

Lucy liked that. "Fabled over time" — as if stories changed and grew, facts and twists sprinkling upon them like sweet white confectioner's sugar from Clara's sifter.

"Pardon me, but one knows just what to think. The bottle's the bottle, a thief's a thief, a traitor's a traitor." And just like that, Sophie was done. Nails in the coffin of this conversation. She rose from her place, stretched, and cracked her knuckles, making Lucy's spine shiver.

"Well," Lucy said, infusing lightness into her voice. "If I encounter Mad Kit Bill, I'll be sure to give him what for."

"What for?" Barnabas piped up. "It won't change the past!" He chuckled at his own joke, but the truth of his words followed Lucy into the night after the teacups were cleared and scrubbed, Lucy drying them and slipping them into Sophie's hands, who spoke nary a word as she put them away.

And that wasn't all that followed her into the night as Lucy headed for her spring cellar. A shuffling sounded behind her, a light touch on her elbow. She nearly jumped out of her skin, half expecting to see a hunchbacked thief strapped down with his pilfered goods.

But it was Violette, her eyes wide. She gestured with her hand — and the look on her face told Lucy she had better go with her. She stepped into shadows darker even than the night, and Lucy followed.

Twenty-One

HMS Avalon
Spring 1811

A shadow descended over Elias Flint in the months that followed his marriage. Frederick saw in Elias both the concern of a man and the old eagerness of the boy determined to sail the world and conquer ships for prize money he would bring home for the girl who held his heart.

The shadow, as Frederick came to think of it, had begun with the letter he received from Juliette when they were in port in Spain. He'd shoved it at Frederick's chest with a grin, asking him to read the letter "from my wife!" His grin, always wide and infectious, spread to new reaches when he said *wife,* and he said it every chance he got. Frederick obliged with pleasure, laughing with Elias at her account of the lambs that had gotten loose and how she'd cornered them in the heather and lured them home with a green hat that looked convincingly like hay.

She may have grown into a young woman and left behind her boyish disguises, but she'd never shed her tomboy spunk. Never would, if Frederick were to wager. And the world was the better for it. He and Elias laughed, imagining the scene, but the letter took a serious turn. Or rather, Elias's reception of it did, when Frederick read aloud:

" 'If you get the chance to steal away home in some six months' time, there will be someone eager to meet you, Elias. A small someone, and if he's anything like his father he — or she — shall have toes of prodigious artistic ability.' "

Frederick halted, waiting for Elias to react.

"Toes of prodigious artistic ability . . ." Frederick repeated.

"You said that. I can't think what she means. Read on," Elias said.

Frederick flopped the letter in his lap. "Someone who sticks their fat toes in the air to draw pictures while lying in his hammock."

"But that's me." He did so now, lying back on his hammock with arms behind his head, without a care in the world. Waving that toe around drawing who knew what.

"Yes . . ." Frederick said, drawing the

word out. Waiting.

"Someone for me to meet who will take after their father who . . ." He pushed his brows together. Sat bolt upright. "Who is *me.*"

Frederick grinned, applauding slowly.

"But that means . . . what? What?"

Frederick hopped down and crossed over to his friend, clapping him on the back. "Congratulations, old friend. You're going to be a father." His grin spread across his face, rejoicing for Elias. For Juliette. For the untainted, pure hope of a life to come.

"I-I'm going to be a father."

Frederick nodded.

"Freddy! Me? A father?" Elias scrunched his face up as he tried the word on, then shook his head in disbelief. He tumbled out of his hammock and began to pace. "But this changes everything. She'll need a bigger home, a place to put the baby."

"I don't believe babies require much room," Frederick offered, seeing a cloud descend over Elias. "Their needs are simple. And don't call me Freddy."

Elias waved him off. "You're an expert in babies, of course." He rolled his eyes.

"They're small," Frederick defended himself. "So I hear."

Elias shook his head. "My child will have

a place to call his own." The way he said it, Frederick would no sooner have wanted to cross a caged lion. He knew Elias had never had such. His own father had left him in a sheep's pen while running caves to smuggle. Tom Heath had found him — much as he'd found Frederick — gathered him up, and calmed down a drunken smuggler when the man pounded on the shepherd's cottage, accusing him of kidnapping his son. He'd kept a faithful eye on Elias as he'd grown, offering him honest work when the call of the smugglers — the family trade — was strong.

Yes, Frederick could well understand why providing a good home was important to that boy abandoned in the sheep pen.

"Your child shall have an excellent home."

"Aye, he will at that. I plan to put enough coin away to take them both to the Windward Isles someday," he said. "Away from sheep and fish and toiling. You'll see."

Frederick thought of the homey fire at Juliette's farm. The way the simple breakfast had filled his belly so long ago. Juliette knew how to make any place a home. A good thing, he thought, for Elias. God had a way of redeeming wounds with the strengths in others. Elias and his home among rocks and seaweed . . . matched with Juliette, and her home — indeed, her *life* — of fortitude and sunshine. It had redemption written all over it.

Frederick clapped Elias on the shoulder. "Juliette is already living in the best home for your child." But in the days that followed, the cloud did not ascend from its place over his friend. In fact, it grew darker with each passing day.

Soon after they docked in Dover, while the others met for a hot meal at the tavern, Elias was nowhere to be found. He could be a stormy fellow, and sometimes it just took some time for the wind to blow that storm back out of his soul. Frederick prayed he had just gone for a climb, or a swim, as he sometimes did when they were in port. Perhaps he would return to the *Avalon* restored.

When they boarded the ship again, Frederick was pleased to see Elias's wide grin and the way he ruffled the hair of the powder monkeys. He jigged that night to the sound of Killian Blackaby's fiddle, roaring in laughter at the impromptu ballads Killian spun to match his music. The balladmonger-turned-sailor was always and ever on the hunt for his one great tale, and every night was an audition to see how the men reacted to his latest work.

But when the balladmonger began his recitation, as he was wont to do whenever the rowdy crew quieted enough, this time something changed.

"Ah, blokes, now gather 'round and hear the ballad of the poor cotton weaver. A sorry tale, if ever there was one."

He cleared his throat and began to sing. And when he sang, everything ridiculous about Killian Blackaby became suddenly solemn. His baritone voice rose to the beams above as if it had been hewn and mellowed right along with the wood.

He sang of a weaver and his wife who had naught to eat and had worn their clothes to threads, and had not sixpence to their names. They lived on nettles and Waterloo porridge — a thin excuse for a meal. When the bailiffs came to collect payment, they took all they had, including a stool, and left them sick of body and heart.

"Said to our Margrit as we lay upon
  t'floor:
We shall never be lower in this world, I
  am sure.
But if we alter, I'm sure we must mend,
For I think in my heart we are both at far
  end,
For meat we have none, nor looms to

weave on,
Egad, they're as well lost as found . . .

The men jeered about the poor weaver. "He'd as well get to sea, aye? Bring home prize money and buy his Margrit everything she needs!"

A jolly cry arose as the men toasted one another, and the merriment continued. But the yellow lantern light split around beams, cast long shadows whose tips barely touched Elias, who sat statue-like in a corner.

Frederick approached, pulling up a seat. "Chin up, old friend," he said.

Elias's jaw twitched.

"Just a ballad, after all. You know Blackaby. Likes to spout a sad tale whenever he can." Still silent. "I think he imagines it picks up the spirits of the men. Gives them something sorrier than all this" — Frederick swept his arm over the scene — "to compare their lot to."

Elias bored holes into the table before him with his stare. "You haven't known hunger," he said at last. Something of the old wrath was in his eyes when he looked upon Frederick. "You've never slept among the rocks and had seaweed as your mattress on the soggy shore with naught to eat for days on end."

Frederick watched his friend. What torment was this? "True," he said slowly, respecting what Elias had endured. "But if you worry for your child —"

"No child of mine will ever know hunger. Not like that." His voice was so low, so vehement, it could have burned the table before them into ashes.

"Of course not," Frederick said. Reassuring.

"Of *course* not," Elias said. Declaring.

And that was the last Frederick saw of Elias for two nights and three days. He tried not to worry — a day or two of not seeing someone was common on a ship the size of the *Avalon,* especially when docked in a bustling port like Dover.

So Frederick passed the time like the others — exploring city streets, taking in hot meals fit for kings, in that they were not riddled with maggots.

But it felt incomplete to walk the streets alone when his comrade in arms — who would be spinning horrible puns and matching him step for step — was just . . . gone.

He took to the crow's nest at nights, fixing his view across the Channel, where he knew the French port of Calais bustled just as Dover did. He searched the skies, spotting a star here or there but falling asleep for long spells of cloud cover and darkness.

He awoke in the middle of the third night to a pit in his stomach. Whether from nightmare or inexplicable premonition, he did not know. But he could not stop thinking of Juliette, of a babe on the way, of her sitting beside that fire he had once awoken beside. And of her love never returning.

Something had happened. He knew it. His spine was hollow with the feeling of it. He pried his eyes open and in his sleep-clouded, fear-shrouded mind, landed his gaze on the clearest view he had ever seen of the constellation Gemini.

The brothers.

He sat up, head throbbing and neck stiff. Narrowing his eyes, he traced the constellations' frames. Castor, it had always seemed to him, pulling Pollux along. Pollux, whose far leg looked broken. Bent at the star Propus. Leaning on his brother's shoulder.

There was no story to match this interpretation. Reskell would've scolded him, told him to let the Greeks have their myths and leave it be. But tonight — stars so bright they seemed to emanate heaven itself against that canvas of deepest blue — the brothers smote him.

A brother is born for adversity.

Elias could fend for himself, wherever he

was. Frederick knew that. But it wasn't his physical well-being he feared for. It was his soul.

A gust of chill wind billowed the sails above, blocking his view of the sky. And when they settled back down, like ghosts going still, a blanket of cloud covered his celestial theatre.

The brothers were gone.

He shuddered, gritting his teeth against the cold. Conviction settled like ballast in his belly — all was not well. Perhaps his friend had fallen into a pit. Found himself with feet of clay, as Holy Joe, the ship's chaplain, would say.

By the third night, knowing the ship would be setting sail to patrol the Channel with or without Elias, Frederick stood staring at his friend's kit — where all his worldly possessions were stowed. He stared, and stared, willing them to give up some answer — but he knew they would not. Not without him rummaging through. But could he do that?

As if in answer, a shuffling sounded behind him. "Fixing to rob me like the bailiffs did the cotton weaver?"

Frederick turned to face Elias, ready to deny that claim, when he saw Elias's old smirk, the one that told Frederick he was only kidding, that he was back to his old self again.

The weight of a thousand chains fell away. And that night, watching Elias shovel beans into his face with the hunger of a pride of lions, remorse overtook Frederick.

He kicked himself for thinking his friend could have been tempted into illicit activity. The opportunities were plentiful, especially with Bonaparte opening protected smugglers' havens across the Channel in Dunkirk and Gravelines — the *Ville des Smoglers* — but Elias had sworn off all that. Frederick would never forget the conviction with which he'd spoken of his past and future, all wrapped in one statement: *"I will never forsake my family for ill-gotten coin."*

Frederick had seen a soul broken in those words — harm done to him by his own father. And now that he had the chance to stand guard against that legacy in the life of his own child, Elias would choose right, a thousand times over. Frederick had been a fool to doubt it.

He glanced around before sliding his meager share of hardtack into the folds of his shirt. Elias was on watch tonight. Frederick planned to steal up to the crow's nest to spot Canis Minor, with the first entirely clear night in a fortnight. First he stopped in the blanket bay, where Elias's hammock stood rolled into a narrow size, perfect for storage, while those in use were slung between beams and weighed down by sleeping sailors, three of whom were snoring in varying keys.

He tucked the hardtack atop it for his friend. An offering of secret remorse for his suspicions. It toppled to the boards below, and Frederick knew the first sailor to happen by would snatch it up in two shakes. Food was anything but abundant belowdecks.

He looked around for something to cover it with and spotted the kit once more. Relieved to no longer have the questions urging him to dig through Elias's entire world, he undid the flap just enough to set the roll inside. Cinching it closed, he took two strides and heard a *thud.*

The whole thing had toppled like a drunken sailor. He picked it up, and the hardtack tumbled out along with a few other things, spilling into the shadows of the swaying hammocks and the symphony of snoring. Light crisscrossed from flickering lanterns. He moved to right it, plucking up a bundle of shore clothes and the food, and slid his hand farther into the corner to retrieve the last thing. His hand met a packet of paper — Elias was fastidious about keeping his letters from Juliette. He would trace the letters in the dim light and try to sound out the words — his wife teaching him to read, as it were, from across the ocean.

Frederick pulled the packet into the light . . . and froze.

It was not a letter from Juliette.

Newsprint. *London Gazette. Oxford Register. Le Courier de L'Egypte.* These were papers dated only twenty days prior. Perhaps not much to look at and certainly nothing to worry over, except . . . Cold steel settled in Frederick's belly.

Elias did not read.

What, then, was he doing in possession of newspapers? Glancing over his shoulder as his heart pounded, he opened one of the papers written in French.

Troubles dans l'armée Français, it read. Frederick scanned the lines that followed. His French was not good — but some words, he was able to pick out. *Insurrection. Désertion. Battre en retraite.* Uprising. Desertion. Retreat.

His mind flew to Reskell's lectures about Karl Schulmeister. The man had delivered falsified newspapers to mislead Austria's army, giving them false confidence. The French paper . . . looked authentic. But what would Elias be doing with it? And Frederick had heard nothing of uprisings and retreats in France's fleets and forces.

Reskell's voice was in his head again. *"Line up the factors, Master Frederick. Add them up with all logic, and the answer will become clear."*

A board creaked on the steps down to the blanket bay. He slid the papers back into the sack, planting his peace offering atop it. He felt sick, looking at the hardtack. It was intended to celebrate, even if Elias was never privy to the fact, that his fears over his friend were vanquished. The sight of it lying against the backdrop of evidence to the contrary burned.

With each footstep that fell, bringing someone closer on the stairs, another factor in the equation fell into line.

Step. Elias's joy at the news of his child — and the way that joy was eclipsed in shadowed ferocity.

Step. Elias vanishing for days.

Step. The newspapers.

Step . . .

Elias stood, hands in pockets, looking for all the world as if he'd just had a visit with the king himself. His grin froze, though, as his eyes went from Frederick, to the bag, and back.

"Interrupting something, am I?" Wariness crept into his forcefully easy demeanor.

Frederick gulped. He would not lie to his friend. "Where were you?" he whispered, not wishing for the slumbering sailors to take in this confrontation.

"Above deck. I told you, I'm on watch tonight. Only just popped down to get my hat." The lightness in his tone was forced.

"No. Where *were* you."

Elias knew what he meant. For all his joking and bandying about, Elias was the quickest lad he knew. Cunning and witty, he did not miss so much as a splinter out of place aboard this ship. It was what had made him soar through the ranks alongside Frederick, into the admiral's trust, and far, so far, from his humble beginnings.

But where else was that cunning taking Elias? Especially when he was gone for days?

Elias crossed over to him, looked from his kit to Frederick. And with teeth gritted and voice so low that none but him would hear, he uttered one word.

"Gravelines."

The city of smugglers.

TWENTY-TWO

For days after any battle at sea, smoke and death hovered in every sinew of every board on every deck of the *Avalon.* Footsteps, and footsteps, and always more footsteps, as men put the floating battleground to rights. Mending sails and planks, knotting ropes, shoring holes, stemming tides. Stitching wounded bodies of men, and stitching hammocks-turned-coffins about bodies no longer alive. Watery graves. Prayers.

It was hard work, grueling to body and spirit. And yet there was always a gritty goodness beneath the open wound of it all. They were protecting their island nation, their families.

They sold the possessions of the men who died — midshipmen giving their last pennies to purchase things they did not need, at prices much higher than were warranted, all because they knew the proceeds would be given to the fallen sailor's family.

It was awful. And it was awe-full. It was blood and heart and terrible and good.

That was battle aboard the *Avalon.* As unnatural as it all was, Frederick knew how to carry on in the wake of death. In many ways, he had been doing it ever since his mother's music had stopped.

But this? What was he to do about a friend intent on betraying his country?

After Frederick's confrontation, and as the *Avalon* pulled away from the stretch between Dover and Calais, Elias tucked the papers in his shirt, and they went down to the hold, the deepest part of the ship, on the pretext of rat duty. Though the task of hunting down vermin was unpleasant to say the least, and not required of sailors of their ranks, it provided the only private place for confrontation on this entire ship.

"It's shortsighted," Frederick argued. "Not to mention foolhardy, dangerous, and . . . oh, yes, *treasonous.*"

"How am I to know that?" Elias said. "All I will do is transfer papers from one hand to another. I cannot read. For all I know, I'm handing over poetry and plays and laundry lists."

"You know *exactly* what you're doing. But to be clear, I'll tell you, so that you have no excuse. You are better than this."

He jabbed a finger into Elias's chest. Heard the crunch of the offending papers. "You are providing them information that might affect our fleet's plans. *Our fleet.* You are taking from them falsified newspapers in their language. Whomever you are transferring them to in England will place it in the hands of trusting men who will take it as truth, who will put stock in printed reports of uprisings within the French army, who will presume that army to therefore be weakened. They will make their plans accordingly, leaving our fleet — *and our nation* — vulnerable."

He was out of breath and had half a mind to whack his friend with the stick he'd been given to hunt down rats. Because in this moment, his immovable friend certainly fit the bill.

But that would do no good.

"It puts a target on your child's back," Frederick said. It was a low blow, ruthless. But he would do anything to crack through Elias's blinders.

"And what do you know of targets on backs?" Elias said, his fists furling. "Always looking down on us all from your high tower." His words were infused with bitterness that must have been buried deep down, festering for years, so sour it tainted the dark air around them.

If Elias would but let his fists fly, let his anger land on Frederick — *Please, God* — instead of allowing it to steer him into smugglers' cities and shadowed dealings.

"Do it," Frederick said. "Hit me."

For a moment, Elias worked his jaw, looking like he would. As if the darkness were gathering about him, rallying to seep into him, he pulled an arm back.

But then he met Frederick's eyes . . . and his bitter expression flickered across Frederick's pleading one. Something snapped inside him — Frederick could see it. Some shackle broke its hold, and he slumped over a heap of barrels, face buried.

Frederick waited. He knew not what more to say, nor what to do. So he waited. Letting this battle play out within his friend, letting battle wage in prayer inside his own soul.

Keep him, Lord. Break him free.

Elias's shoulders shook.

Frederick drew near. "You do not need to do these things," he said. "Think, my friend. If you are found out, they'll put you in the leg irons. You'll get the cat-o'-nine-tails. The admiral, he . . ."

Frederick winced, thinking of the time he'd seen a man caught signaling another ship of their plans. And that had only been a Dutch ship — an ally. *"Enemy might be watching,"* the admiral had said. *"You cannot signal our plans without permission and expect there to be no consequences."* The man had been made to walk an avenue of men, lined up and whipping him, aboard every single ship in the fleet. He had come back barely recognizable, and had spent weeks festering in a sick bay.

Frederick could not imagine what would happen to a man caught in true treason.

Rather, he *could* imagine. He knew very well what would happen. And that thought made him physically ill.

"It'll be the gallows, and you know it. Public disgrace as a traitor. Your family . . . How will they ever live after that?"

Elias raised red-rimmed eyes, bracing himself against a barrel in a wide-shouldered stance, like a dog readying for a fight. " 'Tis a fair thing to ask," he said. "But you go too far in your question. If I do not provide for them, Frederick . . . how will they live?"

Frederick thought of Juliette — dressed to sail a ship, working the land as a child, cooking up a feast out of nothing with her mother.

"You think wrongly," he said, staring intently at Elias. "They will live very well.

And you *are* providing for them every day you spend on this ship."

Elias's fingers fisted, every muscle taut in this battle between temptation and truth.

Frederick thought the man might explode, right here in the hold, that the anger inside would boil up and burst past his last shred of common sense and reason.

But . . . there. His hand relaxed, eerily controlled. His spine unfurled just as slowly. "Very well."

Frederick nodded, but it wasn't enough. Flashes of their shipboard youth lined up in his mind: the two of them fighting in battles, saving each other's lives, coming to blows over it, sleeping with the pigs. Standing side by side at Elias's wedding.

My brother.

Their bond gave him boldness, gave voice to his demand.

"Promise," he said.

Elias shifted his eyes to the side, jaw clenched.

Frederick waited. And waited.

"Very well," Elias said.

"Very well, what?"

"I promise."

"You promise what?"

Elias thwacked him on the shoulder with the stick meant for scaring out the rats.

"Who died and made you king, your royal highness?"

"I'm not royal anything. But you must promise right now that you will do nothing to put your family in danger."

He could have worded it a thousand ways: *That you will not betray your king and country. That you will not convey information between enemies. That you will not be stupid, you big lout.* But he knew the one that had the best chance of sticking was the one that kept Juliette in his mind's eye.

"I promise I will not do anything to put my family in danger." And then, with a shrug, he was Elias again. Making light of rats and groaning over what they'd find at the mess table.

But just as they were to head up to that mess table, which their growling stomachs were drawing them mightily to, he turned. Face serious, eyes earnest. Looking for all the world like a boy again — the one left among seaweed by his own father, and the one whose rough edges fit so perfectly into Juliette's fire-lit ways that the two of them softened each other, somehow.

"You're the best friend a bloke could ask for, Freddy. You know that."

And with that, he was gone. Swallowed into the dark of the stairwell.

■ ■ ■ ■

After a little more than a week of patrolling the Channel, the *Avalon* docked again in Dover. Frederick had seen little of Elias during that time, but they had both been busy and the times they crossed paths, Elias had been friendly, if a little distracted.

But he didn't come to mess the second night in port. Nor the morning after. Killian Blackaby knew nothing of his whereabouts, and Killian knew everyone's whereabouts, always. More often than not, he was writing it — and who knew what else — in that book of his.

When Elias was nowhere to be found that day, Frederick knew.

He knew it when Elias finally did return. Knew it when an official-looking boat rowed out to them from shore, when the men in the blue jackets and brass buttons conferred with the admiral. When the men who had been to shore were lined up, questioned.

"One of you deposited these papers into a stone wall, in a place known to us as a receptacle of information to our enemies. We will not leave until we know which of you it was."

One by one, the men gave their accounts

and alibies, corroborated one another's stories. Until at last, only Elias and one other man remained. Each of them held their chins high in fierce pride. Each of them confident, it seemed, of their innocence.

But Frederick saw a lightning-fast flash of sheer terror in Elias's eyes when he swallowed and met his friend's stare for less than an instant.

And it was then Frederick stepped forward.

For Juliette. For Elias. For the child. For the shepherd, who had given his life so that Frederick could be here today.

He held out his hands, wrists together. Ready to be bound.

"Take me," he said.

Twenty-Three

Stone's Throw Farm
2020

Lucy followed Violette around to the back of the farmhouse, down the moonlit footpath, to what looked to be a former creamery. It was a humble place to behold — the round building settled at the slightest tilt, the lovely stone of ages before, a thatched roof. Two high windows peered at their approach, panes dripping with the sag of time but glinting all the same. The whole place held an air of time-worn curiosity.

Violette slowed as they neared, glancing at Lucy as if unsure. This was her haven, Lucy sensed. A place sacred to Violette. From what Sophie and Clara had said, the girl soaked in privacy and quiet as if it were the air she breathed.

And here she was, on the verge of letting Lucy into her sanctuary.

"I can wait here, if you'd like," Lucy offered.

Violette pursed her lips, studying Lucy like a book to read. Apparently what she read settled well, for the hesitation eased into a tentative sort of invitation. She tipped her head, gestured with a palm — *Come,* she was saying — and led the way with her clunky black wellies over the threshold of the old building.

Entering was an exquisite clash of the senses. The stone building cooled Lucy's warm skin, while moonlight spilled through the two tiny windows like chutes from the sky, landing upon a cozy sitting area near a stone hearth constructed of a different stone than outside. Brown, rather than grey, likely installed long after the place had ceased being used as a creamery. She was cooled and warmed at the same time. Felt at once as if she had stepped into a fairy tale . . . and yet that she had also, stepped into a haven.

For it was clearly, above all, a home, with all the comforts of a worn green armchair in the corner and a chipped Royal Doulton teacup washed with care and set to dry on the stone windowsill.

Lucy recalled an American book Dash had once loaned her. He had liked it for the mystery and adventure of the four orphaned siblings, but she had most of all loved the way they had turned an old boxcar into a home, furnishing it with treasures found in rubbish piles and cleaned in pure river water. This home of Violette's had that same air of timeless innocence and lovely resourcefulness, with care given to guard such life-giving pleasures.

A rolltop desk sat in the corner opposite the stove, and Lucy smiled to see it faced the fireplace rather than away from it. As if Violette preferred to let the light and warmth fall upon her as she worked.

It was to this desk Violette went now, looking of another era with her wispy form and calico dress and wool sweater. Wide-eyed, she nodded that same invitation — *Come.*

Lucy did. Violette rested her hands on the knobs of the rolltop, breathed in deeply, and paused.

The sense of the fairy tale continued, and Lucy's mind began conjuring imaginings of what might hide in this covered desk. Judging by Violette's reaction to the tale of Mad Kit Bill, it surely must be related. A relic of his pilfered goods? A map to his would-be treasure? Or perhaps the story was darker, and it was part of Mad Kit Bill's skeleton.

Lucy chided herself, looking again at the chipped teacup, the bookcase where a potted fern billowed and well-loved volumes of poetry lined its humble wooden planks, which leaned slightly toward the old armchair. This was not the home of a bone collector.

Then again, Lucy herself ran about the countryside chasing down fabled tales of seafaring traitors and ships long lost, so who was she to judge?

Lucy's pulse quickened as Violette began to roll back the desk, the *clack-clack-clack* of the old wooden slats mellow with age. The girl paused and looked earnestly at Lucy, eyes pleading. She pressed a finger to her own lips, and Lucy nodded. A promise to keep her secret. Whatever shadowed relics or dastardly evidence or . . .

The desk was up.

Violette slid something into the light . . .

A laptop. She gripped it and grimaced, her pale cheeks flushing pink.

"You . . . have a computer?"

Violette nodded, eyes closed in shame. She opened one eye and peered at Lucy.

Lucy raised her eyebrows in a friendly way, inviting more explanation. "Is it against the rules to have a computer here? I hope not. I brought mine, and I've used it often."

Violette pursed her lips, twirling a finger in a small circle in the empty air.

Clara's pride at being "completely wireless" flew into Lucy's mind. "You *do* have the Internet."

Violette confirmed this with a sheepish nod and opened the black laptop — small and dated. Rather clunky, and whirring as if it hurt for it to come alive. As the screen lit up, Violette tapped in a password, and what looked like a virtual bulletin board filled the screen. Images of different post-it notes were lined up, each with notes in a typewriter-like font.

Mad Kit Bill — connection to Killian Blackaby?

Killian Blackaby — connection to traitor in Blackaby poem?

Traitor — Mad Kit Bill?

Something quickened inside Lucy. "You have theories of a traitor?"

Violette nodded.

"Do you mean Frederick Hanford?"

A shrug, and she pointed to another "sticky note." This one said, *Killian Blackaby = Traitor? Or Mad Kit Bill = Traitor? Or . . . ?*

Lucy nodded. "Theories," she said. "And you're chasing down evidence?"

Violette nodded, the first small smile breaking through her apprehension. She pulled out the desk drawer and removed a paper. Tapping it twice, she handed it to

Lucy. It was a photocopy, folded thrice as if it had been taken from the post.

Lucy scanned the page. It was some sort of poem . . . or a story told in verse. She flipped through her vague memories of the literature classes she'd had to take at Oxford. An epic, perhaps. But this was short, just a page long. A ballad?

"Son of the House of Hanford."

She froze. There it was. *Hanford.* A name she knew as well as her own.

Lucy flipped the paper over. Blank. Flipped it back to the front and looked to Violette for permission. She nodded, her fair face even paler than usual.

Lucy began to read aloud.

"Son of the House of Hanford
A Ballad in Six Parts
By the Most Humble Killian Blackaby"

The scrawl was ink and pen, looped and slanted in the style of yesteryear, difficult to read. Lucy ran her eyes over the words, letting them adjust before continuing.

"1
Cast thee down, and cast thee up,
And cast thee in between,

And there has gone the Traitor-Man,
Ne'er more shall he be seen.

2
Covered is he, from deep to deep,
His sins have brought him there.
And there has gone the Traitor-Man,
His sorrows for to bear.

3
Sisters seven, seven more,
cloistered in their cove.
His secret keep, this Traitor-Man
In death for to betroth.

4
The tides do come, the tides do go,
And with them mark the time.
The Traitor-Man did rise on them,
To depths in dark sublime.

5
And there his story rests, says I,
Beyond in Weldensea.
We lay to rest the Traitor-Man,
His tale, with words, bury.

6 . . ."

Lucy broke off. Flipped the paper over,

and back again.

"That's it," she said, curving the words into the puzzle that they were. "Where is the sixth part?" The photocopy just stared blankly back at her, speckled where its original was worn with time.

"Mad Kit Bill," Violette said, her voice somewhat hoarse from disuse.

Lucy recalled the way she'd gone ashen at the earlier mention of Mad Kit Bill. "I'm sorry," she said. "I don't see the connection. Frederick Hanford was a traitor . . . Mad Kit Bill was a robber . . . Do you think they knew each other?"

Her eyes flew open wide. "Do you suppose Bill might have broken him free of his shackles?" No one had ever figured out how Frederick had broken loose from his chains aboard the *Jubilee*. But all the theories had been so confident he'd had no assistance that she'd never even considered the possibility of an accomplice.

Violette went to her Dutch door, opening its top and pointing into the dark. Lucy did not know the area well, but she remembered the distant ruins on the cliff, the only structure for miles in the direction Violette pointed.

"Ah," she said. "I see. It was Frederick's

home that Bill was supposed to have burgled."

Now Violette's look was one of pity, and Lucy felt very much like a schoolgirl who could not, despite the teacher's best efforts, follow the story that was right in front of her. Violette's pity morphed into a look of tentative hope as she bit her lip. She looked from Lucy, to the computer, to the dark night outside, as if weighing something.

The computer dinged. Violette's cheeks flushed bright red, eyes wide.

"You have a message?" Lucy ventured.

Violette nodded and then, as if it cost her everything she held dear, gave a small nod of invitation to follow. "Come," she said, voice small.

Curious, Lucy did, and watched as Violette opened up a chat box with someone by the screen name of *MrWaterWaterEvrywhr.*

Violette pulled up a purple chair that had once been painted red, and before that, white, and before that, stained dark wood. The chipped surface revealed these layers here and there, attesting to eras long past. The young woman watched Lucy expectantly, fingers poised over computer keys.

Contraband keys. She suppressed a smile,

recalling Clara's stand against the "Inter-met."

"You have quite the operation here," Lucy said. She saw Photoshop on the desktop, and shortcuts to vacation rental websites. "You run the reservations, Clara said."

"Word of mouth." Violette winked, pointing at the screen. "See?"

And so it was.

Violette paused, gesturing for Lucy to pull up a chair. Accepting Violette's permission, Lucy surveyed the chat:

☐ **MrWaterWaterEvrywhr:** Greetings!

☐ **VioletteSkye:** Hi

"Skye," Lucy said. "Is that your middle name?"

Violette nodded, smile shy, and fixed her eyes right back on the screen.

"Pretty," Lucy said. "Like a poem."

If Violette heard, she did not take time to acknowledge the comment. She was mid-chat with MrWaterWaterEvrywhr:

☐ **VioletteSkye:** How are you? Were you able to find out anything about Killian Blackaby?

☐ **MrWaterWaterEvrywhr:** I'm faring well on this auspicious evening. And how are you, my lady?

Violette glanced at Lucy, as if keenly aware that people did not speak this way, that this fellow was perhaps a little bit . . . singular.

☐ **VioletteSkye:** I'm fine, thank you.

Her hands hovered over the keys for a moment.

☐ I'm here with a friend.

☐ **MrWaterWaterEvrywhr:** Ah! Greetings to your friend, as well.

Lucy smiled her acknowledgement and gave a small wave.

☐ **VioletteSkye:** She says hello. I found an old volume of Browning's *Sonnets from the Portuguese.* Over a hundred years old! Just sitting in the old farmhouse, and I never knew. I've been paying better attention to bookcases ever since we talked about the way books are history living right in the present.

☐ **MrWaterWaterEvrywhr:** The Brownings! Now there was a pair for the ages.

A few seconds passed, and then —

☐ **MrWaterWaterEvrywhr:** I DID find something of your Mr. Blackaby. In addition to the ballad from the village museum I sent.

Violette sat up bolt straight in her chair and perched on its edge. Whatever Lucy had stepped into felt like a conversation between old and dear friends. Perhaps — if she wasn't mistaken, judging by the smile she had never seen on Violette's face — more than dear friends? Tonight was proving to be quite the night of revelations.

☐ **VioletteSkye:** What did you find out?

And then, as if suddenly remembering her manners and the fact that she was apparently speaking to a modern-day embodiment of verbal chivalry:

☐ That is, if you don't mind sharing.

☐ **MrWaterWaterEvrywhr:** My dearest Violette, I am at your service. What will my time at Oxford mean, if I cannot better serve those with an interest in excellent maritime poetry? I have discovered a volume of Killian Blackaby's ballads at the Bodleian Library.

Lucy placed her hands on the desk, leaning in. "Oxford? I was at university there. I wish I could've done something to help you out. ,. ,,"

Violette looked at her pityingly again. "This is to help *you* out, Lucy." The fullest sentence she'd spoken, and it zinged with spunk.

Lucy watched as she typed out the start of several questions, deleting each one in sequence:

☐ **VioletteSky:** Is it — [delete]

☐ Have you — [delete]

☐ Could I possibly — [delete]

☐ Is there anything of the unfinished ballad in it?

☐ **MrWaterWaterEvrywhr:** There appear to be several whose form fits that of the one you identified. But it doesn't appear definitively. Perhaps there are hints in his other works. I would have checked the book out and mailed it your way . . . but it is a first edition. Indeed, I wonder, looking at it, if it is the ONLY edition. It is part of their special collections and can only be read there, handled with gloves, all of the pomp that the ageless manuscripts have there. No photographs allowed. . . .

☐ **VioletteSkye:** Oh . . . I see.

Lucy's heart hurt, watching the way Violette's shoulders sagged, her crestfallen spirit nearly tangible. And then her heart hurt even more, watching her try so hard to buoy herself right back up, this girl who asked so very little of the world, who stayed close to home, her entire universe here, making safe places for creatures in danger.

☐ **VioletteSkye:** Well, I'm thrilled that you found it. At least now we know Killian Blackaby was not a phantom writer invented in folklore!

☐ **MrWaterWaterEvrywhr:** Indeed, he was not. He was a sailor. Pressed into service, it would appear from some of his poetry, and he spent years at sea during the Napoleonic wars. What a change that must have been, going from ballad monger, travelling the country roads and hawking his words at county fairs and open markets, to firing cannons and furling sails and I know not what!

☐ **VioletteSkye:** Yes, such a change.

The chat went silent for a few minutes, and Lucy wondered if she should slip out, let this conversation resolve without the added pressure of an onlooker. An onlooker who was jumping in her skin to urge Violette to go see this book that apparently meant so much to her. But was that her place? How could she presume to suggest something to someone she knew so little?

☐ **MrWaterWaterEvrywhr:** You . . . could come see me.

☐ **VioletteSkye:** [blinking cursor]

☐ **MrWaterWaterEvrywhr:** I mean . . . come see it. The book. I . . . could show it to you, if you like.

He was suddenly endearingly clunky in his words.

□ **VioletteSkye:** I would like that very much. And I would like very much to meet you. But things are . . . complex.

□ **MrWaterWaterEvrywhr:** I live for the complex!

The poor man. Lucy wished she could jump through the screen, embrace him for his enthusiasm over Violette, but whisper a few words about the woman he clearly regarded. Of how she barely spoke, did not leave the farm she came to as a youth, not ever. Did not see the world . . . but oh, the worlds that lived in her, as evidenced by her tender spirit, her shelves lined in epics and poems. Her sketchbook filled to the brim with glimpses so deep, the world needed this soul in it.

□ **VioletteSkye:** ***I*** — [delete]

She looked at Lucy. A collision of desires and abilities. So much depth to her, like the bounding sea was trapped, tide rising, with nowhere to go.

Lucy nodded, encouragingly. "You can go, Violette. I'll go with you." Perhaps a day trip might deliver some much-needed perspective to her, too. "If you like, that is."

Violette's fingers hovered, her right index moving ever-so-tentatively over the Y key — and then she closed her computer. Placed her head in her hands.

"It's all right, Violette. There's no rush."

Violette raised her head. She opened her mouth. "But" — she spoke so quietly, Lucy thought she might have imagined it — "there is."

Twenty-Four

On the way back to what was fast becoming her spring-cellar haven, Lucy met Dash leaving the farmyard, his head once again in the stars. She filled him in on all she had learned during her visit with Violette — and that she had offered to take her to Oxford . . . but the girl wasn't ready. Dash had plans for the next day, and Lucy hoped to visit a neighboring village for more research, so they agreed they would meet up tomorrow evening before the star party.

Lucy's sleep came in fitful bursts. Dreams of bandits traversing the moor with eerie bundles interspersed themselves with her spring cellar's stream song. When morning came, it was an out-of-place sound of scraping that woke her.

Sitting up, she saw someone had slid a crisp white piece of paper beneath her door. Sunlight spilled from the little circle window, beckoning her into the light of day, and whatever awaited her on the paper.

Unfolding it, her breath caught when Dash's signature stick-straight permanent marker writing met her.

COMPENDIUM OF WONDER

She smiled, running her thumb over the words. She knew, even before reading on, what this was. A continuation of his gift given in that cloud document — an addition to the collection of stories.

Stories he now knew she had lost. He was gifting one of them back to her. Wiping away quick tears, she read on:

As told in questionably accurate detail by Dashel Greene, who might have not cared a whit for grammar and the like when this was told to him, and therefore might tell it kinda badly now, too.

"The tide keeps the time almost as faithfully as a clock, Dash and Lucy." The watchmaker had a way of always linking their names together, as if they were one of the inseparable pairs of the universe, like tea and cream, or clouds and sky, or Castor and Pollux in the sky. He tinkered with his pocket watch again — he had that magnifying monocle thing over one eye and grinned when he winked up at them, looking like an absent-minded professor. Or a mad scientist.

Dash took the bait. "Almost?"

"Picture it," he said. "A coastline studded with treacherous rocks, so tall and fierce no ship would venture near, not even in calm seas. Too many had been destroyed by those very rocks. And yet the sea is a living thing that rises and falls, reaches and pulls —" His screwdriver slipped. Lucy handed him a handkerchief, and he wiped it all clean, as he was in the habit of doing whenever he needed a fresh start.

"Thank you," he said, handing it back.

Lucy tucked it into her dress pocket. She scrunched her nose up at Dash when she saw he was looking at her as if she herself were the relic from the past, not just the hankie in her hand. "Our family is old-souled and odd," she'd told him once, "so you'd better get used to it." He, in fact, liked that about them. They were a constant, in a crazy world.

The watchmaker continued. "What do you think happened when a man decided he must find a way to make those rocks . . . disappear?" He did the thing with his fingers again, waggling them as if performing a magic trick.

Lucy laughed. "He waited," she said. She was thirteen now, and had not one but three volumes of oceanography stacked on the family bookshelf. "The rising tide would be the only way for every stone to disappear at once."

The watchmaker straightened and lifted his monocle thing (that's the technical name for it, by the way) so it pointed straight up like an antenna. He beheld her, dumbfounded. Whether truly dumbfounded or acting for their benefit, Dash and Lucy did not know.

"Now what makes you say that, Matchstick Girl?"

She blushed, darting her gaze to Dash. She seemed embarrassed by the use of the nickname, but nothing could fit a soul better.

"I must be a genius," she said, making ready to feign brilliance.

"Yeah, or you must have done your lit homework last week," Dash said. She gave him a look that told him he was a traitor.

"Mrs. Hamsmith has been assigning stories from The Canterbury Tales," he told her father. "Your Matchstick Girl here was just griping about the old language last week."

That much was true. It was Dash who helped her decipher that the man in the story had gone to a "magician" to find a calculation on when the tides would reach high enough to make the rocks disappear, that he might win a lady's love.

"But it's just a story, Dad. The tides don't reach that high. If they did, we would know about it."

Father crossed his arms over his chest, nodding solemnly. "I see what you mean," he said, raising a finger. "But consider the source. Your Chaucer was not just a spinner of tales."

"I know," Lucy said. "He was a jumbler of language."

"Yes, and a student of the sciences. Stars, sea, mechanical things. You might like some of his work, Lucy."

Lucy looked dubious.

"The tides surprise us, sometimes. Remember," the watchmaker said, "they keep time almost as faithfully as a clock." He winked. "Almost." He passed a pin and a watch hand to Dash, and a pair of tweezers to Lucy, picking up some sort of gear and inserting it into the watch's back, then twisting. "There is none who can stop them. You know the story of King Canute?"

Lucy thought they were still speaking of The Canterbury Tales. "We haven't gotten to that one yet," she said.

"Nor will you," he said. "Canute was a real king. Four hundred years before Chaucer. But I'd venture a guess that Chaucer knew his story well. Canute was a beloved king in this land. And king of Denmark and Norway, too. There were many who were convinced there was nothing he could not do. Some today think him the most effective king in the history of these lands."

"Did he study the stars, too?" Dash asked.

"Perhaps. He was a keen observer of things. You see, the people were so trusting of him, they let their trust grow to admiration, their admiration to respect, their respect to flattery, and their flattery almost to a point of worship. This troubled the king. One day, he took a walk to the shore. He had a chair brought down and set it right at the place where the waves broke, foaming about his feet. He told everyone there that he would now command the tide to stop."

A smile spread across the watchmaker's face, gentle lines of genuine respect. "How did the historian put it? 'He spoke to the rising tide.' He commanded it not to encroach upon his land, or wet his feet or clothing. And do you know what happened?"

Canute must be like King Arthur, Lucy thought. If he was about to say the tide stopped, truth and legend had intermingled over time into the magic of myth. She said as much: "The tide stopped."

Father laughed, and she was sure she'd gotten it right.

"The tide . . . rose and drenched right through the king's pantaloons."

"Dad!" Lucy's cheeks were crimson.

Dash cleared his throat and looked away. "Is that true?" he said. "Why'd he do it, if he knew it would fail?"

Dash, ever the hero (if the recorder of this tale does say so himself), diverted the conversation.

The watchmaker smiled. "The historian wrote that he jumped back and proclaimed, 'Let all the world know that the power of kings is empty and worthless, and there is no king worthy of the name save Him by whose will heaven, earth, and sea obey eternal laws.' "

Lucy and Dash waited, not understanding.

"He did it to humble himself in their sight," the watchmaker said. "To show that no matter what the world said of a man, it did not change who the true king is."

"So what does Canute have to do with Chaucer?"

"Nothing. And everything. Do you know there's a scientist now, over in America, who is using the stars to pinpoint when in history certain things happened? Forensic Astronomy, they call it. He figured out exactly when Chaucer's tale could have actually happened. Mega-tides, which can rise up over impossible rocks just as easily as waves can rise up around King Canute's ankles. Just think! Nothing is impossible, you two. Nothing. Remember that."

"Just think." Lucy murmured her father's favorite words, folding Dash's page back up and pressing it close to her heart, praying the other stories, in time, might return to her, too.

After her day of research, Lucy returned that evening to list out exactly what she knew of the puzzle so far. She sat outside her spring cellar, scratching notes down on paper:

Frederick Hanford. Traitor and Deserter.
Ballad: Son of the House of Hanford.
Killian Blackaby — balladmonger-turned-sailor. Shipmate of Frederick Hanford.

The last she had learned during some late-night "Intermet" searching the night before, thanks to Violette's covertly offered password.

Killian Blackaby had sailed aboard the HMS *Avalon* with Frederick Hanford for seven years. During that time, he had written innumerable ballads, including *The Albatross, White Flag,* and *Wooden Monarch.* None of them had reached any acclaim until long after his death. *Son of the House of Hanford* was one that had fallen into obscurity, and Violette had only come across it because of her correspondence with a Bodleian Visiting Fellow at Oxford, an expert in maritime poetry based out of New England. A quick search of Spencer T. Ripley's biography page showed him to be perhaps in his early forties, with a boyish enthusiasm about him behind his wire-rimmed spectacles. He would only be there another two weeks, explaining Violette's urgency to find what answers she could.

Lucy scratched more puzzle pieces onto her list:

Painting — The Way Home
Artist "J."
Edgecliffe Estate, the Towers. The view matching The Way Home.
Mad Kit Bill
The Jubilee. Hurd's Deep? Or . . . ? Dash thinks it could be somewhere else. But where?

"This is madness," she said, sighing. The list looked like a collection of completely unrelated folklore.

And yet, she knew it was more. There was something connecting these pieces. They circled her, spinning about her mind and tangling this way and that, trying different combinations but always falling flat. She, at the center of the puzzle pieces in their chaos, felt as much a question mark as they seemed.

She looked up to see Dash leaving his observatory — a mobile shed he had built to move anywhere on the property. It could have been one of those tiny houses, for all its charm and character. In fact, part of it was his home. He'd built a bunk lofted above a desk, brewed his coffee in a French press, and kept his books on a tall shelf. She would have gone mad living in a space as small as a storage closet.

"But I don't live *here,"* Dash had said, when she'd given him a hard time about it. *"I just sleep here. I live out there."* He'd gestured at the rolling green pastures. *"Know anyone else who measures their living space in acreage instead of square footage? Besides, I'm used to living in small spaces."*

She could well believe it, with all his travels, the sky his only constant.

He approached now, as the coloured sky over the distant Channel slipped from a waltz of pastels into a muted grey.

The moon slipped from behind a cloud on the horizon, a herald of the night sky to come.

"I saw it first!" they said at the same time, their childhood competition for the first to spot the moon resurrecting effortlessly.

"Fine," Lucy chuckled. "I'll give you this one. But you know I'll get you next time," she said.

"Ready for the star party, Matchstick Girl?"

She rose from her place on the boulder, her legs stiff from sitting so long. She shook out her notebook, her list of puzzle pieces dancing upon the page.

"Definitely. But I owe you a thanks first," she said. "The Compendium. The story you left me."

He scratched the top of his baseball hat sheepishly.

"I don't know how to thank you, Dash. It meant the world. Really."

"It's the least I could do," he said. "I wish I could do more — give every story back to you. But I bet they're going to return to you, Lucy."

"I hope so," she said. "But in the meantime, I have a gem of a story to tide me over, thanks to you."

She looped her arm through his offered one, and they started toward the party. How could it feel so natural? Like no time had passed at all? That, too, was a mystery.

"Let me ask you something," she said. "Do you think Killian Blackaby could be Mad Kit Bill? Do you think he could have somehow helped Frederick Hanford escape?"

Dash puffed out his cheeks, letting his breath go. "I don't know," he said. "It's possible. But since the beginning the authorities were so confident no one could have snuck onto that boat — the possibility has never been considered. And why would Blackaby help a traitor?"

Lucy shrugged. "I don't know."

"Hmm. What about Oxford? Can't the

professor guy just tell Violette what's in the poem?"

"He could," Lucy said. "But I get the feeling . . ." She paused. "I think they want to meet."

Dash wrinkled his forehead as if she'd just told him the sky was water and the sea was sky. "You really think Violette wants to leave the farm to meet some guy?"

"I think a part of her does." Lucy thought of her own comfort zone in London, of how it had taken Dash's urging to break her out. Could she do the same for Violette? "Maybe it would be easier for her if you offered to join us. Plus, we could run up to London after that to get the painting I found."

"Needing a dose of art in your life?"

Lucy laughed. "More like needing to make sure I haven't abandoned my senses. I want to be sure."

"You haven't 'abandoned your senses.' " Dash attempted a horrible excuse for a British accent as he quoted her. He'd been away much too long.

"Trust your gut, Lucy. You have better instincts than you give yourself credit for." He stretched his arms to the sky and then locked his fingers behind his head in his familiar easy manner. Encouragement breathed from Dash like rivers to the sea.

She'd forgotten this about him. "In the meantime, did you get any information about that Hanford journal?"

She had told him the day before of Frederick Hanford's journal, which was housed at the British Library beneath a glass case, for all to see. A few inquiries, and she'd received digital excerpts of it a couple of hours ago.

"I did, in an email this afternoon." She leaned in conspiratorially. "Did you know about Violette's secret Internet?"

"Everyone knows. I think even Clara knows, deep down, though she's convinced that advertising that the farm is wireless — for her meaning without Internet — adds to the draw of this place. So we all pretend it's not here and only use it when we have to. And life is better without it, honestly. It's nice not being constantly connected. It makes us . . . more connected, ironically."

"I can see that," Lucy said with a smile. "But then again, it was very nice receiving a document in the cloud via email a couple years back."

"So tell me about the journal," Dash redirected, looking endearingly embarrassed about his compendium.

"This entry was written right there at Edgecliffe, when Frederick Hanford was just a kid. Twelve years old." She shook her head. "It's a shame he took the route he did eventually. I think you'd have been friends, Dash. He made notes of the constellations, the direction of the wind . . . extraordinarily scientific mind."

"Read it to me?"

"Sure." She flipped through her notebook, pulled out the printed pages, and began to read, keenly aware of Dash's intense study of her. Or of the words she spoke. The latter, surely.

"Twelfth of August, 1805

Skies: Constellation Draco in the sky. Constellation Gemini dimly visible.

Wind: North

Observed: Millie the parlormaid makes landscapes with the ashes before she sweeps them from the hearth."

Lucy paused. "How does a soul like that — who notices parlormaids and literal beauty from ashes — become a traitor?" She shook her head. "So sad. He seems such a soulful person. I do wonder if he was the one to paint *The Way Home.*"

"But you said it had a J in the corner."

"Right. So perhaps not. Or maybe it's J for *Jubilee*? Though that doesn't quite add up, either."

"What else did they send?"

"His last entry. May 13th, 1811. That would have been four days before his trial and disappearance. He says . . .

"Thirteenth of May, 1811

Skies: Constellation Gemini — Castor and Pollux — clouded over.

Moon: Waning crescent. Grows smaller every night.

Wind: North by Northeast

Observed: The admiral's mourning dove sings from her cage. I hear it on the wind. I remember her story well.

"He sounds . . . sad," Lucy said. Fading light, mourning doves. She, along with every other maritime scholar, knew the story of Cuthbert Forsythe's rescue of the sacrificial mourning dove. When the admiral was killed at sea in battle off the coast of San Sebastián nearly two years after this journal entry, it was in coming against a French ship engaged in battle with a much smaller British frigate. The dove had become a legend, symbolizing the man's life and death. One of courage in the form of sacrifice.

Dash nodded. "He does. But Mr. Melancholy gives us a lot to go off of in those few lines."

"He does?"

"Crescent moon waning, for one thing. Cloud cover. That could tell us a lot about the tides, a possible storm — both things that could determine where a ship might end up in the days following that entry."

Hope collided in an overwhelming crash with the immensity of what they were up against, research-wise. They would need multiple ships' logs to cross-reference, from vessels out in the Channel. Tide charts, if they even existed from that time period. And even then, it could be a wild-goose chase, trying to track down a rogue ship's whereabouts with just those factors. Still, Dash's words brought a skitter of anticipation to Lucy's heart.

"Come on," Dash said. "Let it simmer for a few hours. We can make a plan after the star party."

Twenty-Five

And so they traversed the path to the far pasture, where the star party was to be. "Less ambient light leads to better star viewing," Dash explained.

"Right," Lucy said. "I seem to remember a certain kid making me wear sunglasses indoors to make my eyes adjust."

"Sounds like a smart kid. And I bet you looked pretty cool, too."

Lucy laughed. "The coolest."

Dash laughed slow and easy, knocking into her with his elbow. "You put up with a lot from me back then, Lu."

"I could say the same thing about you," she said.

They fell into easy silence as they walked on.

The far pasture, as it turned out, was half a mile down the road, in a green field with bobbing buttercups and trees fully lining the perimeter.

"That's unusual for these parts," she said, pointing at the thick wall of trees.

"All the better for us. We're far removed from the village and any lights from neighboring farms. With the wall of trees and the shadow of Welden Hill, it's the perfect place for stargazing."

Lucy wasn't sure what she'd expected — perhaps a few academic types gathered, notebooks and maps in hand, ready to debate astrophysics and theorems — but something in the air defied any expectations she'd had. The lilting sound of an Irish flute piping a reel floated their way on snatches of wind.

"Betty's here," Dash said. "She owns the bakery in town and brings her tin whistle most weeks."

Beatrix came trotting down the path to greet them, floppy Basset ears swinging.

"Hi, Beatrix." Lucy knelt to pet the hound with soulful eyes, and Beatrix leaned into her and followed once she rose to continue.

"Look at that," Dash said. "She doesn't take to anyone like that. Good girl, Beatrix." The dog's tags jingled as she trotted after them, the perfect percussion to Betty's tune.

As they approached the gathering, Violette turned from her place near a campfire, her cheeks bright. Her eyes lit up when she saw Dash. And her smile spread when she saw Lucy. She motioned them over.

As Dash approached Violette, it occurred to Lucy that she hadn't seen Dash and Violette closely interacting before. He was easy in her presence, and she in his. He rambled on about the summer triangle appearing early if they kept watch, and she tilted her head to watch the sky as if it were as much home to her as it was to him.

Something felt bereft inside Lucy as she watched the two of them. Were they a couple? It didn't entirely seem so, but she didn't know. She'd been so caught up in all things *Jubilee,* she hadn't really asked much about Dash's life. That fact smote her, as did the bereft feeling. What right did she have to any such reaction? She liked Dash. She liked Violette. They both deserved places to belong, people to belong with, after all they'd been through. They were alike, Lucy realized. Two souls who'd lost parents early on, able to understand each other.

With a fresh wave, it hit her — she was now like them, too.

Dash turned, his gaze landing on her with a quizzical tilt to his head. He scooped the air, motioning her between them. Violette handed her a cup of cider and a pair of sunglasses.

"Ah, so Dash is up to his old tricks," Lucy said, donning the glasses.

"Hey, if it's not broke . . ."

Lucy laughed. "So where's your telescope?"

"Around the back of the cottage." He pointed to a small stone structure she hadn't noticed, tucked into the corner of the pasture. "Roger and I keep the telescopes back there to block the firelight."

"That's right," Clara said, stirring a pot sitting on a grate by the fire. "Dash insisted we have no light at first, but I told him, 'You can't look at burning balls of fire in the sky while you're freezing. That's too iconic.' "

"Ironic, Clara," Barnabas said from his perch on a nearby boulder.

"Yes, that's what I said."

Barnabas rolled his eyes and smiled affectionately at his sister. "Right. Well, we have a great grand fire here. Clara was right. What're we doin', lookin' at a fire while freezing our toes off, says I? Too spacely minded to be of any earthly good. So? Here we are."

Barnabas grabbed a paper bag from a stack and held it out to Clara, who gave him a look and shoveled something caramelly and smelling of the heavens from a bucket and into his bag.

"Pass those around," she said. "Guests first."

Barnabas froze with a handful of the confection halfway to his mouth.

He ate his quickly, then took fresh bags from Clara and did as he was told. "Candied almonds," he said. "Good as gold." And they were. Buttery and sweet and salty, with just the right crunch.

Somewhere in the distance, church bells began to toll. Strange, for a quick look at her pocket watch told Lucy it wasn't marking a new hour. "What is that?" she said. "A wedding?"

Clara narrowed her eyes, thinking. "It could be the Shepherd's Bells."

Lucy leaned in. "What are the Shepherd's Bells?"

"Well, legend has it that a beloved shepherd was lost to these parts a couple hundred years ago. He was so well-loved, in fact, that an anonymous benefactor paid to have the bells rung in his memory every year for some time after that. When the benefactor's payments stopped, it had become so much a tradition that the people could no sooner think of stopping than they could stop needing food and water. Tradition is like oxygen around here, you see. So every year, the Shepherd's Bells ring, and we remember."

Lucy thought of the noises that filled her world back home. Wake-up alarms and message alerts and broadcasts that ushered her forward and forward, always forward. These bells seemed to do the opposite. They called her to pause. Breathe. Consider a soul who loved well and was well loved. "I like that," she said. "We could do with a great deal more remembering."

And she tucked those bells into her heart.

Soon, they all moved to the back of the cottage, where two telescopes stood. Dash and Roger each stood near one, Dash's black and shiny and connected with a cord to some mechanized apparatus. "It's a go-to telescope," he said. "I put in the coordinates, and it searches the sky and hones in on it. Meanwhile, Roger over there takes his relic and races me by hand. Checking his maps and charts —"

"Or using my head," the jolly man spouted.

"And we race. We'll show you, after the star talk," he said. "When it's nice and dark."

"Can we find the Plough?"

"The Plough," Dash said with a smirk. "I think you mean the Big Dipper."

"Well, if you're going to be all American about it, then yes. The Big Dipper. Could we find that?"

"Sure! Anything you like, if it's in season. The universe is yours, Matchstick Girl."

She laughed, enjoying seeing his world. "It really is amazing," she said. "Seems impossible, sometimes. All those stars, and the ones we see are only a fraction of what's out there."

"Nothing is impossible," Dash said.

That phrase had her once again sitting at her dad's workbench, listening to his tales. Wondering where it was all going. Having it all boil down to a truth he repeated regularly — *nothing is impossible.*

They stood looking at the approaching-night sky, awestruck. "Do you still think of going up there, Dash?" She thought of the books lining his roving observatory. The papers he had stashed on the bottom shelf, peer reviewed and published in scientific journals. The certifications, and the map with pins marking where he'd studied: Palomar. Griffith Observatory. Great Basin. Houston. Maryland. St. Petersburg.

He shuffled beside her, and for a moment, he was that bespectacled gangly youth once more, stumbling over his past and future, tripping and landing in the safety net of her home.

His silence stretched, billowing between them.

She fixed her eyes on him — he fixed his on the stars. "Dash?"

"There's nothing up there for me," he said. "Nothing that I don't already have."

This didn't sound like Dash. He was the boy who would've given his right arm to be among the beacons in the sky.

He finally looked to her. "You ever hear that quote, shoot for the moon, and even if you miss, you'll land among the stars?"

Lucy nodded. Her undergraduate advisor had had that taped to her wall. She'd always looked away, for the pang in her heart, thinking of Dash off chasing the moon and stars.

But he was shaking his head, slow and thoughtful. "I think of your parents, sitting on the back stoop in that tiny garden, with the bushes blocking out the light. They — and you — gave me more in that minuscule plot of land than anything up there ever could. Because what people are chasing up there all amounts to one thing. It took me a decade and a half to learn this, but what they're chasing . . . it was present right there with the crickets in that garden."

Her breath came thick, as if her lungs knew the words she meant to speak could cost her much. "What was it?"

"Hope. Wonder. Light. All wrapped up in the stories, in truth."

"They were fairy tales, though," she said. "Weren't they?"

"Parts of them. But don't you remember the way he used the fairy tales to tell us the true stories, after? The more I studied this universe — the more places I went — the more I realized what your parents were doing."

She waited.

"They were building us a scaffolding. Story upon story, account after account, of true, impossible things — to hold up the truest story of all, when we would find it later."

He paused, and she sensed he was holding something back. Some shadowed part of his story he was not ready to let her in on, yet. He stuffed his hands in his pockets, looking at the stars. "There's nothing up there that can't be found here," he said. "It took a long time to realize that. And I learned it the hard way. The longest way."

There was still admiration in his voice when he spoke of the heavens, calling the stars by their Roman names like they were good chums, no hint of disillusionment or bitterness. But neither was there a worshipful reverence directed toward them.

"The stars are magnificent, Lucy. Always have been, always will be. But no more magnificent or miraculous than the ground beneath our feet, where life grows from dirt and water and sunlight. Or the depths of your ocean. Or the very air we breathe. It all points to the same truth."

He stuffed his hands in his pockets and fell silent, but she could tell he wasn't finished. After several seconds, he spoke again, an edge of nerves causing his words to come out choppy. "Lucy, you should know . . . there was a time . . . I-I mean, I went —"

"Dash." Sophie neared them, looking warily at their closeness. Seeing Beatrix leaning against Lucy, she stopped in her tracks. "She doesn't do that," she said, stooping to pet her dog. "Not to anyone. Not since . . ." She stood, puzzling over Lucy. Her gaze softening from censure into something more nostalgic. "Well. Anyway. Dash, the guests are ready for your star talk."

Lucy shivered, wishing she'd brought a heavier sweater.

"Cold snap," Dash said. "I should've

warned you. Go hang out by the fire. I'll meet up with you after."

Lucy nodded. She would've loved to hear his talk, but her chattering teeth might have been a distraction to his guests.

"You can tell me then," she said, wanting to be sure he knew she saw him, heard him. Wanted to hear whatever was proving so difficult to say.

At the fire, Clara sat in a wood-slat chair and patted the one next to her. She spread her blanket over Lucy's lap and smiled at the sound of Dash beginning his lecture. He certainly did know how to keep a crowd.

"We've got an expert in our own backyard," Clara said, proud. "Think of what it would do for this place if he would let us advertise that. But I can't say I blame him for not wanting to make himself known."

"But doesn't he? I saw his name on the posters in the village," Lucy said. "Dashel Greene, PhD and star guide."

Clara's smile dipped a little, giving way to puzzlement in the firelight.

"Yes, dear, but . . ." Her voice hushed. "You don't know."

"Know what?" Lucy tilted her head, taking a sip of tea Clara had poured for her from a Thermos.

"He's not just a star guide, Lucy. He could

give tours in person. He's a star *veteran.*"

Lucy took another sip, nodding. "Yes," she laughed. "He told me he was a dark ranger." She chuckled, recalling the Great Basin Observatory's name for the late-night park rangers he had briefly been a part of, giving star talks out in the desert for campers.

"Lucy. Dear. Your Dash . . ." Clara set her mug down and placed her hand gently on Lucy's shoulder. "Did you ever wonder why he didn't come to you in London when you lost your father? From what he's told us, yours were the closest thing to parents he ever knew."

She had wondered. Again and again, until she couldn't wonder any more, else it turn her heart bitter and break it all over again.

She gave a small nod, pulled her sweater cuffs up over her fingers, which were trembling despite holding the warm mug.

"He couldn't go to you." She pointed at the sky. "He was up there."

Lucy swallowed her tea, concern washing over her. Clara was eccentric in the warmest, most endearing of ways, but this was something more troubling. Did she think Dash had passed into the next life and somehow come back? Compassion washed over her, wondering how to gently speak truth to this kind soul before her.

And yet the woman looked at *her* with that same sympathy. With pity and patience — waiting for her to realize something.

Dash's earlier words tiptoed up in the dark, swirling about her in a whisper. *"There's nothing up there that can't be found here . . . I learned it the hard way. The longest way."*

And it hit her. By the look on her face, Clara saw it happen, saw the widening of Lucy's eyes, the way she set down her mug suddenly on the wooden arm of the chair, fearing she'd drop it.

"No," she whispered. "He didn't —"

Clara nodded.

"He did?"

"He most certainly did."

Lucy shook her head no. "He hasn't been . . . But that's not possible."

"He most certainly has, dear. And it most certainly is. Little thing they call the International Space Station. I confess I hadn't even heard of it, 'til our Dashel came along."

Our Dashel. Hearing those words did something to Lucy's heart as she thought of the lost boy having someone call him their own. It warmed her gently and made her ache, all at the same time.

Lucy looked to the pinpricks in the dark

sky above. And over her shoulder, as if the empty cottage would open up and let her see right through it, right to the down-to-earth man pointing out constellations. The boy who used to throw wads of paper at her when she got too immersed in her ocean books and teased her for having her head in the clouds.

It appeared she had much to learn about him. And the night would not pass before the truth unrolled between them.

After the star talk, and wrapped in one of Clara's spare blankets warmed by the fire, Lucy joined the clutch of guests and village friends gathered around the telescopes. Dash and Roger stood poised like unlikely track stars. Roger with his wide stance and Dash's height making him look lankier than usual against the night sky. Their silhouettes were jubilant. Barnabas stood between them, hands in the air.

"Your constellation is . . . Pleiades. Ready . . . steady . . . go!"

And they were off. Dash typed something into his computerized telescope, its robotic gears kicking into action and moving it ever-so-slowly, with a mechanical whir.

Roger, meanwhile, stood stock-still. As she drew near, Lucy saw his eyes pressed closed, intense concentration wrinkling his forehead beneath his news cap, fingers running back and forth over his brows. Suddenly, he froze. Eyes flew open, intense with purpose, entirely unfazed by the fact that Dash's scope was shifting its pitch higher, lower, higher, showing its process was nearing an end.

Roger moved his telescope smoothly, swiftly, like a fisherman dipping his oar into placid waters, scooping the sky until he stilled.

"Just . . . like . . . that," Roger said, a slow grin spreading across his face.

"Got it!" Dash said, barely behind Roger and grinning just as wide.

Each of them stepped aside, opening his hand toward his telescope, inviting the onlookers to see the heavens through their scope.

"Come and see, Clara," Roger said, imploring as he opened his arm toward the telescope.

Hesitantly, she did, bending and looking, face a pinch of puzzlement until it broke into a wide smile. When Clara smiled, her whole countenance smiled. "I see it," she said. "Oh, my. 'Canst thou bind the cluster of the Pleiades . . .' " She sighed contentedly. "Such freedom, to know our limits. And to know the God who has none."

"Aye, Clara. And He'll see us through, you know," Roger replied.

Lucy felt herself an eavesdropper, suddenly, and stepped over to Dash's telescope.

"What happened with those two?" she asked quietly, thinking of the closeness they had so visibly shared in the family photo album.

"More like what didn't happen. They're in love," Dash said. "They both know it. But Roger's waited a lifetime to say anything. He finally asked her to the Smugglers' Ball this year, and it scared her out of her wits.

"Sophie says she's afraid she'll lose her closest friend if it doesn't work out. Barnabas says she's doing exactly that by pushing him away. So there you have it." Dash tipped his head subtly toward the pair who were dancing about each other on a floor of eggshells.

Roger noticed their gaze and smiled.

Dash bent to peer through Roger's "dinosaur," as he called the dated telescope. "Bested me again, Rog," Dash said, holding his hands up in surrender. "Don't think I'll ever know the skies as well as you do."

"Oh, aye" — Roger slapped him on the back and winked — "says the man who —"

"No, no, you're the reigning champion,

and that's all there is to it." Dash glanced at Lucy sheepishly, making the lines of his face look suddenly boyish. He tipped his head at her, beckoning her over.

As she neared the telescope, she had to remind herself this was the boy with whom she'd shared this ritual more times than she could count. And yet . . . this was a man entirely new to her, too. His presence strong and kind, and smelling of clean pine and cold air.

"Have a look," he said. Just like he used to when he'd push his glasses up on his nose in the garden of the glass house, letting her into his world.

She inhaled and squinted, her eyelashes blinking clumsily against the finder scope until they, too, remembered that she knew this. Searching the night sky was a part of her, as deep in her bones as the sea.

She did not see the constellation right away, but the memory of her father's laughing voice coached her. *"Just wait, Lucy. You'll see the light. You just have to wait."*

So she did. And slowly, sure as the dawn, the darkness sparked with pricks of light so pure white they pierced right into her. The warmth of Dash hovered beside her, and she sensed him grinning his contagious grin. So with her eyes fixed to his homeland of the sky, she decided to come right out and say it. "You did it, Dash."

"No." His voice was light. "Roger beat me again. But one of these days, if I can garner half the knowledge of the sky that he has engraved on his brain . . ."

Lucy laughed gently, gazing still at the Pleiades. The Seven Sisters, she recalled. "I mean, you *did* it." She straightened, looked at him, searching.

The corners of his grin sobered. Knowing.

"You made it up there." Wonder slipped into her voice, a laugh skipping across her words.

"Sort of," Dash said, his foot pivoting back and forth on his heel like a windscreen wiper. He still had his tell, the way she knew he was nervous or embarrassed.

Lucy raised her eyebrows. "You made it onto the International Space Station. That thing that orbits the earth a billion times a day."

"Sixteen times," he said, looking sheepish.

"And you say 'sort of'? Dash. You *did* it."

She remembered his words on his postcard from Harvard: *Next stop — the moon! But not before stopping back at Candlewick to pick you up, Lucy.* A tinge of melancholy twisted in her chest — which was ridiculous.

Dash couldn't have packed her in a suitcase and smuggled her on board. Still, that old feeling of being left behind reared its head. *This is not about you, Lucy.* She put it in its place and focused on her friend.

He pursed his mouth, scrunching up his nose. "Okay, yah, I did, once . . . or twice?"

"Once or twice?"

"Maybe more like twice."

Lucy opened her mouth but no words came. She shook her head, speechless. So her arm reverted to its old habit and whacked his elbow in mock censure. "Way to bury the lead, astronaut Dash! Why didn't you tell me?"

He stared up at the stars, shaking his head. "I still can't believe it, most of the time. How can I expect others to believe it?"

"Dash. It's me. I took down your notes when you dictated your flight plan in the reading room when you were twelve years old. I would have believed you."

He nodded. "You're right. You would have. I know you . . ."

She heard a *but* in his voice and waited.

"But there are other things, too. When people find out, suddenly they think I'm something special."

Lucy tipped her head to the side. "Well,

you are."

"Not any better or different than anyone else. My physical body just happened to be in a different physical place. I'm still me."

Lucy ached to find out what he loved. What he didn't love. But more than anything, she wanted him to know that she saw *him.* And she figured the best way to do that was to call him out, like they always did for each other.

"Dash."

"Hmm?" He scuffed the dirt some more.

"Of course you're still you. Nothing can or will change that. But you have to tell me."

"Tell you what?"

"What was it like?" she whispered.

His face broke into pure delight. "It's amazing. It's huge. Outside, in space, I mean. And inside it's so small. It's boundless, but with more boundaries and barcodes than I've ever seen in my life. Everything is catalogued and recorded. Every single thing. Every extreme you can think of, you're right there in the middle of it all. Dark and light. Expanse and confinement. The cold of space, the heat of the sun. The earth up there looks like the blue marble, just like they call it, but it's so much more than what you see in the pictures. Tides rising and falling. Oceans moving. Storms gathering.

Clouds swirling. All four seasons and sixteen sunrises, sixteen sunsets every single day. I picked out this random spot up in Maine, where the sun rises first in the States, and I'd pray for them. For whoever was watching, and whatever it was that drove them to the edge of their world to find light."

"Light you saw over and over again," Lucy said.

Dash nodded. "When night moved over the earth, I watched thousands upon thousands of lights in cities — tiny echoes of the massive lights burning above them in space. All those lights represented people making their way through life." He shook his head. "I wanted to reach down and tell them, 'I see you. And everything's okay up here in space. And I hope everything's okay for you, too.' "

"What cities?" Lucy pictured him saying those things.

He shrugged. "Any of them. New York. Abu Dhabi. Dublin. Buenos Aires. Tokyo." He studied her. "And . . . London. Always."

Lucy swallowed, thinking of the times she sat on the back stoop looking through the old telescope with her father — the scene never complete without Dash. Perhaps there were times they were actually looking right at him and hadn't even known.

"Dad would've been over-the-moon proud," Lucy said. "No pun intended. And Mum, too. They'd have been busting with joy for you, Dash."

He seemed ready to say something, then dropped his stare. "I wish you could've seen it, Lucy. You'd love it."

Silence bloomed, airy and great, the whole of space seeming to reach down and stir the space between them.

"But there was a time I would've given anything to be off that station and with you, Lucy." Regret etched his voice.

She pulled her sweater more tightly around herself. She would've given anything for that, too, that day alone on the Thames.

"I . . . I've been making my way back to you ever since." He inhaled, and his eyes shadowed, dropping away their jesting and morphing into pools of sincerity born of brokenness.

She looked at him, questioning. And he looked back, a mirror of her questions. When he left, the magic of Candlewick Commons began to dissipate. And after Dad had died, it had just been a shell of a place. Nothing of the home it had once been. But here, standing before her, was all of the warmth and life of those lost years, in human form.

Here . . . was home. Come knocking on her front door, when she'd thought it lost forever.

"I'm glad you came back."

Later, in her room she treasured up these remembrances, stacked up questions born of them.

Her fingers hovered over the keyboard with the search engine page open, its bright letters staring at her much too quixotically. *Why didn't Dad tell me he was writing to my oldest friend?* She wished she could type her questions and have the answers stack up in search results, catalogued for her to peruse. *What did they talk about in all those letters?*

But the plucky, colorful search engine letters stared back at her blank-faced, the blinking cursor ticking seconds away. *Dashel Greene,* she typed. *International Space Station.*

A lengthy list of articles cropped up — detailing his selection, his years-long training skipping from Houston, to Star City in Russia, to Canada. His time served on a back-up crew before he became part of the primary crew. Old articles came up featuring him as a visiting fellow at universities, as a resident astronomer at observatories far and wide, from Hawaii to the Great Basin to Brazil to Baltimore to St. Petersburg.

"His teachers were right," she murmured. Dash had been, and still was, a genius. That guy with the goofy grin and the Astros baseball cap and dimples, so humble she'd had to hear from another that he'd made it to space.

She clicked on a link to his Twitter profile, dormant for some time now. Scrolling, she read his tweets from space — part of the astronaut's duties, apparently, and he'd made a grand time of it.

@Dashintospace — Bumped into the commander in the Columbus module today. Had to Apollo-gize. **#spacepuns #lightmatters**

Lucy laughed. She could almost hear him, see his laughing eyes, merry at his own pun. She read on, a few tweets about life on the ISS, about getting the stargazer prototype working.

@Dashintospace — An astronomer in space is kind of like an optometrist diving into an eyeball. Suddenly surrounded by the thing he's looked at from afar for so long . . . and let me tell you, this intergalactic eyeball is incredible. #**starsupclose** #**lightmatters**

A picture of him, hair standing on end in the lack of gravity, posed with scissors in one hand about to snip a chunk of that dark hair. His face registering exaggerated concern, like he and the viewer shared an inside joke. Dash was always so good at making people feel at home. Even, apparently, when he was out of this world. She laughed out loud when she read his caption:

How does an astronaut cut his hair? . . . Eclipse it! #**spacepuns** #**hairysituation**

And then he waxed philosophical with just as much ease.

@Dashintospace — That sunrise — incredible. Especially from way up here. But no more a miracle than the match you strike to light your home fire (N. Hemisphere — we see that blizzard coming your way, Ohio!) or your patio candle (S. Hemisphere) tonight. #**lifeisbeautiful** #**physicsastound** #**lightmatters**

She slowed as she neared the end of his tweets, not wanting this glimpse to end.

These snippets from Dash's time in the place he had so longed for was a joy beyond what she could describe. So filling her lungs and feeling the warmth of a full heart, she began reading his last tweet.

> **@Dashintospace** — There are times, out here in the universe, when you'd give anything to cross it just to be with the people you love. Hold tight the people who are your universe. #lightmatters #match stickgirl

She stopped. Her eyes glued to the screen. Read it twice, three times . . . and then took in the date.

She knew that date. It was seared into her very existence. The date of her father's memorial service, her walk by the Thames. When she'd looked at the heavens and right there, surrounded by lights in one of the oldest, biggest cities in the world, felt entirely alone.

The night she nearly tossed her phone into the Thames, but was stopped by the arrival of that document in the cloud.

Dash.

That had been the night he'd sent her the beginnings of the compendium. The night she'd seen his words appearing on the screen before her, a heartbeat in her silence. A ray of light.

At the time she'd thought it ironic that the boy with his head in the stars was writing to her from the cloud. But now . . . it was anything but ironic. He had not written to her from the cloud. He had been in space, orbiting, looking down on her bright city perhaps even that moment. And with all the world before him . . . he'd thought of her.

The balm of a promise kept smoothed over the ragged places in her heart.

Her father's familiar words gave chase in her heart. *"Don't you forget it, Lucy my girl. The God of the stars . . . He is coming, and coming, and coming after you. Always. The heart of a father who will never forget his daughter."*

Her heart beat with the pulse of the words. Had the God of the stars been there that night? Reaching her heart through the words of a dear friend? Her throat ached with a truth that felt too large.

She shivered, but she had a hunch that had less to do with the temperature and more to do with the warmth of the company, the tight-woven fabric of family and community she had seen at the campfire tonight. It swelled her soul and carved the longing deeper in her to find such community herself.

Earlier that evening, as the star party had been wrapping up, Violette came to Lucy shyly, tentatively. "Will you still go with me?"

Confused, Lucy had put a hand on Violette's shoulder. "Where?"

"I want to go . . . to Oxford, I mean. I talked to . . . Spencer. That's his name." She shook her head slowly, as if all the words were too much for her.

Lucy understood how much of a stretch this was for the reclusive woman, so she'd just smiled and whispered, "Yes, Violette. Let's go."

So tomorrow they would venture to Oxford. Meet Violette's mystery man. Find out all they could about Killian Blackaby and his writing, and perhaps find more answers to the *Jubilee* mystery. And maybe — just maybe — she would continue to pick up the pieces of her heart, which seemed to be surfacing from hollows and shadows by the wayside.

TWENTY-SIX

HMS Avalon
May 17, 1811
Imminent death was a paradox. Each moment lived in sharp relief, then engulfed into a numbing blur. It began with Admiral Forsythe looking down on Frederick in the small boat where he sat bound and ready to be lowered to the ocean below and thence on to the prison ship, the *Jubilee.* Miniature compared with the *Avalon,* the *Jubilee* looked cheery and ridiculous as she bobbed upon the tide. Frederick thought she also looked a bit naïve, that she knew not what she had become. What the marks upon her prison walls meant, or whence her residents marched to after departing her decks.

"Why," the admiral uttered.

Why. A statement, a demand, a question, a plea.

Frederick looked up. The sails snapped like great white wings above the man, giving the grave appearance of an angel in uniform.

"Why, Hanford. Tell me."

To explain would take a lifetime. It had taken a lifetime to live it. So he gave the admiral the only key by which he could be made to understand.

"Your mourning dove," Frederick said, remembering the bird who had led Forsythe away from its young, to give them a chance at life. "It's . . . it's because of the mourning dove."

He could not look the admiral in the eye. But in that instant, he felt the man's countenance ease. A flicker of understanding in his stance, respect. And then just as quickly, that respect took on a note of vengeance.

"Elias Flint!" the man barked. Elias appeared, face white as the sails, forcing his chin up. Forsythe held up a wax-sealed letter. "I hear you do not read. So I will be very clear. This details Frederick Hanford's accused crimes. Be sure to place it in the bailiff's hands," he said, arresting Elias with a cold stare, "so that the man responsible can be brought to justice."

Forsythe held his stare and gripped the letter for a few seconds after Elias reached out to take it. Elias gulped. Forsythe raised his brows. Frederick's insides cinched in pain. Perhaps Forsythe understood what Frederick had done . . . but it seemed he was intent on making it as excruciating for Elias as possible.

Forsythe clapped Elias on the back, sending him stumbling into the skiff with Frederick, and the crew lowered them, faces grim.

As they approached port, Frederick gripped Elias's forearm with strength that would not be questioned. He gritted his teeth, schooled the desperation rising into three words muttered beneath his breath.

"Go to her."

And they were twelve again, a pair of scared boys in an alley, facing the press gang, Frederick pleading with the cloaked figure. *"Go to her."*

Only this time, Elias would listen. He must. Frederick saw in the hollow desperation in Elias's eyes that his friend understood every imploring unspoken word. *Do not continue your traitorous ways. Go to her. Go, and sin no more.* The age-old plea. *Do right by her.*

He would go to Juliette. He had to. There was no chance on God's green earth that he would resort to further treason. Frederick's sacrifice had dashed his friend hard against the sharp shore of reality. Coming face-to-face with the unseen reaches of his own sin, Elias looked every bit the scared child left among rocks and seaweed, betrayed by a father who was meant to have cared for him. Elias Flint's torment ran so deep it would either drive the man mad or knock sense into him for the rest of all time.

At last, Elias spoke. "I . . ." He met Frederick's eyes with his own red-rimmed, fear-wrung ones. "I will do good," he said. "I promise. This shall not be for nothing, Frederick."

No *Freddy.* No punch on the shoulder. Only solemnity. Frederick prayed it was a mark of turning.

He could not speak in reply, only nodded as the skiff drew up next to the HMS *Jubilee.* With thick black paint and gilded carvings wherever there was room for such, she loomed in ornate mockery. Frederick had a sense he was landing in some ridiculous fairy tale, one that left him sick to his stomach.

As he was ushered aboard, Frederick looked over his shoulder one last time. Elias looked back and folded his arm, bringing his fist to his heart, just as he had the night after that first battle aboard the *Avalon.*

Frederick pressed his eyes closed around this image of Elias Flint. His brother. And saw him no more.

The moments funneled into a numb blur after that, less sharp, each one serving, he knew, to tick the clock closer toward the moment he would die.

Frederick was shoved onto the *Jubilee*'s deck as if he were an overgrown maggot — tossed down and left by his former crew-mates, who did not so much as glance back at him.

A gruff man with shiny buttons and a slur to his words saluted Frederick in mockery. "Welcome aboard the ship of doom. Your own prison palace, from now 'til kingdom come." He secured Frederick into a dark hold belowdecks and promptly fell into a snoring slumber, flask lying tipped over beneath leaden fingers.

For three days and two nights he suffered in the belly of the ship as it bobbed and pitched with an unsteadiness that could make even the most seaworthy sailor retch. All Frederick could think of was Jonah in the whale. But Frederick had chosen this. Jonah had not.

Frederick made friends with the ship, for it was to be his last companion on earth. He felt sorry for the old girl. 'Twas not her fault that, with scrolled corbels, ornate figurehead, and baubles and bells galore, she'd been decorated to the point of defeat. He'd known life like that, once upon a time.

He recalled Reskell quizzing him about the *Jubilee. "Naught but a blight to the fleet, and a spectacle at that,"* he'd said. But he'd not mentioned the smell of mellowed wood and seasoned sea, the wood grain his fingertips now traced, the tally marks of men who had come before him, counting down their days alive.

His third and final night before his trial, he was brought above deck to sleep beneath the stars. A kindness, or a cruelty, given as tradition to men on the eve of their trials. Trials that were mere formalities, so clear were the articles of war when it came to espionage and treason.

He slept little, letting his gaze fall among his old friends in the sky. He awoke to spears of sunlight slicing past ropes and masts. Slicing, too, through the fog of the past few days with cold truth:

Today he would surely die.

His trial and end would be swift, at least. And he need not lie, of that he was sure. He needed only say all he'd said so far: *Take me.* The guilt in his eyes enough to convince any judge, magistrate, or jury — though they would not know the guilt was for a wrong committed nearly ten years ago against a humble country shepherd and his family.

He clung to these same words in the skiff that took him ashore to his trial. It was high tide, and the ocean sloshed oddly far over the sea wall, as if it had heard it had a traitor to carry ashore, and meant to do it expediently.

As his guard led him by ropes like a beast of the field, Frederick held fast to the vision of a courageous bird feigning its wound, that life elsewhere might have a chance.

The crowd awaiting him on shore was armed with spittle and insults and jeering, twisting his name every which way they could. "Frederick Hanford, scum of the earth. Gettin' what ye deserve, and none too quickly. Good-for-nothin', sellin' yer soul for a shilling and no more. Your soul ain't worth no more'n a half-penny piece, if ye even have one. Bring yer friend? Where's yer friend? Ol' Elias Flint, no better'n you, we wager. Where is he? Elias Flint, scum o' the earth. Where is he now?"

Safe, Frederick hoped. Gone to see Juliette while ashore. But a deep sickness stirred in his belly. What would the crowd know of Elias? Nothing. They should know nothing of him, unless something had happened to make his name known.

"Elias Flint," he said beneath his breath, countering the jeers of the crowd who scorned that name, remembering him as the man who had saved him, the man who loved Juliette well, the man who would do better. His brother.

"Elias Flint," he repeated. "Truest friend a man could know." His chin scratching his neck with the unshaven growth of days past. He planted his feet slowly, surely upon those words, letting the crunch of his boots echo honor into that name. *Elias Flint. Elias Flint. E—*

"Elias!"

The cry was that of love, and desperation, and disbelief, and hope — all in one fierce, stalwart, feminine voice.

He wrenched his eyes from the ground, and though his mind told him not to, he met her gaze.

Juliette. Beneath a hood, her growing figure hidden by a billowing, threadbare cape.

Even in such a state, she was a force, parting the crowd. He saw fire in her eyes. She refused to be kept from her love.

But then she saw *him.* And stopped cold in her tracks, mouth parted around the unspoken word — *Elias?*

Her eyes grew wide. She looked beyond

Frederick, looked desperately around, searching, not knowing. Thinking, he imagined, that Frederick had been caught up in whatever Elias had been caught up in. That they were both here.

His stomach sank.

That meant he had not gone to her. In all the uncertainty, in all the darkness in all the world, there were a few things Frederick could be certain of. One of them was that nothing could or would keep Elias Flint from Juliette.

Which meant something had happened.

Oh, God, he prayed . . . and knew not what more to say. For his prayer was choked by his own mangled mess. Could words even make it past his web of schemes and on to heaven? Surely they were caught somewhere in the in-between. A ceiling between him and God. Tossed about the ever-flapping sails of the flightless *Jubilee,* perhaps.

And yet had not Jesus himself marched to a trial, innocent? Taken on a death sentence, that others might live?

Frederick swallowed, willed Juliette to look at him, to see him shaking his head. To understand.

And she did. Those green eyes flashed tragedy. Rage. The smallest flicker of fear. And written on the draw of her mouth . . .

deepest sorrow.

She plowed forth, reaching him. Walking beside him, shoving aside the arm of the guard.

"We had word in Weldensea that you . . . you died at Gravelines. That Elias was on trial here today."

Frederick stopped.

"But you live." Juliette's shoulders heaved. "So where . . ." Her voice tripped over her question, over the answer she knew before it even had time to find words. "Where . . ."

Where is Elias?

Frederick's chest thudded hard, heart slamming against ribs.

In the blink of an eye, Juliette was lost in the crowd. One look back showed an ashen face, a lifeless sorrow so grim and resigned she became as a statue. The crowd flowed around her like water around a rock in a riverbed, until she was swallowed up in it, and he was in the courtroom. His last glimpse of her was as a hooded man approached. Tall, something familiar about his gait. It did not look to be Elias — but he could hope.

His guard marched him in and bade him stand. Frederick was numb. Somehow, beyond the hum of cold realization, the strangeness of this place reached its icy fingers into him. The precipice of life and death, where wigged men looked on in ambivalent business, apparently deaf to the jeering crowd outside, the shrieks of women whose entire universes had just been obliterated, as with cannon fire, in a single-word verdict.

A rustling sounded, and the magistrate entered. He moved with steady slowness that seemed inhuman, as if he were the ship traversing the sea of this room — and it was in his wake that all present would be buoyed or pulled asunder.

Someone pronounced Frederick's crimes of treason in a monotone that matched the cold, white light of the courtroom. Waves of murmuring stirred the murky waters of those in attendance. Frederick felt their glances like hot darts, spearing him with whispered commentary.

Good. Let them. The faster the better, that he might carry out his purpose swiftly. He could not shake a heavy urgency. As long as he lingered, he held the door open for wrath to come upon Juliette, Elias, and their child. If he could but close that door, nail the coffin, and seal his own name as traitor first . . . they might yet live free of the stigma that could smother even so blazing a soul as Juliette's.

He dared a glance around, in search of her. Thanks be to God, she was not there.

"I ask once more," the judge said, impatience in his voice. "Have you anyone to speak on your behalf as to your character?"

"None fit to speak for the likes of 'im but Davy Jones 'imself," someone said from the gallery rising behind. A chorus of hearty voices rose to a slow boil, and the magistrate employed his gavel.

"No, sir," Frederick said. He held his chin high. Not a look of defiance but rather an act of facing the crimes before him with clear mind and ready heart. That, at least, was true.

The judge studied him, his pale eyes seeming to hollow Frederick out in an effort to lay him bare, examine his insides. "You might be interested to know what your captain had to say about your character."

"Admiral," Frederick said in monotone.

"Pardon?"

"Not captain. Admiral. And I need not know what he said."

"I see. Well, despite your lack of eagerness to hear his —" his droll voice trailed off as he examined a paper before him — "very clear opinion of your character, it has been submitted as written testimony." The judge gestured for a barrister — a young man who stood with great importance and cleared his throat to read from the letter.

As he began, the door behind Frederick opened.

"Wait."

The judge narrowed his eyes against the sun that came in around a figure in the doorway. He could not see clearly who he was dealing with . . . but Frederick knew in the assured voice that sounded.

And he would not put it past her to turn this court on its head. To unmask his charade and undo any chance she had at an untainted future.

He had taken enough from her. He would not now take that, too.

"Your honor," Frederick said. "I wish to plead guilty."

"He is not guilty," Juliette said at the same time.

Ballast dropped in his stomach. The room, which had been so tremorous with murmurings just moments before, was stone silent.

What was she doing? He caught her eye and shook his head. If she spoke again — it could all come tumbling down about her in ruins.

To save her — from herself, from himself, from all of it — he stepped forward, summoned more volume and force than he had ever infused into his voice.

"She does not know of what she speaks," he said, despising how very cold his voice sounded, when all he wanted to do was offer her the world.

"How very unusual," the magistrate said, his dull voice piquing with interest for the first time in, Frederick suspected, decades. "And who, pray tell, *is* she?" He studied her with keen sight, eyes resting a moment at her midsection.

She, not missing a thing, jutted her chin out and turned to better face the judge, to better conceal the protrusion that apparently made her a spectacle.

"Your wife, I presume?"

He bit his tongue.

"I am not," she said.

The magistrate's eyes, so light blue they seemed transparent beneath his yellowing wig of horsehair, took in her swollen form.

"I see," he said.

He did *not* see. Ire rose in Frederick at the implication.

"I am sympathetic to your plight, miss. And I advise you to leave. This is sure to be distressing." He gestured to the clerk, who nodded to one of the officers of the court, who made to lead Juliette from the room.

" 'Tisn't a kindness, miss," the officer said

quietly. "Not t'you nor t'him. Come out into the fresh air, and it'll be better."

"You do wrong," she said, chin held high. "He is innocent. I've just had word that this man is most assuredly not guilty of the crimes he is charged with."

The magistrate's brows puckered, and he leaned to confer with one of the barristers. Their voices were low, but then he nodded gravely and said, "Hysteria. Understandably. Poor woman. Story older than time."

He nodded again, and the officer guided Juliette gently — and then firmly, when he realized he was dealing with a gale more than a mere human — from the courtroom.

She wrested herself from him at the threshold and stood, shoulders heaving, as the judge ordered the barrister to give account to his character, as detailed by Admiral Forsythe's letter.

Frederick swallowed, bile in his throat.

" 'The man guilty of these crimes is, if the court will pardon the vulgarity of this sadly necessary account, the lowest vermin to ever infest the bowels of the *Avalon.*' "

The barrister, in all his youth and eagerness to prove himself worthy of this moment, read with great volume. Enunciating every word so that each one was a trumpet blast. Or a death knell.

He continued. " 'He has, since his arrival, shown obstinacy, insubordination, disloyalty leading to desertion, and ultimately, treason.' "

Frederick thought of Elias. The run-ins he had had with the midshipmen when they were boys. With the officers when they were midshipmen. The times he had worked hard, the times he had undone all of that work by going missing for days.

This account was written about Elias. Forsythe had determined to give account of the real traitor, it seemed.

The man continued his reading. " 'It was no great surprise, then, when he was found to have sold information to the enemy. Information that would have thwarted a most important campaign, had his transfer been successful. One which will, if all the delicate details align, free many of England's captive men from the tyrannical imprisonment of the French. He attempted to involve his deck mate in his schemes. But the deck mate stayed true to his commission to stand guard over the mascot of the ship, a mourning dove.' "

The barrister raised his eyebrows, looking apologetic for the sudden tangential nature of the account.

For someone who detested the transmission of encrypted messages, Admiral Forsythe had written much between the lines. The man was writing directly to Frederick, it seemed.

" 'The man guilty of these crimes is a scourge to His Majesty's Royal Navy. A scourge to his family. A blight upon history.' "

The room began to spin. Frederick bit his tongue, a molten flow of words rising up in defense of his friend. He hardly knew where the charade began and the truth hid. He wanted to rise up against this testimony of Elias, to declare that this same "scourge" was one who stopped the beginnings of a mutiny belowdecks, who regularly went without to give a scrawny newcomer his hardtack. But he could not defend him, for to do so would forsake his chance at assuming his friend's place.

Frederick felt an invisible writhing from the direction of Juliette, still standing at the threshold. He struggled to resist the pull to look at her. What did she care of his fate? What did she mind if he was accounted as a scourge, a blight?

But in the end, he could not resist — and a great chasm split open in his chest. She looked shattered, as if she knew these words were spoken of her beloved. But that was not possible.

Unless . . . Who had the hooded man in the street been? And where was he now?

Urgency rose anew. If someone who could undo all of Frederick's efforts lurked, time was of the essence.

And so, with prayer driving his pounding pulse, he returned to Juliette's gaze . . . and saw pleading. For it all to be erased. For every word the man had spoken to vanish.

Time slowed as he tore his eyes away, skimmed the dark wood wall panels, the yellowing candles of tallow wax — one of them tilting, oddly akilter, ready to spill wax in its crippled form that its meager light might shine still.

And he lifted his sight once more to the judge, who was grave, his mouth moving around words that came in spats. "Guilty . . . hanged by the neck . . .

"May God have mercy on your soul."

Twenty-Seven

Frederick did not sleep that night. Looming execution — scheduled to the minute, no less — turned the world extraordinarily dark and extraordinarily light, all at once. He would be hanged from the neck until dead at nine o'clock the next morning. The eighteenth of May. A day which, until today, had been only one in a string of shapeless days in a calendar reaching afar into the future.

He ached with the heaviness of a friend lost, ached with the hope of life for that friend. He savored the sweetness of night air at sea. How had he never tasted it before? How had he never felt the miracle of it pulsing through him, carrying life to his every limb, feeling to his fingers? He opened those fingers to the night, feeling them crack as the mud slung by the mocking crowds on his march from the tribunal fell away. He lifted those hands to the stars, feeling the emptiness of his palms — the absolute absence of worldly possessions — and watched them fill with distant, miraculous starlight.

He had nothing. Not a thing to call his own. He would be known only as traitor, for all of time. It would break his father's heart.

But oh, it might give another child a chance to know a father. If Elias would but turn and do right, all could be well.

Struggling to his feet, he stood. Empty palms to the sky, grief and joy twining about him until they cinched his lungs tight. He ached with every beat of his heart, drinking in hope as if it were air. A flood of May air filled him with hints of a summer he would never see. He shivered, gulped that air as tears ran down his face.

He looked mad, he knew. But that knowledge only made him laugh. What did that matter? There was the beautiful irony that here . . . here, in a death sentence, was freedom. He reached farther into the darkness, closing his eyes to those stars, imagining he could rake his fingers through their shimmer, gather up their light. Oh, that he could wrap that light in a parcel of brown paper, tie it with string, and send it to the wee child growing within Juliette. He was desperate to tell him — or her — to look to the skies when things were dark. For there always would be light. Steady and sure.

He had no words, no companion to pass his last hours with. Not even the guard, whose flask had proven companion enough for the man, and who now lay again in drunken slumber.

It mattered not. Frederick would not be going anywhere. Ankles shackled and arms spread wide, he was free in this prison.

He surveyed the heavens. The stars of the Northern Cross barely touched the horizon, steadfast and sure. He was suddenly a young boy, back on the roof of Edgecliffe, flipping through the pages of *Uranometria,* untangling stars into shapes and feeling so much smaller — and so much better, in his smallness. While floors beneath him, a bellowing father and the reckoning forces of piano fortes collided in a battle worthy of the old myths, up here these beacons shone on, night after night, projecting stories for the ages before him and the ages to follow.

Overcome, Frederick fell to his knees, felt the press of worn-smooth wood on his forehead as he let the cool planks cradle his head.

Broken. Whole. Alive. The three twisted and twisted and summoned his mother's song, which used to do battle for him, warding off the dark. Setting the stars alight.

He was no musician, had no melody in him. But the words came. Ragged and splintered.

" 'Let us break their bonds asunder . . .' "

It was not melodic in the least. Handel would have cringed, surely. The staccato bright notes and runs and trills of piano keys were nowhere to be heard — but shadows of them lived in his somber declarations.

"Eh?" The guard rustled to a somewhat-conscious stupor.

" 'Let us break their bonds asunder,' " Frederick sang, stronger this time, bass notes anchoring vestiges of a melody to the words.

"They all go mad," the guard muttered. He rose, teetering, and made his way toward Frederick. Pushed his shoulder hard, as if to tear right through him and save the gallows a victim. "Ye'll not be breakin' no bonds here, m'friend."

Slamming into the mast behind him, Frederick's head throbbed. He rocked back, dark spots exploding into his vision like pools of ink. *Set the stars alight.*

"Asunder . . ." he sang, clinging to consciousness. *Please, God. Let this break their bonds asunder.* He pictured Elias, Juliette. The tiny feet of a babe, swaddled and safe.

He recalled the letter Elias had sent her from Spain, including a ribbon to commemorate the eighteenth anniversary of her arrival in the world, then just a few weeks away. Perhaps Elias had arrived on her doorstep himself, instead. Frederick did not know the precise date of her birth, but he pictured the two of them together. Perhaps she had left the trial, gone home, and found him there — and they'd eaten blackberry pie, her favorite thing, as he had learned in being Elias's scribe over the years.

This, then, was what his life would mean. The giving of it.

And it was good.

A swift kick to his gut drew Frederick's knees up into his stomach. The black pools of ink parted long enough to watch heavy boots walk away unsteadily, carrying the guard to a rope ladder dangling over the side of the ship. The sound of oars and raucous off-key singing faded, and with it, Frederick's last glimpse of those stars.

When he awoke, the whole world rocked about him, cloaked in night. His head pounded with the force of hammering steel, the more when he attempted to raise it. He looked first to the prison guard's perch and found it empty. So he was gone, still. Off debauching himself, congratulating himself and the world of purging itself of such a one as Frederick Hanford.

Straining his protesting muscles, he drew up into a barely sitting position, stopping when his shackles reminded him he could not move far.

A dark figure stood at the helm, perhaps five feet away, back to him. The wheel rocked back and forth in his hands. The lights of the port were nowhere to be seen. Only moonlit cliffs of white, off in the distance.

He was at sea.

In the *Jubilee.*

Clearly, he was dreaming.

"I knew you didn't steal my sheep," the figure said, voice quiet, hollowed out — and distinctly feminine.

That proved it. He was asleep. Or delirious.

He watched her, recalling another time he had thought her a boy, another time she'd been out steering a ship.

She turned, and there was no disguising her now. Hair loose and long, tossing in shadows on the wind. Her belly round in silhouette.

"Juliette . . ." he said, trying to reconcile this, trying to prove it a dream.

"Do not speak," she said. Or hissed, rather. "I shall not be lied to."

Frederick raised his hand to his mouth, pain smiting him. Dried blood flaked onto his hand. Did blood do that in dreams?

But in case this was not a dream . . .

"You cannot do this," he said.

"*You* cannot do this. I am only doing what Elias — the true Elias, the one we both know — would do. Not the one swallowed in some madness. . . ." Her voice broke, its wound deep and fresh. "This is what he would do." She nodded, chin set. Resolute.

The sight before him had all the markings of a dream. Nonsensical — for Juliette could not be here, and this boat could not be underway. By the way she studied the blackness before her and adjusted the ship's wheel like a finely choreographed dance, the figure before him was sailing in earnest — or at least believed herself to be. The *Jubilee* could not sail. All of England knew that.

No, this was not real. He was imprisoned. He would be dead in a few hours' time. When morning light came, it would all be over, and Juliette — wherever she really was, in the real world, not in this dream realm

— would be free to find Elias.

And yet . . . it felt different than a dream.

The scene before him blurred. His vision protested against whatever caged creature was thrashing about his brain.

"Juliette." He inhaled, biting hard against a wave of sickness. Dream or no, this would be his only chance to say what needed to be said.

"I am sorry. For your father. For so many things. Go. Be happy. Live a full life with Elias. He will turn around. He will make it right."

Frederick did not know how she had become privy to Elias's treason and Frederick's actions — another reason this was surely imagination — but he continued. "I know it to my very bones. He promised." He flinched against the darkening pain. "He loves you, Juliette."

She stood still so long — with waves lapping, and wind whipping, and sails snapping above — he thought she must have turned statue, in this dream.

But slowly, finger by finger, she released the wheel as if releasing something much, much more precious. As if it killed her to do so.

"Elias . . ." she said, voice flat, "is dead."

The sea lifted up beneath them like a great

hand reaching, turning, tossing this ill-begotten ship hard to starboard. Frederick rose to his feet, scrambling against the cloud overtaking his sight again, and saw before him great chalk cliffs reaching white against blackest night. *"Like veiled mourners."* Reskell's voice haunting the sight.

Up was down and down was up, and the surging waves tossed them to and fro until the cliffs seemed a metronome, moving back and forth, back and forth. With the Northern Cross watching and time swallowed in a blur, the *Jubilee* rose, and rose, and rose on an unending tide. Fingers reached from the sea — five of them, like the tips of bones from a great hand beneath, a chasm yawning into the cliff beyond. They were familiar. He pressed his eyes closed, opened them again. Were they not the sea stacks he had viewed a thousand times?

They could not be. They were too short, water churning about them, nearly covering them over.

And yet . . . perched beyond, a sight appeared that pummeled him.

Edgecliffe. Dark, but for a single window alight. Twenty-seven chimneys standing watch over the boy, now grown, now a convicted traitor, who had once kept watch behind them.

These were the waters Juliette knew. The ones she'd navigated since she was a girl. Of course she had brought them here.

In this dream. For certainly, this was a dark and fevered dream, ushering him into the day of his end.

A beam broke loose from a mast and swung around. His instincts burst through the haze surrounding his mind, and he flung himself on it, thrusting out his heels to slow it so it would not injure Juliette. It socked the air out of him, slamming pain through his entire being — and yet it was nothing when held against Juliette's shocking declaration. *Elias . . . dead.*

She stood at the wheel, great with child, swiping tears into sea spray, navigating the Jubilee into what he knew would be an impossible forest of sea stacks.

But . . . the stacks were disappearing. White froth gathered about each one as what little was still visible of them slipped beneath the surface, pulling back like retreating sentries beneath the dark.

"Fast, then," Juliette said, more to herself as the wind snatched her words away. And then with eyes narrowed and skimming past Frederick, " 'Tis the sea flood. It'll lock us away in the cave, and there's none who'll find you there."

"Sea flood," he muttered, pulling himself up to help but wincing at webbing pain, everywhere. *Sea flood.* It was . . . real? He recalled Juliette's mother's tale of it, a visitor nearly every two decades. 'Twas the stuff of legend. Only lore of the village folk, was it not?

The ship listed hard to starboard. Juliette gripped the wheel fiercely to stop its spinning, then doubled over, slid to the deck, embracing her belly with a cry of great pain.

Frederick wrested himself from this fog and in a tangle of instinct, extended his shackles and braced the wheel. Juliette crawled to it, pulling herself up on it.

Pain cinched him inside at the sight of her anguish. "Rest. Sit back." His own vision blurred as winds tore between them. "Please." It was as much a prayer to God above as plea to the woman who held his gaze a fleeting moment. Long enough to nod.

"Together, then," she said.

There was not time to argue, for the cove and its waves had no rhyme nor reason.

In a thrum of motion, instinct, flurry, and flight, the pair wrestled the *Jubilee* out of her skidding dance and into the black yawning mouth of the cave.

All fell quiet about them, the storm behind

dissipating into the eerie quiet of pitch-darkness.

Frederick's head throbbed. What dream this was, he did not know. But all . . . went . . . black.

Twenty-Eight

Stone's Throw Farm to Oxford
2020

All went black as Lucy closed her eyes to the thrum of the train. Oxford-bound, and with Dash at her side and Violette across the aisle, she felt an inexplicable sense of going home. A pilgrimage to places where she'd left pieces of herself along the way. In the libraries and greens and walking paths of Oxford, and in the heart of the man beside her.

She opened her eyes and turned to look at him. He was fast asleep, mouth slightly open and head tilting toward her. He looked younger in his sleep and more like the Dash of the past. More like the lost boy who'd come knocking at the glass house, who came knocking at her heart. His hand lay palm up, fingers relaxed, and a shift of the train slid it over to where his small finger touched hers, making it look strong and sure beside her slight one.

He had held her hand on a train once before. A memory she felt so keenly it hurt. So she closed her eyes, wishing for sleep, wishing to remember and to forget, all at once.

Sleep blurred the line between past and present, taking her back to her parents' living room, where her father's voice unfurled into a dream of recollection.

"There was an old woman, lived under a hill. If she's not gone, she lives there still! Pass me the magnet, Lucy my girl."

Lucy slapped the tool into the watchmaker's open palm, and turned her eyes back to her book. *Unsolved Mysteries of the Sea* and its tales of vanished crews were a touch more captivating to a twelve-year-old than a nursery rhyme.

"What's it about?" Dash asked with inquisitive brilliance, flicking her book cover. "You know it's not polite to ignore charming friends from far-off lands for the sake of dusty old books." He gave a cheeky grin.

"The traitor Frederick Hanford and the lost ship *Jubilee,*" she said. She had a way of sounding like a robot, or so Dash told her teasingly, when she was reading. "And America is not that far off, you know."

He shrugged, as if he wasn't so sure. She

felt a pang of remorse, then. Every once in a while, she glimpsed a quiet sort of homesickness in Dash.

Not sure what to do with her blunder, her eyes darted back over the rows of words. Dash, too, wandered awkwardly from her hasty words, and bent over the watchmaker's project with him. "That woman under the hill," he said. "Do you think there ever was such a woman?"

Lucy breathed easier. Right. Stories. Return to the stories. Safety lay there, for they had nothing of the real world in them. And yet — sometimes they felt like the realest thing she and Dash knew.

The watchmaker let his laugh roll from deep inside him. "Who can say? Kids since before the dawn of time have been learning that old nursery rhyme. But you never know." He handed the kid the tool and snapped the watch shut.

"It's not likely," Lucy said. "No more than an old woman who lived in a shoe."

Concern wrinkled the watchmaker's forehead. "Perhaps," he said. "But one thing I do know. Made-up tales that stand through time . . . they are echoes."

"Echoes of what?"

He thought for a moment. "Truth."

It didn't make sense. But the watchmaker's

demeanor was serious and inviting. His words seemed important to him. Weighty, even.

"But how? If they're not true, how can they echo truth?" Dash seemed desperate for an answer.

"There's a secret in that. Usually, the true stories are even more fantastical than the made-up ones."

Dash folded his arms, half contemplation and half disbelief.

"What do you mean?"

"Well, take that woman under the hill. It's fanciful and full of imagination and that's why we've told that rhyme to generation after generation for hundreds of years. And we all know there is no such woman. Or at least — that if she's not gone, she lives there still." He winked.

"I never heard it," Dash said, looking embarrassed. He'd once told Lucy that growing up all over the planet with varying and obscure relatives had made him kind of an oddball, and had left him with all sorts of random gaps in the solid foundation of tradition and tale that most kids seemed to possess.

"Well," the watchmaker said, "we've fixed that now, haven't we? But I'd venture you never heard the one about the theatre in the sky, either?"

This one pulled Lucy's eyes from the pages

of her book. "I've never heard that one, either," she said.

The watchmaker went on. "The theatre in the sky," he said, "was a vision to behold. Ladies would wear their finest gowns, gentlemen would top their heads with black hats that looked like chimney pipes, and they would venture out in the dark of night in a cold, cold world, to enter a world of light. A theatre whose curtains draped tall and heavy, like velvet hung from heaven itself. The auditorium could hardly be called that. It should rather have been called an ornamentium, for it was more ornately appointed than anything in its world. Balcony upon balcony, arches adorning them, rooms that reached and stretched. Its stage was never silent. Even when the theatre was closed and empty, that stage was yawning, preparing, awaiting its next act. You could fairly smell the music there. Shadows of ballets that had filled its expanse. Phantom notes, lingering in the dark from orchestras, operas, operettas . . . its very walls were alive with every performance it had ever held."

"But couldn't that be true of any theatre?"

He shook his head. "You haven't heard about the staircase, yet."

The kids waited.

"Forget the theatre for a moment," he said.

"Imagine a house, instead. Imagine a family living within its walls — laughter, tears, joy, fears — all the things that come with living. Imagine them climbing the stairs at night to enter their bedrooms, and laying their heads upon their pillows." He paused. Blinked, opening his palms. "Well? Go on, imagine it!"

Lucy and Dash looked at each other, both on the precipice of that place where fairy stories and imaginings seemed not to fit easily in their skin any longer. She shrugged. He shrugged. He closed his eyes, a goofy grin on his face. She laughed when he peeked through one eye, and then did likewise.

"Good," the watchmaker said. "Now tuck that family into bed and remember the fine ladies and top-hatted gentlemen of the theatre. Imagine them venturing out, leaving the cares of their own lives behind in order to be amazed, if only for a few hours. Do you know how they got into that theatre in the sky? Ascended to those reaching arched balconies?"

The two loved a good riddle and were deliciously frustrated at being unable to put these pieces together.

"How?" Dash said. Lucy peeked, and he was peeking back at her, too, one eye squinty-opened. He slammed it shut. Opened it again slowly and hissed, "no peeking."

"They ascended the grand staircase. Wide and sweeping, with its lush carpet and smooth banisters. And that staircase, though they did not know it, lifted their slippered and booted feet right into the very air above the roof of that happy home you imagined."

"That's not possible." The girl shook her head.

"Anything is possible, Matchstick Girl. Now, pay very close attention. This theatre — the Boston Theatre —"

"American!" The kid fisted his hand into the air victoriously.

"Indeed. They tore it down, fine building that it was."

The kid slowly retracted his fist from the air. "American." He shook his head.

"And when they did," the watchmaker continued, "they found something encased within that grand staircase. And it was . . ." He beat his fingers upon the table, shaking the telescope they were building.

Lucy dipped her head, an invitation for Father to continue. "A house! Just think. An entire two-story house. No one had even known it was there. No one could account for it being there. All those ladies and gentlemen, all those fancy dresses swishing and monocles gleaming and footsteps climbing for decades and decades — right atop the very air where dreams once ascended from sleeping children tucked into beds, none the wiser that one day orchestras and operas and operettas and ballets would carry those dreams onto stage.

"Just think," the watchmaker said. "One never knows what ground one is treading upon." He stopped turning his screwdriver into the tripod, and looked at them expectantly. "Well? Say it!"

They exchanged a glance and muttered together as they'd been coached to: "Just think."

Twenty-Nine

"Just think." Lucy awoke whispering the words. Realizing she'd succumbed to sleep on the train, she looked around, taking in her surroundings and straightening from her slump.

She felt the warmth of Dash's gaze beside her. The look on his face was one she recognized so well — of lingered sorrow, longing, joy, and belonging. He used to look from her to her parents with this expression, and it was this look that had earned him the moniker the Lost Boy.

But now his expression ran deeper. The longing and belonging stirred the ribbon of space between them until her chest ached with an echo of it. Their gazes met, and he lingered a moment longer before closing his eyes.

A slow smile took over her face as she recalled the dream. "Dash," she said. "I remembered." The words soared inside her chest.

He opened his eyes, her words embodied in his infectious grin. "You did?" he said. "I mean, of course you did! Which one?"

She loved how he knew she spoke of Dad's forgotten tales, without her having to explain. She'd forgotten what it felt like to be so much a part of someone, and they a part of her.

"The Theatre in the Sky," she said.

"With the staircase house."

She laughed. "Yes, exactly."

He looked at her, shaking his head, mouth slightly agape, as if she'd just told him the most astounding thing in history. And just as quickly, he stuck his hand up in the air and waited.

"High five, Matchstick Girl!"

She laughed. Dash. Miraculous and down to earth. He did her heart good in so many ways. She slapped his hand and loved the way his smile lingered, holding her victory inside himself like a treasure.

"Listen," he said, shifting gears suddenly. "I was thinking while you were sleeping. Is this the right thing?"

She gulped. "I-I don't know." Leave it to Dash to put words to this puzzle of their relationship, right then and there. His mind was always working, always three steps ahead of her. She wasn't prepared to have *this* conversation right out of sleep and a dream. She needed to buy herself time to think, to catch up. "What do . . . you think?"

"Violette hasn't left that farm in . . ." He shook his head. "A decade, at least. Is it . . . kind, to take her so far, the first time away?"

Oh. So this wasn't *that* conversation. Relief and regret washed over her.

Dash studied Lucy, his gaze open, curious, waiting. She leaned across Dash to study Violette across the aisle. And Violette studied the green countryside zipping past as they made their way north.

"I'm not sure," Lucy admitted. "But you should have seen the look on her face when she said she wanted to go. If nothing else, even if this proves to be a wild-goose chase . . . look at what we're witnessing."

Dash followed her gaze to Violette, whose foot tapped wildly, but whose every other feature was schooled into determination. Determination gilded with the lightest, brightest coat of hope.

"Isn't that kind of wonder worth it?" Lucy asked.

"I know. It's rare. But I've seen it before."

Lucy looked at him, trying to temper her response. To make it come out slowly, not as desperate and demanding as it felt. She was so thirsty for such light in a world that had felt cold and dark for so long. "Where?"

His brown eyes stayed on her, steady, as he tilted his head, shaking it ever so slightly. "In you."

His words collided in the air and dropped in pieces into her lap. They did not make sense. She was pragmatic Lucy, the skeptic at her father's elbow.

"Not me," she said, the words nearly a whisper. She felt ashamed, somehow, saying them. But she felt a fraud holding them in. "I wish that could be true. But look at her." She lowered her voice. "She's lived on a hillside — nearly *in* a hillside — for years and rarely spoken to a single soul. Such a quiet creature, but I wonder if there isn't more meaningful dialogue going on inside of her than in the whole of London."

She'd watched Violette, the way the girl soaked in the world around her, gathered treasures, and searched for miracles — and found them right where she walked and breathed and lived her moments. Hers was a rich, deep, expansive life right there on that farm.

And then there was Lucy, quite literally plumbing the depths of the world's oceans across the expanses of channels and seas and continents . . . and coming up with empty hands from shallow waters.

She opened those empty hands, as if her palms and fingers might give some explanation for this paradox.

Dash ever so briefly laid his hand on hers, and whispered so that only she could hear, below the steady rumble of the train. "Maybe you're an M4."

"A what?"

"M4. Look it up." He gestured at her flip phone in jest. He'd been giving her a hard time about her lack of smartphone. She hadn't had one since that night at the Thames. Though she hadn't thrown her smartphone into the river, in that moment she'd craved simplicity and hunted down a relic of a mobile phone to replace it.

"Why don't you tell me about the M4."

He raised his eyebrows. "I think I just did." He scrunched his nose up, eyes to the ceiling mock-searching for confirmation, and found it. "Yes, yes I did."

Lucy whacked his arm with the back of her palm, and he laughed. It had been easy slipping back into their old camaraderie. And yet . . . that easiness seemed to tiptoe over a layer of thinnest ice that threatened to crack into the great dark depths below at any moment.

Thankfully, he buried himself, baseball cap and all, in an e-book and she turned to face her window, where more pastureland galloped past. It seemed odd to know that somewhere out there, beyond the green meadows and shadows stretching across the landscape, her little London cottage sat empty. And if scenes from the past could be harbored there, her childhood self would be crouched by a fireplace, a gangly Dash sitting next to her, the two of them bent over a project and wrapped in a story.

Yet here they were, fifteen years after he left, charging into Oxford on a train with a girl who would hardly speak and had not left home in just as much time. And for what? Chasing a few lines from centuries before? Meeting a supposedly helpful person from a chat box on the Internet?

As absurd as the journey seemed, the thrill that used to overtake her soul when Father began one of his stories rose within her now. Something was afoot. Something waited — she could feel it — in the history-shrouded buildings of Oxford.

Soon they were stepping from the train with its yellow-and-blue paint bright against the stone-and-brick of Oxford. Teahouse aromas swirled into the streets, pubs touted fish and chips and gravy, and sidewalks unrolled in cobbles and unseen footsteps of writers and reformers and politicians of eras gone by.

Lucy inhaled. It had been years since she'd been here, a wide-eyed first year with her head buried in a pamphlet map. She remembered reading a list of "notables" who had come here before her, the likes of C. S. Lewis and Dorothy Sayers, Lewis Carroll, John Locke, Jonathan Swift, John Wesley, John Donne, and John Wycliffe. Apparently all the Johns in all of history. She remembered catching a glimpse of herself in a plate glass window of a pub and thinking, *All the Johns and me. But who am I?* She'd spent the years that followed paddling in that sea of wonder and wondering.

"No way." Dash nearly fell off the sidewalk and into the path of a red double-decker bus.

"Dash!" Lucy grabbed his elbow.

"The Eagle and Child," he sputtered, pointing at a pub. It was as if he were twelve again, absorbed in the pages of the book he'd claimed proved "ordinary people can do extraordinary things."

"We have to go in," he said. "This is where hobbits were honed into heroes!" His stomach rumbled.

"Time for second breakfast?" Lucy asked, teasing.

"What can I say? Tolkien makes me hungry."

As much as she loved whiling time away in the Rabbit Room, where Lewis and Tolkien and their Inkling group had met and shared stories and poems for critique, she looked longingly in the direction of the Bodleian Library, where the domed roof of the Radcliffe Camera sat upon the skyline. She checked her watch. "There's so much . . . librarying to do," she said, her smile sheepish.

In the silent tension between each of their plans, Violette's stomach growled, too. Her eyes flew open wide, and her hands flew to her middle. Looking embarrassed, she said, "Tea . . . does sound nice."

"Go on," Dash said to Lucy. He dipped his head toward the Bodleian. "It's waiting for you."

Lucy's smile overtook her face, and she could feel herself glowing. "But . . . no. No, let's eat first. The Bod has stood there four-hundred-some-odd years," she said. "I suppose it'll wait half an hour more."

"Go." Dash gave a light push at the small of her back. "Violette and I will eat and meet you at the Divinity School. We'll bring you something. We're not meeting Mr. Internet for another hour, anyway."

Lucy studied them, wondering again at the easy camaraderie the two shared. Dash clearly had a soft spot for Violette.

"Yes, all right," she said. "Very good. You drink your scones and eat your elevenses, and . . ."

Violette stifled a laugh. What? Had she said something wrong? She never could be trusted to be a clear-thinking person when the cloud of library-induced delight descended upon her.

"We'll do just that," Dash said. "Get thee to a library, Lucy."

And just like that, she was headed back to Oxford. She, Lucy Claremont, counter clerk at Cecil Court Clock Shop, who was trying to prove herself worthy to operate measuring equipment in the Channel — she was back to the school of her heart.

And she knew just where to begin.

"I'm researching the M4," Lucy said, trying and failing to sound as if she knew what she was speaking of.

The young man manning the inquiry desk in the Radcliffe Science Library glanced up from his computer screen. "You mean MI5?" His forehead wrinkled as if to ask what sort of proper British citizen could mix up the Secret Intelligence Service so abysmally. "This is the sciences library. I don't think you'll find much in the way of espionage history here. But perhaps All Souls College library might have something. They like that sort of thing over there."

The Oxford library system was vast, housed in its different colleges, housed off-site, housed on-site. The sheer volume of letters upon pages that crossed the circulation desks was mind-boggling.

"No, I mean . . ." Had she heard Dash correctly? He'd looked almost conspiratorial when he'd said *M4,* maybe it was a riddle she was meant to have understood. But it rang no bells, summoned no memories. "It's . . ." Her voice came out louder than she'd meant for it to. "It has something to do with stars. Or galaxies."

"Ah," he said, his face lighting up. "In that case . . ." His fingers flew over the keys on his computer. Then he scratched out a few notes on a small white paper and handed it to her. "Try this," he said. "More star books than you'll know what to do with."

She feared as much. What was she getting herself into? She needed to rejoin Dash and Violette before too long, and this was completely out of her realm.

"And . . ." He typed something else and scribbled *M4* along with a string of numbers. He tapped it with his black plastic pen. "There," he said. "That book should have something."

Climbing the stairs to the sixth level, she at last found her destination. The rolling set of stairs squeaked painfully as she moved it stealthily into place and climbed, praying the pages might hold an answer for her. It was times like this — rare times, indeed — she missed having a smartphone to type questions into and get instant answers.

But where was the magic in the glowing screen of kilowatts staring at her in white-screened splendor? There was nothing of the chase in it, nothing of the dust upon pages of books, the way touching the spines of old tomes was like touching a world outside one's lifetime. Reaching into the past and fingering pages that some other soul hundreds of years before had last touched.

She began to breathe easier, her soul filling. It felt good to be back in a library. Life at Stone's Throw had been stunningly brilliant. Bright days full to the brim and exhausting, too . . . yet always foreign. Here she slipped into the sound of turning pages as a queen into a trailing cape, finding their adornment safe and boundless.

Afternoon sun poured in through the windows as she pulled a slim dissertation from the shelf. *Astroseismology and the Observance of Song through Light.* She double-checked its numbers against the note from the inquiry desk and descended the stairs. She looked around at the tables in the long aisle, the chairs tucked next to windows . . . and sat on the bottom of the stairs. With the aid of the index, she flipped to page thirty-two and ran her finger line by line until . . . *There.* Three-quarters of the way down the page:

Astronomers at the University of Birmingham's School of Physics and Astronomy have observed song in one of the galaxy's most ancient star clusters, M4.

Lucy scrunched her nose. *"Perhaps you're M4,"* Dash had said. Did he mean . . . she was ancient? He'd always told her she was an old soul, but . . . that didn't seem to fit his conspiratorial tone on the train ride.

She read on, of how the sound from turbulence was trapped inside stars, causing it to resonate — to glow brighter, to fade dimmer, back and forth and back again. A visual dance, it seemed, to the song silenced within.

Lucy read the explanation three times,

then photocopied the two pages and folded them into her messenger bag before returning the book and hurrying to meet the others.

She crossed the gleaming black-and-white-checked floor and went out into the spring air, her feet carrying her past buildings and bobbing daffodils and into the Bodleian Library, with its iconic domed roof.

Inside, a rich hush encircled her. The sound of pages turning, footsteps falling, the occasional door opening, all punctuated an atmosphere of peace. She followed the signs to the Divinity School and paid two pounds to enter. At the threshold, she paused, the long rectangular room stealing her breath.

A ceiling carved in stone centuries ago hovered loftily, like radiating lacework vaulted into the sky and frozen in time. Peaked arches of dark wood ushered her toward the far end, where a man was talking to Dash and Violette, their backs to her. Approaching, she had a sense his was the sort of speech that came at a person with all the power of a train and all the urgency of a snail. A forceful, passionate, kindly snail who liked large words. Stepping closer, she saw a rapt look on Violette's face.

"He was an anomaly, you see. Killian Blackaby, the balladmonger-turned-seaman who spent his life recording things he found remarkable, or tragic, or exemplary, or good."

Lucy stepped beside Violette to join the group. "I don't mean to interrupt," she said. "Mr. Water, Water, Everywhere, I presume. Big fan of Coleridge, are you?"

"Quite! *The Rime of the Ancient Mariner* is a tome to be reckoned with. A fine example of maritime literature for the ages."

She offered her hand. "Lucy Claremont."

"An honor, Miss Claremont. A true honor. I am Spencer T. Ripley. Your humble servant, ready to usher you into the halls of greatness."

Where had this fellow come from? She'd gotten the basics from her Internet search, but he seemed rather more like a visitor from the past who had landed in the wrong era, and was as happy as could be to make everyone aware of the wonders of his true time. His dark eyes shone behind his wire-rimmed glasses, radiating some sort of eternal youth.

And Violette was radiating, too. A gentle joy as her wonder-rounded eyes fixed upon this gentleman.

"Shall we?" he said, offering an elbow.

Violette — the same Violette who sometimes jumped at her own shadow back on the farm and thought the daily trip to the mailbox up the road was a grand adventure — nodded eagerly. She placed her hand in the crook of his arm and gave him a look that warned if he tried anything or imagined she didn't have a good head on her shoulders, he'd live to regret it. *Well done, Violette.*

"Now, what we have here, my friends, is a conundrum. A confounding conundrum, truth be told. I inquired with the librarian-in-charge in hopes of granting you access to the book as my visitors, but wouldn't you know? It's in the special collections, and the special collections reading room is in the Weston Library, and the Weston Library is one of two that do not permit visitors." He shook his head mournfully. "Shame, that."

Lucy slowed. "So . . . we can't see the book after all?" She felt puzzlement take over her expression. "Then where are you taking us, Mr. Ripley? If you don't mind my asking."

The man gulped, a flush creeping up his neck and overtaking his face. He pulled at the tie that he wore beneath his sports coat and looked shiftily in every direction.

"Look." He pulled a tablet from inside his

jacket, as if dealing in some sort of contraband. "I photographed the whole thing for you just before you came."

"The whole thing? All of Killian Blackaby's ballads." Violette took the offered tablet, turning it on with the expression of a child on Christmas morning.

"Yes, ma'am. Here, if you'll look at this one, it's the one you were asking about."

She passed it to Lucy, then on to Dash, who scanned the poem.

" 'Sisters seven, seven more, cloistered in their cove.' What do you think that means?"

Spencer took the tablet and read the third stanza aloud.

"Sisters seven, seven more,
cloistered in their cove
His secret keep, this Traitor-Man
In death for to betroth."

"It begs two questions," he said. "What's his secret — is it simply his hiding place? And which sisters are keeping it? It sounds as though he's wedded death, so I'd submit that we can presume he did perish sometime after his escape."

"You mean to say he's not still around?" Violette quipped. Violette. Quiet, reserved Violette, venturing a joke.

Spencer laughed. Not so much an eruption of laughter, like Barnabas, or a spilling, like Dash, but rather he tripped about in his own choppy laughs, in and out, up and down. "That was clever," he said, pointing at Violette, who beamed.

"Now, are there any convents, abbeys, ruins of convents or abbeys anywhere near Weldensea? Sisters could speak of nuns, with whom he could have taken refuge. Think of Jean Valjean," he said. "*Les Miserables.* Something like that."

Lucy thought of the area, what little she knew of it. "There's the chapel near the village," she said. "St. Thomas's."

"Hmmm. Worth looking at, certainly, but likely not home to nuns. Anything else? The tricky thing is, it could be anything. With the religious history of this country, abbeys being shut down several hundred years ago, abbeys resuming since, some having fallen into ruins, some being incorporated into homes — it could truly be anywhere."

Something triggered in Lucy's mind. "What did you say?"

"I said it could be anywhere."

"Before that," she said. "About some being incorporated into homes. Edgecliffe's ballroom was once a priory." Her pulse quickened, a smile spreading. "And the painting I found matched the view from that very place. I'm sure of it."

"Well . . ." Spencer's face broke into a slow smile. "There you have it."

Violette reached for the tablet, scrolling through the pictures. "There's still no sixth stanza."

"Maybe he wrote the number but couldn't come up with anything else to write," Dash said.

"Perhaps," Spencer said. "But one of the hallmarks of Blackaby is that every letter and space has purpose. His meter fits like puzzle pieces, his alliteration beats like a drum — the details were the icing on the cake for him. Don't give up on that stanza quite yet."

The heavy doors opened at the far end of the hall, and the attendant poked her head in. "Time's up, I'm afraid," she said. "There's a tour group headed here shortly."

They packed up and left through Duke Humfrey's Library. With deepest wood shelves upon warmest wood floors, light spilling a walkway between rows of medieval texts, it had an entirely different feel than the Radcliffe Camera or the Divinity School. A young man perched near the top of a rolling ladder, his face buried in a book and completely oblivious to their presence.

"The train'll be off in two hours' time," Violette whispered.

Spencer held the outside door open for them, looking suddenly nervous. He shifted his weight between his oxford-clad feet, taking his glasses off and rubbing his eyes. "Oh, I-I mean I don't suppose you . . . Is there any chance you'd like to have lunch with me?"

Violette had just eaten, Lucy knew, but her "Yes!" rushed out faster and surer than she'd ever heard the girl speak.

And it was settled. Violette would have lunch with Spencer. Lucy and Dash would meet her at the train station, where they would all travel not home but to London. It was time to get that painting.

Thirty

A week ago, Lucy had struggled to sleep in the glass house, for all its quiet and empty. Never did she dare dream she'd return with Dash — who was on the garden green outside her window spreading a sleeping bag beneath his stars — and a new friend reading a book on the sofa by the fireplace.

How . . . had this happened? The return of the boy who had been so much of the reason this cottage had been home. It had felt so empty for the past two years, to the point that she'd usually dreaded returning. And now . . . it felt like home again. Because family, gathered from odd corners of the earth and pieced together in growing friendship, was here.

Dash knocked softly at the arched doorway and came in. "I thought I'd run up to Greenwich since we're so close," he said. "Check in with some colleagues and see how the observatory work is going. Anyone want to come?"

"Sure," Lucy said.

"No, thanks," Violette said through a yawn.

"Oh . . . then I'll stay, too," Lucy said, not wanting to leave Violette alone on her first night away from the farm.

"I'm fine," Violette said. "Ready to drop off to sleep, actually." It had been an incredibly full day.

"Will the observatory even be open?" Lucy asked.

"Observatories come alive at night. Something about the . . . stars, I think?" He feigned confusion. "And even if they didn't . . ." Dash held his hand up, dangling a key. "Perks of being a nerd," he said.

"You mean *star veteran.* That's what Clara called you."

"I like it." Dash pointed, then tipped his head. "Ready?"

And they were off, walking past their fountain, through the wrought iron gates of Candlewick Commons, to the Tube station that used to play the part of the dragon in Father's stories. As they boarded, making sure to "mind the gap," as the recording congenially reminded them, Lucy quieted.

Candlewick to Greenwich. They had ridden this route before, too many times to count. It was a route that had changed her forever.

"You okay?" Dash said.

"Just remembering."

Dash studied her, an invitation in his eyes.

"You remember . . . the blackout?"

He nodded, solemn, sharing her silent remembering. Here they were again, riding that same line, the train all but empty this late in the evening.

Soon they reached Greenwich station and walked through the stone-and-iron gates to climb the long uphill path to the observatory. Dash whistled a tune with his easy stride as they passed brick buildings with black domed tops, white columned stairs, and apartments of royal astronomers.

Two men passed them, and one of them nodded. "Dashel."

"Hey, Jerry!" And Dash strode on.

They approached the building that housed the grand equatorial telescope, the one they'd called "the onion" when they were young, for the white dome atop the stone building looked indeed like a white onion. But they'd never gone in.

"Come on," Dash said when she slowed her pace.

"Are you sure? I don't know if I'm allowed . . ."

He looked up at the darkening sky and then back at her. Let the door shut. "Know what this telescope was built for? To study two-star systems."

He looked as if he'd just proven a point, but she didn't know what it was.

"Stars that orbit each other," he said. "Like Capella A and Capella B. To us, they're so close they look like one bright star. But they're two separate stars that keep crossing into each other's space. Over and over, until they become one to anyone looking on."

"I had no idea," Lucy said, and then hesitantly added, "but . . . I'm not sure why that means I'm allowed in."

He looked flustered. Not frustrated. Just tongue-tied, at a loss for how to complete his explanation. Which was completely unlike him. His eyes lingered on her, pleading for her to understand the message beneath his words.

A two-star system. *Us.* She swallowed, eyes wide.

"Come on in, Lucy." Dash held the door open again. "You'll be fine."

They entered into what felt like the inner realm — right into the domed room that reached higher and higher into the sky. In the center, a gigantic beige apparatus stood, a cluster of people conferring at its base.

"Hey, Dash!" a girl said brightly. "You're back!"

"Guilty," Dash said, and introduced Lucy around. "She's a maritime archaeologist of the highest order. Wait 'til you see her research. She —"

Just then, the dome began to open. With a great creaking groan of metal, it parted, peeled away as if someone had sliced into the onion, and unleashed the telescope.

Dash got to talking stars with those gathered, and Lucy stepped back, loving watching him in his element. Congenial and charged with energy. No end to his curiosity.

"When the Pleiades rise . . ." one of them was saying.

"Oh, no, don't bring the sisters into this *again,*" another bantered back. "It's not always about them. There are other constellations, you know."

The star talk went on — data and coordinates and deep space. A foreign language to her, but fascinating.

When she and Dash finally crossed back over the brown-checked linoleum and into the night, her heart was full, having seen him in his element.

They walked on until they'd reached the

cobbled courtyard with the metal line embedded into it. Its brass gleamed in the walkway lights. Dash stopped, facing her.

"Some things never change," he said. "You're in the west . . ."

She looked down, at her toes pointed directly at his, with the prime meridian running right between them. "And you're in the east," she said. "Worlds apart."

"And yet . . ." His fingers reached for hers, knuckles brushing and waiting. Patient, steady, as she slowly laced hers between his. Familiar and yet . . . so different from when he'd held her hand on the Tube as teens. So very, very different. As if every moment between then and now had been leading up to this, the homecoming of their hands.

"Lucy. Maybe I don't have the right to say this. I've been gone from your life for so long — and that's my fault."

"Mine, too." She dropped her gaze, studying the city names and coordinates inlaid in the cement beneath their feet. *Athens. Tokyo. Jerusalem.* Places he had seen from far above, hundreds of times.

She could have reached out to him, asked how he was, rather than being entirely consumed by her own loss. He had been the closest thing she'd had to a brother. And — an opening deep in her chest cracked wider — so much more.

He brought her hands up, right over that line in the ground. A London wind tumbled up the hill, swirling about them and sending a shiver up Lucy's spine as Dash's palms met hers, warmth radiating.

The wind pricked tears into her eyes. It had to be the wind, for surely it was not this swelling inside of her, this hope of a moment she had longed for and walled away in a secret place, where it could not hurt her anymore.

That hope was breaking out of that secret room now. Slowly, tenderly, Dash kissed the fingertips of the watchmaker's daughter, right there where time began. Fingertip by fingertip, brick by brick, that room in her heart opened up. A perfect swirl of purest joy. Deepest fear. Longest hope. And truest, dearest Dashel Greene.

"I'm here now," he said. "If that's okay with you."

His eyes were wide, waiting. Looking a little like the lost boy again . . . all grown up. And this time, it was her turn to find him.

With a heart filling, she pulled his hands to her lips, and kissed the fingers that searched the stars.

To speak would have been to shatter this

moment. She wanted to hold it close, to protect it from everything outside of themselves. Surrendering her hand to his encompassing grip as he traced her face with his free hand, they walked in silence back down the hill and on toward home.

That night, with Violette sleeping soundly on the sofa and Dash sleeping deeply outside, Lucy pried the old floorboard up once more. Retrieving the painting, she curled up in her bed and ran her fingers along its torn edge.

"The Way Home," she murmured, wondering what it meant. Wondering what all of it — this whole tangled story — meant, and what her part in it was now, more than two centuries later.

Lucy drifted off on dreams of pairs of stars that danced together in the great beyond. It wasn't until the far reaches of the early morning that the snippets she'd overheard at the observatory took hold of her in a new way.

The Pleiades. Sisters.

Seven sisters, seven more.

While it was yet dark, she pulled her atlases out of their moving box, found one of Dad's old star charts, and entered a realm far outside her own. Emerging at the breakfast table looking like Medusa, escaped hairs sticking out from her lopsided ponytail, she held two maps up to a stunned Violette and Dash.

"Seven sisters, seven more," she said, talking too fast. The two pots of Earl Grey she'd already had were making her words come out supercharged.

"See?" She tapped the map of the coast. The white cliffs that stood to the west of Pevensey. "The Seven Sisters. And see?" She planted the star chart on the wobbly table, causing their breakfast dishes to rock. "The Pleiades. Also called the Seven Sisters. Right?"

She looked at them — Violette, chewing her pancakes slowly, eyes narrow, and Dash, standing, taking off his Astros hat and running his thumb and fingers over his forehead. "Fourteen," he said. "Seven sisters, seven more."

He surveyed the room, his gaze landing on a pad of Dad's graph paper. Pulling one of his Sharpies from his pocket, he started calculations. Scratched words like *ascension, intersection.* Studied his numbers, eyes flicking back and forth between the graph paper and the map. Finally, he planted his pen on the map — just beyond Edgecliffe, in the cove guarded by the sea stacks.

"If you follow the line of the cliffs, and

the place where the Pleiades rise directly above Weldensea, this is where they would intersect."

It was nothing. Or . . . next to nothing. Just a country road a tiny bit inland. She looked at Violette. "You know the area best."

"I'm no expert. . . ."

Dash gave a half grin. "She's being modest. She knows the area like the back of her hand."

"And . . . do you know what would be here?" Lucy said, spinning the book so that it faced Violette.

"That's St. Thomas's. The chapel."

"All right, Killian Blackaby," Lucy said. "Let's see what you know about the *Jubilee.*"

Thirty-One

HMS Jubilee
1811
So this was death.

His body shivered — his body, and not himself, for he felt strangely detached from it, as if he were looking on and pitying this poor soul who could only register darkness.

And cold. It was colder than he'd expected. Yet . . . there was a stillness here that he could sink into happily. Stillness, carried along by the sound of water dripping somewhere. He felt it folding around him, swallowing him up. Perhaps this quiet, then, was heaven.

He'd thought there was not supposed to be pain in heaven. He did not know much of theology and the afterlife, but he'd expected to see streets of gold, and light. Perhaps he was only partway there. Though that did not sound right, either.

His eyes flew open.

He assumed he was in heaven. But here he was, in darkness so thick it was unlike any he'd ever encountered. He was in great pain. Could it be . . . Had he . . . miscalculated his faith? Was he in . . . the other region? A deep fear snaked through him, bringing the urge to retch.

Oh, God. Please, God. The prayers blazed across his consciousness, and he spoke them, too. There was an echo here. So eerie and alone. Were his prayers too late?

The throbbing in his head grew fiercer, and he clasped his head desperately with both hands. Hands that had no chains. He blinked hard, willing his eyes to see something, urging his ears to hear something besides the incessant dripping. Shouldn't there be a choir of heavenly host singing, or some other celestial sound? Harps, perhaps? If he were indeed in the lower regions — he could not bring himself to call them by name — should it not be unspeakably hot? Where *was* he?

Show me, God. If I be in heaven, show me an angel. He laughed dryly. It was a bold prayer. Death, apparently, made one audacious.

Through the darkness he heard a sound so incongruous it tangled his thoughts all the more. Handel's *Messiah* — not as his mother had played it, but slowed and gentled into the cadence of a lullaby, hummed in a hoarse, sweet voice. Was it . . . Mother?

Frederick was no scholar of the canon, but none of this seemed to rightly reflect the afterlife. Surely he had misheard. He shook his head, casting the thought away. He was delirious, clearly. That was the only explanation.

But as the song stopped a new sound joined — a soft footfall, somewhere in the dark. *An angel.* His prayer was being answered.

He strained to see, but to no avail. But then the metallic scrape of a strike sounded, flint on steel as flame jumped to life. Its orange light fell on a face streaked with grime, wild eyes against gaunt face, looking at him as if he were to blame for everything unfortunate under the sun and all the travesties in the world.

He swallowed and held back a holler, beholding this truly fearsome sight. This was no angel. But Frederick could not — or would not — look away from this goblin-like creature. Somewhere beneath the fierce grime he saw something that drew him in, something vaguely familiar. Reminiscent of another time he had collided with a fierce creature, but that time out on the pastures of Edgecliffe.

"Juliette?" Her name came out up and down, like an impossible riddle. Which she was, always. "I . . . I mean Miss Heath."

No. That wasn't right, either. As affirmed by the scalding look she gave. "Mrs. Flint," he rectified.

The figure raised the flame to a lantern, and the glow grew until he could make out looming silhouettes of masts. The world bobbed gently, and recollection gathered. He was on board the *Jubilee.* Yet where was the sky?

He had the inexplicable perception that somehow there was a ceiling above him, and walls around him, though he could not see them through the darkness. And how, after all, could there be a ceiling above the masts?

He rubbed his throbbing temples. How hard had he hit this thick head of his?

"You're not real," he said thickly, through parched mouth.

"Really." The figure spoke dubiously. The figure, for it could not truly be Juliette Flint, and he could not truly be cloistered with her aboard a ship, in some great cavern. "The binding of your wound would tell a different tale."

She took hold of his hand, which was bandaged — when had that happened? —

unwrapped it carefully, though never letting her guarded look leave her face. An angry wound emerged, and her quick study of it sent her into the shadows, where she soon emerged with a canteen.

"You're lucky some old captain had a taste for the drink." She unscrewed the lid, and the sharp-sweet smell of brandy pierced the air, unhinging his stomach afresh. Before he could think, she poured the amber liquid over his hand. Everything in him recoiled. His muscles anchored his hand in place amid the flame of pain.

A flash of something softened the emotionless resolve on her face . . . but vanished just as quickly.

"You were singing," he said through gritted teeth, trying to distract himself.

"Aye. I sing to the babe." She stood, brushing her skirts, and that was when he saw, in the fall of flamed shadows, the way they fell over her swollen middle.

"That song . . . how do you know it?"

She screwed the lid back on the canteen. "Used to drift on the wind and over the fields, from the great house," she said. "Got itself inside of me, and it's been locked away there ever since."

His mind etched a vision of her, standing over her sheep in the fields, hair whipping about in the same wind that carried his mother's song.

He had thought himself alone then.

He'd thought his life at an end now.

He seemed to be having a rather startling run of being . . . well, wrong. "How . . . how are you here?" And where was *here*? His head would clear. This would all fade away, and he would be anchored in port, awaiting his doom.

"You don't remember." Her eyes narrowed, pensive. She lifted her hand to his face and held her fingers to his temple. "You took a blow to the head."

"And . . . how did that happen?"

His questions hung unanswered, covered in a cloak of troubled spirit. She did not appear to be ignoring them of sheer obstinacy, though he knew she would if she had a mind to. No . . . something more was at work.

She picked up the pooled muslin and began to tear, making a long strip that matched the bandage she'd removed from his hand. She gripped the fabric much harder than it warranted, and the tearing sound split through the darkness around them until it snagged. He could see how she drew herself up, how she pulled in deep breaths, how all of it was walling away a flood of sorrow. Her eyes brimmed but she would not let a speck of it past the fortress she'd constructed.

Wincing in pain, he stood and stepped toward her, took hold of the muslin. She held fast, and he laid a hand upon hers where it trembled. She flicked her gaze at him so quickly he nearly missed it, but in that instant he saw a world of hurt.

He remembered then. Only a flash — Juliette in the night. *"Elias is dead."*

His eyes lingered on Juliette's, his hand around hers, and her stiffness bespoke the searing truth.

Frederick did not know aught of stonework. But in that moment, a great invisible chisel pounded into his soul, carving out a piece of him that would never grow back. A void with edges sharp and depths unseen, so empty it nearly broke him. Perhaps that was what this was — this cave, or cavern, or whatever darkness they now occupied. It was a manifestation of their loss.

But no. The bile in his mouth told the truth. This was real. Elias . . . was gone.

His eyes burned, and Juliette seemed to plead with him. To forbid him to cry. He would not. He *would not.*

So he swallowed the heat and sharp edges into the silent growing void and set his chin against the grief.

She pulled her hand back and dashed her tears away with a quick swipe.

Confusion swirled. How had she learned of his end? How had this all come to be?

Seeming to sense his colliding grief and confusion, she drew a ragged breath and spoke. "I had word," she said. "About Elias."

How much did she know?

"At your trial, a friend of yours stopped me outside."

He remembered the cloaked figure, the change in her countenance. But what friend had he now, in all the world?

"A man from your ship. Mr. Blackaby. He . . . he told me everything," she said. "I came for you because of him."

Snatches of memory pelted in the dark. . . . A silhouette. The loosing of his bonds. The ship creaking in voyage, just hours before he was meant to have been marching to the gallows.

"You cannot die, Frederick, for something you did not do. Elias would not want that." She bit her lip. "I do not want that. And so I came."

He could hardly reconcile it all. The dripping in the distance plodded on. "But . . . where are we?"

This summoned a dry laugh. "D'ye not

know your own land? Hanford land?"

The dark disappeared into darker-still crevices around them.

"Or perhaps ye've never ventured beneath it before," she said. "Elias and I . . . . We knew a way in, down the cliffs. We used to build a fire when tide was low and plan for the farm we would one day have." A dream covered in the lapping tide now, by the sound of water beneath them.

"We're in the cave," Frederick said. "But that's impossible."

"Aye. 'Tis. But some say nothing is impossible. D'ye know of the sea flood?"

He did, and nodded.

"It lifted us over the sea stacks. We sailed in. None shall seek us here. 'Tis a good thing, too, for you are worse than a traitor now. Ye be a wanted man, surely, and word'll spread faster'n the wind — trust that. And I-I'm no better. I may've been seen. The widow of a man killed in an act of betrayal against his king . . ." She shook her head. "There'll be none who look too kindly upon either of us. We'll need to stay put, for now."

Then the pieces of the puzzle began to slide into place, and he felt hot shame. He had done all this to spare Elias's child the fatherless life he and Elias had both known too well. In doing so, he had put Juliette and the baby in great peril. His plans had all unraveled, and Juliette had landed in the worst place possible, with no good name, no husband, and no father for her child.

Her hollow expression told him these were the least of her burdens. She had lost her friend. Her very heart.

Looking at her now, seeing a flicker of the young girl whose heart he'd broken, he felt the pull to touch her face, to brush away the pain he had caused her again. But this was Elias's Juliette, who quite frankly was looking at his hand as if it were a poisonous insect and that if he dared touch her, it would be obliterated accordingly.

He kept his hand firmly at his side.

"You did not need to do this for me," he said, his voice low.

"I did *not* do it for you." She pierced him with her look. "I did it for him. Elias —" A shadow came over her, her arms wrapping her round stomach.

"Are you all right?"

Her form bent. "I'm fine," she said, but her face pinched in pain. " 'Tis nothing." She straightened again. "Elias lost his way," she said defensively.

Frederick hung his head, understanding the need she had to state this, to clear the man she'd loved. And though that lost way was wrong, he understood.

She continued. "'Twas only his love for this child that drove him to do things he shouldn't." Her voice was fierce, but he heard a quaver that told him she was as much in need of convincing as he. "After delivering you to the *Jubilee,* he . . . he went to meet with a known smuggler for France. Delivered some papers to him. Mr. Blackaby followed. He said he is sure Elias was telling the man he would no longer work with him." Her jaw worked, eyes shifting, and Frederick saw she was not convinced. "But we shall never know. He delivered his papers, received his pay, and . . ." Her voice broke. Dropped to a whisper. "He was shot."

Frederick winced at the word. An image came to him unbidden: Elias crumpling to the ground. The rightful road he was fighting to choose, lying ever untrodden before him.

His whole being lurched in pain of it. *My brother.*

He watched her standing there, cloaked in soiled white. An angel, indeed. And for the first time in . . . he imagined for the first time in her life, Juliette Flint looked frightened. Not just frightened but bordering on broken, there with her arms circled beneath the child within her. She was child and woman herself. And as she stood in that light in the dark, this woman who had taken on an entire impossible sea all on her own — and in her condition — looked at once invincible . . . and unspeakably vulnerable.

He furrowed his brow, summoned words from behind the throbbing, and reached for a prayer. *Lord, soften this blow. Do not leave her side.* Though Frederick knew little, he knew at least that He was a God well acquainted with grief, who knew what it was to be left by His friends in His hour of greatest need. He would not then desert Juliette, His beloved.

"Elias . . ." he began.

Juliette shot him a glance that was half fire, half thirst. Daring him to speak anything of her beloved, yet begging for hope.

Gentle this blow, Lord. Give me wisdom.

He swallowed. "You are right, Juliette." Her name felt rare and precious on his lips, here in this broken place. "Elias lived and breathed for his child. And for you."

He opened his mouth to say more, but she shoved out a hand as if to dam his incoming words with sheer will. And as she did, she doubled over, face pinched into pain.

Realization rolled in and over him like a

crashing wave. It was her time. Heat stole over his face — his hands numb and exceedingly clumsy, of a sudden. What did one do in times such as this?

"You're in need of a doctor," he said.

She only closed her eyes tighter, shaking her head no.

"A-a midwife," he said. That was right. Wasn't it? His face burned, chest pounding.

But she shook her head more fervently.

"A woman's help, then. I'll go for someone —"

A laugh of derision. "How," she said. "You're fair crippled, and know not where you are. And I-I am not ready." She swallowed, fear flickering over her. "My child is not ready."

In the shadows of memory, Frederick was reading Juliette's words to Elias. *"If you get the chance to steal away home in some six months' time, there will be someone eager to meet you, Elias."* But that had been, what? A mere four months earlier. And even accounting for the time it took for a letter to reach a ship . . . He knew little of these things but knew, at the very least, that it was not time.

But he had heard of this before. Distressing news bringing pains upon a woman with child. He had vowed to give his life for

Elias's in a heartbeat, but what of Elias's child?

He looked at the woman bracing herself now with both hands against the helm.

" 'Tis nothing," she said. "I shall be fine. The child shall be fine."

Please, God. Let it be so.

Thirty-Two

The fog lifted slowly there beneath the ground, days and nights unfolding in one shapeless stretch. Juliette's pains subsided. Frederick's injuries faded into a dull ache, an ache that propelled him to move, to be rid of it.

Always, he felt a shadow behind him, hounding him with the question of how long they could remain here. Caves along the coast were havens for smugglers who brought goods in and absconded with prisoners to take with them back across the Channel. They were known to go to great lengths to keep their activities hidden. If they were to discover an entire ship in this cave, it would become a thing to be pillaged, taken away piece by piece.

He held a foggy hope that the cave, being so unreachable, was not frequented by smugglers, but he couldn't take the chance that this, her prison and only haven, could be taken.

So at low tide one day he wrapped a length of the ship's broken bow in sailcloth, doused it in oil, and lit it. Then, with the ache of his muscles urging him on, he climbed down from the ship and sloshed through wet gravel and mud, feeling his way back into the cave.

At first, all its damp walls and the water stain ten feet up the cave wall told him was what he already knew: the tide came and went twice a day, lifting the *Jubilee,* sailing her nowhere, and setting her back down again when it withdrew. 'Twas like a rocking of an enormous cradle by the hand of a sea, in great swells of tide.

He followed the walls, hands running along the cold, damp stone. Light from his torch bounced long shadows, and he did not so much see the heights above him as catch glimmers tucked high above. Wet and shining, but for all the world looking like stars up there in the dark.

He rounded the back of the cave . . . and something sank inside him. While the cave hadn't seemed terribly deep, he had thought — hoped — there might be more to it. That perhaps, somehow, he might happen upon a kindly old smuggler who had repented of his ways, who might then just happen to tell them how to live here, or how to escape. But the back was solid, rounding gently to lead him again to the *Jubilee* and beyond it, to the mouth of the cave.

His head ached fiercely. Finding a place where the wall of the cave jutted out into a rolling ledge, he rested. Elbows to knees, forehead to hands, he closed his eyes and prayed. He did not have eloquent words and was rather thankful just now that the ceiling above him was that of a rugged cave, and not that of a soaring cathedral. It seemed fitting for the state of his heart, his life. The mess he'd made of it all. His thoughts ran into prayers like the rivulets at his feet, which joined into one trickling stream glistening in the dark.

That stream ran between his feet, its melody seeming to tease him. As if it were telling him a riddle, or asking him to follow it.

"I'll not follow the likes of you," he said. His grip on reality must be slipping for him to be conversing with water. "You brought me here, and here I'll stay."

But the water chattered on, heedless of his mad ramblings. He stood to go, took three steps back into the cave, and froze. There *was* something about that water.

It was not flowing into the sea from the cave.

It was flowing toward the cave. More than that, it was flowing *beyond* it.

In two strides, the ache forgotten, he was kneeling palm to floor, feeling the current over his roughened hand. Yes . . . it was flowing beneath the back of the cave. And not pooling in the way of a caught thing. It was going somewhere.

But the cave stopped here. Did it not?

He retraced his steps, ignoring the protests of his leg. This time, he ran his hand vertically as well as horizontally against the cave wall, stopping to examine every contour. When he reached the back again and ran his fingers around the smooth stone, he just barely brushed a rough patch, where wind and waves had not smoothed it in the same way as the rest of the surface. A fissure just wide enough to reach his arm through and confirm that, yes, something lay behind it.

Raising the torch, flickering light revealed that the fissure widened, and widened, as he drew his gaze up and up.

His chest pounding, breathing labored by the exertion he'd spent to ignore his injury, he willed to ignore it further. Retrieving one crate and then another from the *Jubilee,* he worked until he had a makeshift stair tall enough to see into the widened portion of the fissure.

And he saw it — a chasm ascending into a shelf of a floor, a dome-like room within. He cast a glance back. Juliette was sleeping on a pallet he'd fashioned for her in the ornate captain's quarters. He could not leave her long with the pains that had been coming. They had quieted the past days, but if they returned . . . Well, he knew not what the clumsy hands of a sailor could do at such a time, but he owed her any help he could give.

Still, the chasm pulled at him as if some force were anchoring a rope about his soul and hauling him in. He would take a quick look. Nothing more. Only to ascertain whether the room there went on or stopped there. If the former — what might he find beyond? And if the latter, it was still a safer haven than the open cave. He couldn't help but think of another such hovel, so long ago in Bethlehem, where a wee one was ushered into the world in a place of humble dark. Could this be Juliette's manger? A safe place for her, and for the child? Walled away from the tide . . . and from anyone who might come seeking the reward of the price surely on their heads.

Even with torch in hand, oppressive dark

enveloped him inside the chasm. It made the cave, with its window to the world, seem like the noonday sun. His eyes straining, he ventured forth to the shelf. Feeling the rock to see if it was sound, he hoisted himself up, shone the torch in, urgency driving him harder, faster, to discover what was there.

What he found was dark, and dark, and continued dark. It should have swallowed him with dread, but something foreign quickened within him. A spark, a lifting . . . a hope.

There was room here. Passages, some cobwebbed, some clear, all of similar height and width, as if someone had taken care to make this place traversable. He'd heard the tales of smugglers of a hundred years back hewing tunneled networks from sea to towns, storing all manner of goods along the way.

He went on to discover more rooms. He hoped to find a second entrance, a place he might escape to procure good things for Juliette.

Juliette.

How long had he been gone? By the scrapes on his skin and the pounding in his head and the way his torch sputtered — he did not like the answer.

"Fool!" He spat the word into the darkness, loathing himself for straying so far. In the same breath, his torch gave one last heave of light, and sizzled to a sickening black. Smoke cinched his lungs.

A low moan tumbled through the corridor, chased by the sound of faraway surf. He spun, listening. The moan repeated, louder this time, longer. His heart lodged in his throat. Those moans were — they had to be — the sounds of a woman who had come to her time.

THIRTY-THREE

"Juliette!" Frederick shouted, not for the first time. "I'm coming, Juliette!"

How could he have been so stupid? To leave like that, to assume he'd be able to find his way back with no issue. As it was, he was navigating blind and by dim memories. Juliette's moaning echoed through the caverns, reaching out like some unfurling, unseen hand to beckon him back.

He followed in the dark, turn after turn until he was hopelessly lost — and her voice went silent.

Only the faraway dripping of water answered his calls.

Now fear was the hand reaching in the dark, and it threatened to choke him. Was she . . . ? Had she . . . ?

Please, God. He continued on, limping — nearly dragging his leg now. As he rounded a corner, the distant sound of surf shot hope straight into him.

"Juliette!"

Only waves, upon waves, and then — a sound so small he barely heard it, and yet it sent a surge of life through him: the tiny cry of a baby.

He could see a shaft of light now. The room he'd first entered, and beyond it, the crack in the earth. Heedless of the screaming pain in his leg — for surely it was nothing compared to what Juliette had endured — he hauled himself up and through the jagged opening. He sloshed through rising tide and clambered up the makeshift stair of outcroppings in the cave's side to board the ship again.

Pulse pounding, he followed the sound of the cries, and swallowed at the sight of Juliette leaned against the wall, eyes closed, chin lifted, a bundle in her arms wrapped in sailcloth. A pool of blood-soaked rags surrounded her, her skirts bloodied but tucked about her with care. A knife glinted next to a flickering kerosene lamp.

"Juliette?"

Not a hint of movement. Dread pummeled him, sinking into his stomach like lead. He knelt and watched for the rise of her shoulders. *Please . . .*

With the lightest of flutters, her eyelids lifted, green eyes searching, falling on him, and then down into the face wrapped with care, tracing a rosy cheek.

"I . . ." He swallowed. A man had no place here, he knew. And certainly had no place in a room of birth as a woman labored. Yet still, he felt the heavy cloak of failure for not having been there for her. They were not living in the world of societal norms any longer. He was the only human being who could have given support to her during her ordeal. And he had failed.

He shook his head. "I'm sorry you did this alone."

"I was always going to do this alone," she said. And when she beheld him with weary, haunted eyes, he knew she spoke of more than his absence in the cave.

When he looked at Juliette, he'd always seen fierceness. A beautiful fierceness that had captivated Elias. A fierceness that had driven Frederick to a distance, unsure what to do with a creature who seemed to hold the wind in her very soul. But here — with evening's golden sunlight stealing into the dark and splashing a gentle glow about her uneven plait of hair and tired features — he saw vulnerability. Softness. Love — and fear, too — as she gazed upon the tiny face in her arms.

"A daughter," she murmured, voice

hushed in awe.

A daughter. Frederick looked upon the pair, seeing hope. And seeing history repeated. Two daughters before him, both of them fatherless.

"What is her name?" he asked, voice husky.

Heaviness descended. "Elias was to name her," she said. "I can't . . ." Her voice grew thick, a tear rolling down her cheek.

Frederick reached out, brushing that tear, laying a hand on her shoulder. It was the first time he'd ever touched her, and he was breaking his very first promise to her to do so. Yet how could he not, here in this moment, if he could but erase his question, her pain.

"In time," he said, willing those two words to push out the walls closing in upon her, to give her room.

Give her room. The words struck him, and suddenly he knew what he could do.

It was seven days before he could show her. Seven days of hauling pieces of the ship away, secreting them into the tunnels, evading her questions and wary looks as she tended the baby. Seven days of cringing when he dropped materials, giving away his whereabouts far beyond the main room of the cave. Seven days of bringing her fish and hardtack and "tea" — water collected from the cave's condensation, where it had been stripped of its salt, boiled over a driftwood fire, steeped with old tea leaves from the galley that he hoped to get just one more cup out of . . . again, and again, and again. She should be dining on silver-plated dishes of steaming eggs and sausages after all she had done. He was determined she would have her tea, such as it was.

On that seventh day, when she was moving with a bit more ease — and when he thought she'd go mad with the frustration of continued confinement — he put a torch in her hand and waited.

"What's this?" she asked, looking at it as if a fallen star had just landed before her.

"A torch," he said simply.

She gave him a look. "I can see that. What do you mean by it?"

He lifted his brows. "We'll need it where we're going. Come and see." He opened a hand to her. "Bring the stowaway." He nodded at the child, who was sleeping on deck in a nest of her tattered shawl.

"Stowaway." She laughed, and her smile gentled around the nickname. "Aye."

Babe in one arm, she returned the torch to him and together they disembarked the

Jubilee.

The torch was inadequate for such a reaching place. But somehow its small light set the stage for what he saw play out across Juliette's features. He did not pay attention to their terrain, except to guide her over boulders and through fissures and around bends that he had come to know so well he could walk them blind. Instead, his glances were directed at her. Stolen ones, to see wariness spark into surprise. Surprise give way to curiosity. And curiosity — as it was meant to from the time God breathed life into the great wide world — made way for wonder.

All was hushed as they entered the room he had prepared deep into the labyrinth. He stopped at the threshold, where he could see in, and she could not. One more step, and she would behold all that he'd toiled over. As he watched flames glancing over the scene, heavy doubt surged. This . . . was what his hands had bled for? It looked suddenly meager and spare. But he stepped aside, making way for Juliette to behold her new home.

He followed her gaze as she took in the sights: a makeshift pallet of a bed, laid with musty straw gathered from the *Jubilee*'s hold. A worn blanket pulled taut over it.

Three lanterns he'd found on the ship, with enough oil to last several months if they were careful with its use.

A candle, already burned down to a stub, rested in its tarnished silver holder, the finest thing he could find in the *Jubilee*'s captain's quarters. That and about twenty other such tiny candle stubs he'd gathered into a cracked clay pot pulled from the galley and stored in a small carved-out shelf in the wall of the cave. Beside it, the lone book, a psalter of sea hymns.

Heated shame crept up Frederick's neck as he realized how the place must look to her. With the rivulet of water running down the wall on the far side of the cave, and a great dark void filling the rest, it was little more than a hovel. Perhaps, more accurately, little *less* than a hovel. To think he had sworn to give her Edgecliffe one day. She deserved a palace — and all he'd given her was a hole in the ground.

But he'd prepared for this moment, and though it may be foolish, he began his speech. "There" — he pointed at the rivulet — "is your own waterfall."

She looked askance at him. But when she crossed to it and let the thin veil of water run over her fingers, something gentled around her demeanor.

"And your own private library." He strode over to the small carved-out shelf, just large enough for the psalter and pot of candle stubs.

She picked up the book with reverence, and for the first time in . . . well, for the first time ever, he saw a flicker of timidity in Juliette Flint's features. With her free hand, she ran her roughened fingertips over the book, tracing the long-faded gilt details of the cover. "Ps . . . psalter," she read slowly, pronouncing the *P* in a way that made her seem suddenly more schoolgirl than maven of the sea.

A smile warmed him straight through. He did not correct her. He knew Juliette had not had formal schooling. She could read, and write, as evidenced by the letters he had held in his own hands. But it was a hard-won labor of true love for her. Her plight was common among the village children, another fact he had long intended to amend once he was master of Edgecliffe.

The warmth faded. That day would not come now. But there was one child he might yet — if it pleased God — make some small difference for.

"What is that?" Juliette set the book back down, narrowing her eyes at a squat silhouette in the shadowed foot of the bed.

Frederick's heart pounded. *Everything,* seemed the only true answer to that question. He hoped — he prayed — it might be a balm, and not salt in the wound of her circumstances. She crossed the cave room, footfalls soft upon the hard stone floor, and touched it. She tilted her head, running her palm over the side, which had been sanded by the wind itself. "The crow's nest?"

"Yes," he blurted. "I mean, no." He swallowed. "I mean . . . it was. But now it's hers." *Blubbering idiot.* Why could he suddenly not put two intelligible words together? "For the baby. A cradle." The word felt so foreign to speak, and he felt himself the imposter that he was, standing here, giving Juliette's child a cradle. That was Elias's place.

She tentatively reached a hand out to where he'd cut the oversized barrel in half and laid it on its side. He'd formed a platform of some of the wreckage and nestled it with the softest scrap of cloth he could find in the belly of the ship. It was meant for wiping down mess tables, he knew, but with the *Jubilee*'s unfortunate history it had hardly, if ever, been used. He had washed it with seawater, hung it to dry at the mouth of the cave in the sun, and tucked it in with care.

"It was a poor idea," he said, interpreting her silence so she would not have to find a way to say so. She was truthful, yet he knew even beneath all her bluster and blow, a current of kindness flowed from her — else she would not have risked life and limb to save him from the gallows.

"I'll take it back." He shook his head. "It's no place for a baby. I-I see that now. It has seen too many horrors." It had been a lookout in battle and witnessed cannon fire and the fall of sailors in the distance. But . . . it had also witnessed the child's mother steal aboard a ship and sail it — with more skill than many a sailor — to safety.

Juliette lifted her hand from the cradle. She was silent, not jumping to reassure him or fire away his doubts, as she usually did. But that was the magic of her. Or the puzzle of her. She had a way of speaking truth, cutting to the heart of a matter. No finishing school or regimen of dance and deportment to have polished that gift away.

"Aye," she said at last. "It has seen much violence." She paused, considering . . . and then gave a small nod, as if a decision had been made. "But it also saw a man give his life for his friend. Or nearly do so," she said. It took a moment before his muddled embarrassment understood that she was speaking of . . . of *him.*

"Elias spoke his letters to you," she said, "so you could write to me." It was a fact. He nodded. "So you know he informed me that a midshipman named Frederick clambered to another crow's nest at night to see the stars."

His face burned. He remembered Elias telling Juliette so, and in fact had refused to write that line. *"Tell her,"* he'd said, that indefatigable grin of mischief on his face. *"Tell her my addle-brained friend leaves the scant comfort of his hammock — leaves his sleep, the fool, when sleep is the only luxury permitted on this floating Hades of a vessel."*

Frederick had tossed a stale roll at him and flinched as it bounced off Elias's head with a *thud. "Sorry,"* he'd said, and it was only to prove his remorse that he actually penned some version of those words. *Frederick climbs to the crow's nest at night.* No further explanation.

And now Juliette was measuring this fact with eyebrows raised in curiosity, hand upon the crow's-nest-turned-cradle. "I always wondered about that."

He pressed his lips closed. "Not much to tell."

"I can spot a fib even in this thick dark."

Juliette laughed. "A sea-worn sailor doesn't abandon the few blinks of sleep he can get to climb a mast in the middle of the night for no reason. Why?"

Frederick faltered. Her question crashed into the one corner of this world that had been untouched by loss. He did not open his mouth, holding on to the hope that refusal might protect that place out there on the ocean. But to ignore her entirely would be entirely rude. He bowed his head and gave the simplest explanation he could. "It felt like home."

Juliette studied him and then lifted her hand to trace her daughter's sleeping face. " 'Tis the kindest gift a body could give her." She lifted her gaze and slowly turned a full rotation, taking in the room. "Home. 'Tis *all* a kindness, Frederick. I thank ye."

Thirty-Four

Stone's Throw Farm
2020

"Hurry back!" Clara called after Lucy. "We've got to get you all shipshape for the smugglers!"

Lucy laughed. It sounded as if the dear woman planned to condition her to fight fiends in their contraband dealings — not as if she wanted to bedeck her in one of the fine gowns kept in the attic especially for the Smugglers' Ball.

"You too, Clara," Lucy said. "We'll help each other!" She saw the woman's cheeks darken to a pleasant pink behind her nervous smile. She had told Roger she would attend the ball with him, *"because that's what friends are for,"* and he'd been swinging his cane and doffing his cap to everyone he saw ever since.

Lucy swelled with joy, hoping good things for both of them. It surely was a scary thing to put a cherished friendship on the line. She glanced at Dash, recalling his hands upon hers, his lips upon her fingers, over the Prime Meridian. Neither had spoken of it since, but that moment — and this blooming place inside of her that had her breath hitching — had scarcely left her thoughts.

Quickly, she turned her mind to the mission ahead. She and Dash were headed to St. Thomas's to see what secrets the "sisters" kept cloistered in their cove.

"This is madness," Lucy said, as they walked up the footpath to the little stone church on a small rise. "I know I should be charting tides and checking your books to see what might propel us on to Hurd's Deep. But if Frederick Hanford really does have a history kept somewhere here . . ."

"Definitive evidence," Dash said. "Isn't that what the committee wanted?"

Lucy nodded. "It just all feels too surreal. Dad told you he thought you might like it here. Do you think he could have known all of this, somehow?"

"I don't see how he could have," Dash said. "But I wouldn't put anything past the watchmaker."

"Right," Lucy said. "Life was one great magic riddle to him."

Dash's smile grew serious. "Yeah. But

more, too. It was as if everything on earth was a sermon to him."

" 'And this our life . . . finds tongues in trees, books in the running brooks, sermons in stones, and good in everything.' "

"Lucy Claremont, if that was you quoting Shakespeare, then I'll be watching the skies for flying pigs next."

Her cheeks burned. She had taken a Shakespeare course her first year at university, pining for the boy who had taken to muttering the bard's lines in the reading room.

"Well, it's like Dad always said — the stories are echoes of truth. And I wonder what this story is all about."

"What do you mean?"

They crossed a footbridge, the trickling water mimicking the flow of her thoughts. "I can't shake the feeling that we've somehow found ourselves right smack in the middle of one of his tales. But instead of hearing it, we're living it."

Dash nodded. "Like he was dropping bread crumbs all those years ago for us to pick up and follow."

Lucy slowed as they neared the church graveyard. There was a hushed reverence here, as if by walking through these tall grasses and leaning stones, they walked among memories and moments. After scanning several grave markers of varying ages, she paused at one grave so humble in its simple presentation — common fieldstone, crudely engraved — it drew her:

TOM HEATH
FAITHFUL HUSBAND TO MARGARET
LOVING FATHER TO JULIETTE
SHEPHERD, FRIEND

She remembered Clara's story of the Shepherd's Bells. "Do you ever wonder what one life can mean?"

Dash laid a hand on her shoulder, concerned.

She shook her head. "I don't mean that in a hopeless way. I just mean . . . this man, for instance. What if he had never lived? Never walked these fields, shepherded his sheep?" The stone was smudged where a rivulet of muddy water had splashed over the word *Friend.* Lucy knelt, pulling her cuff over her hand and using it to brush away the shepherd's stone. She did the same to the one next to it, a Margaret Heath. His wife, she presumed. No children — or at least, none who had lived and died in the same area. Perhaps they'd married or moved away, for there were no further Heaths to be seen. Smiths, Jones, Rivers, and even Hanfords — Barnard and his wife, Maria, and the generations before them — but no further Heaths. And of course no Frederick Hanford.

She ran her hand over Admiral Hanford's gravestone, and as she did, a glinting white object caught her eye. Stooping, she found it near-buried in the earth. With hands well practiced in easing treasure from soil, coached by her mother the gardener for so long, she gently unearthed the relic: a single white pawn. It seemed hand carved with care from stone to rival the brightness of the nearby sea cliffs.

"I wonder if it's even possible to overestimate the significance of a single life," she said, brushing bits of dirt from the pawn and standing it with care upon the old headstone. "Words spoken, hearts changed, a meal provided to a hungry sojourner — who knows? Who knows how far everyday actions reach? It's incredible, when you think of it."

Dash stared at her, his eyes warming.

"What?"

"You sound like your father," he said. "Everything a miracle."

That sobered her. She should have paid more attention to his stories, heeded the truth of them more. She'd never known how right he was when it came to the underlying truths.

Dash offered a hand to pull her up, and entering, they found the church empty. Pews waiting for those who would stop to pray. The church bells still for the time being. Light falling through a small square window filled with sea and sky.

"What do you suppose we're looking for, exactly?" Lucy said.

"No idea," said Dash. "Anything to do with stars, or cliffs, or traitors . . . I don't know. When would this all have taken place?"

"1811," Lucy spouted, the date engraved on her mind. The year Frederick Hanford had absconded with the *Jubilee,* never to be seen again.

"There we go," he said. "Maybe we'll see something with that date."

"I was thinking more along the lines of a hidden key or a secret code. Possibly a pew that's secretly a portal to a hidden cellar."

"Okay, now you *really* sound like your father."

This made her proud. But half an hour later, they had scoured every nook and cranny of the church, finding only holy history and evidence of a community in worship.

Lucy was about to call it a day when she took one last peek behind a hanging tapestry of the twenty-third Psalm. A row of books filled a single shelf. "Parish records," she breathed. "Births, deaths, marriages." She pulled the deaths book out. 1811 held only one name: *Elias Flint, survived by Juliette Flint.*

Such a unique spelling of that name — Juliette. And yet it matched that of the shepherd's daughter on Tom Heath's gravestone. So much loss for one life. . . . Lucy's eyes pricked with tears.

Scanning the rest of the page, she found no mention of Frederick Hanford. The births book she skipped, letting her finger rest on the marriages book spine.

" 'In death for to betroth,' " she said, quoting a line of Blackaby's ballad. "Perhaps there's something in the marriages register." She pulled out the volume.

Turning the pages gently, she ran her fingers down the date column. There was only one marriage listed in 1811.

"Rivers," Lucy said.

"Rivers, who?"

"That's all it says." Lucy flipped the page gently, searching for an addendum containing first names, a maiden name — anything. But the only other note beside it, in the parish priest's careful hand, read simply: *Married in St. Thomas annex.*

"Annex?" Dash said, and strode out the door. Lucy replaced the book and joined him, scanning the building, the horizon, for an annex, outbuilding, or addition, anything that might fit that description.

But they saw only stretching pastures of green, berry bramble hedges here and there, and the peaceful bleating of sheep. No annex.

"That's strange," Lucy said.

"Rivers could be anyone," Dash said. "They probably have nothing to do with the *Jubilee.*"

"Perhaps," she said. "But if that's the case, why is that entry so strange? No given names, a nonexistent location . . . It feels clandestine."

"I wish I could tell you, Matchstick Girl. But one thing I do know . . ." he said, face serious.

"What's that?"

"Clara will have your hide if you're not back in time to get ready for the Smugglers' Ball."

Clara, as it turned out, did not have hides

in mind, but rather piles and piles of dresses. "Smugglers' Balls for a lifetime will fill one's attic," she said, laughing sheepishly at the swarm of chiffon and lace. For the rest of the afternoon she draped Lucy and Violette in different dresses until she was satisfied with the final effect, proclaiming them "morning and evening" — Violette dressed in a periwinkle floor-length gown that set her eyes to brilliance. Her countenance, shining indeed like the morning sun, had more to do with a visiting fellow at Oxford who had made the trip down for the event and planned to meet her there.

Lucy was dressed in deepest blue, a gown that felt like water in fabric form, the way it waterfalled to the floor in runnels and rivulets of flowing chiffon. Simple beading ascending from the hem caught the light like stars, and Clara had done wonders with her simple black bob, twisting it into a chignon of curls at the base of her neck.

"Starry night in human form — that's what you are," Clara said. "Implicit."

"I think you mean *exquisite,* sister," Sophie said, quirking a brow and . . . had she actually smiled at Lucy?

"Quite." Clara picked a flyaway bit of fleece from Lucy's dress.

The sisters, too, looked lovely in their

dresses, Clara insisting that "this old thing" — the new dress she'd bought in the village that day in a cheery yellow — was nothing to fuss about.

Preparations finally finished, they stood at the start of a path lined with flickering candles in simple white paper bags. In the near-dark, Lucy saw that the grass sloped on three sides and dipped into what Dash had accurately described as being "like a sunken amphitheatre." Where once a roof of earth had capped the former cave, emerging stars lit the sky above. Ladies in fine gowns, men in top hats and bowler hats and sometimes no hats at all — strolled the unlikely path on the strains of a violin. The scene before her unrolled like a storybook.

This . . . is the Smugglers' Ball? She wasn't sure what she'd expected; possibly people dressed as pirates, and songs about bottles on the wall, and props of crates and burlap sacks and buckets of gold.

She trailed behind the others, feeling a strange sense of familiarity.

The theatre in the sky, she thought. That grand stair in Boston. The hidden kingdom. Entertainment, whimsy, delight, built right on the surface of catastrophe. Only instead of a frozen river, it was a caved-in tunnel. Oh, if Dad could but see this. Mum, too.

He would be spinning her on the dance floor as if she wore fine satin gloves instead of remnants of lilac-perfumed soil beneath her fingernails.

A black-and-white-checkered dance floor had been brought in for the occasion. Strains of country fiddle music fairly jigged into the night, perfect for the airy scene. A white tent set up to the side offered punch, tea, coffee, and cake. Twinkle lights strung back and forth where the ground — or ceiling? — once was made the whole thing enchanting.

Seeing Roger clasp Clara's hands, looking at her with shining eyes, Lucy smiled. And then, even though it was unseasonably warm, Roger shrugged out of his oversized jacket and placed it on Clara's shoulders. Lucy expected her to scold him, jest, as they were wont to do. But she simply laid a hand on the shoulder of the jacket and fingered the lapel as if she had never seen one before. Turning to him with a timid smile, she simply said, "Thank you."

It seemed the Smugglers' Ball truly was a place of miracles.

Lucy stood happily against the earthen wall where the ballroom was its deepest, watching children jump in circling dances. Violette strolled arm-in-arm around the dance floor with Spencer T. Ripley, who was gesticulating wildly, speaking of Masefield and Coleridge, pausing to listen intently when she proffered something about Joseph Conrad. They made a good pair. He was perhaps a bit older than Violette, but rarely had she seen two souls better matched.

There was no DJ, no master of ceremonies. Only simple programmes that had been distributed like old-fashioned dance cards, listing the order of the evening. As the quartet struck up again, this time with the wild fiddle strains gentled into those of Bach, Lucy spotted Dash headed toward Sophie. She watched as he said something to the prickly woman, stuffing his hands in his pockets. Looking at the ground. Waiting.

Sophie looked ashen. She pursed her lips tightly, took a step back. Dash pulled a hand out of his pocket to wave it in apology, saying something else. But Sophie caught his hand midair, lifted her chin, and — this much Lucy could decipher across the room — said a simple "Yes."

And they stepped out on the dance floor.

Curious, Lucy opened her programme and found the waltz playing. Beside it, typed: *Annual Mother-Son Dance.*

Her heart stilled and eyes pricked as she watched Dash's fumbling feet, his tall legs unsure, but his smile sincere.

She thought back to that photo album, of Sophie's son, Jesse.

"Violette," she said, tapping the girl on the shoulder the next time she and Spencer passed on their rounds. "This may be presumptuous of me to ask, but — how old would Jesse have been?"

Violette stopped in her tracks, her smile fading. "My cousin?" She tilted her head. She narrowed her eyes. "He was a few years younger than I. So . . . about thirty-three?"

Lucy did a quick calculation in her head, watching Dash as he laughed, staring at his feet, trying hard to catch the steps.

"About the same as Dash," she said. And her heart grew at least three sizes then for both Dash and Sophie. Yes, the Smugglers' Ball was a place of miracles.

She felt intrusive watching the sonless mother and the motherless son, this bond forging between them. Perhaps that was why Sophie bristled so at Lucy, an air of protection about her.

She slowly walked the perimeter of the pseudo-room, running her finger around the beams and rocks embedded in earthen walls. As she neared the tea tent, Sophie approached her, glowing. "It's a sight to behold, isn't it," she said, catching her breath from the dance and awaiting Lucy's reply.

"It is indeed," Lucy said. "Not even the grandest ballroom in the grandest home in the grandest era of balls could compare."

Sophie choked a little on her punch. "If only your father could've heard you say so. He was none too keen on the Smugglers' Ball." She laughed.

Lucy's astonishment at Sophie's teasing conversational manner was eclipsed immediately by what the woman had said.

"Dad . . . was here?"

"His family came here quite a few years when he was a boy. . . ." She seemed on the verge of saying more but stopped. "He never mentioned it?"

"I had never heard of Stone's Throw Farm until Dash told me about it," she said. She turned, seeing the place with new wonder, trying to imagine what her father, in his boyhood, would have been like here.

"What was he like? As a boy, I mean. I never knew my grandparents, and Mum didn't know him as a child, so I never heard those sorts of stories."

Sophie narrowed her eyes, remembering. "We had a lot of people coming and going, back then. We had just opened the farm for visitors. I remember we'd play all over the sheep fields, he and my siblings. We had a tire swing beneath the old yew tree, and he spun and *spun* on it."

"He always liked spinning things." Lucy chuckled, remembering his gears. "Why did his family come?"

Sophie shook her head slowly. "It was their family tradition to take holiday around here," she said. "Claremonts and their kind had been coming to Weldensea for generations."

"I never knew," Lucy said, feeling both ashamed and thrilled to her core. Perhaps the sense of home that she felt here wasn't so far from the truth.

Clara came and stole Sophie away for a jig, and with Dash nowhere in sight, Lucy continued walking along the grass-covered wall of the ballroom. At its far end, a small overhang of the former ceiling remained in the form of a splintered beam holding up the earth. Beyond it, a wall of rocks blocked off whatever had once connected here. Made up mostly of mortared-in earth and sod, it looked less like a pile of rubble and more like a strikingly rocky knoll. Barnabas had told her the network of tunnels beyond had been long closed off, since before the Napoleonic wars. *"That's when she caved in, and when the pirates and smugglers went elsewhere. No shortage of cliffs and tunnels on this coast."*

She placed her hand on one of the white rocks, closing her eyes and imagining dark tunnels and contraband goods, a time long past. Hooded figures and clandestine meetings, underhanded dealings and —

A tap on her shoulder made her jump and her eyes flew open.

"Whoa," Dash said, putting his hands up between them and backing off "Just looking for a dance partner. I'm quite a catch on the dance floor, if you didn't notice. I only tripped eleven times."

Lucy laughed.

"But Sophie taught me a thing or two and I am now ready to sweep you off your feet, Matchstick Girl." He held out a hand, grinning that lopsided grin.

She slipped her hand into his, and when his fingers closed around hers she felt so much . . . peace — more so with each step.

A lilting, quirky waltz began to play, one with a skip in its step and an occasional minor chord, one with a sense of wonder as much as a sense of humor.

Like it had been written for the two of them.

In proper Smugglers' Ball Victorian form, he held her one hand in the air and rested his other on the back of her starry-night dress. Lucy swallowed as they began to dance.

This was Dash. Her Dash. Lanky, gangly Dash, whose narrow face used to make his glasses look like an entire galaxy, they were so big on him. Dash, who would trip over his too-big feet whenever she came into the room . . . The same Dash was traversing the dance floor with that same goofy swagger. Only he'd grown into his feet, into his lankiness and gangly limbs. Now his glasses, when he wore them, gave him an air of friendly gravitas that, coupled with his lopsided grin, hid the fact that brilliant knowledge of universes lived behind those eyes. But her Dash was . . . not hers, anymore. Was he?

His eyes settled on her now, his hand guiding her with gentle strength and familiar steadiness. How had she come to be here — in an honest and true ball, fancy gown and all? She was dancing beneath the ground, of all things, with Dashel Greene.

"We . . . should probably talk," he suggested. "That's what people do, right, when they dance?"

"Last time I waltzed in a subterranean ballroom, yes, that was the norm," Lucy quipped. "What should we talk about?"

He shrugged a shoulder, smiling. "Shakespeare, maybe? As I recall, you're his biggest fan."

She laughed. She'd so enjoyed their sparring of Shakespearean quotes, but she had none to offer him now. "No Shakespeare today, but will you answer a question for me?"

"Anything," he said.

"What did you mean, Dash?"

"Which time? I hardly ever know what I mean."

"You *always* know what you mean." It was one of the things about him she'd missed terribly when he'd gone. He always said what he thought. He always asked what he wondered. And he blazed right past small talk and into the heart of the matter, whether the matter be his undying love of marmalade, or the meaning of life as gleaned from his observance of the stars.

But he was not going to let her off easily. He just lifted that quizzical brow, waiting.

She sighed, playing into his game. "You said I was an M4."

"Ah, she divulges her secrets at last," he said, eyes twinkling with candlelight. "The M4, eh? My bet says you've already dug up just what I meant."

"You don't know that," Lucy said, her offense only half real.

He narrowed his eyes, nodding. "You're right. I don't. But I do know you conveniently disappeared at the Bodleian. I do know you went in the general direction of the science library. *And* . . ." He let the word trail out dramatically. "I once knew a girl who would never let a question hang over her for more than two seconds before pounding an answer out of the universe. And I have a hunch that girl is alive and well somewhere. . . ." He craned his neck, looking around the room.

"Dash," Lucy whispered, beginning to blush.

"Hold on. She's here, I know it."

"Dash." Her whisper intensified, and he stopped dancing and turned, scanning the crowd of people, bumping into the couple behind them.

"So sorry," he said to them. "Just looking for an old friend." The couple spun off, perplexed, and Dash turned to face her. "Ah," he said, face softening into a familiarity so warm it felt like coming home. "There is something of her here, I think."

"We're not talking about me," Lucy said.

Dash grasped her hand and they began dancing again. "Aren't we? I thought you wanted to know what I meant about the M4."

"Well? Did you mean I'm ancient? Because if you did, I will happily remind you that you are two and sometimes three years older than me."

He tilted his head, feigning confusion. "You have an interesting understanding of time, for a watchmaker's daughter."

"You know what I mean. So tell me about the M4."

He inhaled, looking at the stars above the strung lights. "As I'm guessing you already know, an M4 is an ancient star cluster. And as you may have read, researchers have recently discovered that they sing."

"The stars sing," Lucy said. "Forgive me, but how could researchers possibly know? Isn't that a little like the whole 'if a tree falls in the forest and there's no one around to hear it, does it make a sound?' thing?"

"Their song gets trapped," he said. "It springs from energy, from turbulence. And so it gets trapped and comes out in a pulse of light, instead. In its very existence." He waited a moment, then finished. "Like you."

She dropped her gaze, not knowing what to say.

"You . . . fell silent," he said. "After my email. I thought you might respond."

Her hand stiffened inside of his, the dancing slowing to a barely there sway.

She looked up at him, saw in his eyes not the mirth so typical of him, but deep sorrow, and a pleading, too. For understanding, perhaps. Or . . . or a pleading with the past.

"Where did you go, Lucy?"

He scanned the room, solemnly this time, and gently led her toward a quiet corner by the rock cave-in, and then continued down a small corridor she hadn't seen before, a vestige of the old tunnel. Its quiet enfolded them, pulling them away from the music, the energy, the crowd, and into its silent cloister of dark.

She heard her pulse pounding out answers, just as Dash had said — the girl who would not let a question sleep. But this time, the ache in her throat prompted words that would reveal far too much of her young self, alone in the courtyard, watching the stars through an abandoned telescope.

"I understand why you didn't jump to answer my email," he said, "with that ridiculous compendium. And maybe I didn't have any right to send it. But, Lucy, I would've given anything to walk through that time with you. I truly hoped you would respond, given time."

She nodded, blinking back tears, railing against this notion that perhaps some of their fissure had been her own fault. She'd felt so alone.

"I didn't know what to do, Dash. How to be. You were just . . . gone." Her voice broke as it crossed that single-syllable word, revealing scars she had covered so well, for so long. Her voice was ragged. She could only manage, in a whisper, "You . . . forgot me." She hated how frail those words sounded.

And then she looked at him. If all the sorrow in all the world could gather up and land inside a single soul, it had done so in Dash. Eyes wide and unguarded poured out a silent regret so thick it cinched her heart.

He reached a hand up, let his palm come up alongside her jawline, cradled it as his thumb swept a single tear from her cheek, and lingered.

"I'm sorry," he said, voice scraping over coals, and full of soul.

And oh, did it anger her. Oh, did it dredge up the pain and the emptiness of the courtyard and the way she'd let him in, only to be deserted, only to be left to walk the road alone when she needed the one who loved her parents as much as she had.

But rising above the anger and the hurt,

his two words — *I'm sorry* — reached inside her with tenderness, an offering of himself. Vulnerable, honest, caring. Calling her into his heart again. He had known just as much loss in his life — more, even. The anger and the hurt rolled up and dropped away. She reached up to grasp his hand.

"I should have written more," he said. "Part of me was ashamed. Everywhere I went, I felt homesick for a home that wasn't mine. For you, and your parents, and that little patch of grass with the homemade telescope."

"It *was* your home. It never felt the same after you left. You always had a place there, Dash." He always would.

He scuffed a foot on the ground. "I found the website you made for the store. The one with the clock with gears spinning, keeping real time."

Lucy smiled. To fill her time after Dash left, she'd worked for two months to learn how to make a website, and when she'd slapped that widget on the site, Father had declared she could never outdo herself, and she'd never touched the website again.

"I watched that clock while I worked on my college applications. I was determined to make something of myself, to come back someday and thank him. But undergraduate turned into grad school, and grad school turned into waiting lists for observatories and submitting papers to be published in scientific journals. . . ."

"Oh, and going to space," she said, lightening the mood.

"And that, yeah. Which is not that big a deal, by the way. Hundreds of people have been on that thing."

"Numbers have nothing to do with how extraordinary something is."

He tipped his head, admitting defeat. "Anyway. Someday just . . ."

"Got away." Lucy hung her head, knowing too well that sorrow.

He shook his head. "I waited too long."

"But you found a way to reach out," she said. "You sent that email."

"I nearly didn't. I was too ashamed, thought I was too long gone, that your loss was not mine. But, Lucy, I would close my eyes at night and see this picture of you sitting alone in that courtyard, knees drawn up, not even touching that old telescope, or your books. Maybe I was crazy, but I . . . had to do something."

So he'd created a compendium of wonder and reached across the miles, right past his own brokenness to touch hers.

"You did something," she said. "You'll

never know what that meant to me. I should've told you, returned your email."

She shivered, and Dash pulled her close. She leaned in, taking in his heartbeat. "I'm sorry," she said, "for going silent."

His hands ran down her arms. "M4, even in your silence, you find a way to sing. Carving light from darkness, chasing down lost ships, giving a crazy guy like me a chance to know you again. My Matchstick Girl."

There in the eyes of the lost boy grown up, she saw an entire universe reaching out, pulling her in.

Her breath hitched. He stepped toward her, and her heart somersaulted. He lifted a hand — the same long fingers that had dialed in focus knobs on telescopes and helped her up when she'd tripped at the courtyard fountain — and traced her face. Slowly, deliberately. Her hand reached up to meet his, to lace her fingers between his.

The boy who had held her hand through the darkness of the Underground, who had sat with her behind the house when they were locked out and scooted to give her the driest spot when all heaven unleashed its downpour, had given everything he had, always. And now . . .

She pressed her eyes shut, fear shooting through her as she imagined herself holding out her heart, unveiled — there for the taking.

On the wings of the fiddle and the waves far beyond, the wind swooping into the tunnel and spinning about them, the girl and the boy who had crossed hemispheres and atmospheres and everywhere in between, stepped together — and their lips met. Soft, safe, warm, strong.

Lucy's heart swelled within her, both aching with fear of losing him again and spilling over with joy at being in his arms.

Her Dash.

Perhaps Father had been right. Nothing was impossible.

Thirty-Five

Summer 1811
The Cave

Hearing the cry of new life takes a man's very breath. To hear it, then, tumbling down corridors beneath the earth where the sun does not reach . . . pierces a man's soul. The three of them settled into a rhythm in their maze of tunnels. Juliette tending the wee stowaway as she grew from a babe in arms to a creature pushing her curious self up, belly to earthen floor, as she watched her small world. Frederick bunking in a sparse alcove, keeping watch. Strangers, the three of them, yet the only inhabitants of this deep world.

They made a life there beneath ground, and as the rest of the world reveled in the joys of summer . . . Juliette was wilting. Not her fortitude, for she was as courageous as ever. More so, even. But there was a quietude that fell upon her often, and the freckles that had always sprinkled her face were now faded, skin pale, the rosy glow of spunk replaced by a white sheet of determination.

She deserved more. She was a creature of the sun, made to live in the light of that bright star.

While exploring the honeycomb of cave rooms and network of tunnels, Frederick had discovered an opening in the ceiling of the cave that came out on the rise behind Weldensea. It was difficult for him to see it at first because it was heavily covered by tangled barbs of raspberries. But the sound of birdsong had summoned him, and the birds had taken flight from their brambly roost the moment their song was interrupted by a hand reaching from their haven of sticks.

From there, he had excavated an exit, taking care always to cover it over with the brambled hedge, a living fortress for his small family — or his wards, he corrected himself. He dared not presume to call them family. It was too intimate. Too . . . good.

Frederick watched and waited for a stormy night that covered the moon and stars, and finally, when all was safe with his secret exit, he stole out into the night, skirting the village, noting the shadowy landmarks along the way: a view down into the alley where he and Elias were first pressed into service, the tree where Tom Heath had found him, the graveyard where that same shepherd now lay. These things drove him on, reminders of why he now must sneak into the home of his inheritance and steal goods like a common thief.

At a crossroads, he stopped to read a sign hanging on a post. Looking carefully around, he took a chance and struck steel to flint, lighting a small flame to read. It was a list of war criminals — deserters and the like — known to be in the area. At the bottom of the wooden sign, painted in white lettering, he saw it:

Wanted, though presumed dead: Frederick Hanford. Deserter, traitor, coward, and fiend. 200 pound reward.

He tossed the flame to the ground — stomped on it.

The words branded his very being. He pressed on, but now the shadows reached longer, voices around corners more sinister, and his own reflection more ghostly.

This, then, was what had become of him. He did not know why it settled so heavily within him. He had chosen to be labeled traitor, taken his friend's sentence upon himself. But he had never figured on being alive to witness the long legacy of it. Seeing it there, spelled out without hope of defense, with Edgecliffe looming on the rise beyond . . . he began to realize his actions had reached farther than he had ever considered.

Sneaking into Edgecliffe was like entering a haunted place, and that sign helped him understand why. A skeleton staff was running the place, as evidenced by the essentially empty downstairs servants' quarters, where once a veritable army of servants had slumbered at night. The sleeping room doors stood open but for those of the butler, housekeeper, and two housemaids.

From the servants' quarters, using his routes in the walls, he visited his mother's chamber and his old room. He gathered odd-shaped bundles of clothing, books, food, another lantern, and more oil . . . and finally, he made it to his old perch on the roof and retrieved his telescope. Encrusted now with dust and the weathering work of sea wind, it had sat forlorn since the night of his impressment.

"Hello, old friend." His voice was as rusty as the telescope, so little did he have occasion to speak. But he strapped it onto his back, determined to give it new life. "Come with me. There's someone I'd like you to meet."

A vague thought tugged at him, telling him he'd lost his head, talking to a telescope and carrying it off to a woman beneath ground. He laughed dryly, shaking his head. Life was a wonder, that it could spin into such a tale.

At the threshold of the servant's exit the night air drew him. He drank it in as if it were life, so unaccustomed was he to being inside. Still, something stopped him. The silence called him back to corridors that had once thundered in battle, halls that bore echoes of fencing matches long silent . . . and to his father — the man who had commanded a fleet and the respect of a nation but who had missed the son beneath his own roof.

Frederick's chest ached. Everything in him told him to press on away from Edgecliffe, to never look back.

But something summoned him back — the same thing that had driven him to ring the bells for the shepherd, to till the soil with the farmers, to march before the magistrates for Elias. The silent voice, so strong in him that he had begun to recognize the tender grip of it as being heaven born.

Go to him.

So he did. Back into the labyrinth he stole, turning and turning, first to his father's empty bedchamber, and then into the heart of his study.

In the room hung dark, thick sorrow. The embers of a fire lay in the hearth, and a form so altered he barely recognized The Admiral slumped over in his chair, a nearly drained glass of brandy at his elbow.

A deep sorrow like he had never known split through Frederick, blindsiding him unexpectedly. In Frederick's disgrace, the proud man had lost his last hope at continued prestige for their family in his cherished Royal Navy. And worse, Frederick had muddied the distinguished family name.

A shrouded rectangle loomed on the wall. It called to him, luring him until he lifted the drop cloth that veiled it.

It was him. His portrait. He hardly recognized himself, for the proud look the artist had given him, with his hand tucked inside the navy cutaway jacket and bicorn hat perched like a great black crown. Brass buttons gleamed as if heaven itself shone upon him, declaring a bright future. He was a stranger, the man in this depiction. All of his father's hopes wrapped up in that shell of a man.

The artist had gotten one thing right, though. There was a longing in his dark eyes. Hunger, ambition — like any good man of the sea, his father might say. But the truth of it reverberated straight through Frederick. It was the expression of a man cut loose. Without home, without family, without belonging.

And he knew right then — through his trial, Juliette's heroic rescue, and the birth of a babe — all that had changed.

He turned, taking in the scene spread before him. Newspapers piled upon the empty chair across from Father, where Frederick had once sat. The chess table stood just as it had on the night of his impressment . . . but for one marked difference. The ebony square where his pawn had been poised to overtake Father's king . . . was empty.

"You'll distinguish yourself, Frederick. Don't look so doubtful. The house of Hanford is intended for great things, and this is your path. And one day you shall inherit all I possess."

All of his father's hopes, dashed. Silently, carefully, Frederick retrieved the black poker and stoked the embers, placing a log upon them until it glowed with warming flame. This smallest act, at least, he could offer.

Frederick reached out and hovered his hand over his father's, so close he could feel its warmth. He looked older, much older, than warranted by the eight years elapsed since his father had suspended their match. How much of that was Frederick's fault?

He moved to retract his hand and ever so slightly brushed his father's fingers by accident. They opened, barely. The glow of the fire cast a tendril of light over something cradled in his father's palm.

Frederick moved, changing his angle to see better, and realized it was the pawn. There in the hand that had never reached out to take his.

A yawning ache expanded in Frederick, urging him to somehow make it all right, to breathe hope into his father's shriveling soul, to undo the great hurt that fairly pulsed in the room.

But he could not undo it. To return now would further sully the Hanford name. But perhaps there was something else he could give the man.

Traversing the long hall to his mother's conservatory, he passed through a curtain of cobwebs. This place that had once embodied light and beauty was now so unlike her. During one of his drunken benders, his father had forbidden the upkeep of the place after her passing, but he had never thought the man would let things go for so long. The years had spun gossamer webs that formed an eerie shawl about the place. Bathed in blue moonlight, it looked like an ice palace.

And there, still on the piano, was her Bible.

Hands numb, he reached out and took the book from the cobwebs' clutches. He blew off the dust, watched it fall like snow in the moonlight. Returning to his father's study, he placed it in the middle of the chess board and, with great care, plucked the small pawn from his father's fingers. He ran his thumb over its smooth, rounded surface, this relic he had last touched as a twelve-year-old so unsure of the future, of the world, of his place in it.

But rather than returning it to its place on the board, or executing that final move Father had preserved for so long, he instead laid the pawn down on the open Bible, pointing to a verse he had repeated to himself over and over while imprisoned: *Greater love hath no man than this, that a man lay down his life for his friends.*

It was not the full story. He might never be in a place where he was free to communicate the whole story, but as he snuck away from Edgecliffe, he prayed that his offering might give his father some measure of peace — and even more, some measure of hope.

He stole across the pasture, goods strapped on his back in a great awkward lump. And when he lowered himself back into the cave, stored his supplies, and laid a couple of his mother's gowns at the foot of Juliette's bed of straw when she was away walking the restless child through the corridors, he told himself once more that it was not stealing. He was no thief, taking these things from the home of his inheritance. And truly, when one considered the geography, he wasn't even removing these things from the estate, but rather relocating them to a story below. That was all.

Thirty-Six

Frederick ventured out other nights to pluck berries or procure eggs from the Edgecliffe hens betimes, but he never darkened the doors of the house again. When the first wisps of dawn floated across the sky, and the sound of sleepy sheep's bells jingled softly across the hills, he knew lights in the fishing village would soon be glowing, boats heading out to pull in nets — and it was his signal to return home.

He would lower himself through the hole, cover it over again with the tapestry of fallen branches and brambles, just one of a thousand such structures over the landscape harboring birds and squirrels. Shepherds none the wiser that a small family was living out their days in the dark beneath.

But he again corrected himself. They were not a family. If they were a family, Juliette would not try to hide her tears the way she did, by wandering to the farthest reaches of the tunnels before letting those tears fall.

If a family, he would not try to hide the widening desire within him that burned to wrap his arms about her small frame and catch those tears. As it was, he not only hid it but beat it back with everything in him, finding other ways to take care of the two souls who now lived engraved upon his very being.

After one of his nights of foraging, he dropped down to the floor of the cave room he had come to call the chapel, for it was the one place the heavens shone down into this abyss. He felt the cool of the cavern floor against his palms and remained there, crouched and staring into a puddle. When he'd first thought of this room as the chapel, he had mopped that puddle up whenever the rain trickled through the hedge and bracken above. But after a time, he began to find solace in the way it summoned bits of lantern light reflected in ripples caused by droplets descending from dew. Majesty, right there in the dark.

But as he now stared at the reflection he saw only a lost soul with dark eyes. A man with no name — for his own name was that of a man presumed dead. He and the child shared more than a cave, after all. They were both nameless. The only nameless people in all the world, perhaps. What was he doing, anyway? The woman he was sharing this life with — if a few shared meals each day could be called so — had saved his life. And what sort of life was he giving her in return? One devoid of even the most basic comforts? Devoid of joy? Robbed of . . . of love, itself?

Angry at the man in the reflection, he swiped at it and winced as something gashed his palm.

He had sought to give them life, by laying his down. How had he muddied things so badly?

Pressing his wounded hand into the other, he stared at the rippling reflection again.

That man stared back . . . and issued a challenge. *So give them your life.*

"How?" His question came out raspy. How could he help? He, a wanted man, who if he made himself known would only drag the woman and the child even farther down than he already had. And — he laughed derisively — they were living in a cave, after all, so that was a good way down.

Give them your life. Pledge it.

"I have." Had he not? He had tried. He had been ready to face the gallows for them.

And he would do so again, though Juliette had pleaded with him months back to never turn himself in. "Elias's crime required a death to pay for it," she'd said, with eyes afire. "A price that he has paid."

He could not argue against her logic, though it all seemed such a muddle. But would he trade the gallows for an altar? His life, he knew, was meant to be given for her, poured out for her. And there was only one way to do that, short of turning himself in — which she would never agree to. And even if he did, who would care for her and the babe?

Marry her.

The words ricocheted off of the walls, pounding him with preposterousness.

She would never have him. Why would she? He was the reason her husband was gone. He was the one warned never to speak to her again, all those years ago.

"I cannot do that to her," he said, silencing the earlier echoes with defiance.

But as hard as he fought it, the questions hovered around every corner. *Why can you not? How can you not?* It was the unseen thread that cinched tight the space between them as she insisted she bind the open wound on his palm, tying the bandage off and brushing his palm with her thumb, lingering a moment longer than he could account for.

The shadow of this question — *How can*

you not? — chased him across the moor as he foraged supplies. And it was the incessant pounding of it that kept him company as he built for her the one thing he had to give, besides his life.

He worked among the brambles under the cover of darkness, pulling branches off the hillside and into walls that disguised his entry and exit to and from the earth. He harvested more berry brambles from the wild, transplanted them over hill and dale, to become living walls. A room he hoped Juliette could emerge into with some measure of cover.

One night, when he dropped down from his preparations, she looked at him with surprise and asked, "What are you wearing?"

Until that day he'd worn only houseservants' clothing he'd pilfered from the manor, not quite ready to wear the fieldworker's clothing he'd also collected from their place hidden beneath the base of his wardrobe. They had been oversized on his wiry body when, as a boy, he had procured the shirt and pants from an Edgecliffe gardener, who had only shrugged and handed them over when Frederick had asked for an old pair of his clothing. They fit him now as he summoned the old remembered motions of breaking earth to plant things.

Juliette laughed. "Did you rob the gardener's shack?"

Dropping his gaze, he wondered how much to tell her. "They're mine," he said simply, planning to leave it at that.

"Yours," she said, shaping the word like the mystery it was. "But why? When would you have worn clothing such as those?"

She was asking in, asking to be a part of his story, or at least to understand it.

She studied him, her eyes wide, expectant.

"You remember that morning your father brought me to your home," he said.

She nodded, somber.

"You . . . and he . . . and even Elias and your mother gave me a taste for what it meant to do good work. To be tired from it. To see something changed because of the toil of your hands. Once I got a bit older, it made me want to understand more." He went on, telling her of the tenant farmers he had come to work with, becoming plain old Fred. The other workers giving the nickname Rivers, soggy string bean that he'd been after falling into the River Welden that first day in the field.

She looked shocked . . . and then narrowed her eyes. "You mean to say you took payment from the very farmers who were already paying your father exorbitant amounts of money to farm the land they poured their very souls into?"

The girl could jump to conclusions faster than sparks flew from fire. Though he had witnessed a kind and tender side of her, she still had the fury of the wind, too. A passion for justice.

"You could put it that way," he said. "Though I did have worthy use for that money." She needed not know why.

But he should have known better. Juliette Flint was not one to let something go so easily. She took a step closer, the tendrils of unanswered questions pulling her in. "What could you have needed the pay of a hired hand for?" She shook her head, her questions void of any bitterness or incredulity now. Only true wondering.

He did not want to tell her. 'Twould spoil the bells for her, knowing the man who paid to have them rung was the man responsible for her father's death in the first place.

Above them, floating down through the branch-covered window to the sky, the church bell tolled eight o'clock. He gripped the shovel tighter, clenched his jaw more, willed away the heat rising to his face.

And she, hearing the bells, seeing his manner, understood. He saw it on her face. The surprise of her eyebrows. The narrowing and then softening of her eyes. The tilting of her head.

"It was you," she breathed. "The bells." And when he did not answer, she had her reply. She shifted the babe to her other side, and placed a hand on his arm. "All along, it was you," she said, tears rimming those lingering eyes.

He met her gaze and gave a single nod. "He deserved much more."

A tear broke loose from those pooling upon her lashes.

He lifted his hand, and caught one as it coursed down her cheek.

"I didn't know if it would matter," he said. "Ringing them every year."

"It did. It does." She sniffed, her jaw warm in his hand. "It meant the world, Frederick."

She lingered there long that night, the silence comfortable. After that, a slow warmth sprinkled their interactions, growing and growing, summoning the calling pounding inside of him: *Pledge yourself. Give yourself.*

And so one night, after watching, and waiting, and observing the heavens for the brightest moon — since it was all the jewel he was prepared to offer her — he brought

Juliette Flint and her six-month-old daughter up to the house of brambles and he cloaked them in a blanket beneath the high moon. Standing here beside them, as she turned slowly to take in the low hedges, the makeshift table, and chairs of odd-sized stumps he had rolled into place, he saw how rudimentary his offering was. Childlike, even. It had felt grandiose as he built it, but now he felt his face burn, felt the veil drop away and saw only prickly thorns and remnants of trees long dead . . . and Juliette taking it all in, clothed in the gown of a lady of the manor.

The contrast was enough to silence him. For as much as her lack of reaction smote him, what was to come would be the nails in the coffin. But he must speak the words. It had become his very heartbeat. If ever a man knew what thing he must do, it was this — here and now.

Juliette spoke. "What is this place?"

He tried to weigh her tone, find any trace of distaste there. But it was clear and open, a simple question. With no simple answer.

Frederick beheld the dark soil, so recently upturned as he transplanted the hedges. In the distance, Edgecliffe loomed against the stars. "This place," he began, "is everything it should not be."

Juliette tilted her head in a question.

He filled his lungs, and began to explain the impossible. "I . . . I meant to give you a safe, happy home with Elias, and I have not. I meant to give you my inheritance, and now I cannot. If I had a good name to offer you, I-I would."

He felt heat grip his throat, doubt pressing back the words. But he saw understanding in her wide, round eyes — she knew what he meant. There was no turning back now. Had there ever been? Since that day her father gathered him up and gave him life? Was his life not one long unfolding of giving to Juliette Flint? It seemed so to him now, looking back. And down in his very soul it seemed . . . right. His chest pumped, pushing blood through him, urging him on to do what he had been born to do.

He swallowed. "Juliette, all I have is the air in my lungs, the work of my hands. Not even the soil beneath us is mine any longer. To join yourself to such a person would surely be . . ." He shook his head, the admission coming so much faster and easier than anything else he had yet spoken. "It would be madness. But if it is a madness you can bear" — he dropped to his knees and took her hand — "I offer myself to you. I do not ask for love. I know to whom your heart belongs. And I will guard that."

Breath was short and quick in his lungs. The soil was damp against his knees. She pulled her hand from his, but her gaze did not leave him. He felt her eyes upon him but could not bring himself to lift his eyes to meet her stare.

Behold her. The pumping in his chest commanded it — and the pull of her eyes summoned it. Until he turned his face toward hers, and what he saw there took his breath. It was not refusal. Neither was it assent. It was not, thanks be to God, horror.

It was . . . searching. As if she were peeling back the layers of him. Letting him sink into her soul, considering what she felt there.

And he waited. He had not felt such a thing since that day so long ago when he'd sat at her family's fireside. It was . . . what it meant to be seen. To have one's heart held. *"To be known is no shame,"* her mother had told him.

And suddenly, everything in him ached to hold Juliette's heart — the one he understood as well as his own, having lived in a single, intertwined heartbeat for month upon month upon spellbinding, otherworldly month. The little fingers and toes and laughs and cries of the stowaway stitching their hearts together.

"You would marry me, Frederick?"

He tried to read her voice, her face, the way she held the sleeping child, whose arms draped over her shoulder. Juliette's thumb stroked back and forth across the child's frock she'd fashioned out of one of his mother's old dresses. He wondered what Mother would think if she could see her garments now, wrapping a sunbeam, a wee bundle of light.

"I would." His voice husky with sincere longing and desperate conviction. "But even if you refuse, I will give my life in any fashion to make a place for you, and for the stowaway." He pinned his hands to his side, though he wished with everything in him to reach out, let his hand land upon the wee girl's back . . . the touch of a father.

Oh, the terror that shot through him then. What if Juliette banished him? The stowaway had wended her way into Frederick's heart until it was impossible to imagine a world without her pure, sweet presence.

"I will make a way to take you north of here. Or sail you away to Australia, or America, or . . . or anywhere, to give you both a life. Someplace she can run in the sunshine."

He shook his head slowly, the ache inside

of him growing. "This girl was made for the sun, and the sun for her. She cannot grow up in hiding, slinking about smugglers' tunnels, never knowing what it is to breathe fresh, bright air. And neither should you be confined to such a life, Juliette. So be it by marriage, or be it by working the rest of my life to make a new place for you, I will get you away from here," he said, resolve shaking his voice.

Juliette's eyes moved over him, following his hand as he, at last, reached out and stroked the babe's slim shoulder. It hurt him that she was such a twig of a thing. She should be dining on custards and cakes and every good thing that could brighten a little girl's world.

"D'ye not know, Frederick?" She curved the question downward in a melody.

His eyes stung. "Know what?"

"These months . . . this home ye've made for us. The cradle, the space you fashioned for her to one day run free in these depths . . . and now this place." She laid her hand upon his, where the babe's soft breathing rose and fell beneath their tentatively locked fingers.

"Ye've given us *life,* Frederick."

Her words fell like dew upon a parched land, the soil of his heart marked with the dark spreading hope of them.

He cleared his throat to loosen his voice, frozen in disbelief. "I brought you stale food and stolen clothing, and you dwelled in a hovel. You deserve so much more. You deserve everything, Juliette." And it was true. She did. The girl who had been light to him from the moment he awakened to her curious face, haloed in wild, sun-gilt hair as he lay ill by her fire. She had been the sun to him.

He forced himself to stand straight, await her refusal, and rest in the knowledge that he would at least have offered everything. He would swallow his doubts, his fears, his pride, to surrender all.

"D'ye not hear me?" She laughed. "Ye've given us a palace, where we were destined for a poorhouse. Life, when the world would have nothin' to do with us. And more than all of that . . . ye've already given us yourself. Every day, and every night, and every moment in between."

She cast her face toward the moon, and its light baptized her. She closed her eyes and basked in it, as if it held the warmth of the day.

Perhaps she did not understand. Perhaps, after all, he needed to say the words more clearly. To spit them out, clunky as they were.

"Juliette." He rested his eyes upon hers, long and deep. "Will you have me to be your husband?"

Silence knocked the ends right out of the box of their small world. It stretched itself out like a drawbridge, ushering in the sounds of the surf, of the frogs in a nearby farm pond, singing their great gulping chorus, which sounded suddenly like a symphony when stacked up against his clumsy speech.

He dropped his gaze, understanding. The silence was her answer. She was too gracious to say it outright. "I understand," he said. "And I will find a way to make a home for you both. Somewhere you'll be safe — known only for your true selves and not the story that marks you here. I will leave you be, but will make plans for your provision."

He went on, naming the port he would sail from for Australia. There was work there, he had seen in a leaflet. He named the solicitor he would entrust his pay to, to be passed on to her. The details rattled out with ease — for it did not cost him what his ill-fated proposal had.

But Juliette's touch to his face stopped him.

Those eyes — the ones that had always held fire in them — beheld him with depth that left nowhere to hide. He had laid bare his soul, and in this touch, she was reaching through the walls that divided them and gathering that soul up.

"I will," she said.

The flood of sound about them seemed to ebb, to pull back and let her words shimmer in the night. But surely she did not mean . . .

"You will . . . go?"

She shook her head. "I will marry you, Frederick." The way she said his name — she was trying it on, deliberate kindness there. It was not the love of the ages, with the passion or spunk she had as a girl with Elias. But it was something chosen. And by the steady light in her eyes, something true.

The parish priest wed them that week. They came to him quietly of an evening, knocking on his door in humble clothes, no wedding laces or top hats, but with a friend in tow — procured from a ship in port several towns away. It was clear what he surmised of their circumstances, babe in arms and not a penny to their names. But bless the man, he congratulated them on doing what was right in the eyes of God and asked no further questions, not even mentioning the publishing of banns for the customary three weeks.

"I've seen the oldest story, redeemed by the ancient story, more times than I can count. Each one a miracle," he said.

He wed Juliette and Fred Rivers in a chapel beneath the ground. The priest, so taken with it, promised to protect their secret, claiming he would record the location as annex to the chapel. It would always be a holy place, where the kindly man had united two battered souls. There was only one witness to the humble ceremony. A man accustomed to the writing of ballads, who had watched their story from near beginning and vowed to see it kept for the ages.

"Promise me you won't tell," Frederick said, clutching the man's parchment when he brought quill to it as the moon rose that night. "It must never be known," he said. "Or they'll be ruined."

Killian Blackaby raised a finger, a twinkle in his eye. "My life has but one mission, my boy — to find a ballad for the ages, to preserve it. But it does not follow that I shall make it known. All shall be cloaked, all shall be veiled."

And so they'd lived on, Blackaby returning to the sea, and the small Rivers family hoping against hope that he would be true to his word.

THIRTY-SEVEN

How does a world shift? Frederick did not know, but he felt it tilt and upend, as surely as the dawn he rarely saw. Outside, cannons blazed in the ongoing war, parliament raged, matrimonial matches maneuvered in ballrooms, and ships upon seas traversed the world. And yet here in the belly of the earth . . . all he felt was air. All he saw was light. And oh, did the light deepen, for he knew he should never have been afforded this time.

When they had been wed a number of weeks, he rounded a corner and spotted Juliette lying on her side on her bed, with the stowaway nestled on her arm. Her finger traced her little girl's cheek, softly, slowly, as though the act might infuse the child with all the strength and fight Juliette feared she would need in her life.

It became suddenly hard for Frederick to swallow. Retreating, he pressed himself against the corridor, unsure why it should matter whether she knew he'd seen that tenderness toward his daughter. His *daughter* — heaven be praised for such a mercy. Awakening sprang up in him at the miracle of it.

And that awakening soon took on a life of its own. It quickened at the unlikeliest times. When Juliette dropped down from the garden room one night trailing dirt behind her, she held out her cupped hands and offered freshly picked berries — her favorite thing, given to him. The night air had enlivened her whole spirit. He felt it. He saw it on her face. When she stomped her feet to shake the soil loose from her boots, he froze. In the lantern light, he saw that she'd slipped her small feet into his large boots, and worn them into the garden.

"What?" she said, her eyes smiling. "Lacing boots is the most perfect waste of time in the world. Yours are big on me. All I have to do is pull them on. See?" She tromped down the corridor, clunking clumsily, and turning to rest her hands on her hips while she beamed with pride. "No lacing needed."

He laughed, and the laughter dug that contented place inside of him deeper and wider. Would she have touched his boots with even a rotting branch a year or two before? Never. And now here she was, wearing them, and laughing.

Her garden trips grew more frequent. One night, with his boots strapped on about her tiny feet, and the baby asleep in the cradle, she clutched a basket and made to go up for berries again. At the arch leading away from their respective caverns and into the tunnel, she paused, hand on the wall, and turned.

"Come," she said. So simply, just dropping the single syllable into the night as naturally as one of the drops from the spring rains.

He set his book down, leaned forward. Surely he had not heard right.

"Or don't," she said, and shrugged. She disappeared around the corner, her footsteps receding into the echoing yonder. He dashed after her. There, where the night sky spilled starlight down into the dark of the earth, she turned. "Coming with me?"

"Yes," he sputtered, hating the way his face flushed at how fast he'd spoken. But he never imagined that Juliette Flint — Juliette *Rivers* — would invite him to join her, unless she meant to trick him into falling into a volcano. But she was not that same girl — and he was not that same boy.

Above ground, silence settled over them

easily. The earth struck up a quiet song of night herons, wind through the heather beyond, and the steady soft landing of berries in a basket. Soon even that fell silent.

Frederick looked to her, saw grief written upon her face as she beheld the stars.

At last, she spoke. "Do you ever wonder . . . about him?"

"Yes." He did not need an explanation. He knew exactly who she meant. "Every day."

Juliette turned to face him, eyes pooling. "What happened?" Two words that surely required immeasurable amounts of courage, for the way they laid bare every fortress wall she had constructed around the subject of Elias. As she'd said them, he'd felt the laying down of something.

Frederick inhaled. Closed his eyes. When he opened them again, she was searching him, biting her lip.

"Come." He gestured to the cracked-log bench beneath the budding lilac. She followed and sat.

For this tale he did not feel right sitting next to her, nor standing before her, nor sitting on the ground. So he sat on a nearby low boulder, careful not to let his knees touch hers, though their distance was so close he felt her warmth.

"Elias . . . he just . . . He fell, I think."

Juliette narrowed her eyes, nodding, inviting more, asking him for the specifics he did not wish to hurt her with. He spoke of his friend's radiance upon receiving her letters. He spoke of the way his soul seemed to double in size when he learned he would be a father. He told of the way the past came biting at his heels — how Frederick watched him fight it back, as if he held a club in his hands. Yet the battle bloodied him, the lies and doubts thick like soupy fog, and the lure of the smugglers' city drew him.

"And he was caught," she said.

Frederick nodded. "It was a slow fall, at first. And he did fight it. But he believed one small lie, and it led to another, and another. One lie at a time, one step at a time, until he was there at the gates of the City of Smugglers. I believe with everything in me, Juliette, that had someone asked him first thing, straight out, to go to the city and take those documents, he would have refused. He would've revolted at the thought. But it started with smaller things, which bigger things built on again and again, until the big betrayal no longer felt like a plunge to him. It was a small — almost natural — next step."

Frederick had spent the past months reliving every moment of it all, piecing together the fall of Elias, wondering what he could have done differently, haunted by the terror in his friend's eyes, and he heard himself speak it again in the telling to Juliette. *"Take me,"* he'd said. Elias had shaken his head violently, and Frederick had silenced him with a look of steady determination.

"I knew some of it," she said. "From Killian Blackaby, the day of your trial. But not all. What made you do it?"

Frederick leaned forward, resting his elbows on his knees as he looked at the ground. He did not wish to bring her more pain. But he knew her now, knew she would see right through him if he gave her less than the truth.

"That day . . . when your father found me under the yew tree."

"You think of that, still?"

"I think of it always. The boy he found had nothing."

She watched him. She could have scoffed at his claim so easily. But she did not scoff, and to him that spoke volumes.

White clouds veiled the stars above in wisps. "That boy had only a heart so heavy he could not carry it any longer. He did not know where to go, what to do, what his place in this world was." He spoke of yearning to do something that mattered, but he did not know what that could be in a world where he seemed always to be shuffled into corners or bellowed at. When his mother, his one good thing, was taken by fever, he'd had nothing left. And so *he* left.

"I imagine that shepherd thought he was simply helping a lost lad. What he did not know — what I wish he *had* known — was the moment he saw him and stopped and laid aside everything in order to carry that boy to a good place . . . he moved heaven and earth. He gave me hope."

Juliette watched on solemnly, when Frederick raised his head to meet her gaze, opened her hand a moment, motioned for him to continue.

"That is why I did it. I begged God beside your father's grave, asked Him to take me into the earth instead of him. To bring you life once more and help me somehow make it right."

"Seems your prayers were answered," she said, softly, earnestly.

Frederick thought back to what he had said. "Aye, he did take me into the earth after all. Thanks to you." He gave a sad laugh.

Juliette opened her mouth, but apparently

thought better of whatever she had meant to say, and waited for him to continue.

"I took your father's life," he said.

Juliette shook her head slowly. "Frederick, no. We were just children. 'Twas a sickness that took many a life. Yes, I blamed you, but . . . well, it was Elias who showed me you had lost your mother to the same fever, that you nearly lost your own life, too. We could not know, for certain, from whence came Father's affliction. I should never have blamed you."

Frederick searched her, words failing.

"You mean that, Juliette?"

"I do," she said, conviction lacing the words with resolute truth.

Frederick shook his head. "Thank you." He did not know whether he would ever be as sure as she that the shepherd's death was not his doing. But her words embodied grace he had not known his soul longed for.

He continued. "I thought . . . if I could give your child a chance to know her father . . . though it send me to the ends of the earth, or cost me my very life, I would do it. In an instant. Just like that kind shepherd did for me."

"And you did that very thing." Her words were hushed. "Frederick, Elias burned hard and fast at whatever he did. Father saw that early on and worried for him. He used to say all that burn would run his candle out before his time."

This Frederick agreed with.

"It was not your fault, Frederick."

Frederick's every muscle froze, every bone so still for fear of destroying these words she spoke. He dared not ask what she meant, for it shamed him that there were so very many things she could be referring to. Her father . . . her husband . . . the fact that her only company now was once her sworn enemy . . . the fact that she — and her child, for heaven's sake — lived in obscurity in a cave.

She reached across the dark and grabbed his hand, and in the reaching bridged two universes, broke right through their barriers and cast a fortress of truth around him.

"You have done well," she said. "Elias is — was — what Father said. He was a fire burning hot and fast. And most of the time, it was good. I loved him for that."

Frederick laughed. "Aye. Did he ever tell you of the time he gave two midshipmen the scare of their lives?"

The look of surprise and doubt on her face told him no. He laughed, recounting the way some of the older lads had taken to stealing blankets right off of sleeping sailors in the middle of the night, using fishhooks and twine.

"After they stole mine and I spent the next two nights shivering in my hammock, he decided to strike back. He made a deal with the cook and collected all the chicken feathers he could. Then he stitched them inside his own blanket and waited. When they stole his blanket, he pretended to be asleep. And when the culprits fell asleep, one of them draped in my blanket, one in Elias's, Elias crept over and pulled the thread out that he'd closed his blanket up in, drizzled treacle over the fellow's face and hair and clothes, and snuck back into his own hammock. He was asleep within a minute."

Juliette narrowed her eyes. "What happened?"

"When the fellow's watch came, he flung his blanket aside, and a cloud of feathers billowed into the night, falling all over him and sticking to the treacle." Frederick laughed, remembering the way lantern light had ringed the falling feathers in yellow light as they floated every which way, mocking him. "He was picking feathers out of his hair for three days. And our blankets mysteriously reappeared in their rightful hammocks."

She laughed, and it was good. Music in

the dark night. "I can see it," she said. "That was Elias, sure as the sun do rise." Her smile met his.

It was good to remember his friend this way — for this part of Elias was no less true than the choice he made in the end.

Juliette sighed. "He did not often speak to me of life on the ship."

Frederick leaned forward, resting his chin on hands fisted around themselves. If he could but keep this moment for her, stretch it out long, for her. "What did he speak of?"

She shook her head, smiling, her cheeks creasing with warm remembrance. "Dreams. You knew him. Surely he filled your head with the same dreams. Dreams of the farm. Never did a man dream such grand dreams for a sheep farm." Her eyes creased into a gentle smile. "Do you know he thought we would one day supply wool for King George?" She shook her head. "And always, above all, that ridiculous dream he got in his head to make for the Windward Isles."

Their laughter sobered at the mention of the land that had meant so much to him, swayed his choices — and in some ways, perhaps, taken his life.

"Do you know how we met?" She raised her eyes, rolling a pebble between her finger and thumb.

Frederick searched his memory. "Do you know, for all the tales he told me, he never recounted that one."

She smiled. "It was my fault."

"You say that like it was a catastrophe." He meant to offer it as a jest, to lighten her heart. But a pensive look flashed across her features.

"I do wonder sometimes," she said.

He reached for words to amend, to invite the tale. "He mentioned that your father became like a father to him."

"Aye, he did look out for him when he was small. But after that, when he was older, he tumbled into our lives again. I was on the roof, you see."

He froze, every sense suddenly fixed on Juliette. The roof was his place.

He cleared his throat. "Wh-which roof?"

"The spring cellar," she said, as if it should have been the only apparent answer. "I used to go up there sometimes, to be away from things. To be closer to the clouds."

He pictured her there, across the pastures, him upon his roof to be away from things, closer to the stars. Perhaps she was not as foreign a being as he had judged her back then.

"I was meant to fly that day," she continued. "I'd been watching the gulls off the cliffs, and decided that if they could do it, why shouldn't I? I dug through our attic to find something for wings. The only thing I could find was an old pair of Father's long johns. I snipped and stitched and patched until I had the most horrific looking pair of threadbare wings a body ever saw, and I climbed up to the top of the roof from the hill that covers behind it, and —"

"You talked sense into yourself and climbed back down?"

"Clearly you did not know young Juliette well."

He laughed. "A body can hope."

"Well, she jumped." Her eyes were wide, her words rounded, emphasizing.

"So you did fly."

"If by *fly,* you mean, 'nearly squash the boy dashing by to bury smuggled beans in the woods beyond,' then yes, I did fly that day."

Frederick studied her. "He broke your fall."

Juliette nodded. "Though he used to say I was the one to break his fall. Him dropping the outlawed things in order to take me up. Always seein' a deeper meaning in things, he was."

"You broke his fall," he said with conviction. He would affirm that for Elias until the day he died. "Though you gave up your flight to do it, you broke that fall."

She smiled sadly. "That's just it, though. I don't know that I gave up the flight. I guess I would say that was the place the flight began, that life with him."

Frederick studied her, captivated. What he would give, to set her to flight once more. "I have an idea," he said, offering a hand to help her up, walking her back toward the tunnels. "Meet me tomorrow morning, back at the *Jubilee*."

Thirty-Eight

Frederick had worked the night through, securing rigging and making sure it was safe. It had been long since he'd done this himself — not since he was a powder monkey, really. He now paced the deck with the stowaway in his arms, laughing aloud at the open-mouthed smile she saved just for him. "Where is your mum?" he asked. "What's taking her so long?"

"What's taking me so long are these." Juliette emerged from the captain's quarters. "It's been a deal of time since I wore something like this," she said, tugging at a rope that cinched the old trousers tight around her waist.

Frederick tried to stifle a laugh but could not.

"What's so funny?"

"Nothing," he said, regaining composure. "It's just been a deal of time since I saw you in something like that. Last I saw you in trousers, you were ten years old and had just finished piloting Mr. Swain's cutter."

"Just an imp," she said.

He recalled the way her hair had stuck out from beneath her cap, her freckles setting green eyes vividly afire. "A captivating imp," he said.

Her cheeks grew rosy at that. "Now. What are we doing?"

Frederick set the stowaway down in the barricade he'd fashioned for her of crates, where she set to a string of happy cooing as she played.

"Up there." He pointed to where the crow's nest — the half not used for the cradle — was lashed afresh to the mast. "There's something up there you should see." He offered his hand there on the rigging, and she only looked at him, head tilted as if he had lost his last bit of sanity.

"Offerin' help to the damsel, are ye?" she asked, a twinkle in her eye. "Have ye forgotten which of us sailed this old girl here to begin with?"

"Right." Frederick laughed. "I won't tell you how long it took me to get to where I didn't flop like a fish from the rigging."

She laughed, genuinely enjoying herself. It seemed so, anyway, and he prayed it to be true.

"Come on, then." He led the way, she racing up the netting beside him. He sped up, giving her a challenge, and the look of sheer delight on her face was priceless.

At the top of the rigging, he gripped a rope. It was a line running from the main mast nearly to the bow. Half the length of the ship, from crow's nest to deck. The beating in his chest grew louder, both from exercise and anticipation.

She was all curiosity now. Something in the way the corners of her mouth turned up . . . it seemed hope, too, might live there.

"When we first met, you told your father the day you were mistress of the land would be the day you could fly."

She narrowed her eyes, searching her memory. He watched as she landed upon the conversation from the day of the mud fight. "How do you recall such a thing?"

"*You* said it," he said, dropping his voice. "I remember everything about you, Juliette."

Her study of him made him self-conscious, and he moved on quickly. "You've married the master and have no home. You are mistress of the land and live beneath it. Your child shall have a home there, if ever I can find a way back, find a way to make our name right for her again. But until then . . . there is yet one thing I might do."

She waited, and he slid his hand behind her back, wrapping the rope gently there, feeling her against his arm and using every bit of self-control not to pull her closer. He unfolded her fingers, pressed them closed about the rope.

"Fly," he said.

She took the rope with a wary look in her eye. "You're mad."

"At sea we called it skylarking," he said. "You've the trousers for it. If you take hold with your knees, the rope shan't burn your hands. But just in case . . ." He took her hands. They were cold, and could it be — was she shaking? He looked around, noticing the torn sail hanging limply beside them. Picking it up, he tore one strip and then another. He reached out his hand, pausing before his fingers brushed hers, seeking permission in her eyes.

She swallowed. The slightest of nods. His fingers touched hers, and they were surprisingly soft. She, the wind in human form, was human, after all. He slid his palm beneath hers, lifting it, and began to wrap. Layer overlapping layer, until the ragged sail cloaked her hands, readying her for flight. He clasped her other hand and did the same, then, her hands in his, wrapped her fingers around the rope. Her hair brushed his chin, and her small form was warm next to his. His arms, which had cradled her babe but had never so much as brushed her shoulder, ached as if they were near home.

And they burned then, as he stepped back instead. Slowly.

When she looked over her shoulder, girlish anticipation on her face, he nodded. She shuffled her small feet close to the edge of the platform, her shoulders raised as she filled her lungs . . . and in an instant, she was gone.

He nearly slammed himself across the crow's nest, to see the wind in human form take flight. As he watched her closing her eyes, smile spreading, the world seemed to slow. Her hair flew behind her as her hands and knees skimmed the rope that guided her toward deck, her spirit soaring.

The aching in his arms grew, spreading deep into his chest as he clambered back down the rigging to meet her.

Frederick knew not what he expected. A smile, he hoped. Perhaps one of her conviction-laced declarations about her flight.

Never in a thousand years would he have dared dream of encountering a Juliette whose entire trouser-clad, wild-haired being seemed to drink him in as he approached.

But she did.

He slowed, meeting that gaze. Daring to let the depth of longing in his soul, hidden painstakingly for so long, to show at last.

Without a word she stopped, toe-to-toe with him. Wordlessly waiting, eyes sparking — air between them sparking, too.

Time stopped there in the cave as Frederick circled her slowly, deliberately in his arms. And when she did not pull away — when, indeed, she entered into his embrace until he could feel his wife's heartbeat against his own — he lowered his lips to hers.

Here they were. Two souls, buried alive beneath the earth, beside the sea, in a place of nowhere — an empty cave that felt impossibly full as Juliette took flight where there was no sky.

This was a place of impossible.

And what a beautiful impossible it was.

Thirty-Nine

2020

Twenty-one days. Twenty-one days of her thirty permitted had passed since Lucy had gone before the committee, full of hopes and fully convinced the *Jubilee* lay at the bottom of a sea trench. And a mere three days since the dearest friend of her heart had taken her into his arms . . . and right into his heart.

So much had changed, not the least of which was that she seemed connected, somehow, to the *Jubilee.* On a professional level, yes, but it was more than that. Looking back, it was clear her parents had been dogged in their commitment to give Dash and her a strong foundation to open their minds to seemingly impossible things being possible. Why? And why had a painting of the sea stacks from Edgecliffe been stowed beneath their floorboards?

Was it crazy to think her attachment to

the *Jubilee* had not been a coincidence, that they had been planting seeds all along, watering them through their stories?

She had left her cozy "home" in the chill of the early morning to walk among the ruins again. Sheep's bells and gentle bleating mingled with gulls were sweet sounds for pondering.

A footfall sounded behind her and she turned. "Sophie," she said, surprised.

The woman stood in chaps and riding boots, her hair pulled back into a long braid. She had a timeless sort of beauty about her, one that belied the rugged strength she demonstrated every day running this farm.

"I saw you out walking," Sophie said.

Lucy could not read her voice. It sounded gruff, as usual, but the woman held out a red plaid wool blanket. "It's a cold morning," she said. "You'll be wanting that."

She turned to go.

"Sophie." Lucy stopped her, not quite sure what she wanted to say. "Thank you. For the blanket. And . . . for letting me stay at the farm so long."

Sophie nodded. She lingered, as if she had something to say, too.

"You be careful," she said.

Lucy looked around at the ruins. They didn't seem treacherous, but Sophie knew better than she. "I will."

"Good. That's good. And . . . be careful with him." She nodded toward Dash's tiny house in the distance, tucked beneath the ancient yew tree.

Lucy understood. Sophie had lost much, and Dash had become like a son to her. A son who had also lost much, and whom she did not want to see hurt.

Lucy nodded. "Dash is . . . one of a kind." She meant it with all her heart.

"He is at that." Sophie looked as if she might say more but stopped.

Lucy felt a wavering connection and did not want to let that vanish. "Is he very much like him?" she asked, praying to God she was not presuming. "Your son, I mean."

Sophie pursed her lips, standing straighter, looking out over the sea, considering.

For a long time, Lucy thought she might not speak.

"No. And yes. In some ways. Jesse was . . . I've never seen so much life in a single soul," she said. "Except in his father."

She remembered the wedding picture — the man who looked so kind, the way Sophie beamed at him. "I'm so sorry for your losses," she said, wishing there were words that did not sound so . . . cliché. But she meant them, truly.

"Yes, I am, too. Every day. But the losses would have been greater if I'd never known them. That's the gift of it all," she said. "That's what I told myself when we were married. I knew his time would be short and that there was a chance he would pass his condition on to any children we might have. But . . ."

"Numbers have nothing to do with how extraordinary something is," she murmured, remembering her conversation with Dash.

Sophie darted her assessing gaze to Lucy, reading her.

Lucy considered how best to explain. "I just mean . . . in a world where everything is measured, calculated, sometimes we miss the biggest blessings of all."

Sophie jutted her chin out. "Yes, you could say that. And I'd do it a thousand times over again for the gift of loving those two men. No matter how short the time. A single life can make more of a difference than we can possibly imagine." When Lucy agreed, Sophie's manner softened, and she crossed the rubble to stand overlooking the sea stacks. Lucy held the painting in her hand, and she half hid it now, uncertain of how to explain her possession of such a thing.

But Sophie did not miss much. "What's that?"

Lucy, with no other explanation to offer, showed her.

"Remarkable," she said, turning the aged paper in her hands gently. "How old do you think it is?"

Lucy had wondered that, too, and had done some research on the paper used. "A century or two old, I'd guess."

"Is that all," Sophie muttered. Lucy looked askance at her and was rewarded with a rare half smile.

She explained where she'd found it, and her father's recommendation of Stone's Throw Farm to Dash. How it all seemed too interconnected to be coincidental.

"Hmmm. Well, anything is possible. That's what he used to tell you, right?"

And she was off, leaving Lucy to ponder. Leaving Lucy to jolt upright when the thought struck — how had Sophie known what Father used to tell her?

She ran from the rubble out onto the moor. "Sophie!" she called after the woman who had seemingly vanished without a trace. "Mental note," Lucy said. "Find out what Sophie knows."

Walking east along the cliff, Lucy pulled a paper from her pocket — she'd written down Killian's ballad — and read it for the umpteenth time. She'd thought it a dirge, at first, with all the talk of death and laying to rest. But what if it wasn't?

There seemed to be something between the lines, but she could not pin it down.

" 'Cast thee down, cast thee up, cast thee in between . . .' " Her footfalls crunched to the rhythm of the words. She ran her finger down the page. " 'Covered is he, from deep to deep.' " She'd thought that had meant Hurd's Deep. Definitive evidence — or at least something akin to that — that she could present to the committee. But with the talk of the sisters, his secrets cloistered in their cove, the mention of Weldensea — all signs pointed to . . . well, *not* to Hurd's Deep.

She should have been crestfallen. She'd staked everything on that theory. But instead, a quickening of her spirit sped her on to the next lines of the ballad. The thrill of the chase — of solving this puzzle at last — drove her. Her pace picked up, as if she were unraveling the mystery with every step she took.

" 'The tides do come, the tides do go; The Traitor-Man did rise on them, To depths in dark sublime.' " This was the line that stumped her every time and filled her with delicious curiosity. Tides were her language, after all. But how did one rise to depths? The two seemed polar opposites.

"Think, Lucy. Think." The waves crashed against the cliffs in echo: *Think . . . think . . . think.*

The ballad spoke of burial, being covered over. But where could a vessel that large take cover, if not beneath the waters? Waters that sounded oddly near just now.

Her pace quickened, her pulse with it, the nearness of the answer just out of reach. Her toe snagged on a rock that held its grip long enough to send her sprawling headfirst toward a gaping hole in the ground.

The blowhole. White mist rushed up at her as she braced her hands, heart in her throat. Landing with a crack, she watched Killian's ballad slip through the protective grate that had just saved her from falling. The painting fluttered and spun atop the grate, and she grabbed it just as it was about to follow the ballad into the hole.

She lay frozen, shoulders heaving, eyes smarting. Two thoughts clashed like resounding cymbals, sharp and cutting:

She might have died, if not for the grate.

And she knew where the *Jubilee* was.

No. No, that wasn't possible. Was it possible? How had she not noticed before?

She took off running, straight for the yew tree and the man who lived beneath it.

Forty

Her fist was starting to throb from pounding at Dash's observatory. He must be gone. Turning to go, she stopped at the sound of an opening door. The sight of him looking at her with befuddled, half-asleep eyes smote her.

"You were asleep," she said. "I'm sorry. I'll come back later."

His hand went around her arm, stopping her with gentle warmth. "I can sleep anytime," he said. "You're almost jumping out of your skin. What's going on?"

Where to start? "I tripped at the blowhole and —"

His gentle grip around her tightened into a protective one. "Are you okay?" He braced both of her arms, looking her over. "You're okay. Are you?"

"I'm fine. But, Dash, I-I remember another one."

His brown eyes grew round in amazed

excitement. "Your dad's stories?"

She nodded quick and furious. "Remember the one about the stone carvers?"

He scratched his head. "I'm not sure . . . tell me."

She couldn't be sure whether he was feigning ignorance just to give her the chance to speak it, to hear her newly found story in her own voice, but she was happy to comply.

"We had just finished building the telescope and were out back where the shrub blocked the streetlamp, waiting for dark. You were looking so hard at the sky, like if you looked hard enough, you could peel daylight back and crack through to the distant galaxies."

Dash whistled a descending scale. "Way to be dramatic, Matchstick Girl."

She grinned, feeling the rush of adrenaline as the memories stacked up, one behind another, begging to burst to the surface. "Dad told us a riddle."

She pressed her eyes closed around the words, making sure she found the right ones before she opened her eyes again. "What do seashells, ballrooms, Winston Churchill, and hospitals have in common? You said they were all timeless British institutions. I said they all had good foundations. And Dad said they were all under the earth."

"And then you groaned and said he couldn't talk about Churchill that way," Dash said.

"Right! He said he was speaking of Churchill during the war, and that the answer came back to the stone carvers. Unseen workers of wonders. He said, 'While your stars move about the heavens, the stone carvers are hard at work in the obscure dark, carving away great swaths of stone with the simple giving of themselves.' "

Dash tilted his head. "That's . . . really specific."

"I only remember because I gave him a hard time for his dramatic descriptions of ordinary things. I finally asked him what the stone carvers were, and he said I would love it . . . because they were water."

"I remember," Dash said. "He talked about the waves hollowing out caverns from the cliffs, and drops diving into cracks where they froze and expanded —"

"And over time" — Lucy sucked in a breath — "caves were born."

"Which got turned into tunnels, and Churchill used them in wartime."

"Right. Dad went on and on. About the tunnels in the white cliffs of Dover being used for war rooms and shelters and hospitals. About a farmer and his son discovering a hole in their field far inland while trying to dig a duck pond — and how it was encrusted with shells in intricate designs, and nobody knew why. He talked about Oxford using an old salt mine to store their library books. And smugglers and pirates' lairs, and a cave in Victorian times being used to host a ball."

He laughed. She'd had no idea he had actually *been* to that ball, or at least a modern version of it, in his boyhood. The memory was so strong now, she almost could see it, and hear him, and feel how the far-off tremble of the Underground had sounded during his story, a tribute to his treatise on subterranean life.

"Just think, Lucy," he'd said. *"You sleep in a room where glass was ground down, and adhered to tiny sticks of wood. Little makers of light. Dashel, you watch planets and stars because of pieces of glass in a long metal tube. Glass placed into a device, hundreds and hundreds of years ago, all because a maker of spectacles and some schoolchildren in his shop accidentally discovered what glass could do, when lenses were stacked one upon another. Just think . . . that glass was made from heat, from fire. And now you use it to see fire in the sky."*

"Just think." Father had been on a roll. He had been hard to keep up with when he got like that. *"An entire underground shell kingdom was discovered because of a duck pond. The Dead Sea Scrolls were discovered in a cave because of a shepherd boy looking for a lost goat. I heard of a man who immigrated from Sicily to California and found the farmland useless in the heat. Do you suppose he gave up? No! He began to dig. Grottoes and tunnels for miles and acres and stories beneath ground, planting trees. Trees! Underground! Day lighting the tops of them to receive sun. An entire world in his underground trenches."* Dad had chuckled and shook his head with a smile. *"Ducks, goats, trees, caves — anything is possible. Remember that."*

"Anything is possible," Lucy said, bringing herself back to the present, and readying herself to tell Dash the most preposterous thing she had ever thought of.

"Dash . . . I think the *Jubilee* is in the sea cave." It sounded even more ridiculous spoken aloud. People would've found it by now if it were true. It could never have fit. A thousand voices told her it was impossible . . . but one echoed steadily within her: *Anything is possible.* "It could only have gotten past the sea stacks if one thing came into play."

Dash's forehead pinched. "A miracle?"

"Yes. In the form of the spring tide."

"Spring tide," Dash said, rubbing the last traces of sleepiness from his eyes. "Are you sure?"

"I'm anything but sure. But think about it. The spring tide brings the strongest high tides, with the new moon. But then there are those times when it gets taken one step further . . ."

"The earth, the new moon, and the sun all lined up perfectly during a spring tide. You're talking about a super tide."

"Or . . . ?" She waited, and he stared blankly. "A sea flood. Isn't that what they call it around here?"

Now she had his attention.

"You're the one who said you thought the local girl who vanished the night of the sea flood could be connected to the *Jubilee.* Same night, right? So?"

She shoved the picture into his hands, tapping the sea stacks. "What if . . . ?"

"What if what?"

Words were failing her. She caught her breath. "What if she helped Frederick Hanford escape? What if she somehow got on board the *Jubilee,* and they sailed her into the cave beneath Edgecliffe?"

He studied the coastline and the sea stacks in the distance. "The sea flood could have lifted them right over them. But the timing would have had to be exactly right. They would have had to know this intricate coast. So many things would have to line up, Lucy, I don't know. I hate to say it, but it seems . . ."

"Impossible?" She waited, breathless. The word had been gifted to them all their lives as a challenge. A lens to see wonder where others saw walls.

"Yeah," he said, a smile spreading slowly.

And so the plan was hatched. Borrowing Barnabas's powerboat, they would navigate the sea stacks and enter the cave.

Violette and Spencer would come along — indeed, would not have been kept from the expedition, once they were filled in.

Lucy's feet itched as she thought about the possibility the *Jubilee* was beneath them, just waiting to be rediscovered.

Forty-One

Stone's Throw Farm had gone to sleep, but Lucy's soul was a barrage of steadily marching memories. Tomorrow they would enter the cave, and she felt as if she were following bread crumbs of a tale dropped into her life every step of the way. Running through the stories in her mind, she could not sleep. They were coming, and coming, and coming after her. Knocking at her soul, lining up and waiting to be transmitted from the invisible world to the actual world.

"God is the pursuer of your heart, Lucy," Dad had said. *"He is coming, and coming, and coming after you. In every sunset, in every snatch of birdsong. In everything that stirs deep into you and makes you hungry for bigger things, eternal things. That is Him, pursuing you with tenderest grace. In the places so hard they wring your soul. In the places so beautiful they steal your breath. He is there, filling your soul, giving you breath."*

To believe these words now was frightening. For the truth of them called her out from the familiar, from the dark confines of her springhouse, to meet truth in the sky.

Lucy gripped pen and paper. An act of defiance against the voice inside her that told her to lay down her pursuit of truth. To stay in the dark, to resurrect the wall between her heart and her past.

The return of these memories was a gift. But the recollection was hard.

She climbed onto the slope of her springhouse roof, where the blades of soft grass were so long, they whispered an embrace about her as she sat.

This time it would not be Dash unraveling the story for her. He had done his work, returned what he could to her.

It was her turn now.

She closed her eyes and remembered the one story that could never have made it into Dash's compendium. The one her father had tried to tell her, his last night.

Her hand shaking, she set pen to paper . . . and wrote.

The watchmaker's time was at an end.

"Tempus custodit veritatem," he said to the girl, all grown up.

"Time is truth's keeper," she said back,

holding tightly to his hand. Not ready.

"Remember that," he said, tapping the watch in her pocket. "And remember" — his voice had been quiet, but his words were just as full of life as they had always been — "baby . . . in a cave, cradle . . . from the sky. Man . . . gives his life, and love . . . lives."

It was the ancient story. The one he'd lived with every bit of his life. He had loved Christmastime, the way it brought this Nativity tale to the top of people's hearts. "Nothing . . . is impossible."

Lucy's pen slowed on the last word, and when she lifted it, she felt the weight of this truth.

"Let that be so." She whispered her prayer into the far-off sounds of the waves that would carry her straight into the impossible when morning came.

Forty-Two

The earth seemed to shiver around Lucy. Her heart followed suit, skittering as they climbed from the blaring white of the cliff into the dark yawning of the cave. Water droplets plinking and plunking from all directions in different notes and skipping cadences mixed with the thumping of Barnabas's boat as it bobbed on the shore to spin a curious melody.

She was glad to have disembarked. Though the vessel was small enough to navigate between the sea stacks, it had been a tumultuous passage as churning surf at the stacks' bases had done its best to toss them asunder.

The cavern was massive. As her eyes adjusted, Lucy caught glimmers of light reflected from wet sheen on a ceiling far up. In a craggy arch, the ceiling spread and sloped down into walls. Lucy closed her eyes, imagining. Could an entire ship truly have landed here? There was certainly no ship here now, but wasn't that to be expected? Wreckers and storms over the years would surely have picked the old girl apart, taken her piece by piece. But surely there would be some trace, if she had been here.

The very thought dropped a veil over the scene, and she imagined the years disappearing like tendrils of sea smoke.

Dash leaned close, his arm pressing gently against hers. "Anything is possible, Matchstick Girl."

She faced him, eyes wide. He was reading her thoughts, it seemed. Or perhaps he was feeling the same thing — the sense they were stepping foot inside of Father's stories, the stories coming alive into one living, breathing thing.

He winked at her, adding that tilting jot of character to a somehow sacred scene. When they came to a rise in the cave floor, Dash offered a hand to help Lucy step up. Out of the corner of her eye she saw Spencer do the same for Violette, who eyed his hand as if to say *What's that for?* and lifted her brow. Lucy smiled. She could nearly hear Violette's silent question, *D'ye think I'm a helpless lass?*

Spencer, to his credit, took her reaction in stride, busying himself with a head torch, switching it on and then giving one to each of them.

Dash led the way, surveying the wall before them with eyes accustomed to patient study of the dark. They all stood in a line beside him, and Lucy had a vision of what they must look like, standing as if they were waiting for the stone wall itself to open before them.

She eyed Dash and saw a glimpse of the boy he'd once been in the way he stood as if awaiting the starting gun to fire at a race, his shoulders rising and falling in syncopated anticipation.

She desperately wanted to hold on to their friendship forever. To never, ever lose it — as they once had, for so long. And yet . . . she hoped even more to hear particular words from his lips, words she dared not even give name to.

Stepping forward, she placed her palm against the wall. It was cold and wet, its craggy terrain smoothed from winds and waves and years gone by. She began following it, feeling it draw her on. Had Frederick or the girl — Juliette Flint, she recalled, from the records at St. Thomas's — done the same once?

They had returned to examine the birth records and discovered that the young widow had also been the baby born the night of the sea flood eighteen years prior to Elias Flint's death.

Suddenly, she stopped. "Here." Her fingers curved around, following the contour of the cave back. It beckoned her on, until she turned and a reaching black schism stood before her.

If she had thought, upon entering the cave, that it was dark — she had been mistaken. For ahead she saw only black beyond black, so tangible it seemed ready to swallow them all. One step, and then another, a climb over a low-lying boulder that seemed to be standing guard — and she was in another world.

The next hour they picked their way along dark corridors illuminated only by their head torches, placed palms against cool walls carved from stone. Graph paper and pen in hand, Spencer scratched out a map along the way, tracing their path.

It was a bit eerie, the way the light beams sliced and wove, crisscrossed and circled, then dissipated off into the desolate unknown. And yet, for all that desolation, Lucy felt something else. Unseen embers, somewhere, of a story kept. Waiting.

At length, they stopped in a cloister of sorts, where shelves carved into the walls held bottles long empty, wooden boxes long splintered, and a small web in the corner where a lone spider perched.

"How came you here, little one?" Lucy whispered, glad the others were gathered over Spencer's map and did not hear her imagination. But if that spider could talk, what would it say? Was it part of some ancient remnant of life down here? Had its predecessors witnessed all that they now pursued? It seemed laughable, somehow, that an eight-legged creature might — if this were a fairy story — know everything that four grown inquisitors did not.

Without giving answer, the spider skittered away, and Lucy's eyes followed its path to the bit of wall between two of the hewn shelves.

She stepped back, narrowing her eyes, willing her beam to shine brighter, for before her on the wall . . .

"Are those words?"

The others were at her side in an instant. Violette brushed cobwebs away, and Spencer scribbled madly.

"I can't believe it," he said. "It's the last stanza. The lost one. It has to be! Verse six, remember? It's the same meter, and it is definitely Blackaby's cadence. Most definitely."

Dash read aloud slowly:

"He gave his life to spare his friend.
He gave himself indeed.
For he was not a Traitor-Man
Despite what all may read."

Lucy pressed her eyes closed, recalling the words she'd read so often she'd memorized them. " 'We lay to rest the Traitor-Man, His tale, with words, bury.' "

"What does that mean?" Violette narrowed her eyes.

"The story is quite literally buried," she said. "The cave is guarding it."

Silence fell over them as they each looked from the inscription, to the branching tunnels. The two passageways diverged before them like a great, spreading riddle.

"Which way is guarding the rest of the story, then?" Spencer asked. "Perhaps there are more stanzas! The implications of this in the literary world are . . ." He stopped, shaking his head. Speechless, miracle of miracles.

"How about we split up?" Dash asked.

A lump rose inside of Lucy. "N-no."

Violette held Spencer's map straight out in front of her, as if it would provide a clue. "Yes," she said. "We'll meet back here and compare what we've found." She seemed to notice Lucy's hesitancy and softened. "It's either that, or we spend twice as long to discover half as much."

Dash looked befuddled at that math but agreed, taking Spencer's map and copying it down on another piece of paper.

Then all eyes were on Lucy. She filled her lungs with the air, which had traded its cloak of sea salt for the spice of chalk earth. "All right." She thrust her hand into her pocket and, fingering her pocket watch, added, "But let's meet back here in an hour — no matter what."

Violette looked at Spencer, who shrugged, and the two seemed to be having a silent conversation. Violette was extraordinarily expressive in ways other than speaking, but this connection between them was something more.

"Make that two hours," Spencer countered, "and you have yourself a deal."

Forty-Three

The deeper she and Dash went, the deeper the quiet grew, until it was a presence in itself. The corridor stretched on and on. Ducking her head to cast the torch's beam upon her pocket watch, she saw that nearly a half hour had passed.

"Dash," she said, clearing her throat to speak past the lump forming there. "Do you think . . ." She trailed off, afraid to speak it, afraid that saying it aloud might make it true. "Never mind."

"Never mind?" Dash repeated. "Too late for that. Tell me, so I can mind."

"Do you think this is a fool's errand?"

He stopped, looking into the reaching avenue of nothingness that unfurled before them.

"Are you calling me a fool, Matchstick Girl?"

For a moment, all she could see was a vision of Dash at fourteen, his feet too big even for his tall body, bumping into console tables with his sunglasses on in the corridor at Candlewick. If they'd been anywhere but a tunnel under tons of earth, she would have laughed at the memory, punched him on the shoulder like old times, and given him back as good as he gave in a battle of wits.

But they were wandering in an uncharted cave, hunting down a legend pieced together from threads and snippets of what felt like a thousand wispy stories, in a tunnel wending deeper into the dark belly of the earth.

"You know what I mean, Dash. Why are we here? England has as many legends — true, fabricated, and everywhere in between — as it has cups of tea."

"Too many to count?"

"Precisely. So again, why are we here? Why are you — an astrophysicist with three degrees and two trips to a scientific laboratory in outer space under your belt — here?"

He stood silent. Picked up his left foot and scratched his right shin with its heel. He lifted his face to meet her eyes — and there, in his suddenly serious, pleading eyes was answer enough.

Everything in him answered with one unspoken word: *you.*

But she dared not believe it.

So much hung in Dash's gaze — and she

could not bear to think of what might crumble if whatever words were spoken next were not the words she longed to hear. What would it cost her to lose him again? And more, what would it cost him? Would he once again lose the only home he had if this proved to be a fool's errand? What if he'd gone and attached his name to her research proposal, only to be ruined by it?

Breathless at the gift of what it seemed he was wordlessly offering her — himself — she shifted her gaze. And as she did, the shadowed room beyond reached to her in specters and odd shadows, different from anything she'd seen so far.

"Dash," she breathed, shining her head torch in that direction. "Look."

Together they stepped into the small room and stood caught in the middle of a tale frozen in time. There was a narrow bed, its blanket pulled neatly into place as if its owner had merely stepped out for the day's work. Only the additional blanket of dust declared otherwise. Beside it, a barrel lay on its side, gently slanting stoppers appearing like four feet.

Lucy drew near enough to peer inside. "Someone's built a platform at the bottom. Almost like . . . a cradle." She pictured a pink-cheeked cherub lying within, smiling up at her.

Dash leaned in to look, running his hand around the edge. It appeared to have been sanded with care, nary a splinter to be seen. "These notches," he said, pointing at two half circles carved from one end. "What do you make of that?"

Lucy's stomach did a little flip, the sight striking a familiar chord. "Of course," she said, shaking her head in slow wonder. "It's a crow's nest, from a ship." She touched the grooves, nodding. "They'd have rested their spyglasses here. To leave for the next watchman, to have them in arm's reach at a moment's notice. They made a cradle of a warship's lookout," she said. She did not know if it was beautiful, or tragic, or somewhere in between.

She and Dash moved about the small cave room that had likely once been used to stow smuggled goods but had become a refuge. For a woman and her child, by the look of things. She shook her head, thinking of another baby in another cave, long ago in Bethlehem.

Baby in a cave. Those words hit her like a landslide. She was at her father's bedside again, fingers laced within his. He was not entirely lucid, breaths coming harder, words dredging up from deeper places. Or perhaps he'd been more lucid than she'd thought.

"Baby in a cave . . . Cradle from the sky . . . Man gives his life . . . Tempus custodit veritatem."

She'd assumed he'd been speaking of the Nativity. And perhaps he had, but . . .

Her heart picked up speed, snatches of stories flying into the darkness like bats on the loose. Her consciousness grabbed at them, head pounding.

"Lucy?"

She shook her head, turning slowly, as if the walls would speak.

Dash touched her elbow. "What is it?"

She faced him, searched his eyes. "It's just . . . look at us. Standing in a cave beneath the ground. A place of impossible life — a hidden kingdom. An underground city, like the people of Coober Pedy. From a rising tide, like the one he spoke of. Was Dad telling us this story all along? Giving us one giant riddle, our whole lives through?"

Dash looked back and forth, as if dredging up those stories of old, reconciling them with what she was saying.

"So many times he told me, 'We keep the stories.' He said we pass them on — it is our duty . . . and our honor. In a world as dark as this, people forget how to see the light, so we need to remind them by telling the truth. Paying attention . . . setting the stars alight."

"It sounds like him," he said. "But why? Why him? What would he know of all of this?"

The pieces did not all fit neatly together. There was still much to discover. But this room kindled the embers within her, gave her hope that more answers were tucked into this cave.

She paused at what appeared to be a curtain. The once-white cloth hung limp and crooked, snagged by a few rough spots of the cave wall. A small gathering of sticks rolled as Lucy's toe nudged them by accident. But no . . . they were not mere sticks. They were black bits of burnt wood fashioned into rudimentary writing utensils.

Noticing that her light was growing dimmer, Lucy knew that they should be turning back before this world plunged into darkness, but she couldn't stop now, not yet. Gently, she pulled the curtain back, as one might pull aside a sheer silken curtain to gaze out upon a vast and captivating view.

But what she saw instead captivated her all the more: a scene drawn in charcoal. A man holding a baby. A woman watching on in the corner.

At the bottom Lucy saw writing. Dash stepped behind her as she knelt to read it, narrowing her eyes to see. Each jot, each stick of every letter, each quirky curve of the letter *s* . . . was a gift carved with care. A shiver ran through her as she began to read.

Forty-Four

Slowly, haltingly to puzzle over the smudged bits, she read aloud.

> "Here a man lived, and gave the truest thing that ever he could. He gave his life to three souls. Everything in him. For one of those souls, he took on shame, all to give the man a chance at truth and life. And for two of those souls, he carved a simple life in this cave. By turns, his giving led to love."

There was more . . . but it was too smudged. She leaned closer, nose nearly touching the wall, and saw that the charcoal had been carefully etched over with something sharp. Again and again, carving the words into the wall. Ensuring they would last, treasures stored up for the ages.

She reached a finger to trace the script and read in a whisper. " 'And he was loved.' "

She could not explain the way those simple words made her want to weep.

And he was loved.

Her heart flooded with it. For Frederick Hanford's sake — whose tale she had a feeling they were just barely scratching the surface of — and for the sake of another lost boy, who had spent his life in search of home, and who had crossed the world to explore this dark abyss with her, to discover the light of this story.

The nearness of that very soul warmed her, and she let her fingers lace his. They stood, facing each other in this place where time stood frozen. Preserved, it seemed, just for them. As wars raged above, and the fire of the sun blazed above that, and a thousand fires greater still shone beyond that in the vast unknown . . . this quiet, endless moment spun itself around them.

She opened her mouth to speak only to come up empty. What to say to a love carved in the depths in so many ways? To the yearning that it opened inside of her, which reached into the dark for her friend's heart.

He squeezed her hand. Gone were the ever-present smile-crinkles around his eyes. In their place, story upon story upon story were written, reaching wordlessly right into her.

He gently tugged on her hand, surely sensing a sort of reverence in this room, as if they had tread into a place where wonder slumbered, and though they would leave, it would cling to them forever.

It trailed them in gossamer threads as they ventured farther down the corridor, and they found the story was still unfolding as they stepped over a threshold into what felt like a hushed and holy place.

Before them stood an old pew, one of its legs splintered and repaired with care. Stepping closer, she saw a hymnal upon it, laid open as if the place had been waiting for them so the service could begin. There was no pulpit, but there was a large rock, and upon it a communion chalice carved from what appeared to be driftwood. A wedding bower stood with bunches of heather tied in simple twine. Crisp, and most of it long decayed away, but enough was left that Lucy could picture a man constructing this bower for his bride and stealing above ground to bundle heather for her.

Somewhere above them, melodic ringing began to sound. A bell, slow, thoughtful, remembering.

"That's close," Lucy said.

"Really close." Dash tipped his head, studying the ceiling. "Could we be near St. Thomas's?"

Lucy tried to trace their path in her head, envision it in relation to the village above. "It very well may be," she said. The tolling went on, somber and slow. There was no mistaking it now — they were near the chapel. Right in the middle of a wedding ceremony frozen in time.

"This is the annex," Lucy breathed, her voice a whisper of wonder. If her growing theory was correct, this hovel in the ground, blasted and carved by marauders and smugglers . . . had been witness to three lives united in the impossible. A fresh start. New life.

The truest story . . .

As she turned, soaking it all in, her head torch starting to shimmer. Lucy's eyes landed on the far wall . . . and she stopped. Swallowed.

"Dash," she said. Pointing, in case he hadn't seen.

But he had seen. They both froze in place, as if one breath more would undo the sight before them.

A slide of rocks, arrested in time. Spilled from the earth in a river of stone, their path unmistakable. The rocks had, at one time, been set on filling this room, on burying any who stood where Lucy and Dash now stood. A splintered beam jutted here and there from the rubble — vestiges of a safeguard from the smugglers, she remembered from Barnabas's explanation of the ballroom.

The rockslide appeared stuck in suspended animation, restrained by the intentional damming of wooden planks, hammered with care into a makeshift wall rising waist high.

But those were no ordinary wooden planks.

"What on earth . . . ?" Lucy moved to step forward, and Dash held her in place.

"Be careful, Lucy. I don't think it's safe. I can take a picture, zoom in."

She studied the debris, the way the rocks rested against one another. The slide had occurred at least a decade ago, if not centuries before, by the looks of things. By now, she hoped they were surely settled well together, but they had no way of knowing.

Dash was right. It was unpredictable. But Lucy couldn't resist the draw of those planks — they were a siren call. If they were what she thought they were, they could change everything.

"I think it's all right," she said. "Whatever

falling those rocks were doing stopped long ago. Someone made sure of that."

Dash warily stepped forward. The two of them approached the wall. He with leery curiosity, she with disbelieving wonder.

She ran her hands over the planks and beams. She knew this wood. The black of it, the gilded detail carved in ornate relief. She had studied it. She had hoped to go in search of it — on the floor of the English Channel. And, if she was not mistaken, it was the same wood she'd taken tea on at the kitchen table at Stone's Throw, and that of her very own bed stand in the spring cellar.

Dash, too, ran his hands along it. He stooped to examine the handiwork, to tug tentatively, then firmly, and find it immovable.

"Impossible," they said at the same time.

They looked at each other, and a smile tugged at Lucy's mouth. "It's from the *Jubilee,*" she said. "These carvings, the black walnut — there is no other ship this could possibly be. Do you realize what this means?"

"That someone chose some expensive wood to make this old scaffolding?" Dash's smile lines were back.

"Understatement of the century," Lucy

said, laughter buoying her voice. "And it's been right under our noses this whole time. Literally."

Just as boldness seeped into her bones, whispering to her that she was safe here, that she should take a plank, just one, her light blinked out.

She reached up and tapped her head torch. "It's done."

Dash put his hand on her arm. "We need to go, Lucy. We have no way of knowing how long my lamp is going to last. I'll lead the way. Stay close."

He turned and started for the exit tunnel.

"Okay, but I just . . ."

How could she leave without a piece of the *Jubilee*'s beautifully carved wood? She had searched for so long. Without the light of her head torch, the rockslide was filled with shadows, but she stepped toward a piece she knew would be a perfect specimen. She paused, the pull of the wood barricaded by an instinct even stronger. If she unleashed a landslide — if she hurt Dash — nothing was worth risking that.

"I'll be back for you," she whispered. Turning to follow Dash, she felt her sweater snag on something behind. Glancing back, her eyes widened as the plank slid from its place in obedience, the sickening scrape of rock upon rock sounding. Lucy lunged to stop it as Dash's light swung to light the rockslide.

"Lucy, no!"

A *crack* sounded above them.

And the roar of a dragon unleashed.

FORTY-FIVE

In a cave in the ground a babe was born.

In a cave in the ground a man from a cross was buried.

In a cave in the ground the trees grew.

In a cave in the ground the light was mined.

In a cave . . . in a cave . . . in a cave . . . light broke into dark.

Again, and again, and again. The story of the ages. The story of life.

And in a cave in the ground Lucy Claremont lay with those splintered thoughts burrowing up from the past.

She swam in a dreamland so dark and so cold — a fog of sirens unfurling into pouring rain, Lucy trapped in a wrecked car. Sick with fear in a stranded car on the Jubilee line of the Underground. A burst of bubbles as her cell phone submerged into the murky waters of the Thames, flickering bright with *THE HIDDEN KINGDOM* before going entirely dark.

But that last hadn't happened — only almost happened. The hint of the untrue sent her clambering up from those snatches of past. The barrage of cold rain slowed as memory slid into foggy consciousness and the rain became a distant dripping, echoing somewhere far away, as if she were in a tunnel. Nothing, not even that thick, hot dark of the Tube, felt as heavy and hopeless as this.

She was twelve again, sitting in the dark on the Jubilee line. *Close your eyes,* she told herself. That was what Dash had said, all those years ago.

"It'll still be dark . . ."

"But it's a natural dark, Lucy. Nothing to be afraid of."

"But . . . it'll still be dark."

"True . . . and I'll still be with you."

She reached in the dark for her friend. Her heart.

And blinked awake into pain, not knowing where she was or why she could not move her arms and legs. But she did know one thing. The hand she was finally able to move was not empty. Running her fingers over the warmth within them, she knew the carved contours and ridges.

"Dash?" Her voice came out thick and dry. Why was it so hard to utter his name?

Blinking, she strained to see in an effort that made her head pound.

The cave. It hit her in a flood of memories. She'd pulled a plank of carved wood from a pile of stones. It had been an accident, yes, but one that would never have happened had she not lingered so close to the temptation. Her blood ran cold as she remembered one thing clearly — the warmth of Dash diving toward her, pushing her away from the path of the sliding rocks. And all going black.

"Dash." Her chest hurt. He was not moving. He did not reply. "Dash. *Dash.*" Frantic now, she struggled to move her left hand — pain seared as it scraped loose. Freed, she sucked painful air through clenched teeth.

Twisting her body toward the man who was her very heart, she felt in the dark until she found a shoulder. Sliding her hand gently until she felt the buttons on his shirt, she waited, listened.

"Please." A prayer unto heaven. And a plea to Dash. Her heart raced, and she pressed her eyes closed, as if that could silence the pounding that she might hear past it, hear his heartbeat.

She pressed her palm firmer to Dash's chest . . . and there it was. Buried deep but reaching up from wherever he was in his sea of unconsciousness, touching her hand with his pulse. *Thump. Thump. Thump.*

"Oh, Dash," she breathed. "I'm so sorry. This is all my fault."

In the silence she felt tears pooling, but she refused to break down. She closed her eyes to blink away the tears. *Think, Lucy.*

Opening them again, she realized there was enough light that she could see silhouettes of rocks and Dash lying next to her. His head torch was gone. It must have been buried, still putting out this meager amount of light.

The next moments of twisting, contorting, and moving rocks were a blur. She felt the scrapes and strains and maybe sprains or breaks as a collective fog, wincing against the pain and pushing through it with one thought in her mind: *Dash.*

The impossibility of it all struck her with a cruel irony. The man who'd orbited the earth was now shackled by it. Rock by rock, she blindly worked, until she heard it.

"Lucy . . ." His voice. Raspy, but it was his voice.

She crouched down. "I'm here, Dash. Are you all right?" It was a ridiculous question. Of course he wasn't all right.

"Great." The word scraped out of him. He pulled at his limbs, and she stilled him with her hands.

"I'll get you out," Lucy said, looking around as if the darkness might suddenly reveal a solution for her. "I promise." She moved the last rocks until, finally, Dash was free, but she was pretty sure it was a bad idea to try to move him — or let him move. She had to find a way out. "Stay still, Dash. Don't move."

She scrambled to her feet, trying to orient herself. "Help!" she yelled, her voice coming out in a thin ribbon. "Help!" But the call did not echo. The cavern did not carry it along on a current of ricocheting sound. It swallowed the single syllable up, just as it had swallowed them.

Once again, Lucy turned to the question of where the meager light was coming from. But as she turned to explore, Dash struggled to rise, so she knelt beside him. He looked at her with one eye squinted. Seeing? Not seeing? She did not know. Then his head dropped heavily. Her hands slid behind it just in time to break his fall. His hair was damp, his skin so clammy — and he grimaced.

"Turn it to Capella," he said.

Lucy's stomach sank. A strand of horror slithered inside of her as she recognized the unmistakable sky-navigator mode he'd slipped into. He did not know where he was.

She thought hard to the first-aid training she'd taken so many years ago. Signs of shock . . . what had they been? Fast pulse, even if weak. Coldness. Sweat. Confusion. And dizziness. With a swallow around the growing lump in her throat, she asked, "How do you feel?"

"Stuck." He barely got the word out, along with a few dry laughs, which led to coughing. "Orbiting."

Orbiting . . . ? Of course, Dashel Greene when pinned in a hopeless state would not just say "dizzy." She wished she could laugh, love him for it — but all she felt was fear, more deeply than she knew possible.

"That's what we do, Lucy. We orbit."

Her thoughts scrambled, and she slipped into a surreal calm, even as her mind raced. Concussion, shock, some hidden injury — these possibilities drove her into mechanical action. Pulling her cardigan off of her shoulders, she spread it over Dash, stretching it to wrap around his shoulders so broad. It wrenched her to wonder if they would rise again.

But such wonderings would do him no good.

Lucy's chest hurt as she returned to his statement. "Yes," she said. "We orbit.

Around and around the sun, like you always said."

Dash laughed. "You and me," he said. "Capella A, Capella B. We orbit each other."

He was naming stars, senselessly, but at least he was talking. If she could keep him talking, maybe get him to where she was sure enough to leave him, to find help.

The very thought of leaving tore something deep inside of her. Hot tears escaped, and she lay down beside him. Got as close as she could, feeling his face more than seeing it. Enough time had passed that Spencer and Violette should soon realize there was a problem and would come looking for them . . . but would it be too late?

"Dash," she said softly, "I have to leave you."

"I know," he said. He began to tremble. "You have to go . . . to the sea."

She reached over him with a light embrace and prayed. Prayed his tremors might still, his pulse might steady. *Clear his mind, Lord.* Her lungs constricted with physical pain at leaving him. "Remember your note, when you left London way back?"

He moaned, and her every sense stung with panic.

"Dash?" Was she losing him?

"The note," he mumbled. "Don't remind

me. Worst mistake of my life."

She laughed at his joke, her heart simultaneously rending within her. "You said you wouldn't say good-bye because it would never be good-bye for us, not ever. You remember that. Don't slip away." She struggled to infuse hope she did not feel into her voice. "I'm coming back for you."

His face next to hers, that light seeping in ever so softly from somewhere, she saw his eyes for the first time. And they looked clear — lucid and seeing, regret and hope all pooled together.

"That's what I always told myself," he said. "I was coming back for you." He coughed, tried to lift an arm and winced. "But I was too late, wasn't I."

No. The word pulsed against her ribs with such strength it would surely have brought the whole cave down upon them had she released it. She caught that wild word in its thrashing state, harnessed it with every ounce of self-control she had, and uttered it into the cave in a whisper. "No." She swallowed. "Never too late, Dash." A beat of silence stretched into eternity. "How can you be late for always?"

Gently, tentatively, she reached a hand up to his hair, ran her fingers slowly through it. That he would understand that she was not ready — would never be ready — to say good-bye to him.

His eyes lingered, reading hers. " 'I have' " — his voice was patchy, like it had been dragged over the rubble surrounding them — " 'loved . . . the stars too fondly . . .' "

Lucy choked back a wave of heat that threatened to break into a sob. But she would not do that to him, would not cover this moment in the despair she felt. She would instead finish the words of "The Old Astronomer" that he could not.

" '. . . to be fearful of the night.' " She nodded, unable to stop a tear from falling on his cheek. She brushed it away and ran her thumb over his face.

Never could those two kids stuck in the Underground, whispering of a poem too lofty for the likes of them, have imagined that those words would come back to them this way. *"It's about love,"* Lucy had said. *"It's about dying,"* Dash had said. They had finally agreed it was about hope. Then their heads had bonked and that had been the end of that.

But *this* would not be the end. There was still time. There had to be. His thready breathing quickened her spirit unto action. "I'll be back soon, Dash. Hang on."

And with a prayer, she pulled herself up,

stepped back, picked her way over rubble — and for the first time, felt heavy dread anchor her in place.

For the rockslide had obscured both passageways. Behind and before, they were walled into their own impossible catacomb.

Forty-Six

Her parents had named her "light," placed her in a cradle in a room where glass was once ground, where matchsticks were born. And here she was, drowning in darkness.

Lucy felt the air thinning, the blackness pressing. But behind her, the breathing of her truest friend drove her on.

She clambered up over one pile, thinking to dig her way out, run back, find Spencer and Violette. Someone could go on for help while the others came back for Dash.

But nothing would budge.

She clambered up over the other side. Maybe the rockslide had opened up the long-closed passage. Surely the tunnel went on to the village or beyond — wherever the smugglers had dug.

She finally found a rock that jiggled ever so slightly. *Yes. Thank you!* Wedged her hands behind it, unheeding of the way her skin screamed in protest, bones pinched, muscles strained. She pulled, leaning back with her entire being. It would come. It would be a start! It rocked, and rocked . . . but with a final yank, some contour or unseen lip caught, sending her sprawling back, stumbling to stay upright, to stay alive. *To save Dash.*

She would try again. And did. And failed again.

Oh, God . . . Tears strangled her unfinished prayer, and she quieted herself. She could not cry out, could not let her ominous despair reach Dash's ears.

"What do I do?" she whispered, standing with both feet planted firmly in a mountain of impossible.

"Nothing is impossible." The watchmaker's echoes reached through time, pulled up in memory.

"Just think." This was Mum's voice. The echo of it filling Lucy's mind, inviting her to peel back what lay on the surface and see something remarkable beneath.

"Pay attention, now." Father.

"Ad tendere." Mum.

Eyes pressed closed, Lucy saw her mother sliding that plate of biscuits over, a twinkle in her eye. *"To stretch toward."*

The words, these bits of memories, snatched at Lucy's senses as if they were flakes of snow, drifting down, delivering instructions she did not understand.

Realization hit her. She was losing her mind. The air was surely limited. Would she soon be unconscious?

The thought clawed at her, sent her scrambling higher, straining her eyes to see.

"Just think," she whispered. "Nothing is impossible. Pay attention."

If she could not go back and she could not go forward, there was only one option.

Up. She would dig her way out with her fingernails if she had to.

"Pay attention. Stretch toward." She looked to the ceiling and finally noticed the source of the faint light filling the cavern. Bits of light filtered through what appeared at first to be a solid ceiling.

She scrambled to the pile of rubble beneath the light source and immediately regretted all the loose rocks she had sent tumbling — for she needed them now. And so, rock by rock, climb by climb, unheeding of how much time was passing, she built the mound higher, hollering every now and again to check on Dash. She dreaded the time he would not respond, but for now, he had strength enough for the briefest replies. Enough to keep her digging with increasing ferocity, though her muscles burned.

Finally she reached the spot where tendrils of light filtered through the cavern ceiling and began to run her palms over the surface. She moved her feet to find solid footing. Grains of soil loosened, dusting her with spiced earth that smelled less of must and more of life. She pulled away the thatching of branches and roots that looked decidedly man-made, and the light strengthened.

As she worked, she considered that Frederick might have used this room not just as a place of worship but also as a storehouse of goods. Her breath hitched an odd hiccup of hope . . . as she thought of a witness seeing the legendary Mad Kit Bill vanish into thin air.

"It was you," she whispered, as if Frederick, the carver of this unlikely home, could hear her.

It was far-fetched. *But nothing is impossible.* Hadn't that been the motto of her entire childhood? Trained into her, for such a time as this?

She began to tremble, not daring to name the warmth that overtook her. But deep down she knew it was hope.

She clutched and tugged, tore and snagged, and pulled herself up until she was hanging on the thatching, toes barely touching the rocks beneath. Finally the branches and roots gave way to stalks and stems and brambles — *thorned* brambles, her pricked and scratched hands told her.

Soon the brambles became too thick to continue with her raw hands, so she picked a rock from the pile and hacked away in upward thrusts, defying gravity until . . . at last her fist broke through. By turns, her arms followed, and finally her face turned up into a late-afternoon sky whose brightness burned all the brighter to her cave-conditioned sight.

Tracing the ancient path of Mad Kit Bill, she flew across that pasture, defying time.

FORTY-SEVEN

The hours that followed were a blur of people gathering, rescuers pulling Dash from the cavern, the ambulance carrying him away, and fear clawing at them all. About the same time Lucy had arrived to find help, Spencer and Violette had arrived as well, frantic after being unable to reach them for the rockslide-blocked tunnel.

The hospital waiting room was torture, where gleaming floors held up to Lucy's pacing, and Sophie's hand reached to squeeze hers. An offering of grace that Lucy offered right back.

When the doctor came out to give a report on Dash and his injuries, the details pooled together — bruising, fractures, monitoring. Lucy felt her heart rise into her throat at the mention of his head, that mind proclaimed brilliant from so long ago.

"We have every reason to believe that all will be well," the doctor said, and sent them all home. Lucy lingered, asking to see him even though he was unconscious.

He'd been cleaned up, his hair combed more carefully than she'd ever seen it, not tousled out of place as during the wild chase of his stars. Scratches, bruises, and a few stitched wounds marked him, bringing tears to Lucy's eyes.

"You're quite a pair," a nurse who entered said. "Matching scars, you'll have." Lucy hadn't even given thought to her own face. In the reflection of the glass frame on the wall she saw she was smudged, scratched, and bedraggled. But most of all, she was so thankful.

She spent the night sitting at his side, his hand in hers. At some point she'd fallen asleep and woke to see the most welcome sight — his eyes open, studying her.

"Matchstick Girl," he said, before drifting off to sleep. That was all. And so much more. Stories upon stories, years upon years, love upon love, woven into those words.

In the days that followed, after his release with strict instructions for convalescing, they walked more of Stone's Throw Farm than she'd thought possible. Talking, remembering, dreaming. Short walks at first, and longer each day as Dash's strength returned.

"Well?" he said one afternoon, when they found themselves at the far pasture, where the star party had been. "What now, Lucy?"

"We could rest a bit." She gestured toward the seats near the cold campfire ring. "Or keep on. Maybe walk down the road a bit . . . ?"

He smiled, amused. "I mean, you have done the impossible. You have found the lost ship *Jubilee.* Or what's left of it. I think your committee is going to be more than impressed by your . . . What did they call it? Indisputable evidence?"

"It's ironic, though. Now I have no need of the research funds."

He dipped his head side to side, weighing that. "Maybe. Or maybe you can request a reallocation. There's a lot of the story yet to discover about your Frederick Hanford and the lady Juliette. It'll take some digging. Some time. Less funds than you needed before, but with such 'compelling evidence,' I have a feeling Professor Finchley won't be so stingy with that grant this time around."

Lucy nodded in agreement, but she couldn't help wondering. Frederick and Juliette's story had been protected for so long. She felt compelled to research it, but should it be made public? A part of her believed they might not mind their story finally being told, if it could bring hope to others.

She looked at the stretching patchwork of green pastures, the landscape dotted in houses of stone and white clouds of fleecy sheep. Beatrix bounded toward them ahead of Sophie, who approached slowly across the pasture.

"What do you say?" Dash sounded nervous, suddenly. "Will you stay?"

There was nothing for her in London — only boxes waiting for her move from the cottage that was no longer home, and a promise of a one-room flat from Mr. Bessette. Then she thought of the tiny springhouse that — with its cozy lights and earthen embrace, and the stream running through — had come to feel more a home than any tiny hovel logically should.

She did not know what would come of it all, but she planned to see the story through, whether the committee gave their approval or not, and whether she shared it with the public or not.

"I will stay," she said, the revelation a sweet sound to her own ears. "That is . . . if it's all right with you, Sophie."

"What's that?" The older woman neared

them, an envelope in her hand.

"Might I request a longer stay in the spring cellar?" Lucy bit her lip, waiting. She knew Sophie had been none too keen on her presence at the start.

But miracle of miracles, the corners of Sophie's mouth turned up ever so slightly. "We'd be glad of that," she said. "For as long as you like."

She paused, holding the envelope, running her thumb over it. "You're gathering documents for your research?" she asked.

Lucy nodded. She had much to track down to uncover what had transpired between Frederick and Juliette Rivers. Cross-referencing ship's records and magistrates' records in Portsmouth, clerks' receipts, local art from the time — the work would be intricate and painstaking, and she would love every moment of it.

So many questions remained, so many strands of this tapestry to make sense of yet. And the archaeologist in her was bursting to sit down and dig deep, to question every soul living at Stone's Throw, find out each of their perspectives, the lore passed down over the ages, the holes such tales might fill.

Sophie tapped Lucy on the shoulder with the envelope to prod her from her planning.

"This was given to us many years ago. It might help, I think. Your father . . . came to us just after your mother passed on and stayed for several days." As she stood there in her pearl earrings and flannel plaid shirt and knee-high muck boots, Sophie's compassion was tangible.

"This is where he went," Lucy breathed, thinking of those nights he had called home and then returned different, determined to see her through.

"He was a man on a mission. He walked the pastures and the cliffs, climbed down to the beaches, walked the shores. Day in and day out, searching. Every afternoon we sat him down for scones and tea just where Clara sat you your first day."

Tears sprang. "He sat there?"

"Yes. As boy and man, both. He believed, Lucy, that you would come to us one day, too. I have a feeling he pulled a few strings to be sure of it, urging Dashel here for his research as he did." She winked at Dash, who scuffed his foot in the soil and shrugged.

"A riddle always has a safeguard," Lucy murmured.

Sophie placed a hand on Lucy's shoulder and squeezed it. As engulfing as a full embrace it was, coming from her.

"Thank you, Sophie," she said.

And then Sophie was gone, leaving them to open the envelope.

Inside, crisply folded graph paper unfolded into a letter with handwriting so familiar it felt like an embrace.

Dash drew close to listen as she read.

"Dear Lucy,

So you've found it, have you? The story. I expect you've also figured out that it's one important to our family.

Love letters are as old as time, Lucy. Some folk write in sonnets, some in prose, and some in really terrible songs. But the truest suitor — the one who's been pursuing since time began and who won't stop until it ends — writes His love letter across the very sky. Within the very earth. In every sunset. Every star. Every refuge hewn from caves and mines and seas.

So we keep the stories, Lucy. Matchstick Girl. Keeper of light.

Our family has been entrusted with the keeping of this tale, and how you do it is up to you. Killian Blackaby began the tradition with his ballads. His son Jonathan carried the tradition on in painting, capturing the sea stacks and titling them

'The Way Home.'

Each generation embodies the story in a way fit for them. Some, such as one simple Simon, determined to piece it out, bit by bit, in veiled story while turning gears and telling tales to two wide-eyed kids who needed each other more than they knew.

I have kept that story back, in hopes that you will discover it on your own. You've been chasing it since you were a girl, the Jubilee planting itself in your heart, towing you out to sea. Some stories must be lived to be believed. So I planted the seeds and watered them where I could, and set you free to do something impossible.

You've done it, my girl. I knew you would.

It is up to you now, Lucy, how you keep the stories and pass them on. Board your ship. Chase your mysteries. Wherever you are called, your chance to keep the stories will be there.

The world is dark, so dark we sometimes forget the stars. But they are always there — we need only fight to see these places of brilliant light, these echoes of the truest story. Of a man who gave his life for another — and of a Man, centuries before him, who gave His life for the world. The One who is coming . . . and coming . . . and coming after you. Fighting for your heart. Every breath a gift.

He sets the stars alight, my girl. And we open our eyes to this in benevolent defiance of the dark . . . by remembering.

Take note. Live deeply. And be well, my daughter.

All my love, always,
Dad."

Lucy slipped her hand into Dash's. The Matchstick Girl and the Lost Boy. And together, they walked into a future as bright as the sun.

Epilogue

The village of Weldensea never forgets its legends — part of the enchantment of this land, so they say. Its people gathered the threads of stories like those of the good shepherd; and Mad Kit Bill with his odd-sized bundles, stealing across the dark; and the scandal of the traitor Frederick Hanford. They wove them into the fabric of time, passing them down from generation to generation. Snippets of the story were passed down, too, with no one the wiser that they were vessels. Humming bits of Handel's *Messiah* to babes as they fell asleep. Naming pigs after the one who came before it, and before that, and before even that. Generations of pigs named Salt, nobody dreaming the name sprang from the sty of one of the finest warships ever to traverse the seas in the name of His Majesty the King.

But beneath the canopy of tales and

legends, a story so ordinary it escaped notice planted itself, too. That of the Farmer Rivers and his young wife and child. Aerie was her name, called so after the name for eagles' nests. *"Or crows' nests,"* her father sometimes said with a wink.

If one paid attention, leaned in, they would notice the way this family held one another with a closeness that was almost otherworldy. The family came to Weldensea when the girl was ten, having spent the first years of her life in a northern county. "Letting time pass," they'd said, but one got the feeling there was something time was meant to sweep over in those passing years.

Upon their arrival, they took up residence in an old sheep farm far north on Hanford land and called it Stone's Throw Farm, being it was so far removed. The empty house of Hanford, in Edgecliffe, stood in the distance on the seaside cliff. And villagers swore that from time to time, bits of Handel's *Messiah* could be heard drifting from its abandoned piano, its notes both mournful and healing. Always the refrain of bonds being broken asunder, and always the notes being carried by the sound of the waves beyond.

With the purchase of their farm, the Riverses inherited a prodigiously aged pig named Salt from the village woman who had lived there for some years. They planted trees. Thick and green to border the farm, that they might live an extra quiet life. The girl, Aerie, flew across that pasture, wings on her feet and sunlight in her golden hair.

As years went on, she led three young children — her siblings in perfect stairstep height — through those pastures, sometimes playing crack the whip, and their father watched on, carving figurines from bits of soft stone he'd salvaged from a nearby cave, as he told it. Here the four children herded sheep, learned tunes, lived wild and free beneath the light of the sun and the love of a mother and a father whose devotion knew no bounds.

Sometimes the whole family perched all in a row upon their small thatched roof with a telescope, or sat upon its ridge and listened as the Shepherd's Bells tolled from St. Thomas's chapel.

Every few years or so, they all traipsed down to the seaside cliffs by moonlight to watch the waves climb higher and higher at spring tide, eclipsing rocks and towers, all on their way to greet this family who those same waves had delivered into safety so long ago.

They could be seen, betimes, as figures

cloaked in hushed dusk, approaching the churchyard and leaving bundles of wild heather upon the gravestone of the last master of Edgecliffe Manor.

"Admiral Barnard Hanford," Aerie read reverently from the grave marker one such evening. "Who was he, Father?" Aerie slipped her hand into his, and his wife did likewise, enclosing her fingers in his.

Frederick's jaw twitched as he searched for an answer he still did not fully know, himself.

So he gave her the truest thing he knew. "He was a man who lost much," he said. "But who gained more than he could ever have imagined."

Aerie nodded gravely, not understanding everything and yet grasping the honor in such a moment. As she and the young ones drifted away into the dusk one by one, the farmer lingered long, reaching into his pockets and placing something hidden in the tall grasses lining the marker. Six pawns, carved with care from the walls of the cave beneath Edgecliffe. One for each of those Riverses — The Admiral's legacy.

In the quietness of their life, they were happily forgotten by most. But the story of the Traitor-Man, his betrayal and the scandal, was carried on from generation to generation by people never dreaming that very man had once lived right beneath their noses. Never recognizing the sacrifice, the redemption, or imagining how it shaped generations to come.

But the story was kept faithfully by descendants of the Blackaby line. And if that Blackaby line were able to trace things back and back, they would find their forefather Killian, boots up on the hearth of that stone cottage, taking bread and cheese and tea with the Riverses every few years when he passed through on his rounds. He would play for them his favorite ballad, the great tale he'd spent his life in search of.

The Ballad of the Traitor-Man.

The story of life.

And the story of light.

AUTHOR'S NOTE

Dear reader,

Can I tell you a secret?

I think you might relate.

Sometimes this sitting at the keyboard and tap-tap-tapping out words is . . . hard. I wonder what the black letters on a white screen really mean, whether they matter, whether I should be spending my time doing something else.

But as I wrote this story, God whispered a bit of bolstering encouragement into my heart about it. If I had to assign one word to describe it, it would be this: wonder.

Not wonderful — it felt far from wonderful, as I worked through the various stages of its creation.

Not wondrous — unless you mean wondrously perplexing and how in the world are all these pieces ever going to mesh together, ever?!

No . . . just wonder. An aching word, a thing radiating hope if we will but pay attention and be amazed at the miracles of this life, of this very world.

Because, you see, this world can be a dark place. I don't need to expound. We all know it. We see it every day. We feel the heaviness of it descend when we turn on the news.

But there is something else in this world, too. And it is light. Hope. Truth. Wonder. There is proof all around us, stories in every nook and cranny, promises yearning with joy to be fulfilled. That is what this story is about, at its very core. Wonder. Light that fights the dark. I pray that truth might come through my meager words, that it might breathe life in the spaces between my letters, words, lines.

It was Galileo Galilei who first looked through a telescope pointed beyond our world and toward the moon and stars beyond. He, too, had his breath stolen by the wonders of the universe and, what's more, by the Maker of those wonders. To the detriment of his own safety and good standing in society, he completely revolutionized mankind's understanding of the universe with his "radical" ideas of the planets revolving around the sun. Like Lucy, Dash, and the watchmaker, Simon, in this humble story, Galileo found miracles in both the small and the grand.

He said, "The sun, with all those planets revolving around it and dependent on it, can still ripen a bunch of grapes as if it had nothing else in the universe to do."

I smile reading those words. For isn't that just how God loves us? Shining light intimately into our lives, in personal ways, even though He is simultaneously orchestrating rising tides, star fall, sunrises, and sunsets.

I am a quiet soul. Sporadic even online, harboring hobbit-like tendencies toward tea and comfort and general aversion to adventure . . . but God allows even quiet souls to help fight for that light in this world. He placed a pen in my hand, some words in my heart, and my hope is to use them to fight for that light. For the wonder. For the hope.

I think He has done the same for you, too. He has entrusted you with tools uniquely meant for you. And tools are meant to be used to carve away that darkness and magnify the light.

Be encouraged, friend, in whatever you are setting your hand to today. In His hands, crafted with His heart and placed into yours . . . it matters.

With joy,
Amanda

ACKNOWLEDGMENTS

More than any other story I can recall working on, *Set the Stars Alight* feels to me like one of those wooden nesting dolls, where each doll opens up to reveal another doll inside. On it goes, layer by layer, story upon story. This novel holds within it so many other stories, hearts, and sources of inspiration, without whom it may have turned out to be merely a hollow shell. Here are a few, in no particular order, to whom I offer all my thanks.

Simon Murphy, curator at the London Transport Museum, who gave me an incredibly detailed account of the underground power outage of August 28, 2003. Imagine my shock at the coincidence when I learned that one of the affected lines was the Jubilee Line. This was long after the ship in the story had been named the *Jubilee* . . . and the shiver of coincidence this fact gave me just had to make its way into the story.

Thank you, Mr. Murphy and the LTM, for your care-filled records and willingness to help!

Henry, Archdeacon of Huntington, who wrote in his 1100s chronicle of England's history, *Historia Anglorum,* of King Canute's challenge to the sea, and proclamation thereafter.

The people of Coober Pedy, who carve homes into the earth and pull light from the dark.

The industrious and whimsical London souls who have held festivals on ice, cricket matches on dry riverbeds, mudlarking to find treasure in the muck — and made memorable delight out of potentially disastrous times on the Thames.

To those ladies and gents who climbed the grand stair of the Boston Theatre, never knowing that in doing so, they ascended the air above a house encased beneath. And to Paul Collins, who with the briefest mention of this phenomenon in his memoir, *Sixpence House,* set my mind reeling years ago. How he learned of it, I know not, for it took every ounce of my research-sleuth muscles to dig up the briefest mention of it from a single old newspaper clipping. How a large house beneath an even larger staircase could disappear twice, entirely, from history, I don't know . . . but perhaps the lives it once held can be honored here.

Donald W. Olson, forensic astronomer and astrophysicist at Texas State University, whose book *Celestial Sleuth* explored Geoffrey Chaucer's *Franklin's Tale.* This, along with the true account of a 1773 ship found buried beneath the former site of the World Trade Center, first sparked the idea for this story.

The seventeenth-century Swedish warship *Vasa,* so heavily ornamented and armed, by order of the king as a symbol of his hopes for his reign. Sadly, it proved unseaworthy in its top-heavy state and sank within minutes of embarking on its maiden voyage. It served as subtle inspiration for the *Jubilee*'s origins.

St. Clement's Caves in West Hill, Hastings, East Sussex, which served as one of the cave-network inspirations for the story — and where Victorian balls truly were held beneath ground in the 1800s.

The many other places of subterranean wonder — some of which made their way into the book, and many of which could not, for sheer lack of story space. I'll be sharing more about these on social media when this book releases, and I hope you'll tune in to share the wonder!

The poet Luci Shaw, who drew my attention to the meaning of the phrase, "Pay attention." May we all stretch toward the wonders around us — may we pause to think on their significance.

To the Rabbit Room folks, who brainstormed wonder with me, and brought to my attention the delight of Chimney Swifts, among many other awe-striking things, and who lent a hand with translating Latin to help come up with a motto for the worshipful company of clockmakers: Katie Daniels, Matt Kunz, Jennifer Major (yes, pig latin counts!), Elizabeth Allen, Ima Virginia Justus, Gatlin Bredeson, Beth Bowen, Bill Smithfield, Dustin Ashenfelder (and here is where we ask — how many rabbits does it take to translate four words into Latin? Answer: Depends on how many translations you want!). So thankful to have had such outpouring of help. The Worshipful Company of Clocksmiths thanks you, too.

The "Worshipful Company of Clocksmiths" is a nod to the very real Worshipful Company of Clockworkers. The slight name change has been to honor their own traditions and mottoes, a nod that those included in the story are slightly different from (though definitely inspired by) theirs.

In like manner, the fictional Committee

for Maritime Archaeology borrows its inspiration from the Oxford Centre for Maritime Archaeology. To the OCMA: Many thanks for the intriguing work you do in studying things once-submerged or currently submerged. The fictional CMA surely departs from how things are truly done in the OCMA and was invented to protect the integrity of what you do, not wishing to change it for story's sake.

The Bow Quarter of London, which served as inspiration for Candlewick Commons. Once a matchstick factory, now a hub of London flats and the lives lived there.

Cecil Court, that bookish cobbled road lined with aged tomes. The place in all my London wanderings long ago that felt most like home. And next in line, the British Museum Reading Room. Lucy loved it because I loved it. When in London, friends, do be sure to stop by.

To the kind gentleman at the star party my family attended. You were waiting outside on the patio with your telescope while the lecture transpired inside. And while I tried so hard to track with the astrophysics being discussed within, my silly brain couldn't quite wrap itself around the lofty subjects, and it was my husband whose countenance lit up at it. So I slipped out the side door to take a turn watching our kids run on the lawn, and you graciously explained to me your telescope. How it worked, what we would see first in the sky, and how you used to race with your very cherished friend to see who could find the constellation first. The astrophysics that night were fascinating. The stars were glorious. But it was your story of community and friendship among the star party society that dug its way into this story's heart, and I thank you for sharing yours.

To NASA. Never could I ever have imagined I'd get to thank NASA in the acknowledgments! But thank you, thank you, to the NASA Wallops Island flight facility for allowing me to take part in the launch of the Antares rocket launch carrying the NG-12 Cygnus spacecraft to the International Space Station. The tours, the press conferences, the chance to speak with the scientists and taste the cookies the astronauts would be baking once the oven arrived . . . It was unforgettable. And, of course, so was the launch. You made Dash's work that much more real to me for the writing of this book, and I thank you.

To the crews of the International Space Station. We wave at you often from our driveway in the dark as the ISS passes on by . . . and we hope your days are filled with wonder. You certainly help spin wonder into our lives! Maybe you'll wave back sometime?

The P.A.G.E.S. Crew book launch team — how can I thank you for the way you give of yourselves to help these stories make their way into the world? I'm so grateful for the way you pour your hearts and skills into the bookish world.

To my Ben, who is so embodied in Dash. I had more fun than I can say writing him, writing the easy camaraderie and laughter and cheesy jokes and banter that he and Lucy shared. In many ways, they are us. Their story, reaching so far back, is so akin to ours. I'm thankful for your friendship, I'm thankful for your love. P.S. Thanks for not minding my stealing your shoes.

To Mom and Dad, for giving us stories that echo with the Great Truth.

To my brother and sister and brothers-and-sisters-in-law. Your friendships and examples are treasures to me!

To Raela Schoenherr, who sat with me beneath the redwoods at a writing conference many years ago and first heard the idea for this story. To Raela again, and Karen Schurrer, and Elizabeth Frazier: all three editors extraordinaire along with the entire

Bethany House team, who have ushered this story on to completion and made it better in a thousand ways.

To Wendy Lawton, agent and friend, who believed in this story for so very long and with so much heart.

And to the Maker of the Stars, the Author of Wonder, the Creator of our hearts, who, as the watchmaker says, is "coming, and coming, and coming after you. Always." Thank you for pursuing my heart. For not giving up on me, and for breathing life into this world in the most beautiful ways. You give us hope. You give us life.

ABOUT THE AUTHOR

Amanda Dykes is a drinker of tea, dweller of redemption, and spinner of hope-filled tales who spends most days chasing wonder and words with her family. She's a former English teacher and the author of *Whose Waves These Are,* a *Booklist* 2019 Top Ten Romance debut, as well as three novellas. Find her online at www.amandadykes.com.

The employees of Thorndike Press hope you have enjoyed this Large Print book. All our Thorndike, Wheeler, and Kennebec Large Print titles are designed for easy reading, and all our books are made to last. Other Thorndike Press Large Print books are available at your library, through selected bookstores, or directly from us.

For information about titles, please call:
(800) 223-1244

or visit our website at:
gale.com/thorndike

To share your comments, please write:
Publisher
Thorndike Press
10 Water St., Suite 310
Waterville, ME 04901